SHADOW'S
EDGE

Image Copyright fotoduki, 2012. Used under license from Shutterstock.com
Image Copyright nito, 2012. Used under license from Shutterstock.com
Image Copyright FILATOV ALEXEY, 2012. Used under license from Shutterstock.com
Image Copyright RYGER, 2012. Used under license from Shutterstock.com
Image Copyright Slava Gerj, 2012. Used under license from Shutterstock.com
Image Copyright Ralf Juergen Kraft, 2012. Used under license from Shutterstock.com

Published by Montlake Romance
P.O. Box 400818
Las Vegas, NV 89140

ISBN-13: 9781612183312
ISBN-10: 161218331X

J.T. GEISSINGER

SHADOW'S EDGE

A NIGHT PROWLER NOVEL

To Jay, my knight in shining denim; thank you.

———————————————

To my parents, Jean and Jim, for surviving
the surly teenage years; I owe you big time.

———————————————

And to all those who dare to love...this one's for you.

When love beckons to you follow him,
Though his ways are hard and steep.
And when his wings enfold you yield to him,
Though the sword hidden among his pinions
    may wound you.
And when he speaks to you believe in him,
Though his voice may shatter your dreams as
    the north wind lays waste the garden.

—Khalil Gibran

PROLOGUE

Excerpted from the *Illustrated London News*, October 27, 1888

EGYPTIAN FARMER UNEARTHS ANCIENT CAT TOMBS

According to Sir T.M. Addison Pike, famed Egyptologist and Orientalist, the recent discovery of a massive grave outside Beni Hasan containing more than 300,000 mummified cat remains is of special import and sheds new light on heretofore unconfirmed reports of the unusual esteem in which cats were held by the denizens of ancient Egypt.

A cemetery site located near the Nile River, Beni Hasan was primarily used during the Middle Kingdom, which spanned the 21st to the 17th centuries BCE. The colossal necropolis where the mummified felines were found is believed to be constructed by Hatshepsut and dedicated to the local goddess Pakhet, a lioness war deity.

Hatshepsut, translated as *Foremost of the Noble Ladies*, reigned longer than any other woman of an indigenous dynasty and is considered one of the most powerful and prosperous pharaohs of ancient Egypt. Female rule in Egypt was quite common; another example of a woman who ascended the throne was Cleopatra, the last – and perhaps most notorious – pharaoh of ancient Egypt.

Upon interview of the farmer who discovered the tombs, a colorful local legend emerged. It tells of the *Ikati* – Zulu for "cat warrior" – creatures sublimely beautiful and equally deadly, betimes human in shape but able to take the form of vapor or panther at will.

Apparently, the ancient Egyptians believed these fabled creatures were gods, originating from the darkest heart of the African rainforest, where the Congo disappears into clinging mists and savage wilderness beyond where any man dares to tread. Legend has it that the *Ikati* first civilized the area now known as Egypt, and they built the great pyramids at Giza as well as the Sphinx as an homage to their kind. They were even said to have mated with human women during religious rituals, siring some of the most famous of the Egyptian pharaohs, including the beautiful and cunning Cleopatra herself.

According to said local farmer, only the fall of Egypt to the Roman Empire halted the inevitable proliferation of these dread creatures throughout the globe. Once discovered by the emperor Caesar Augustus, they were declared witches and hunted to near extinction. The few survivors that were left were said to have fled their native shores, ostensibly to take up residence in some other, unknown part of the world...

Sommerley House
Hampshire, England
June 19, 1994

My love,

By the time you receive this, I will be dead. Forgive me.

I have brokered a compromise to save what is most precious to me, a bargain I purchase with my own blood. I agreed to this in order to spare you a lifetime of running, of peering into the shadows as we have been these ten long years, trying to escape the hungry death that pursues us.

They will sheath their claws and let you go, of that I am certain. But one day they will come for our daughter.

Until she is old enough to stand against them, teach her to run. Teach her to hide. Tell her everything about me and my kind, or tell her nothing at all. I leave it to you, my darling wife.

I find myself utterly wretched in my final hours, lost without you. My surrender to you was total, and for that I cannot feel regret, regardless of the price I am made to pay. True love can be a blessing or a curse, and for us I fear it has been both.

But it is the only real thing of value I have known in my life. The one thing I know will last forever.

I do not believe there is an afterlife for creatures such as I, but pray with all my heart I am wrong, so I may hold you once again. Heaven or hell, it matters little. As long as we are together. Until then I remain—

Eternally yours,

Rylan

 ONE

Had she known today would be the last day of her carefully controlled, predictable life, Jenna might not have devoted quite so much time to her mundane routine of errands, shopping, and cleaning her apartment, which hardly seemed worthy endeavors in light of what was about to happen. But as these pivotal days are wont to do, this one began with no hint of what was to come.

It was Sunday, it was July, and it was hot. Blazing hot, the kind of heat rarely seen in Southern California, the kind that shortened tempers and wilted flowerbeds and sent the already overtaxed electrical utility into spasms that created rolling blackouts across much of her tiny beach community. Even the bikini-clad rollerbladers and the oiled weight lifters and the legions of tourists with cameras and plaid shorts that normally populated the beachfront boardwalk in front of her apartment had fled, leaving only groups of wheeling, sharp-eyed seagulls to patrol the bleached sky above.

Because Jenna was immune to temperature extremes—she'd lived everywhere from Africa to Alaska without the slightest discomfort—she was the only one in the grocery store that didn't appear to have just emerged from a sauna. Everyone around her was sweating, shuffling, drooping like so many unwatered houseplants, but even in a fitted wool dress, with the substantial weight of hair so long it fell nearly to her waist in thick, honeyed waves, she remained cool and comfortable, as if encased in a preserving layer of ice.

The butcher, however, did not appear to be encased in ice.

"What'll it be, miss?" Beneath his white paper hat, his eyes were half-lidded, his cheeks were flushed red. His breathing was labored and sweat beaded his brow and upper lip. He seemed on the verge of some kind of cardiac event.

"The rib eye," she said, pointing through the glass case.

"Filet's on sale," he said, listless. "Wouldn't you rather have a nice filet?"

Yes, she would. But she couldn't afford it.

"Thanks, but the rib eye's fine." Along with the salad fixings and bottle of cabernet already in her basket, it would make a nice dinner. She normally ate her meals at work—standing up—but tonight she was off and treating herself.

Moving as if underwater, the butcher wrapped the steak in waxed paper and handed it back over the counter. "Don't overcook it; it just needs four minutes on each side."

She wasn't going to cook it at all, but didn't think he needed that particular bit of information. "Great. Thanks again."

He gave her a wink and a lazy smile that bordered on bedroom.

And that's when it happened.

At first, it was only a slight hot sting, an odd, tangible shock that seemed to come from nowhere—yet everywhere—around her. The concussion of heat twitched her hand so sharply she nearly dropped her handbag. Startled, she glanced at her hand and watched as a rash of goose bumps covered her arm. Then the strange, heated shock rose, vibrating, pressing in toward her core. It was so molten, so intense, she felt as if she might actually be burned by it.

Carefully, moving only her eyes, she glanced around.

Nothing.

Please tell me the butcher isn't giving me hot flashes, she thought, glancing back at him, giving him a closer look. He was still sweating, still smiling, at least twenty years older than she. His thick forearms rested on top of the meat case like two slabs of hairy, tattooed rejects from the refrigerated display below.

No. Definitely not the butcher.

She glanced around again and caught the eye of a tall, silver-haired gentleman standing beside his nattering wife in front of the nearby wine display. He was staring at her in the way she was accustomed to being stared at by men, but no, it wasn't him either.

Who—or what—was it?

And then a terrifying memory surfaced, one that made the goose bumps on her arms spread up to her neck.

If they ever find you... run.

They were her mother's words, a litany repeated daily until she died. An *unexplained* litany and one that left her with a permanent case of paranoia and a suspicion of strangers so profound she was never truly able to make friends.

She reminded herself that her mother had said a lot of strange things she didn't understand—and she drank a lot. "You're just hungry," she muttered to herself, earning a lifted eyebrow from the sweaty butcher. "You're hungry and probably overtired, and it's about a thousand degrees in here. Get a grip."

She headed to the front of the store and entered the express checkout line, behind a man so fat she didn't think he would be able to squeeze through the aisle without ravaging the magazine and candy display racks on either side. She unloaded her cart onto the crawling conveyor belt, then turned and opened the large refrigerated case of drinks that stood between her aisle and the next checkout lane. She chose a soda because there wasn't any milk—whole milk—her second favorite food to steak.

And when she closed the door and turned back, suddenly the very air itself seemed different. Charged somehow, with a heaviness that ate straight down through her bones.

For the second time, a sudden jolt of static electricity spiked the hair on her arms and the back of her neck, sending a shock of awareness through her core as if she'd been lanced with a spear of fire. She gasped and stiffened, earning a lethargic stare from the giant man in line in front of her. An eerie recognition pulsed over her skin.

I see you, the pulse whispered inside her. *I know what you are.*

She shuddered. Her fingers spasmed so tightly around the plastic soda bottle it split and crumpled in her fist. A fine spray of Pepsi shot out, fizzing out in a cold burst over her wrist and fingers, coating the nearby rack of magazines and gum.

"You OK?" the boyishly handsome cashier said, glancing at the ruined plastic bottle in her hand. He frowned, casting a shadow over his clear blue eyes. "That's quite the grip you've got."

"I'm sure it just had a crack," she said through stiff lips. "Dropped during shipping, something like that."

All the blood had drained from her face. The giant man was gazing at her steadily now, inspecting her pale face and shaking hands from beneath two unruly eyebrows that perched like hairy caterpillars on his forehead. The soda dripped into a fizzing pool on the beige linoleum floor.

The cashier pressed a button and spoke into a mike that squealed with feedback over the PA system. "Clean up on checkout five."

She inched forward, stepping carefully in her white strappy sandals around the dark, spreading mess of soda, which looked eerily like a pool of blood coagulating at her feet. The feeling of imminent danger was so acute that she had to fight the pressing urge to run.

So because the giant man had turned his back again and the cashier was now distracted with counting out change, because none of the other shoppers in line behind her could know what she was doing, she closed her eyes and opened her senses, pushing her awareness out like an ever-widening bubble in swift, concentric rings to encompass everything around her.

The low drone of air-conditioning whispering through steel vents high overhead. The faint squeak of shoe soles against linoleum; the even fainter creak of leather. The muffled chink of coins jiggling in a pants pocket somewhere near the back of the store. An argument in the deli section—*you never let me have what I want, not even at the fucking grocery store*—hissed low through clenched teeth. Someone's gaze on the backs of her bare legs, heated and heavy. But not dangerous. Nothing dangerous, not yet.

She pulled in a slow, deep breath through her nose, letting in the overwhelming sensory world she'd learned so long ago to shut out.

And there—there it was.

Animal. *Hungry* animal. A predator—and a large one at that.

Her eyes flew open. Her heart began to hammer. Every nerve in her body screamed *Danger! Disappear! Run!*

But she couldn't run. She was frozen. Hands shaking, heart pounding, every muscle fixed.

"Let's get you another soda," the cashier said, smiling warmly at her.

She was unable to answer or even move her arm to hand him the ruined bottle. She lifted her gaze to his face and he did an immediate double take.

"Wow! Your eyes are amazing! I've never seen that shade of green. Or…yellow? It's so unusual. They're beautiful."

"Contacts," she lied, one of many little white lies she told about herself to mask the truth.

The blaze of fear and fever hit her again, electric and stabbing, like a knife in the gut. She had to grit her teeth against a sudden, wrenching light-headedness. The cashier saw something on her face that made him blink, his brows drawn together. She dropped the ruined plastic bottle on the conveyor belt, stammering excuses.

"I think—I don't really need another soda. In fact, I'm going to leave everything. I'm sorry. I'm not feeling well. I…I have to go."

"You're sure? It won't be any trouble, it'll just take a sec. I'll get one from the fridge at the customer service desk, it's right over there—"

But Jenna had already turned away. She began to push past the giant man, but he was wedged so securely between the counter and the large refrigerated case of drinks there was no way to get past him, and there were ten people in line behind her, pressing close. She was trapped.

So because she was panicked and had no other option, she did something she never allowed herself to do and used her strength.

All of it. In front of everyone.

The collective gasps of twelve people were drowned out beneath the piercing metallic shriek of the refrigerated case as it was dragged across the linoleum, its round feet cutting deep into the steel and cement floor beneath. There was twenty feet of gouged floor between the aisle where she'd been standing and freedom, and it took only a few seconds and a very slight push. She didn't look back as the refrigerated case came to rest against the customer service counter with a muffled *boom,* scattering a stack of coupon flyers into the air like confetti.

She began to run.

She almost made it to the sliding glass doors at the front of the store when she felt the jolt of electricity again. It was a concussion that pierced down into her muscles, into the very marrow of her bones. A rising thick pulse of intuition flooded through her veins and she felt something vast and intangible rushing at her, heated and dark and inevitable as death. She stumbled into a dust-covered display of Duraflame logs stacked in a wire rack and sent row upon row of plastic-wrapped logs bouncing to the floor.

And then, shaking and gasping for breath, gazing out the sliding glass doors into the shimmering heat of the parking lot, Jenna saw them.

Tall and graceful, lithe like dancers, sleek and silent and dark.

They stood on the far side of the parking lot in the long shadows of a tall hedge of shaped ficus trees, staring right back at her from beautiful faces with detached expressions and very sharp eyes. All three were dressed in black clothing, obviously expensive, fitted and formal and distinctly out of place in the bludgeoning summer heat. There was nothing but grace and loveliness about them, nothing to suggest danger, but her skin crawled with bone-deep fear.

Because even from here she saw it. For all their elegance, there was something very wrong.

It could be seen in the planes and angles of their faces, in the slanted set of their eyes, in the cold red curve of their unsmiling lips. Their posture, the lines of their bodies, even their faces were perfect but—odd. Carved and otherworldly, almost elfin. They were beautiful in the way that certain predatory animals are beautiful.

And just as devoid of humanity behind the eyes.

One stood apart, slightly ahead of the others. Like his companions he had ebony hair, honey-bronze skin, feral, flashing eyes. But he was larger, broad-shouldered and substantial, forbidding even with all that perfect symmetry of bone structure, that jawline that seemed sharpened on a diamond cutter's lathe. Something about the mouth: sensual but hard, so hard it seemed he hadn't smiled in years. Or ever.

Their eyes met, and it gave her a jolt like lightning to her toes.

Who, she thought, and then, *what?* Her mind struggled to keep up with the adrenaline that flooded her veins. Her limbs lifted into sudden power and buoyancy, her nerves screamed *RUN!*, but she could only stare at him across the distance of the parking lot, into eyes beast-bright and wondering, luteous green. He stared right back at her with a gaze so intense and burning she thought he might ignite her with it.

On instinct she inhaled and caught the essence of him distilled into one tiny, heady whiff: Male. Potent. Dangerous.

Then he shifted his weight forward on one leg, and with that small movement, everything changed. His expression darkened, sharpened. He looked for a moment like he would cross the parking lot and devour her whole.

Another blistering shock of heat hit her—heart-stopping, blood-curdling—and to her great horror, everything began to slide sideways in one long, nauseating pull. Her body went curiously limp, out of her control. Her eyes blurred and focused, only to lose focus again when she slumped hard against the rack of fake fireplace logs and hit her head on a metal bar.

Spots of color popped and faded in her peripheral vision, the world leached of color. Except for those eyes that remained a constant, phosphorescent glow against the encroaching darkness.

No! she thought, panicked. *No! I'm not—I can't—*

Just before she fainted, Jenna saw the feral green-eyed stranger lick his lips.

TWO

"Well, Leander, she certainly looks charming. Though a bit equilibrium challenged. Are you sure we've got the right blonde?"

Leander didn't turn at the sound of his younger brother Christian's amused voice, nor did he move or blink, or in any way acknowledge he heard him. He only stared, with fevered eyes and a flush of blood creeping over his cheeks, across the parking lot and through the doors to the grocery store, where a small crowd had gathered around the slim female figure recently collapsed onto the floor.

"It's her," Leander said with a calm that hid the way his heart was pounding in his chest. "I know that's her."

From the moment he'd laid eyes on her, he'd known. And not only by the Eyes, by her scent as well. She smelled of something indefinable, lovely and dark and deep, particular to their kind. It was a sensual mix of forest floor, herbs and rain, fresh air and musk and moonlight.

Leander's senses were unmatched. It was one of his Gifts, though not by any means the most powerful one. He'd spent much of his life trying to manage the assault of smells, noises, sensations, and vibrations that emanated from everywhere around him. He'd long ago learned to shut out much of the chaos, to filter how much he absorbed, but he'd opened his senses fully to take her in and now had the taste of her skin lingering on his tongue like afterglow. Every nerve ending in his body felt her. Every pore was filled with her. He was almost dizzy with desire.

"Oh, for God's sake!" came another voice, this one female, from Leander's other side. A dramatic sigh followed, then the sound of leather boots scraping across hot asphalt with the annoyed shifting of her weight. Without looking, Leander knew the boots were Italian, designer, and absurdly expensive. "*That's* her? The wilting flower? The deer-in-the-headlights Snow White?"

"Morgan," Christian said quietly, just the one word. Leander didn't have to see it to feel the look of warning Christian shot at her behind his back. He allowed the smallest of smiles to curl his full lips.

As Alpha, Leander enjoyed not only the elevated rank and accompanying status among his colony but was also afforded the respect of someone with his very rare, very powerful Gifts—Gifts that the girl now being helped up from the floor of the supermarket by a huge, sweating ape of a man possibly had as well.

Not that she knew it. Not yet.

But they were here to find out if she did. If so, she would be brought back to Sommerley to take up her rightful place in the colony. If not—

But Leander didn't want to think about what would happen if she showed no sign of the Gifts. Not after he'd felt her, not after he'd *seen* her.

Though they were all beautiful, even the least Gifted of their kind, she was something else altogether. An exotic sylph with elegance and strength and solid luster, all feminine curves and opalescent skin and a surfeit of raw power simmering beneath. He felt the fine, humming force of her all the way across the parking lot, like a hand caressing his skin.

"What now?" Morgan asked, her tone a tad more civilized, though he sensed her irritation like an angry bee under his skin.

Leander reluctantly turned his eyes away from the girl and met Morgan's level, impatient gaze. Her outfit was so tight it followed every curve of her figure like a second skin—just as she wanted it to, he knew.

She was nothing if not provocative.

"Now we wait," Leander replied evenly. "There's only a week to go. Now that we've found her, we lie back. And we wait."

"And what are we supposed to do in the *meantime?*" Morgan complained, one hand on her slender, leather-clad hip. "Babysit her? Make sure she doesn't trip over a rock and bash her head in? She appears to have the tendency to faint dead away for no particular reason."

She shot a resentful gaze at the doors of the supermarket, where a half dozen men had surrounded the now-standing Jenna to offer assistance. Several more people were running past the doors toward something he couldn't see within the store. Maybe something that had to do with the shriek of grinding metal he'd heard moments before, just before the girl appeared in the entry.

"We go back to the hotel and relax. I can track her now that I've got her scent. We'll have our answer in a week."

Morgan blew glossy black bangs off her forehead with a sharp puff of breath and slanted him a look with her eyes, which were dark and frozen emerald green.

Leander turned away. He didn't want to argue. He didn't want to talk.

He just wanted to look at *her*.

When the subject of a reconnaissance mission was forwarded by the Assembly, Leander hadn't been pleased. He hadn't understood her importance, had thought it all a great bit of folly, time and energy wasted that could be better spent elsewhere.

The colony had more pressing business to attend to, of late.

"Of what interest is she to us?" he argued, standing before the sixteen men and one woman of the Assembly, his jaw set, his hands spread wide.

The East Library, where the Assembly regularly met, was filled with fractured, golden sunlight reflected from the crystal chandelier overhead. The room had a magnificent gilded ceiling and a seventeenth-century marble fireplace, a spectacular view of the river Avon snaking through the New Forest beyond, and was normally Leander's favorite place at Sommerley. It was a place where he could hide from the world and think.

When the Assembly was not in session, that is.

"A half-Blood whose father was executed for treason?" Leander added. He shook his head in frustration. "She's hardly worth a second glance. The probability she has any Gift is beyond remote. She's displayed none of the signs—"

"She has the Eyes," came the quiet response to his right from Edward, Viscount Weymouth. He reclined in a beige and ivory-striped silk Dupioni chair with his hands folded over his waistcoat. Spindly legs stretched out in front of him, round spectacles teetered on the end of a long, aquiline nose. "This has been confirmed by more than one scout," he added.

Leander pursed his lips and considered him.

He was a trusted man, a man who kept a record of the ancestry of each member of the colony, a man who knew all their secrets and every facet of their history back to their ancient days of glory in the equatorial rainforests of Africa.

Viscount Weymouth was Keeper of the Bloodlines, as were his father and grandfather before him, and every other male of his line, back to the beginning.

It was an important job in the colony, a revered one. Because for the *Ikati*, Bloodlines were of secondary importance to only two other things:

Secrecy. Allegiance.

"I believe there have been other half-Bloods in our history who had the Eyes, and few of them showed any other sign. Even fewer were ever able to Shift," Leander reminded the Viscount.

The Viscount stared at him, stony and silent, for one long moment. Then he uttered something that made the other members of the Assembly shift in their seats and murmur to one another in worried agreement.

"What you say is true. But none of the other half-Bloods were *his*."

"Leander."

His brother spoke his name, and the room turned to his voice. Christian sat in second position around the rectangular mahogany table, to the left of Leander, his gilt beechwood armchair with its carved wooden back only slightly less ornate than his brother's.

He was pretending to relax, slouched slightly in his chair, a sardonic smile on his handsome face. His hair spilled in a silken jet tangle over his shoulders. He was the less physically imposing of the two, but equally intelligent, sloe-eyed, and lithe, with the height and grace and dusky coloring all the *Ikati* shared.

And like all the others, he gauged Leander's reaction with every word he spoke. One poorly turned phrase could lead to very unpleasant consequences.

"Perhaps it would be wise to pay this half-Blood a visit," he began slowly. "If only to assure ourselves that she is not a threat. Under normal circumstances, she would have been dealt with at birth. The mere fact that she remains free puts us all at risk."

Leander's only response was an arched eyebrow and thinned lips. Emboldened by Christian's words, Robert Barrington leaned forward over the table, green eyes narrowed in a handsome, leonine face. "I agree. If she were to Shift for the first time outside the walls of the colony, unsupervised, perhaps in plain view of who knows how many people, the results could be disastrous."

Another man, a set of belligerence to his jaw, sat forward. Grayson Sutherland. Newly wed, always confident, he'd competed as a young man against Leander for the attentions of one of the tribe's most sought-after females, a raven-haired beauty with rose petal lips and notoriously free hands. Sutherland had lost.

"They're right, Leander. This little stray could be the undoing of us all. She should immediately be brought here to face the Assembly and her fate."

A few other men around the table made low noises of agreement, all of them privileged, all of them Gifted, every one of them stepping into very dangerous territory.

Leander's face darkened with anger. He felt the blood rise to his face.

Shifter Law—ancient, iron-clad, and utterly patriarchal—was clear on this matter. Though it was allowed for Shifters to dally outside their race with humans—frowned upon but allowed—it was forbidden to marry, expressly forbidden to breed. The punishment for this very rare transgression was death for the human and the offspring and a lifetime of imprisonment for the Shifter.

With a single exception. If the Shifter gave his life in their stead.

Leander's gaze, burning with cold fire, picked out each member of the Assembly, one by one. "A sacrifice was made to ensure her freedom. You know that." Above all, he revered honor and courage, duty and discipline, and therefore admired what Jenna's father had done. Though to admit his admiration would in itself be a kind of treason.

"You *all* know that. An oath was sworn and paid for in blood. My father, Charles McLoughlin, Alpha Lord of this colony before me, exacted the price himself. It was done according to the Law and will stand. She will not be taken."

Though it was quiet and controlled, his voice cracked like a bullwhip across the room, silencing them all.

"Yes," Christian agreed after a long and awkward moment in which the only sound was the ticking of the Belgian clock on the Chippendale burlwood desk. "We cannot break the oath of the Alpha. She and her mother were permitted to live, and so far she has given no other sign but the Eyes. But the risk remains."

Although it was still a foolhardy thing to do, Christian was allowed to challenge Leander, who supposed it was good for him, in a way. It kept him grounded and reminded him he still had family, small though it was now. Since the accident that had claimed his parents three years ago last May, his older sister, Daria, and Christian were all he had left.

"So I suggest we find her current whereabouts and pay her a visit a few days before her birthday. Keep out of sight, no contact, just watch. On her twenty-fifth birthday we'll have our answer, one way or another. I'll go myself, if you like."

He lifted his gaze straight to Leander's and waited, expressionless, still casually slouched in his chair. But Leander felt what simmered beneath his brother's air of casual indifference.

Excitement.

He narrowed his eyes, wondering at the cause, but his brother, still impassive, glanced away. Leander turned his attention back to the gathered men. "And if she is unable to Shift?"

It was Viscount Weymouth who answered him through the heavy silence that suddenly filled the grace and splendor of the East Library.

"Then you know what must be done."

So it had been agreed. Christian and Leander would travel to observe the half-Blood until her birthday, and Morgan would accompany them. She was the only woman who served in the Assembly, a concession hard-won and resented by the old guard, men who were unused to having their authority questioned, unaccustomed to a female usurping their age-old dogma of male superiority. But it had been put to a vote and she had been approved, by a threadbare margin of one.

Leander's was the deciding vote.

Securing her place in the Assembly had been a battle. She'd sustained scars and nursed deep resentments for those who stood against her. But Leander suspected ambition and a shrewd acuity kept her quiet. In truth, her Gifts and intelligence made her worth ten of the men who'd opposed her.

Savagely cunning, an expert hunter, and completely lethal, Morgan possessed the rare Gift of Suggestion, which would make it easier for them to convince an unwilling half-Blood to return to Sommerley, if the need arose. It was also the reason she had ultimately been accepted into the Assembly.

She was also bloody high-maintenance. Leander had experienced firsthand her flair for dramatic displays of emotion, the fine-tuned and overly delicate sense of pride that made her so wary of any imagined insult. She was more prickly than a porcupine.

The plan to visit the half-Blood was implemented with a speed that hadn't marked the Assembly's decision making in years. The trio departed on a private plane on a course for Los Angeles that very night.

Fifteen hours and one too many scotches later, Leander stood on his balcony in the presidential suite at the Four Seasons Beverly Hills, looking over the city as twilight stained it hues of deepest indigo and violet.

As they had innumerable times since leaving Sommerley, his thoughts turned once again to Jenna.

She'd been followed in one way or another her whole life, though she was unaware of it. The Assembly had allowed her father's sacrifice to ensure her freedom but not to erase her from their view completely. To ignore her would be simply unthinkable.

A scout had been assigned to watch her, to track her and report back to the Assembly on her progress. But over the years, as she grew from a child into a woman, Jenna showed no outward sign of the Gift other than the Eyes.

By puberty, when most other Shifters would have begun to exhibit the Gifts of their Blood—the strength, the agility, and the speed that made climbing a tree or clearing a fence a thing of ease, the heightened senses that allowed them to hear the whisper of air over the wings of the birds in the sky and the heartbeats of the little creatures that burrowed below the earth, to smell water from miles off and know if it was fresh or salt, still or running, lake or pond—Jenna had not.

And so, over time, they became convinced she never would.

The scouts were sent only once every few years now but never reported anything unusual. The possibility that she would Shift on her twenty-fifth birthday, the age when all half-Bloods first Shifted, was hardly a possibility at all.

But still, there was a chance…

Leander's pulse quickened as a warm breeze stirred the sheer curtains of the open patio doors, the scent of baked stone and crushed flowers folded within its balmy caress. The pink marble veranda with its balustrades, cascading scarlet bougainvillea, and stone fountain lay quiet and open before him, an invitation to the night.

He raised his gaze to the darkening sky and felt the pulse within him.

The call of the Shift.

Night was when he felt it most strongly, though he, like all others of his kind, could Shift at will. But Leander had a Gift only the most powerful were blessed with. He could become more than just an animal, more than the lethal predator all his kin could become.

He could become vapor and blend without form into the very air itself.

He stepped out of his clothing, his jacket, his shirt, his fine wool trousers, letting them all fall to the warmed marble beneath his bare feet. He closed his eyes and let it rise within him, his heart hammering within his chest as the joy of the Shift took over.

It was like nothing else he'd ever felt, that final moment before disintegration, and nothing on earth compared to it. It was a cascade of sensation, a tremor that became an electric charge that became a weightlessness as his body disappeared. All human flesh was gone, all senses vanished but the silken feel of the air against him. He slipped through it, a fine spray of mist rising up, shimmering, shaping itself through his will and his mind, which remained, though his body did not.

Nothing else could make the turn with him. Not clothing or weapons or food; anything he wore or held in his hands would simply fall to the ground. It was a fact that had proved inconvenient on more than one occasion. But tonight he thought not of this, nor of the Assembly and their Law, nor of Christian and Morgan and the task set before him.

Tonight he thought only of freedom and let himself melt into the heated sanctuary of the indigo sky.

THREE

The champagne was doing little to alleviate her headache, though it was an exquisite 1996 Louis Roederer.

The subtle taste of almonds, hazelnuts, and white flowers glossed over her taste buds on the first sip, accompanied thereafter by the rounded, creamy attack of silken texture, akin to the sinful decadence of a buttery brioche. Scents of straw, citrus, light toast, and buttered corn hit the back of her nose and she almost groaned with pleasure.

This, Jenna thought as she swallowed, *is an orgasm for the tongue.*

It cost more than four hundred dollars a bottle.

It was a gift from her thrice-divorced neighbor, Mrs. Colfax. They were more than acquaintances but not exactly friends, since neither ever divulged anything resembling personal information to each other—which was precisely how they both preferred it. Jenna guessed Mrs. Colfax had her own closet full of rattling skeletons with which to contend.

She watched the lustrous, pale gold liquid effervesce within the elegant confines of the etched Waterford flute—another gift from Mrs. Colfax—and heaved a sigh of frustration.

What happened today was ominously disturbing, though she'd nearly convinced herself she'd imagined the entire episode. The bubble bath was helping, if only to relax the taut muscles in her back. It did nothing to ease the tension in her mind, however, or the lingering static on her skin.

A static that increased every time she let herself think about *him*.

Yet she couldn't get him out of her mind. The stranger with the glossy fringe of ebony hair, the face of a Botticelli angel, the eyes of a hungry wolf.

Something about him seemed so familiar. Though it had been but a glance before she'd passed out, she felt something leap against her skin under the weight of his stare, as if an unknown beast strained sinew and muscle, hungry to surface.

In that moment their eyes met, she suddenly felt like… an animal, awakening.

Jenna stretched her legs out and curled her toes over the edge of the tub, took a deep breath, and closed her eyes, shutting out the candlelit bathroom with its mirrored vanity, marbled counter, and enclosed glass shower. She shook her head to dispel the memory of his face, burning bright as a new penny under her closed lids.

He was just another stranger on the street. The strange electric charge couldn't possibly have come from him. Could she have suffered heat stroke? She chewed on her lower lip and considered it. The symptoms were the same: dizziness, pounding heart, clammy skin, fainting.

But she was never affected by the heat. She never got sick or fainted or felt dizzy. She'd never even had a cavity, for God's sake!

So she did what she always did when confronted with something she couldn't figure out: she put it out of her mind. She sank down farther into the warm, perfumed water and thought about where she was going to do her grocery shopping from now on.

The bathroom was the one place she'd invested money to upgrade her tiny one-bedroom apartment, and it had been money well spent. *The plumbing, though,* she thought as a trickle of water from the faucet ran in a chilly sluice over her left big toe. She was going to have to talk to Saul about the plumbing.

The building was over fifty years old, done in a poorly executed art deco style, and had what her landlord Saul referred to as "character." The faucets dripped, the toilet ran, the kitchen cabinets stuck, the walls were thin as paper. She had become overly familiar with her next-door neighbors' personal problems.

Still, she loved it. It was home, and a home was what she most desperately needed after her mother died.

It wasn't a shock, her mother's early death. No one survived long drinking as much alcohol as she did. But her death had left Jenna, at eighteen years old, with no one, not a single soul in the world to call family. Once her father vanished when she was ten, her mother had adamantly refused to even speak his name.

Jenna had only the most fleeting memories of him. Tall and dark, handsome, somber, mysterious. And the memory of his smell was burned into her mind. He carried the cool scent of night on his skin no matter the time of day.

Her mother had no siblings, her grandparents were long dead...there was simply no one.

College was out of the question. Her mother left her with no money, nothing other than an upside-down mortgage on a small bungalow in the Valley, a few pieces of jewelry, and furniture bought from a secondhand store. Jenna sold it all and used what little money she had left as a down payment on her first month's rent on this apartment.

She'd made her way. And knowing she could survive alone, after the chaos of her childhood, after all the unanswered questions about why she was so different from everyone else, there was nothing she would allow herself to be afraid of.

Except, maybe, what happened today. Which she wasn't thinking about.

"Yoo-hoo, Jeennnaaaaa! It's your fairy godmother!"

Jenna smiled and opened her eyes to the singsong warbling of her neighbor, Mrs. Colfax, calling through the open patio door.

"In here!" Jenna shouted, then hauled herself out of the bath. Bubbles slid in languorous sheets down her naked body. She set her glass of champagne down on the counter and wrapped herself in the lush white embrace of a Turkish cotton towel.

Two short raps on the thin bathroom door, then the elegantly coiffed blonde head of Mrs. Colfax popped through.

"You're taking a bath? In this heat? My dear, are you *mad?*" Mrs. Colfax asked, one perfectly arched eyebrow raised.

She'd been an actress in her youth, beautiful though not particularly talented, and retained both the elocution and melodrama of the theater in her speech.

"That is debatable," Jenna said. She gestured toward the fizzing champagne. "But I have a headache, so I thought a bath and a little bubbly would help."

"Ah, yes," Mrs. Colfax agreed and swung the door open to invade the bathroom with her larger-than-life persona.

She wore one of her signature Chanel suits—this one a powder blue—Valentino patent d'Orsay pumps, a double strand of pearls, and three-hundred-dollar French perfume that smelled of rare orchids and sex. She had seduced, wed, and divorced a succession of wealthy men and made efficient use of them—and of their money. She lived in a sprawling, modern mansion next door that towered over Jenna's tiny apartment complex like a glass Goliath.

"Cristal will do *wonders* for one's level of happiness and good health," Mrs. Colfax added. "I'm glad to see you developing a taste for something more refined than that hideous whole milk you drink."

Jenna reached for another towel to wrap around her head. "You realize there's a *reason* they say milk does a body good, right? Besides, it's more affordable than champagne. Especially the ones you drink."

"Having money for French champagne is far more important than having money for the rent, my dear, never forget that," Mrs. Colfax shot back. "By the way, I ordered the filet from Boa for dinner, darling, I hope you don't mind. I'll be in New York for your birthday next week and thought we could celebrate tonight, since you don't have to work?"

Filet mignon, Jenna thought. *Heaven on a plate.*

She remembered with real regret the thick rib eye she'd left at the checkout this afternoon. The only thing better was a T-bone. Or a New York strip. Or a nice grilled tri-tip. Her mouth began to water. How anyone could be a vegetarian she couldn't fathom.

"You know I can't resist filet mignon." She flipped over at the waist to bundle her long hair into a towel, which she twisted around and flipped back up, leaving her hair wrapped in a towering cotton beehive above her head. "What's in New York?"

Mrs. Colfax twisted her mouth into a roguish smile and gave Jenna a dismissive little wink. "Just a certain gentleman. Nothing for you to worry about, my dear."

Jenna smiled back, satisfied. At least some things would remain reliably the same, even if everything else seemed so confusing.

The doorbell rang. Mrs. Colfax turned to look out the bathroom door, toward the patio, a mere twenty feet away. "Ah! The steaks!" She clicked out of the room in her designer pumps and Jenna shut the door behind her so she could finish drying off and shrug into her clothes. It wasn't two minutes before she heard her name called.

"Come along, princess. Don't let it get cold!"

Jenna made her way to the table and watched Mrs. Colfax plate the filet mignon, along with perfectly steamed asparagus spears and a lavish mound of garlic mashed potatoes. She tossed the empty containers onto the granite bar counter behind the dining table, then sat down. She poured two glasses of champagne and raised her own in a toast.

"To my dear friend Jenna, who is tragically alone, hideously overworked, and grossly underpaid. She truly deserves more from life than what she got." She tipped her head back and drank her champagne in one long draught, then set the glass back down on the table with an elegant flourish of her slender, fine-boned hand.

Jenna just stared at her.

Mrs. Colfax raised her perfectly plucked eyebrows. "What is it, my dear?"

"*That's* my birthday toast? Seriously?"

"Oh, my. That *was* rather lacking, wasn't it?" she replied, completely unchastened. "Shall I try again?" She cut into her filet mignon, took a dainty bite, and chewed, all the while looking at Jenna as if waiting to be amused.

"You're hopeless," Jenna answered with a laugh. She refilled Mrs. Colfax's glass and picked up her own.

With a twinge of sadness, she thought of her mother and the toast she used to make on Jenna's every birthday. She raised her glass and swallowed around the lump in her throat. *This one's for you, Mom.*

"Life is pain and everyone dies, but true love lives forever."

Mrs. Colfax pursed her lips. "Tch. How uplifting. And please don't tell me you believe that hornswoggle, my dear. The myth of true love is one of the greatest self-deceptions ever embraced by the female sex. It's right up there with the ridiculous notion that money can't buy happiness and size doesn't matter. Now eat your steak—and don't tell me it's overcooked; I made sure they prepared it just as you like. Bloody rare."

Hours later—dinner finished, dishes cleared, Mrs. Colfax off to the glass Goliath—Jenna lay in bed, staring up at the shadows crawling over the ceiling, thinking about love and death and self-deception, about a pair of fine green eyes burning bright.

She fell asleep with the image of those eyes still glowing behind her lids.

FOUR

Jenna had been having the same dream since childhood, and though the details varied, the sense of happiness she awoke with never did. She was running through an ancient forest with total abandon, leaping over fallen logs and moss-covered boulders, flying through air swirling so thick with morning mists it seemed to brush against her bare skin like silken tresses of hair. Moist beds of moss and green leaves were crushed into perfume underfoot as she ran, only somehow she felt the loamy forest floor through the soles of four feet instead of two.

But this dream was different. And profoundly disturbing.

It began with the whisper of her name in her ear.

The voice was both familiar and alien, and strangely comforting. She turned toward it, reaching out with a sigh.

Her fingertips met soft skin over a strong jaw, traced the outline of full lips, but her lids were so heavy she was unable to open her eyes to see the face under her hand. The lips moved to her face, brushed her forehead, temple, cheek, then pressed softly against the corner of her mouth. She shivered with pleasure. The barest musk of spice and smoke and summer heat teased her nose.

"Yes," Jenna murmured into the darkness. Then she felt the hands.

A hand with strong, cool fingers curled around the back of her neck, cradling her head. Another softly stroked the slope of her cheek, then moved down the line of her throat to where her pulse beat hot and strong beneath the skin. She felt the lips touch her there, heard her name whispered again.

She arched her back, made a small sound deep in her throat, and whispered, "Yes, please."

The fingers tightened in her hair, pulled her head gently back, exposing her bare throat. A feather-light kiss on her neck turned to a deeper, insistent suck as a warm mouth opened over the column of her throat. Jenna moaned, a sharp ache of longing between her legs.

"Tell me you want me," the voice murmured, husky-sweet, teasing, lips moving over her skin.

"Yes, yes," she said, heartbeat accelerating, breath coming shorter.

"*Say it,*" the voice softly commanded, and she trembled under the current of desire that scorched through her. Goosebumps formed over every inch of her skin, hardening her nipples into raw nerves that longed for the lap of his tongue, the gentle tug of his teeth.

"I want you, I want you, I want—"

But her whispered chant was cut off by the lips crushing down on hers. The fingers dug into the flesh at her hips. Her hands reached out, pulled the face down harder. She twined her fingers into locks of thick, silken hair.

She pressed her body up against a hard chest, wanting more, so much more, but suddenly the kiss was over, the hands were gone, and nothing more remained but a low, throaty laugh that drifted into silence as she jerked upward out of bed, waking, and sat trembling and gasping in the dark room.

It was hours before she fell back to sleep.

When she opened her eyes in the morning, she was lying on her side, knees drawn up, hands folded beneath her cheek, the bed sheets in disarray around her waist. Sunlight slanted through the slit in the heavy blackout shades and fell into a pool of gold on the beige carpet.

A lone seagull cried out somewhere in the distance and the sharp tang of hot espresso reached her nose from the neighbor's kitchen. The alarm clock swam into view, the small bedside table with its reading lamp, framed photo of her mother in a rare smile, her desk with computer and telephone beyond.

The book she was reading before bed lay open upon the nightstand, though she remembered distinctly closing it before setting it down and turning off the light.

She frowned and stared at it for a moment before pushing herself up from the pillow to a sitting position. She *had* closed it, she knew—she remembered thinking at the time that she shouldn't be dog-earing a library book. She picked the book up and looked at it, then decided she'd probably been too tired to remember anything clearly. With a shrug, she set it back down on the nightstand, yawned, and stretched.

She stumbled out of bed, feeling soft carpet then cool tile beneath her feet as she entered the bathroom. Her reflection in the mirror showed evidence of the night: hair knotted and wild from tossing, red, bleary eyes with puffy lids, deep shadows beneath.

She made a face in the mirror, turned on the shower, then bent down under the sink to get her brush, thinking she would try to get some of the knots out of her hair while she waited for the water to get hot.

When she opened the cabinet under the sink, she saw her makeup bag had been moved from its spot in the wire pull-out basket. The lotions and perfumes stored next to it were in slight disarray.

She stood so quickly she almost banged her head against the countertop.

She was fastidiously neat. She had to be, the miniscule size of her apartment dictated it. Everything had its place, every space was utilized and arranged for maximum efficiency. Her cosmetics were always in perfect order.

And now they were not.

She tried not to panic. This was, after all, practically nothing. She must have forgotten to tidy this area yesterday, she'd been too tired, had felt unwell. Yes, that was it. She'd felt unwell and was mixing things up in her mind. She let the cabinet door swing shut and stepped into the shower.

After she dressed, Jenna went to make herself a cup of coffee. As she stood in the kitchen spooning coffee grounds into the filter, she noticed that one of her leather-bound photo albums, kept in a bookshelf in the living room, stood a few inches out from the others, as if it had been returned hurriedly to its place but had not been fully pushed back in.

A serpentine flash of premonition crawled up her spine.

She went to the front door and checked the lock, but it was latched securely, as were all the windows and the patio door.

Jenna stood silent in the living room for a long time, staring out toward the navy strip of ocean shimmering beyond the sand, lost in thought as the mug of coffee in her hand grew cold.

Getting into her locked apartment had been the easy part.

Leander had merely pushed himself through the hairline crack in the upper corner of her bathroom window, the one she would finally notice when it widened enough to be seen by the naked eye.

It was watching her sleep that proved difficult.

She slept with the innocent abandon of a child. Breathing deeply, body slanted across the middle of the queen-sized bed, arms flung wide, hair spilling silken, honeyed gold over the pillows.

He watched from the corner of the dark bedroom as her chest slowly rose and fell, her nude body outlined beneath the sheets.

He'd been through her apartment, trying to find clues. Trying to find anything that would lead him to believe she possessed any of the powers of their kind.

So far, he'd found nothing.

She loved art and music, loved to read, this was plain from the things she kept. Her books, her eclectic CD collection, the ticket stubs to the Molière exhibition at the Getty

Museum. Paystubs from a French restaurant, unopened mail stacked neatly in a wicker basket by the kitchen phone, takeout menus in a drawer.

There was no sign of a lover, no photos of friends, no indication she was close to anyone at all. Her photo album contained only old pictures of her mother, of herself as a child, mementos of places she'd visited, postcards.

Her orderly and sterile apartment illustrated the life of someone utterly alone.

He'd had no thought of coming here when he Shifted, had no destination in mind as he allowed himself to be caught in the updraft of heated night air that lifted him from his veranda at the Four Seasons. The lights and noise of the city grew distant as he melded into the atmosphere, rolling and spinning through thin sapphire clouds, free upon the wind.

He knew her name, he knew her address. He had a picture, though it was a few years outdated and slightly blurry.

But he didn't know *her*, this creature of gilt and satin and feminine curves, skin like roses and cream and sunlight on water where the rest of his kind were dark, with hair as dark as the forest floor at midnight, skin tones of café au lait and buttered rum.

He didn't know that the force of his desire would make him sink to his knees, crouching naked in the dark with his heart in his throat and the scent of her flaming hot in his nose.

He hadn't expected this.

His eyes drank her in and he wondered that she possessed the Gift of beauty all the *Ikati* shared. She was half human, after all, an inferior race evolved from mud, prone to violence, greed, and all manner of disease. He'd never found a single one of them attractive.

But her father had. He'd done the unthinkable and *mated* with a human.

He'd also exacted a promise from his successor that his half-Blood offspring would not be brought back to Sommerley to live a life of confinement until the time of her first Shift as the Law decreed for the circumstance. She would be allowed to grow and live as a creature free from the shackles of protection, duty, and constraint that defined life within the colony.

And for a female, there was more constraint than some could bear.

They'd had deserters in their history as well. Those were dealt with as swiftly and mercilessly as the colony dealt with any other threat.

He watched her until the muscles in his thighs began to ache with inactivity, then stood and walked silently over to her bedside. In human form, he was as silent as a cat. He saw through the darkness as if it were high noon, he retained all the heightened senses of his animal side.

Normally this was a blessing. Now…it was closer to torture.

A book lay on her bedside table. He flipped it open with one finger, read a single paragraph.

Man is the only creature that consumes without producing. He does not give milk, he does not lay eggs, he is too weak to pull the plough, he cannot run fast enough to catch rabbits. Yet he is lord of all the animals. He sets them to work, he gives back to them the bare minimum that will prevent them from starving, and the rest he keeps for himself.

Leander's lips curled into an amused smile. *Animal Farm* by George Orwell.

Ah, the exquisite irony.

He slanted her a look, his gaze lingering over the arc of her lips, her smooth brow, the soft planes of her cheek. Was she more than just this surfeit of sensuality so pleasing to the eye? What of her sense of humor, her intelligence, her passion? Would she fight for her freedom?

But no, one way or another, her time of freedom was coming to an end. If she could Shift, if she was fully one of their kind, he would take her back to Sommerley. Force her, if necessary. She would join their colony, she would learn their ways, she might even one day be his...

It came unbidden into his mind, startled him into stillness with his hand hovering over her open book.

Mine.

He crouched down next to her bed. A long, curling lock of golden hair hung free over the pillow. He picked it up and pressed it to his nose.

And if she cannot Shift, if she is Giftless, he thought, staring hard at her carmine lips half-parted in sleep, *it will fall to the Alpha to kill her. It will fall to me.*

"Jenna," he whispered, an almost noiseless exhalation of sound from his lips.

She shifted on the mattress, made a pretty, feminine sound in her throat. Her back arched beneath the sheets, a drowsy, languid movement that pressed her body taut against the fabric.

The dip of her waist. Her flat belly. Those full, perfect breasts.

"Yes, please," she murmured, then settled back down against the mattress with a sigh.

With a stab of desire so acute it made his mouth water, he realized she was dreaming.

He felt the ground disappear beneath him, his foundation of law and order and tribe, his entire lifetime of duty and sacrifice, safety and silence. She became—with an abrupt alteration of priority that made all else fall away—the only thing and everything he wanted.

But he was the Alpha and she was an unproven half-Blood, daughter of an outlaw, her future hanging on the scales of fate, her very existence uncertain.

She was not his to have.

The strand of her hair slipped between his fingers and he rose, heart pounding, and turned away.

FIVE

When Jenna first interviewed for the coveted job of sommelier at Mélisse, she was twenty-two years old, had no college
degree, no special training, and no relevant experience.

What she had was raw talent.

Her sense of smell was so keen it picked out the single note of lavender, the merest hint of graphite, the faintest rumor of black truffle hidden deep within the aromatic
spice and fruit bouquet of a fine wine.

Though Mélisse was renowned for its wine program—
one which had been overseen since their inception by a quick
succession of middle-aged, snobbish men and contained
over six thousand bottles of the best wine produced throughout the world—they hired Jenna before the conclusion

of her first interview, based on her rather remarkable demonstration of this talent.

The owner of the restaurant, a trim, elderly gentleman named Francois Moreau, set out ten bottles of wine wrapped in plain brown paper bags on the long oak table in the glass-walled private dining room, then poured a single ounce from each into ten unlabeled crystal Riedel wine glasses.

"Tell me," he said in a pronounced French accent as he gestured toward the preposterous lineup, "what is the wine in each glass?"

He adjusted his wire-rimmed spectacles, folded his blue-veined hands over the second button of his camel pinstripe blazer, and smiled at her, serene and sharp.

Jenna smiled back and began.

Not only did she tell him the grape varietal each glass of wine contained, she told him whether it had been grown on hillside or riverbank, in high altitude or at ocean level, and what percentage of varietals contained within each if it was a blend.

Mrs. Colfax, who counted Monsieur Moreau among her beaux and had arranged the interview, had been very generous in sharing her wine and her knowledge of it, and Jenna never forgot a thing. The sense memory came as easily to her as did a great many other things, like her intuition, her strength, her agility, her speed.

Things her mother assiduously trained her to keep to herself.

She started the next night. Jenna loved her job more than anything else in her life, in spite of the inevitable discrimination she endured as a woman in what was considered—by the vast majority of their well-heeled clientele—a man's job.

This particular evening, she had arrived at work nine hours earlier, far ahead of the evening rush, and was now standing on the opposite side of the long, curving bar from Becky, the feisty, ginger-haired bartender recently hired away from a competitor.

It was late, almost closing time, and her feet hurt.

She'd had three difficult customers tonight. They were all older men who eyed her as if wondering how much she'd fetch at auction, then grilled her with questions about the wine list, proper food pairings, and minute differences from one vintage to the next, each finally allowing she might actually know what she was talking about and wasn't just the hat-check girl standing in for the real sommelier—the *male* sommelier.

She was in a foul mood.

When she felt that singular current of crackling electricity spike through her body, she should have known things were about to get worse.

"Ooh, la, *la*," Becky murmured, low so only Jenna heard. Her hand paused in midair over the wine glass she was about to lift into its place on the hanging rack above her head.

Jenna raised her eyes to Becky's freckled, sun-kissed face and took in the admiring stare aimed over her left shoulder at someone who had just come through the front door. She moved her gaze to the mirror that hung on the wall behind Becky, which provided an unobstructed view of the entire restaurant within its colossal, oak-framed border.

A man—tall and dark-haired—stood looking around the restaurant, letting his gaze rove over the graceful interior as if he were looking for someone. He handed over his coat without glancing at the eager hostess who appeared before him to take it.

His suit alone was worth admiring. Precisely cut to showcase broad shoulders, trim waist, long, well-muscled legs, it was a fitted charcoal-gray pinstripe and had the look of absurdly expensive bespoke. He wore beneath a snowy white button-down shirt, open at the collar to reveal a hint of tawny skin at his throat.

But it wasn't his elegant suit that made the chic and sophisticated patrons of Mélisse sit up and take notice of this gorgeous new arrival. It was the unstudied air of confidence and privilege and raw magnetism that surrounded him that drew the eye, the way he simply *took* the room by standing within it.

The maître d', a haughty man named Geoffrey with stooped shoulders and hairy wrists that showed below the starched white cuffs of his shirt, appeared at his side and exchanged a few words with the man. He gave him a curious, low bow.

Jenna lifted an eyebrow at this and watched in curiosity as Geoffrey led his elegant charge to a reserved table at the back—the best table—a graceful curved banquette of dove-gray leather ensconced against walls painted smoky plum.

He seated himself with the lithe movements of a dancer and accepted the menu and wine list from the waiter who materialized at his table. He spoke a few words to Geoffrey, who then scurried away like a terrified rodent, shooing the waiter along before him as he fled.

Then, with slow deliberation and the barest hint of a smile lifting his cheek, the man raised his head and met Jenna's gaze in the mirror.

Under lashes long and black as soot, his eyes were sharp and very green. She saw their phosphorescence through the dim, candlelit air and froze on a breath.

His smile deepened, a slow, slow burn. He did not blink.

"Oh, God." Jenna dropped her gaze and felt heat creep up her neck and flood her cheeks. Her heart began to pound.

The ghosted memory of the vivid dream flitted back to tease her. The hands and lips and tongue.

"It's *him*."

"Him who?"

"I know that man. I've seen him before," she murmured to Becky, trying to speak without moving her lips. She had the uncanny feeling he would be able to read them.

"In the restaurant?" Becky replied, surprised. "I don't remember him." She ran a hand over her unruly red hair, then smoothed it down the curve of her waist, flattening the wrinkled black apron. "I'd *definitely* remember him."

"*Shhh!*" Jenna scowled down at the granite bar top. "He'll hear you!"

Becky finally lifted the wineglass above her head and slid it into the hanging wire rack. "Please. He's all the way across the restaurant, Jenna. He's not going to *hear* me."

Jenna shifted her weight from left foot to right and began shredding a paper cocktail napkin to pieces. She became acutely aware of her body, her bare legs, the warm air on her skin. In spite of the simple black cocktail dress she wore, she suddenly felt *very* naked.

Her pulse had doubled in the space of thirty seconds.

"How do you know him?" Becky asked. She turned to mix a martini for one of the waiters.

Jenna didn't dare lift her eyes to the mirror. The heat that flooded her cheeks had begun to pulse throughout her body. The same throbbing burn she had felt in the grocery store.

This was not good. What the hell was the matter with her?

She inhaled a long, steadying breath, squeezing her hands into fists so they wouldn't shake, and counted to ten before answering.

"I saw him before, I was at the store—"

"Uh-oh," Becky interrupted, her voice turning sour. "Batten down the hatches, here comes Napoleon."

Before Jenna could ask, a voice hissed into her right ear.

"Earl McLoughlin is requesting the sommelier's assistance with his wine selection—*let's not keep him waiting!*" The reek of garlic and dried sweat stung her nose.

Jenna ground her teeth together and exchanged glances with Becky. "I thought we weren't using the first names of the clientele, Geoffrey? Because you think it's '*très gauche*'?"

Next to Jenna's elbow, Geoffrey practically vibrated with smothered apoplexy.

"Earl is not his *name*, you twit, it's his *title!*" he spat. "The concierge from the Four Seasons called in the reservation! He's an *aristocrat, for God's sake!*"

Before she could catch herself, Jenna's gaze flew up to the mirror. Across the restaurant, the earl was studying the wine list—brows stern, face neutral—but she sensed the stifled laughter yearning to break free from his full lips, which were pressed together with firm intent.

"You may refer to him as Your Grace or Your Majesty, but either way, be professional, be smiling, and be *gone!*"

He flapped his hands at her and made shooing noises, as if she were a pigeon begging for crumbs on a park bench.

Jenna didn't budge.

"One does not refer to an earl as Your Grace, Geoffrey, nor does one call him Your Majesty. Those titles are reserved for a duke and a king, respectively," she said coolly, looking down on his balding head.

Geoffrey's mouth formed a startled, moist O, but he didn't reply. He did begin to blink quite rapidly, however. Becky coughed into her hand to hide her laugh and turned away.

In addition to the enjoyment of fine wine, Mrs. Colfax had taught Jenna a few other things about high society.

"I will call him Lord McLoughlin or sir, as is proper etiquette, unless he asks me to call him by his first name, whatever that may be, as it would be '*très gauche*' to continue on with the ridiculous business of titles after that."

Jenna enjoyed the mottled shade of crimson that stained Geoffrey's cheeks. She turned on her heel and walked without hurry across the restaurant and over to the table that housed Lord McLoughlin, trying all the while to force the blood back out of her own cheeks and keep her breathing even.

The earl didn't look up from the wine list as she paused at the edge of the table. For one swift moment she allowed her gaze to linger on the long, tapered fingers that held the leather-bound book. They were tanned, strong, and elegant, like the rest of him.

A fine, humming current took up residence in her abdomen.

"Lord McLoughlin," she said, raising her eyes to his handsome face. "Welcome to Mélisse. How may I be of service?"

With a smooth motion of his arm, he lowered the wine list to the table, then met her gaze. He smiled—a true smile, admiring—and the din of the restaurant seemed to recede abruptly into a bank of muffled fog, leaving the two of them alone together.

"Please, call me Leander."

That voice like velvet, sending a wash of honeyed warmth throughout her body. The glossy fringe of his hair was longer than she remembered, almost brushing the tops of his shoulders, thick and shining jet. The barest hint of stubble glinted copper along his jaw.

Tell me you want me...

"Leander," Jenna repeated, liking the way his name felt on her tongue.

Impossible, she thought. *Too far away. But still...*

She tilted her head and gave him a sidelong look from under her lashes. "Not Your Grace? Your Highness?" she said lightly, testing him.

His answering smile was proof enough, but his words were total confirmation.

"Why bother with the ridiculous business of titles? It's all so..." He snapped his fingers, searching for a word. "Gauche. *Très gauche*, in fact...wouldn't you agree?"

He leaned forward over the table, steepled his fingertips under his chin, and held her gaze. For one brief moment she imagined he heard her heart pounding in her chest.

"Quite," she replied, her mind working furiously.

How did he hear the conversation with Geoffrey? How was that possible? They had been a hundred feet away...at least. And *whispering*.

Her stomach turned over with a twinge of intuition she promptly ignored. There was no one else who could do what she did; no one she'd ever met had those kinds of sensory gifts. He was just another man.

And her mother's cryptic warnings...well, her mother used to drink a lot.

She pushed a stray tendril of hair away from her cheek with the back of her hand and motioned toward the wine list. "May I assist you with a wine selection, Leander?" she said smoothly. "Do you see anything you like?"

Why had he been staring at her at the store? *Had* he been staring at her? What was he doing *here*? Was she just crazy—was the whole thing her imagination?

His smile deepened, dimpling his cheeks. "Why, yes, Miss...?" he lifted his eyebrows, waiting.

"Jenna," she replied.

"Jenna," he repeated slowly. His intense gaze flickered over her figure, once. It came back to rest on her face and a muscle in his jaw twitched. "Yes, I do believe there is something I like."

Under the proper English accent, Jenna detected a slight cadence to his voice, something lilting and familiar, a nuance she couldn't place. The way he was looking at her made her stomach do something strange.

"Wonderful." She cursed her voice for cracking. "What may I bring you this evening?"

Coincidence? Her imagination? Who were the other two? And what *was* that heavenly smell coming off his skin?

"The '61 Latour."

And then she stopped thinking and just blinked at him, trying not to let her mouth hang open. The waiter came and set a silver tray of flatbread and warm rosemary sourdough rolls ensconced in ivory linen upon the table.

"Sparkling or still water for you, sir?" the waiter asked.

Leander's eyes did not move away from Jenna's face. "*Rien, merci,*" he said, his voice silky smooth.

The waiter glanced over at Jenna, then inclined his head and retreated.

"The '61 Latour," Jenna repeated stiffly, her lips puckering. "A fine choice."

At seven thousand nine hundred eighty dollars, it was by far the most expensive bottle on their thirty-nine-page wine list.

It was only there to add gravitas to the wine program; no one in their right mind would spend that much money on such a rare wine at a restaurant. He'd have no way of knowing if it had even been cellared properly. A true collector, someone with both the pocketbook and the palate to appreciate a thing so rare and valuable, would purchase it through a reputable auction house or directly from the château, ensuring the chain of care and the wine's integrity.

Even the movie people and the rappers, who were the restaurant's greatest consumers of fine wine with the least appreciation for it, wouldn't go for the Latour. It would be the Moëlleux or the Screaming Eagle.

Besides, with even the most careful cellaring, a 1961 vintage was most probably past its prime—years past, in fact. It was ridiculous. It was *beyond* ridiculous.

Leander lifted his eyebrows. "Do I detect a hint of surprise?"

"*Surprise?*" she repeated, the two syllables lengthened with disdain.

He had interpreted her ridicule as surprise? As shock? As—heaven forbid—awe?

So: another egotistical, entitled jerk who liked to throw his money around like confetti to impress the unwashed masses. She guessed he treated women in a similar fashion.

He probably thought her dim-witted and out of her league. Number four for the day.

With a poof that was almost audible, Jenna's patience evaporated.

"Of course I'm not surprised. It's the perfect choice for you," she said, the slightest accent on the last word. She ignored the ghost of her mother's warning voice in her head and granted him a smile, small and deliberate.

A fleeting frown crossed his features. It was quickly replaced by an expression of placid neutrality.

"For me?"

He leaned back into the soft leather of the booth and draped one arm casually over the top of the banquette, his gaze never leaving her face. The muscle in his jaw twitched once again.

The waiter materialized silently at the tableside and presented an oval platter with three mouthfuls of food nestled in tiny silver spoons all surrounded by an elaborate drizzled pattern of cucumber-infused froth.

"The *amuse-bouche*, sir." He pointed out the bite-sized portions. "Kumamoto oyster with cucumber gelée, millefeuille of smoked salmon with Osetra caviar, roulade of bluefin tuna with pickled fennel."

He reached to set down the plate in front of Leander just as Geoffrey appeared, wearing a smile that would have looked at home on a shark.

"And how is the wine selection coming along, Your Graceful Lordship? Would you care to hear any of this evening's specials?"

Neither Jenna or Leander acknowledged him. Their eyes were still locked together.

"Yes," Jenna said acidly, "it suits you perfectly. The '61 Latour is the ultimate penis wine."

Geoffrey gasped, the waiter fumbled the plate of *amuse-bouche* and sent it clattering down against the table, but Leander remained taut in his chair, gazing at her, a wintry little smile curving his lips.

"Really?" he said, controlled and calm. "How very amusing. Pray *do* enlighten me."

"My Dearest High Majesty, I apologize *completely*! Let me assure you Mélisse in no way condones this type of—"

Leander made a sharp, dismissive motion to Geoffrey with the hand that was draped over the back of the banquette and kept his wolfish gaze on Jenna's face. "No apology needed. Leave us."

Out of the corner of her eye, Jenna saw Geoffrey's face turn an interesting shade of eggplant. He clutched the waiter's arm and dragged him off toward the kitchen.

"You were saying?" Leander said.

"I call them the penis wines," Jenna replied, keeping the same tone of lightly contemptuous civility though her blood was boiling. She knew there would be hell to pay for this, knew her job was most likely kaput, but for the moment she could not care less.

"They are the ridiculously expensive wines purchased as a show of masculinity by a certain species of men—excuse me, *males*—who have no real appreciation for their value but feel the pathetic need to display their tail feathers."

Her small smile grew larger as his disappeared altogether. "I think a man secure in his masculinity would choose something a little more...substantial, shall we say. A little less *showy*."

A moment passed, not long but wide and cavernous, in which neither of them spoke.

"I've offended you," he finally said. His face betrayed nothing, his tone was quiet and acutely polite. Only his body revealed a hint of anything other than utter detachment. He gripped the edge of the table so hard his knuckles turned white. "How?"

A shade of hostility faded from her posture. She'd expected blustering, outrage, even outright yelling. Most blowhards like him were more than happy to shout at an underling if the opportunity presented itself. She'd been primed and ready for an argument, had even thought of a few more witticisms to snap at him.

But she hadn't expected this. Not this patience. Not this…concern.

Jenna drew in a breath and shifted her weight onto her other foot. She suddenly wished to be anywhere else than here at this moment. She was tired and behaving badly.

All at once the anger drained away, leaving only a faint residue of embarrassment and the strong desire to go home, climb into bed, and pull the covers over her head.

She closed her eyes and swallowed. "Geoffrey was right, that wasn't well done of me." She sighed and passed a hand over her forehead. "I'm sorry, it's been a long night. I'll bring the Latour straightaway."

She turned to leave the table, wondering where she was going to find her next job, when Leander's soft voice called her back.

"Wait, Jenna, please."

He was half out of the booth already, rising to stand before caution held him back, reaching toward her with his hand, his face shadowed by the raphis palm near the table, his eyes troubled.

She looked up at him, surprised by his height and his sudden proximity. He gazed down at her intently, his hand still reaching toward her arm. The intoxicating and eerily familiar scent of spice and night air and virile man swirled around her, filling her nose.

"The '61 Latour was my father's favorite wine," Leander murmured. His eyes gleamed in the low light like polished gems. "He served it at his wedding to my mother, thirty-five years ago."

He inhaled and lightly brushed her bare arm with his fingertips, which sent a current of heat zinging through every nerve. "They were both killed in a car accident three years past. On the rare occasion I find it on a wine list, I order it in memory of them."

Jenna momentarily lost the power of speech. She was, however, acutely aware of his fingers on her skin, the heat and tension that ached between them, and the curious eyes of everyone in the restaurant.

"Oh—I...I'm so—I'm so sorry," she stammered, blushing. His fingers kept a light, distracting pressure on her arm. She confounded herself by blurting out, "My parents are both gone too."

Jenna hadn't spoken of this to anyone in years.

In response, he simply murmured, "Yes."

And then she was falling into his eyes, sucked into their bottomless emerald depths like a swimmer losing the fight against a riptide, a swimmer who *wanted* to drown. A dark, startling rush of déjà vu swept through her, so strong and clear she felt overwhelmed by it.

Yes, her mind echoed. *Yes.*

"Do I know you?" she whispered, urgent. "Have we met somewhere before?"

He remained perfectly still, so motionless and coiled he seemed otherworldly, like he was carved from stone, a piece of marble with incandescent eyes.

He increased the pressure on her arm by a fraction yet didn't speak. "It was *you* in the parking lot at the store, wasn't it? I saw you there...didn't I?" she pressed, breathless. Her heart leapt as their eyes clung together.

A ripple of tension rolled through his chest. His lips parted and he stared down at her, his face blazing with heat. "We—I—"

He seemed just about to say more, but a woman at one of the tables near the piano burst into peals of high, raucous laughter and the moment was gone.

"We have never met before tonight," he said quietly and dropped his hand from her arm. He turned away, then stepped back, angling himself toward his table.

"But—"

"Would you mind—if you please—may I have the Latour?" he asked politely, looking down, hesitating before taking his seat once again. He folded his hands together with his forearms resting against the edge of the table and leaned over, staring down at his plate, his hair gleaming ebony as it brushed against his cheekbone, hiding his expression. He didn't look up.

A flush of scarlet crept up Jenna's neck toward her ears. *Idiot.*

"Certainly," she murmured stiffly, "I'll be right back."

She willed herself to move calmly away from the table, willed her eyes to stare straight ahead to avoid meeting dozens of other inquisitive pairs directed her way as she wove through the restaurant, her legs stiff as boards.

She didn't remember walking to the kitchen, she only knew she had arrived there when Geoffrey found her standing like a zombie in the middle of it, staring into space.

"You are *finished*!" he screeched, his neck veins bulging blue against the starched collar of his shirt.

"Geoffrey—"

"I knew we shouldn't have hired a female sommelier! I *knew* it! Too emotional, too unpredictable, too *unprofessional*!"

Jenna winced and wiped away a fleck of spittle from her cheek while Geoffrey stalked back and forth in front of her, arms flailing.

"We're ruined, you know." He swung around and stabbed his finger into the air in front of Jenna's face. "*Ruined*! What do you think is going to happen when he tells the owner about this? *I'll* be held responsible for your disgusting display of feminism! And the *press*!"

He froze. His skin took on the pallor of a bed sheet. His beady eyes bulged out of his head until she thought they might actually be ejected from their sockets.

"The press," he whispered, his face ashen. He lifted his hands to the sides of his head. "If word gets out to the press that you called His Holy Dignity a *dick*—"

"I did *not*—"

"Geoffrey!"

The hostess, a busty brunette in a clingy black dress with a plunging neckline, burst through the swinging steel doors of the kitchen and looked wildly around, almost panting in panic. "*Geoffrey*!"

"For God's sake, Tiffany, *I'm right here!* What is it?" he spat, turning with a huff.

"The earl," she breathed, pointing over her shoulder toward the dining room. "He's *asking for you.*" She twirled back out through the doors with a flash of tanned leg above a platinum gold Jimmy Choo pump.

Geoffrey turned back to Jenna and narrowed his eyes. "Your employment with Mélisse is terminated, effective immediately. *Get out of my restaurant,*" he snarled.

Before she could open her mouth to speak, Geoffrey vanished through the kitchen doors like an angry poltergeist, leaving only the metallic scent of fury lingering behind.

Jenna drew in a slow breath, checking her anger. She looked around the open kitchen with its black-and-white-tiled floor, enormous walk-in refrigerator, stainless steel sinks, and bustling activity, and said a silent good-bye. She had only her jacket and handbag to retrieve; all the papers and files in her small windowless office belonged to the restaurant.

Once she stepped out the door, it would be as if she hadn't spent the past two years of her life here. It would be as if she'd never existed.

In a daze, she moved through the kitchen toward her tiny office at the back. She slammed the door behind her to block out the snickering from the sous chef and picked up her handbag from the chair where she'd tossed it as she rushed out at the beginning of her shift.

She looked around one final time. The shape of the room, the bookshelves lining one wall, the master sommelier certificate framed above her small desk. The thought that she'd be able to take *one* thing after all—the certificate earned through her own hard work and talent—did nothing to cheer her. After being fired from Mélisse, she doubted she could work anywhere in the city again. She'd soon be bartending at the strip club near the airport.

The pounding of fists against the office door made her jump and spin around.

"Jenna!"

It was Geoffrey, hissing, probably come to take her head away on a platter.

"Give me a *minute*, Geoffrey, I'm just getting my—"

The door swung open to reveal Geoffrey and Tiffany looming large in the doorway, with the entire kitchen staff pressed close behind them, staring in with the look of a lynch mob.

She took a startled step back and bumped into her chair. It clattered to a stop against the desk and everything fell silent but for the faint sizzle of unwatched onions caramelizing in butter on the six-burner range in the kitchen beyond.

Geoffrey held a bottle of wine in his hands and lifted it toward her, his pale and bulbous brow beaded with a fine sheen of sweat.

"The Latour," he rasped, his hands slightly trembling. "He wants you to serve it."

Jenna's gaze jumped back and forth between Geoffrey and Tiffany, who were both stiff and pasty as mannequins. No one else made a peep.

Geoffrey swallowed and held the bottle out as if it were a holy relic. There was a generous layer of dust settled over the glass, a faint smudge of mold on the label; the sign of a perfectly undisturbed, pristinely aged bottle of wine.

"Now. Please," Geoffrey whimpered. The overhead light shone pale against his forehead.

"What is going on here?" Jenna asked.

It was Tiffany who answered. "He's not mad. He wants the wine. *You're the sommelier.*"

Jenna looked over to Geoffrey, eyebrows raised. "Geoffrey?"

He nodded, his head giving a quick up-and-down jerk.

"I'm not fired?"

His head jerked again, this time side to side. No.

"Why not?"

The breath left his lungs in a sharp puff of air as if they'd collapsed. "Please, Jenna—just go! We'll talk about it later! *Please*," he begged, bending his knees and making an odd little hop. "Don't keep him waiting!" He waggled the bottle back and forth in front of her like a lure, sloshing the wine around.

Jenna reached out and delicately pried the bottle free from the sweaty death grip he had on it. "Gently, will you! You're mucking up the sediment, it'll be all cloudy—"

"For God's sake, woman, just *go*!" he practically shrieked into her face.

Jenna paused, the realization dawning that somehow her fortune had turned and the balance of power had tipped to her favor. She had a sneaking suspicion she knew who was responsible for this sudden change.

"Geoffrey," she said and looked him square in the eye.

He clapped both his hands over his face and then shook them apart over his head, a dramatic, silent *What?*

"Get out of my way."

He spun around, collecting Tiffany by the arm as he went, and barged a path through the crowd of visibly disappointed onlookers. "Back to work, you *dégueulasse animaux*, before I fire you all!" he crowed.

Jenna looked down at the bottle of Latour. *He wants you to serve it...*

You want it, you got *it,* she thought grimly. *But be careful what you wish for, Earl McLoughlin.*

She squared her shoulders, raised her chin, stalked out of her office and through the kitchen, holding the Latour in her arms like a child.

Without another glance backward, Jenna strode through the swinging doors.

SIX

Leander watched her approach with equal parts fascination and awe.

It wasn't her figure or her gliding walk or her regal carriage, the determined way she held her head. It wasn't her ivory skin or the shape of her jaw or the mass of shiny golden locks cascading over her shoulders that set her apart, that drew admiring glances from every male as she passed by.

It was simply that she shone like a flame, a flawless diamond breathing living fire among so many dead lumps of coal.

As she moved gracefully through the swinging doors of the kitchen, past the tables of diners, coming toward him through pools of warm candlelight and patches of dappled shadow, slender and lovely and tall, she blazed brighter and more brilliant than the noonday sun, illuming the air around her like a torch.

She stepped past the bar, lifting her arm with the grace of a swan to snare a Bordeaux glass as she passed. The Blood of the *Ikati* was clearly visible in her figure, the sensual lines of her body, the way she floated like a panther hunting its prey in the forest. She was lissome and sleek and glorious.

Her beauty made his skin prickle.

But it was those Eyes that drew him in, strange and clear and haunting, that look of something carefully hidden, something guarded. She was bold on the outside, full of poise and confidence and strength, but every glance revealed a contradiction, a shade of quiet sorrow. Even as she mocked him and called him pathetic, there was some fathomless depth of...

"I suppose I owe you both an apology *and* a thank you," Jenna said primly, eyes downcast as she presented the bottle of Latour, label up, for his inspection.

Her voice, quiet and melodious, sent a fresh shiver crawling up his spine. He was glad for the stiff leather of the banquette against his back, real and grounding. He made a conscious effort to keep his body relaxed, his breathing regular.

"You've already apologized. And no thanks are necessary." Leander stroked a thumb over the fine layer of dust on the Latour's label, keeping his own eyes focused on the bottle.

He nodded toward the bottle, approving.

She set the Bordeaux glass on the white linen tablecloth and used a foil cutter to remove the foil cap over the cork. A corkscrew appeared in her hand.

"I'm sure you must have said something to the maître d'. My job has miraculously been restored." An elegant turn of her wrist released the cork from the bottle. "Not that I deserve it," she added, almost inaudibly.

Leander glanced up at her face. His acute hearing had allowed him to overhear every word that dreadful little rat of a man had spoken to her in the kitchen. He had wanted to take Geoffrey's neck between his hands and squeeze very, very hard.

"I informed him that I plan to dine here every night for the remainder of my...vacation...and simply made clear my expectation that his talented and insightful sommelier would be on hand to assist me with my wine selections."

He accepted the cork she held out to him without further comment. She watched him stroke a finger up and down the slender stem of the wine glass.

"Shall I decant?"

"No," he replied, raising his gaze to the poem of her face. "But you should bring another glass."

"Is someone joining you?"

"Yes. You are."

He saw how that surprised her. Her slender fingers tightened around the neck of the wine bottle. She shifted her weight to her opposite foot.

"Ah..." She shot a glance toward the kitchen doors. "I don't really think that would be the best—"

"Come now," he interrupted with a small smile. "I don't think your maître d' would approve of you denying the request of His Holy Dignity, do you?"

It was a provocation—and a deliberate one. He wanted her to be curious, wanted her to wonder how he knew the ridiculous moniker Geoffrey had called him, wanted her to want to get closer—

Jenna slammed the Latour down upon the table with a jarring *thump*, the wine sloshing in the bottle. Hectic spots of color stained her cheeks.

"Is this some kind of joke?" she said through stiff lips. "Am I on camera or something? *How did you hear that?*"

Leander made a mental note for future reference that she didn't like being provoked. Nor did she appear to have any problem being direct. He forced back the smile that wanted to curl his lips.

"Why don't you sit with me and I'll tell you?" he murmured, holding her fierce gaze.

A fighter, he thought. *Magnificent.*

She remained tense and silent at the edge of the table, breathing raggedly with that flushed face, those glittering eyes.

"Please." He gestured to the empty seat next to him. "I have something I'd like to ask you, at any rate."

Jenna continued to assess him with a long, measuring look, as if she could pluck the very thoughts from his mind.

He hoped to God she could not.

He was close to conceding defeat when she suddenly bent her knees and elegantly slid into the booth next to him. She reached out, picked up the bottle of Latour, and poured it into his glass. A perfect arc of liquid swirled into a pool of smooth claret within the crystal bowl. The color was dark and rich, ruby fading to amber at the edge.

She set the bottle on the table, grasped the stem between her thumb and forefinger, and slid it smoothly across the tablecloth toward him.

"So," she said, turning to fix him with her sharp stare. "I'm sitting. What is it you wanted to ask me?"

He did his best to ignore her eyes of frost, and instead picked up the wine glass, swirled the wine around in the bowl, and lifted it to his nose.

He closed his eyes.

First: the aromas of game, smoky oak, herbs, and vanilla, something indefinable, wild and powerful. Next: truffle, leather, mineral, and sweet, jammy aromatics, viscous texture, cedar, blackberries, currant. Finally: the thick and caressing finish, lingering on his tongue like ambrosia. He tasted the sun and the rain that had nourished the vines, the gravelly soil, the wood barrel it had aged in, harvested from an ancient forest in France.

Tronçais, he thought. *No—Jupilles.* The toasted vanilla flavors had more finesse than wine aged in Tronçais oak.

It moved him every time, this thing of perfect beauty, this work of art, the glory of nature confined within the shape of the bottle.

His father had had exquisite taste. The '61 Latour was quite possibly proof of God's existence.

He felt her shift in the booth next to him, heard the rustle of her silk dress against leather and bare skin as she moved, and handed over the glass without opening his eyes. She took it; he felt the sudden weightlessness in his hand.

"What I wanted to ask you is this," he said quietly. He opened his eyes to stare with full intensity into her pale and unsmiling face. "What do you taste?"

It had surprised him that she was the sommelier, but it gave him hope. This line of work was not for those with dulled senses. It was a clue, a possibility...

Her brows, pale and finely arched, drew together. "Is this some kind of test?"

You've no idea, he thought. But he only shook his head no and looked at her.

She licked her lips and swallowed, then let out a long breath through her nose. "After this, you'll answer *my* questions." She lifted her chin, defiant.

He finally allowed his lips to twist into a smile. He nodded.

She raised the glass to her nose and inhaled.

He saw it then, the way it came over her, the way she opened her senses to allow the flavor in. Her eyes fluttered closed, her lips parted. She held the breath on her tongue and stilled, every sense alight, every fiber and nerve attuned with perfect concentration to the bouquet of the wine in front of her.

Ikati, the animal inside him whispered, rising up to strain against his skin. It was a pulsing sting of recognition, hot and strong and uncontained. *She is Ikati. Like me.*

She took a sip of wine, rolled the liquid over her tongue, paused for one long, silent moment, then swallowed.

"Oh," she said, letting out a little, astonished breath. "Oh, God."

"Tell me," he murmured. He leaned forward on instinct, catching the subtle, feminine perfume of her skin, watching the flush on her cheeks spread down to her neck, her chest.

"I've never...it's..."

She swallowed again and turned to look at him, wonder and reverence evident in every feature of her face. The guarded tension was gone, all the reticence, the quiet melancholy. In its place was amazement, delight, exhilaration. Joy.

He suddenly found it very hard to breathe through the steel band that tightened around his chest.

"It's magnificent," she breathed. "After all these years—after all this time it should be faded, it should be..." She shook her head, blinking. "But it's *perfect.*"

"Yes," he murmured, admiring the way the candlelight glowed amber and honey against her hair. "It is. Just at its peak now, I would say. It may even have another ten years ahead of it."

She set the glass on the table with precise, exaggerated care, then slid it back toward him. "Thank you," she said quietly. "That was incredible. And very—" She hesitated and swallowed, raised her eyes to his. "Very *non*-pathetic." A tiny, wry smile twisted her lips.

Without moving his gaze from her face, he reached for the glass and let his fingers settle over hers, the barest friction between their skin, the slightest pressure possible.

"You haven't answered my question." His voice came out just as quiet as before, but now it was shaded somber, almost tense. "What did you taste?"

She held very still, the tiny smile fading as she gazed back at him, and he became abruptly aware of a heat and ache in his groin and the almost overpowering urge to plunge his hands wrist-deep into her hair and pull her hard against him.

"Black currant," she said. "Toasted oak. Limestone."

He heard her breathing increase, her heart a growing thrum against her ribs, and wondered what caused it, hoped that maybe, somehow, it had something to do with him.

Jesus, he thought, *she is so beautiful. That skin, those lips, that fragile, perfect—*

"Easy," he scoffed quietly, still holding her gaze. He allowed the tip of his index finger to graze the side of her thumb. She didn't move or blink, but her pupils dilated a fraction of an inch.

"What else?" he murmured, leaning toward her, inhaling the scent of her skin. The ache in his groin grew to a throbbing, uncomfortable stiffness.

"Spanish cedarwood. Anise. Cinnamon." She paused. "Woodsmoke."

He raised his eyebrows. "Woodsmoke?"

The tip of her tongue flicked out to moisten her lips and he almost groaned, it was so erotic. "You won't believe me," she said.

He leaned closer and smiled at her. It was a dangerous smile, a hungry smile, he knew by the way her eyes widened when she saw it, but he couldn't help himself. It took all his willpower just to keep from kissing her. "You would be surprised at what I would believe, Jenna," he said, low. "Try me."

She sank her teeth into her lower lip, hesitating, then came to some unspoken decision with the slight lift of one shoulder. "There was a wood fire burning near the vines during the growing season, budbreak to harvest. Flowering prune trees, I think."

He looked at her. Still and lovely, eyes glowing like green embers, she was clearly afraid of his ridicule, of his disbelief. A tremor passed through him. He inched closer.

"Windbreaks."

"I'm sorry?" she said, throaty. Her gaze flickered down to his mouth.

"Prune trees are used as windbreaks around the vineyards in Pauillac," he said, teetering on the brink of self-control. The way she was looking at him, looking at his mouth…"France had an outbreak of phylloxera that season, thousands of trees were infected."

She glanced back up at him and he was pinned by the power of that gaze, the beauty and haunting luminosity of those eyes. Not only were they a startling, clear green, the irises rimmed with shimmering gold, but they contained gorgeous deep flecks of amber and citrine embedded within that sparked fire into their cool emerald depths.

He pictured her reclining atop his massive four-poster bed at Sommerley, her curves nestled into the glossy fur coverlet, those lucid eyes mirroring his own desire, her body nude but for the diamonds he wanted to give her: at her throat, around her wrists, on her finger…

"They had to burn all the trees that year to stop the spread of disease," he whispered.

The desire rising inside him suddenly transformed into a beast, hissing, clawing just under his skin, poised to devour him. His fingers tightened over her own and he parted his lips, letting the flavor of her burn bright against his tongue.

"Windbreaks," she murmured, leaning into him with a dreamy, half-lidded look. "Oh…that's…"

Heart pounding, he bent his head. One second more… one inch more and his lips would be on hers…

Then her eyes clouded. She began to blink. Her brows drew together and her eyes focused sharp. "Can you feel that?" She turned her head, searching the restaurant, her gaze moving toward the black sky framed in the windows that lined one wall, a view to the street.

Leander wondered if Jenna somehow *smelled* his desire for her, so acute was this sense of hers proving to be, but then she turned back to him, grimacing.

"What *is* that?" She seemed close to being sick. Her fingers began to shake under his.

He was abruptly alert, wary, a sense of peril eating through his chest. "Jenna? Are you unwell? What's wrong?"

But she was rising from the table already, her face paling, her eyes wide, her gaze flying around the room. Her lips parted and she breathed out a few words as she tried to steady herself with a shaking hand on the banquette.

"That vibration. That—friction—static—"

She gasped and stumbled.

He was next to her before she could fall, pulling her to him with one arm, supporting her body against his chest. Her heart was pumping a violent, staccato beat. She was satin and fire in his arms, the skin of her bare arms prickled with goose bumps, burning with unnatural heat. His heart began to thunder in panic when she gave a low, keening moan and sagged against him, eyes huge and round and staring at nothing.

Something was wrong. Something was terribly wrong.

Then the shaking began.

SEVEN

Morgan had discovered Rodeo Drive.

And not just in a touristy kind of way, gawking in star-struck wonder as she passed by on the top deck of a sightseeing bus. No, she had gone native.

Which wasn't a precise description for the way she'd spent the past three days, because no one in Beverly Hills seemed to walk anywhere—except for the tourists—and she had walked from Valentino to Prada, from Bulgari to Armani, from Dior to Tiffany.

She loved to walk, having spent her entire life roaming the New Forest, finding all the best spots of damp, wooded earth and soaring vistas glimpsed from the tops of fir trees. Moving her body was second nature. It was easy to walk for miles, carrying packages, the sun on her face, wind playing through her hair. It was being confined within the gilded cage of the Four Seasons Hotel she found difficult.

She hadn't stayed in human form this long for years.

So, to distract herself from the growing discomfort of denying her animal side, she went shopping.

Her purchases were beginning to take over a rather substantial portion of her suite at the hotel. Square red cardboard boxes, rectangular black paper bags with turquoise tissue peeking out, plain white parcels with logos from the most expensive boutiques, and those perfect, darling little robin's-egg blue boxes with the white ribbon. Her favorite.

She couldn't wait to try it all on again.

The fact that she'd charged everything to the credit card Leander had given her—*for emergencies only, Morgan*—made it all the more satisfying. It appeared his little black card had no purchase limit.

Morgan stood barefoot in the middle of the plush butter crème carpet, surveying the damage, feeling rather proud of herself. She'd ordered breakfast again from the fabulous French café just down the street—another luxury thanks to the wonderful little black card—and the remains of what was once a fat, smoked bacon, gruyere, and apple omelet lay on the dining table in the master suite, next to a pot of steaming hot coffee and pastries.

She probably couldn't get out onto the balcony if she wanted to: the glass sliding door was hidden behind a chin-high stack of Ralph Lauren boxes. She briefly wondered how she was going to get it all back to Sommerley, but then shrugged her shoulders and put her hands on her hips. Leander would figure something out for her, he always did.

He was the Alpha. That was his job.

A delighted smile lit up her face.

It was in exactly this posture Leander found her when he came crashing through the door.

"I need you," he growled, curt and tense. A stack of parcels on the glass console table in the foyer toppled over as he shouldered past them, spilling a four-thousand-dollar Hermès crocodile-skin handbag to the white marble floor.

"Don't you *knock?*" Morgan complained, turning to shoot him a flinty stare.

"My suite. Now."

His body was tense in a way she had never seen. He normally moved with a dark grace, stealthy, all poise and menace and feral-eyed vigilance. But now he was visibly distracted—taut as a bowstring, grim-faced, and unshaven—so Morgan only pursed her lips and swallowed the retort on her tongue.

"What is it?"

Without another word, he yanked the door open in one swift, hard motion and disappeared through it. His hair swung in a loose, handsome ruff around his shoulders, black as midnight against the rumpled white silk of his shirt.

Morgan sighed and turned to gaze again, with more than a hint of melancholy, on the piles of expensive plunder. It looked as if her plan for the morning had been derailed.

Trying everything on again would have to wait.

Leander had watched Jenna all night, crouching silent and still in the gloom of her bedroom as she slept, tensed to vanish as vapor into the air if she awoke, waiting for any sign she might not be as fine as she repeatedly told the EMT she was.

They'd been called to Mélisse because of the injuries. Paramedics and firemen and police had been dispatched all over the city to care for the wounded. They were mostly minor things: cuts from shattered glass, scrapes from falling down, contusions, a few cases of shock in the elderly.

No major damage had been reported to any structures, though many buildings—like the one Mélisse was located in—suffered a few broken windows, some cracked plaster, damage to the façade. He'd been told it was one of the milder earthquakes to hit Los Angeles in recent years.

No matter how mild the quake, it caused a major upheaval for him.

At the first ripple in the bedrock, as Jenna sagged against him in that half-faint that made his heart climb into his throat, his animal instincts went into overdrive.

He lifted her up against him—her knees crooked over his left arm, her head lolling against his right—and swept her out the back door of the restaurant to the middle of the wide, brick-paved patio. It was a deserted place, a safe place, cloaked in darkness, free from anything that could fall on them from above.

Amid the dark enclosure of the cypress and oak trees that encircled them like an open-air cathedral, the sky above them smoke and ebony-blue, Leander stood braced against the shaking, his legs open wide, his arms wrapped around her hard.

The boughs of the trees swayed and thrashed above while the eerie groans and creaks of the buildings around them—stressed to their foundations with the earth bucking like a creature alive—tightened his stomach into a fist.

If it weren't for Jenna, lush and passive in his arms, he would have Shifted to panther, climbed the nearest tree, and roared down in fury at the insanity below.

Her face was very clear in the moonlight, pale and beautiful like something forged from marble, her long lashes a dark smudge against the satin perfection of her ivory cheek. He knew she hadn't fainted, though her eyes were closed, her breathing shallow. He knew because she kept a hand pressed firm against his chest.

The heat of her palm burned straight through the fabric of his shirt.

He didn't know if she was seeking reassurance in the steady beat of his heart, or trying to keep him from getting any closer. Could she sense how he longed to touch his lips to her forehead, her hair, her cheek?

He very badly wanted to kiss her, anywhere, everywhere, even as the ground under his feet went mad.

When the shaking stopped and the world settled into a more reasoned lucidity, Jenna opened her eyes and stared straight up at him, beseeching. The electronic clamor of hundreds of sounding car alarms rose into the night air above the city to create a ghostly requiem for the quake. It was underscored by the rising shouts of panic and shock from the restaurant behind them.

"I felt it coming," she whispered up at him, her voice thin and frightened. Her hand curled around the front of his shirt. "I felt it in my bones. I smelled it. I *tasted* it."

It was then Leander realized the Assembly had their answer.

So did he.

He set her gently down on a chaise lounge with a whispered reassurance and left her, briefly, to use the phone inside. A mild pandemonium had broken out inside the restaurant, which Geoffrey was doing little to assuage, being too busy with his alternating fits of screaming, hysterical hand-waving, and hyperventilating. The paramedics arrived within minutes and took control. At his insistence, Jenna was one of the first to receive their attention, but they found nothing wrong with her. Though shaken, she was fit, unhurt, perfectly sound. They advised her to go home and get some sleep, and then they turned their attention to the others.

She pushed away from him when he came back to her, looked at him as if she suddenly knew some terrible secret—*his* secret—and disappeared into the night like a ghost, before he could speak, before he could catch her.

She was wicked fast. She could run even faster than he, though he was stronger, faster than anyone in all the colonies. Faster than any other predator on earth.

Except, evidently, her.

He hadn't been prepared for that either.

When he lost her trail around the dark corner of the bank building at Second Street, when all he could smell when he opened his senses was the vanishing trace of her perfume diffused through the heated, salt-laden air like a memory of something almost forgotten, he very nearly lost his mind.

Her apartment was the only place he could think to go—the only logical place to wait for her, though he kept carefully out of sight. He shed his clothes behind a stinking Dumpster in the back alley as he Shifted, discarding the handmade Italian suit as if it were offal, then rose as a fine mist to settle against the rough stucco wall of her apartment building.

He hovered there for hours in the warm evening air, spread so thin it was uncomfortable, knowing one strong gust of wind could tear him clean apart. He was thankful it wasn't below freezing; there wouldn't even be any bones left if he died like this.

The night was arid, the heated air so much drier than in England, even at the edge of the sea. He didn't need to breathe—spread sheer and disembodied like smoke—or feel his heart beating like a drum or suffer the scorching of his blood through his veins. The sensations and burning passions of his body had disappeared. It was peaceful. Restful.

If only he could shut off his mind too.

He imagined her lost, injured, attacked by drug addicts, rapists, gang members. The longer he waited, the worse his fantasies became. For the first time in his life, he cursed himself. If he had the Gift of Foresight, he would know where to look. He could protect her.

He could *do* something.

She finally came stumbling through the silent, early hours of the morning with the look of a zombie raised from the dead: disheveled and shuffling, gray-faced, wide-eyed, stiff. The elegant lines of her dress were creased and thrown out of kilter, as if she'd slept in her car or fallen down. Repeatedly.

This did little to alleviate his anxiety.

He slid down the uneven wall of the old apartment building, molecule by molecule, flowing softly over cracks and bumps, past dark window panes, melting silently through the climbing ivy and flowering hibiscus until he found her bedroom window.

He settled as a gray plume of mist against the sill and waited.

Jenna came into sight through the dim corridor from the kitchen like a ghost materializing through the night, moving so slowly she seemed drugged, hands lifted slightly out in front of her as if she didn't trust her eyes to lead the way. She didn't turn on any lights. She stood in the doorway to her bedroom with one hand on the doorjamb, just looking around. She stared silently at her bed, the small desk in the corner with its lamp and photo frame, her closet door half-opened, the shoes she'd pulled out and decided not to wear earlier still lying on the carpet at the foot of the bed.

She finally passed a shaking hand over her face, smoothed her hair, and reached behind her neck to unzip her dress.

Leander sank from the windowsill and floated above the bed of mint outside her bedroom window, the fragrant, velvet leaves brushing against him, ruffling his edges. He allowed her the privacy of undressing and climbing into bed without his gaze on her, though it was all he could do to resist breaking down her door, taking her back to Sommerley right then, forcing her to return with him to the place he now knew was her rightful home.

She looked so lost. So frightened. So…vulnerable.

You are Alpha. She is Ikati. Do not fail her!

The need to protect her lashed at him, sudden and insistent. Unmerciful.

It had been done before. There were safeguards in place for these situations, defenses that would keep her bound, provisions in the Law. He could take her back, keep her there, make her safe.

Against the demand of every nerve in his body, he restrained himself, and waited.

Once inside her apartment through the now-familiar crack in the bathroom window, he Shifted to man and watched over her as she slept to make sure she was unhurt, watched for any sign of distress, watched to see if she would need him.

Arms akimbo, hair splayed wild over the pillow, she slept, restless and moaning, tossing the sheets like a drowning swimmer fighting the vast, relentless sea.

It was only when she finally began to stir from her haunted sleep, late in the morning as the sun slanted saffron and gold through the windows, he'd been able to leave her and return to the hotel.

"So it's true, then," said Christian, low. "The little stray can Shift. Who would have thought?"

From the sofa of the presidential suite, Christian watched Leander in the chair opposite with eyes that were unnaturally bright. He was tense and grim and there was something unusual in his voice, a hint of ragged emotion Leander had never seen him display before. Something about his whole demeanor set Leander's nerves on edge, his instincts on high alert. Why would he care if Jenna could Shift or not?

"If she can sense an earthquake, smell the ghost of a decades-old fire in a glass of wine, and outrun *me*, I think she can definitely Shift. In fact," Leander said, carefully watching Christian's face, "she may turn out to be the most Gifted of us all."

Leander kept his gaze on Christian as he stood from the couch, walked over to the glistening expanse of windows, and ran a hand through his thick hair.

"Son of a bitch," Christian murmured, and nothing more.

"You seem...disturbed, brother."

Christian turned to look at him. A muscle flexed in his jaw. "We've found the free-born, half-human, incredibly beautiful daughter of the tribe's most powerful Alpha ever, and you're telling me that not only do you think she can Shift, but that she might turn out to be more Gifted than us all. Yes. I'm disturbed. I'm *definitely* disturbed."

Leander's left eyebrow cocked. "Incredibly beautiful?"

Their gazes held for just a bit longer than Leander liked. Then Christian turned back to the window with a shrug. "None of my business, I suppose," he muttered to the sunny view. "Second sons never get first choice."

"Welcome to my world," Morgan said from behind them as she swept into the room. "How'd you like to never even *have* a choice because what's between your legs happens to not be a penis?"

"For God's sake, Morgan," Leander said sharply, his patience beginning to unravel. He turned to glare at her. "Enough of that! We need to focus on getting Jenna back to Sommerley before she runs away again. Before she Shifts for the first time. Right away. Today. *Now.*"

"No!" Morgan put her hands on her hips and glared right back at him, defiant.

She stood in the middle of the elegantly appointed suite wearing a dress he hadn't seen before. It was made mostly of air, a thin wisp of black silk to her knees with diamond cut-out patterns throughout, revealing large swaths of tanned, perfect skin and sculpted abdominal muscles. He narrowed his eyes and wondered how much it had cost him.

And were those *python* skin heels?

"Absolutely not! We've got another few days before her birthday! There's no reason to rush this—"

"We are not on vacation, Morgan. Our purpose here is not to relax, sightsee, or *shop*—"

"Easy for *you* to say!" Morgan snapped, eyes flashing bright green and blade sharp. "You've been able to come and go as you please! You haven't been cooped up your entire life, waiting for a chance to escape, hoping for—"

"Hoping for *what?*" Leander enunciated, quiet and very calm.

They stared at each other across the room.

"If you think the life of Alpha is better than yours, easier than yours, you are very sadly mistaken, Morgan."

For all his privilege and money, for all the power that came with his position, he often wished, in the secret dark heart of his soul, the role of Alpha had fallen to another.

He alone was the leader. He alone held all their fates in his hands. It was not, as Morgan imagined, an all-access pass to happiness and fulfillment.

No. It was closer to a curse.

Morgan lifted her chin. "And how do you propose we go about this?" she asked icily. She crossed her arms over her chest and tapped one python-clad toe against the plush carpet. "I could use Suggestion to get her to go along for a while, a few hours possibly, but that will only go so far. How are we actually supposed to get her back to Sommerley? Kidnap her?"

"I think we should just tell her the truth," Christian said from his position at the window. "She must know she's different. What if we Shift in front of her and tell her she's one of us?"

"And then what?" Morgan shot back, turning to give him a frosty stare. "Throw a bag over her head and drag her off when she freaks out and runs away?"

Christian ran a hand through his mass of shining black hair again, leaving it in disarray. "No. But we could drug her."

"I was being *sarcastic*, Christian," Morgan said with an exasperated sigh. "There's no way we're going to *manhandle* her, she's not some piece of—"

Leander gripped the carved wood arms of the chair he was sitting in with such force they splintered under his hands. Morgan and Christian fell silent and looked over at him.

"If either of you had paid any attention during the Assembly meeting, you would know the plan," he snapped, eyes blazing. "We will get her alone. We will subdue her with your power of Suggestion, Morgan. We will—"

The phone on the desk rang, interrupting him. He inhaled a long breath, released his grip on the chair, stood stiffly, and walked over to yank the receiver from its base.

"Yes," he said into it, curt and low.

"What's a few days' difference?" Morgan said quietly to Christian, lobbying for his agreement.

He stretched his long arms out and put both palms flat against the glass, looking down at the view of the city below. "Agreed," he murmured, almost to himself. "We should stay here awhile and…get to know her better before we take her back. Before her mind is made up for her."

"What?" Morgan said. "What does that mean?"

He didn't answer, and the tension in his shoulders suggested he wasn't in the mood for more conversation.

She unfolded her arms, and the slender ruby bracelets encircling her right wrist released a knot of fiery sparks in band over faceted band. She shook back a swath of long, glossy locks from her face and glanced over at the ruined arms of Leander's chair. "Anyway, if she isn't home," she persisted, "do we hang around her front door for a few hours, waiting for her to magically appear? Like that won't look suspicious? Or are we supposed to go try to *find* her—"

"We don't need to find her," Leander interrupted quietly, setting the phone back down in its cradle. He turned to gaze at both of them with an odd look on his face, as if he'd just considered something deeply arresting.

"She found *us*. That was the front desk on the phone. She's in the lobby."

EIGHT

Jenna remembered very clearly the last time she saw her father alive.

It was a few days before her tenth birthday and raining very hard. The water sliced like needles down from the sullen, slate-gray sky. This would have been unusual for the month of June in most places, but at that time her family was living on Kauai, one of the smaller of the Hawaiian Islands. It rained almost every day in that green and lovely tropical paradise.

They'd been there a few weeks, no more. Boxes were still half-unpacked in the living room. Her mother never really bothered with completely unpacking all their belongings. They'd be packing them up soon enough again, she knew.

The smell of green vegetation, blooming plumeria, and wet, loamy earth soaked through everything in their small home. Her mother had left all the lights burning to ward off the gloom of a tropical summer storm, but her father had gone around the house in silence, turning off the bulbs one by one, stealthy and taut and ever unfathomable.

It was one of the things Jenna remembered most vividly about him. The way he always preferred to move in the dark, like some nocturnal creature of the forest on the hunt for dinner.

She'd been watching him again from her favorite hiding place, the tiny space under the stairs she'd turned into a warm burrow with pillows and blankets and her love-worn teddy bear. One of Teddy's eyes was missing, the other a jaunty speck of black against plush caramel cheeks.

Her mother said she was too old to keep carrying him around, but Jenna couldn't bear to part with him. Teddy and the clothes on her back were the only solid proof that she had a past.

Her father caught her watching, as he always did. Even when he didn't call her out on it she sensed he knew her eyes were on him. But this time he called her name, motioned with his hand for her to crawl out from under the stairs.

She kept Teddy in her arms as she went over to him and climbed onto his lap in the rocking chair, watching the rain slide down the windowpanes like silvery tears. Through the glass she saw trees and grass and flowers smeared into muted plots of color as the patter of rain increased.

"Jenna," he murmured into her hair. He held her tight in his arms and rocked back and forth, slowly kicking off the wood floor with one strong, bare foot. "Do you know who loves you?"

She was too young then to hear the tremor in his voice, so she smiled and wound her arms around his neck, nuzzling down into the warm space between his shoulder and neck, feeling happy and warm and oh so safe. He'd built a fire in the small fireplace in the living room; it crackled and sparked and threw off lovely waves of wood-scented heat.

"*You* do, Daddy," she answered, the same answer every time.

"And do you know *why* Daddy loves you?" He tipped his head back to gaze down on her with those sparkling green eyes, his handsome face almost fuzzy that close.

She loved seeing him like this, unfocused and blurred in her half-lidded gaze. He seemed more real somehow. The detail of his eyelashes, the dark stubble on his chin, the pure white of his teeth as he smiled all served to make him less of a mystery, more…hers.

The mysterious, ragged scar on his jaw was still fading as it healed, four thin, ugly slashes of red going slowly to white, marring the perfection of his burnished, golden skin. He'd come home with it the day before they moved here.

"No," she said, already knowing the answer but wanting to hear it again.

"Because you are a princess," he whispered into her ear, stroking her back and hugging her even tighter. "Golden blonde and beautiful, strong and brave and worth any sacrifice. My princess who will one day be a queen."

But something bothered her about this answer, something she hadn't thought of before.

"What's a sacrifice, Daddy?" she asked, wrinkling her brow to look up at him. He only smiled and kissed her forehead, rocked her back and forth until she fell asleep, warm and safe and happy against the hard expanse of his chest.

When she awoke the next morning she was in her bed, tucked in with Teddy under the threadbare patchwork quilt, and he was gone.

Since that night, every time it rained Jenna thought of her father and had to swallow the flame of agony that rose in her throat.

It wasn't raining now, as she sat calmly in the lobby bar of the Four Seasons next to an enormous display of aubergine calla lilies and scented jasmine that loomed somewhat ominously over her table. It was blazing hot and so dry her eyes were sticky, but she was thinking of her father just the same.

She was thinking of her father because she had seen his face in Leander's mind.

The first time Leander touched her last night—that light pressure on her arm as he'd explained in his low, attractive voice how he ordered the Latour in memory of his parents—she'd felt a singular tremor course over her skin. The same current of heated electricity that she'd felt so deeply in the store—and again when he met her eyes in the restaurant—passed from his fingertips.

But she was still in denial. She'd dismissed it as nerves.

The next time, it was heat and static and a sudden blur of smeared color that swam before her eyes as his hand rested on hers over the stem of the wineglass. Her heartbeat surged as she tried to concentrate on it, to make the colors coalesce into something coherent.

Jenna forgot all that when the sound of the earth rending a mile below their feet hit her ears minutes before the shaking even began. Then she could only concentrate on standing upright as the vertigo hit with the first shockwaves of pressure, as the acrid smell of heated, fissuring bedrock stung her nose.

But once Leander picked her up in his arms and ran with her through the restaurant to the back patio, she remembered. As her hand rested against his chest, she'd felt the beating of his heart, felt the heat of his skin under her palm, and the smeared blurs of color came again. But this time they cleared into visions of things she'd never seen before.

Memories, though not her own.

His.

So many things at once. So many people and places and a crush of sensation and strange power and throbbing desire but always this:

An elegant manor house, set back on wide, sweeping green lawns, vast and mysterious inside with columns of alabaster and huge gilt-framed paintings of unsmiling people and priceless antiques scattered throughout. A dark forest, dense undergrowth, ancient trees so tall the tops were lost in shrouds of mist with moss draped over the low-hanging boughs, swinging in a night breeze, ethereal. Fangs and claws and muscled sleek bodies, creatures on four legs undulating silently over the forest floor, creatures that growled and roared and disappeared into smoke when they heard an unknown noise.

A wild, faraway land of lush green vales that led to the ancient forest, a surging river with water so clear you saw the mirror flash of trout far below against its rocky bed, a low range of smoke-purple mountains darkening the far horizon. A land filled with people so beautiful they didn't seem real.

People who all looked just like her father.

After the earth stilled, after Leander called the authorities, when he came striding back through the unstrung chaos of the restaurant like some ancient god of war—lean and muscled, body hammered like a blade, face glorious and beautiful and terrifying all at once—he kneeled down in front of her and grasped her arms in his hands.

"Everything is going to be all right," he said, velvet smooth and calm. In spite of his reassuring tone, his expression was hard and severe like a winter-cold beast. His ferocious green eyes stared out of that chiseled face like the eyes of a wild, starving wolf.

But she knew it wouldn't be all right. Because now his palms were burning hot on her bare skin and she saw his memories and his thoughts and his fantasies all at once, flashing before her eyes in a panoramic and terrifying display of movement and color and light, as if she were seeing a three-dimensional movie, as if she were somehow *inside* his mind, at the point of origin.

Jenna had to run away to stop the onslaught of visions. She thought she might never stop running.

But stop she had. And now she was here, waiting for him in the elegant, bustling lobby bar of his hotel.

Her calm suddenly vanished, her heart began to hammer in her chest, her mouth went dry, and her face blazed with heat as Leander came into view around the corner of the room.

She saw him brush past the artfully arranged potted palms as if in slow motion, moving with grace and stealth, exuding a current of raw power and danger, turning heads as he came. His eyes met hers across the empty space between them, and she clenched her hands into fists in her lap to keep them from shaking.

He was alone. He looked as if he'd had a bad night.

"Jenna," he said, coming to a graceful stop at the side of her table. He slanted a cool green look down at her. "The lovely sommelier from Mélisse. What a pleasant surprise."

She looked up at him.

He appeared totally at ease and in control, as if he'd happened upon a casual acquaintance while out for a stroll.

"Are you feeling better today? I'm afraid you gave me a bit of a scare when you ran off like that. I hope you didn't—"

"I know what you are," Jenna said, soft and very still, staring up at his face.

He froze for one long moment, his cool detachment undisturbed but for a tiny twitch in a muscle of his jaw.

"Do you?" he murmured. The chandelier above threw sparks of blue off his black hair as it caught the flow of warm air. The light in the room seemed to grow even brighter and everything smelled of blooming jasmine and relentless heat.

Jenna could not read his expression. It was utterly neutral.

"Yes. You're what I'm supposed to be running away from."

This seemed to startle him as he stood blinking down at her, his lips parted.

He gathered himself and motioned to the chair opposite her. "May I?"

She nodded. He sat down and crossed his legs, letting his gaze fall to the cut glass bowl of mixed nuts on the tabletop between them. He was casually dressed today, in fitted beige trousers and a white silk shirt, sleeves rolled up over his tanned and muscled forearms. A shadow darkened his jaw; he hadn't shaved.

He plucked a walnut from the bowl and began rolling it between his fingers.

Jenna was abstractly aware of the sunlight slicing through the massive glass doors of the lobby behind him, the muffled din of conversation and high heels clicking over marble tiles, the heat that crawled down her back until she could barely breathe, but every molecule of her body, every atom, was focused on him.

"I'm not quite sure how to respond to that," Leander said carefully. He raised piercing eyes to her face, his tone still so neutral. "Perhaps you'd like to elaborate?"

Jenna kept her lasered focus when she answered. "If you're going to play games with me," she said quietly, staring right into his eyes, "I won't go back to Sommerley with you."

His expression still blank, his gaze sharp and frozen green on her face, Leander crushed the walnut to dust between his fingers.

"Excuse me?" he whispered.

She smiled in grim triumph. Not so cool after all.

"Did you think I'd be totally unprepared? Did you overlook the fact that I might have thought about how this moment would play out—that I might have even been expecting you, or someone like you, for years? Do you take me for a complete fool?"

She raised her eyebrows at him, waiting, but he only gaped at her in silence, utterly astonished.

"My mother warned me this day would come, though I'm not sure I ever really believed her," she said, her heart hammering against her ribs. "She told me to run, she showed me how to live a life in hiding, but quite frankly, I got tired of running a long time ago." She paused. When she spoke again, her voice had dropped an octave. "And I'll be damned if I'm going to hide, from you or anyone else."

Jenna was finished with hiding. Finished with secrets.

Since she was an infant, her father had moved the family every few months, never staying anywhere long enough to set down roots. Her childhood was a constant blur of strangers. A succession of transient faces—neighbors, teachers, classmates—materialized in and out of her life as if they were apparitions on a merry-go-round. They made one quick turn then vanished into thin air, never to be seen or heard from again.

And then her father became an apparition as well and vanished like all the rest.

"You are different from other girls, Jenna," her mother would say, which was more than obvious in a thousand different ways. "But you have to pretend you are not. No matter what happens, you have to blend in. Like your father did. It's the only way to stay safe. It's the only way to stay free. And if they ever find you...*run*."

She was utterly certain that something she was supposed to run from was now sitting across the table from her, exotic and coiled and still, like a cobra before it strikes.

"I want to make a bargain with you." She reached over to brush the dust of the crushed nut into a little pile on the starched white tablecloth beneath his frozen hand. "Tell me the truth, and I'll go with you without a fight. I'll go willingly. *If* you tell me the truth. What do you say?"

He didn't move, or blink, or speak. He only stared at her with narrowed eyes, calculating.

"I know it wasn't what you were expecting, but I hope you'll consider it. It's a damn sight better than your own plan, at any rate."

Jenna kept her face carefully neutral and didn't allow the fact that she was mostly bluffing to distract her from what she wanted. She'd seen bits and pieces, had gotten so many images and impressions that much of it had been horribly garbled. But there was no way *he* could know what she'd seen.

She wanted answers. After that...he could go back to Sommerley, wherever that was.

Or he could go straight to hell.

Leander slowly leaned back in his chair and stared at her. He released a long breath through his nose. After a minute in which neither of them spoke and the rising tension in her body felt like a wire pulled close to snapping, the barest of smiles lifted his cheek. His voice, however, did not sound amused. It sounded guarded and shrewd and almost...admiring.

"You can read minds." His fingers unclenched and he brushed the walnut dust from them without moving his appraising gaze from her face. "How very inconvenient."

"Only yours so far. And this is a new development in my life so don't expect too much."

He reached down and began idly tracing an invisible pattern on the tabletop, his gaze following his finger, and when he looked back up at her again everything was between them, everything she'd felt since the first time she'd seen him, the hum of electricity and magic and the menace he exuded like perfume. "You seem remarkably serene for someone who's just discovered something so unusual," he murmured.

A knot formed in her stomach. "My entire *life* has been unusual. Moving from place to place, running from some phantom menace, a father who disappeared without a trace, a mother who drank herself to sleep every night, knowing I was different but never having any answers, never, *ever* knowing the truth."

She stopped herself abruptly, looked down at the table, and blinked away the sudden moisture in her eyes. When she spoke again, her voice came in a whisper. "And believe me when I say I'm not serene. In fact, my breakfast is having some serious thoughts about making a reappearance."

Leander leaned forward in his chair. "Jenna—"

But he broke off as someone new appeared at their table, a handsome young man, lithe and black-haired like Leander, with a widow's peak and knife-blade, lingering eyes that hinted at ruthlessness and sensuality in equal measure. He lowered himself onto one of the chairs, sighed, and stretched his arms over his head.

"Couldn't resist getting out of the room for a bit. Beautiful morning, isn't it?" He grinned at her with an open voraciousness that belied his casual demeanor and slung his arm over the back of his chair.

Jenna knew this one. He was the other one from the parking lot, that first day.

Another followed just after, the stunning dark-haired woman who'd been with Leander that day also, wearing a dress so provocative a man walked straight into a wall as he gaped at her when she passed by. She gracefully sat down at their table as well, disregarding the look of icy fury Leander shot her.

Jenna ignored both of them and shifted her weight forward in the chair. A rush of rash determination flooded through her veins.

"All you have to do now is tell me the truth and I'll keep my word," she said to Leander. "I'll leave with you. I didn't see anything in your mind that made me believe you want to hurt me." A flush of scarlet darkened her cheeks. "Quite the opposite, actually. I believe you may be the only person I've ever met who can answer the questions I have. And I have *a lot* of questions. But if I think you're lying, or holding anything back, there is nothing that will compel me to move from this chair. There is nothing you'll be able to say or do once my trust is gone to get it back. I chose a public place for this meeting for a very good reason. I will sit here in this chair and scream bloody murder until the police come and then I'll run so goddamn far away you'll never be able to find me again."

The sounds of people talking and footsteps echoing and the clink of glassware seemed amplified in the sudden hush that followed. The woman and the younger man sat unmoving in their chairs, surprised. They glanced at each other, then at Leander.

But he was gazing serenely at her, effortlessly handsome and controlled, his composure recovered. "I must admit, I'm...almost at a loss for words. I can't recall the last time that happened. If ever."

"Tragic," she said, to the obvious enjoyment of Christian.

Leander's expression soured. "Just to clarify," he said with an exaggerated patience that suggested his composure wasn't quite so solid, "you will leave your home—all your friends, your work, your life—for places unknown, with persons unknown...just for answers to some questions?"

"Yes," she lied. She had no intention of going anywhere with him.

He shook his head slowly back and forth. "You're making things much easier for me, but, honestly, I don't think I understand your reasoning."

Jenna sat back in her chair, relieved and terrified in equal measure that he didn't deny her accusations, didn't try to assert his innocence, didn't call her crazy.

For better or worse, so far he was going along with her demands.

She brushed her hair away from her face again with a flick of a wrist and gave a one-shouldered shrug. "You're a man. I'm a woman. I'm sure there's a lot of things you can't understand about me."

The beautiful dark-haired woman began to giggle, a soft, girlish laugh she tried to hide behind the perfectly manicured hand that flew to her mouth. But it built to a loud, delighted guffaw, and she threw her head back and gave herself over to belly-clutching laughs while Leander and Jenna stared at each other in silence.

"I think I'm going to like her, Leander. I think I'm going to like her very much," the woman said when she could speak again. She wiped a stray tear from the corner of her eye and regarded Jenna with a new appreciation through her warm green gaze.

"Forgive me," Leander said to Jenna, "for not introducing my companions." He shot a steely glare at the woman first. "This is Morgan."

Morgan smiled wide, her teeth a perfect sheen of white behind scarlet lips, and stuck her hand out, her expression open and direct. Before Jenna could even think of reacting, Leander's hand shot out and snapped Morgan's fingers together in his fist. Morgan froze and glanced over at his face but said nothing.

So he guessed how she had seen his thoughts. Clever. Very well, then. He still couldn't know how *much* she had seen.

"And this is Christian," Leander said, with a sharp nod toward the younger man seated next to him. Their similar features spoke to their relation, but Leander did not add more.

"I must tell you," Christian drawled, gazing at her intently from beneath his lashes. A rakish smile played over his lips. "What a pleasure it is to finally meet you." He broke into a huge grin. "The mysterious little stray gone so long from the nest is finally coming home—shouldn't we have a party or something?"

"Christian," Leander warned, his lips pressed to a thin line, his gaze turned to flint.

Morgan clapped her hands together in delight and sat up in her chair. "Yes! A party! When we all get back to Sommerley I'm going to organize a ball in honor of Jenna's return and we'll have dancing and music and—"

"Stop this, both of you," Leander hissed through clenched teeth. His face had gone dark with a cold fury that silenced them both.

Jenna shifted in her chair, aware on a visceral level of the power play Christian had just orchestrated, of Morgan's innocent accomplice to it, of Leander's outrage with both of them.

"Are you related to my father?" she said to him abruptly, pressing her advantage.

"Yes," Leander said, answering roughly, out of anger, before he could think. He pinched the bridge of his nose between his fingers and closed his eyes. "No, I mean. Not like *you* mean it anyway. It's not as simple as that, it's very—"

"Do you know what happened to him?"

He looked up at her and his eyebrows drew together, casting a shadow over his eyes. "Again, it's not as simple as—"

"Do you know where he is? Is he *alive?*" she said, her voice rising.

"Jenna, for God's sake, this is not the place to be discussing—"

Jenna shot up from the chair, her face blazing in the sudden burst of anger that surged through her. The chair fell over and crashed against the marble floor with a sharp clatter that turned heads around them. She ignored everything else and focused her vision like a laser beam onto Leander's unsmiling face.

"Why have you been following me? What do you want from me? Where is my father?" she demanded.

He knew. He knew everything. He knew and he remained silent as a statue, staring at her with that infuriating look of cold condemnation, as if all he cared about was the scene she was making, as if all that mattered was maintaining decorum.

The truth, you bastard, she thought, bile rising in her throat, *that's what matters.*

Her hands began to tremble, as did her lower lip, her knees, and every nerve within her body. Something inside her snapped.

"*Who the hell are you people?*" she shouted at the top of her lungs.

Everyone and everything in the bar fell into abrupt, complete silence save for Leander's heart. This she heard as clear as a bell, thumping hard within his chest, strong and loud and filled with blood.

He stood up from his chair with an unhurried luxury of motion, every muscle flexed taut as he rose to face her. He regarded her with a gaze so icy it would have frozen molten lava.

"I am willing to answer all of your questions, Jenna, as you requested," he said quietly, the anger obvious beneath the soft tone. "But perhaps it's time we went somewhere less public to continue our discussion, as it seems to be getting rather...heated. I suggest my suite."

Jenna bristled at this, still shaking. "You expect me to go with you, alone, to your suite, where you could do God knows what? If you think I am that gullible, you are *sadly* mistaken."

His gaze thawed a few degrees and he allowed himself a cheerless smile. He lifted his hand and held it out toward her: an invitation. "If you don't believe me..." He turned his palm up. "Satisfy yourself."

Jenna stared at his outstretched hand and then back at his face, handsome and severe. She wouldn't touch him again, she *couldn't*. She wasn't ready for the onslaught, for the terrifying glut of sensation that came with the pressure of his skin on hers. She would never be ready. It occurred to her she might never be able to touch anyone again, and she was so upside down she didn't know if that bothered her or not.

So...she would just have to trust him.

"Fine. Your suite then," Jenna said, curling her hands into fists again to control their shaking. "But we're leaving the door *open*."

Leander inclined his head without breaking her gaze. His voice low, he said, "Follow me."

The *if you dare* was left unsaid, but she heard it clear as day anyway.

She didn't go first. She followed the three of them as they moved silently through the lobby with its gargantuan flower displays and glistening mirrors, past the serene glassed atrium filled with tropical plants and a dark pond with restless orange koi, through the glass doors that opened outward with a burst of hot, rose-scented air. Those doors led to the back gardens and the private staircase that wound up to the presidential suite on the top floor.

She had refused to get into the elevator with the three of them.

She couldn't take her eyes off them as they moved, seeing the animal in each one. The way their feet stepped without noise over marble and concrete and grass, the way their limbs moved, supple and elegant, powerful and lissome, every turn and bend revealing their true nature, every motion a symphony of natural, dangerous, perfect grace.

Jenna couldn't help but picture them moving through a darkened forest, on the prowl.

Hunting.

When they reached the top of the stairs, Leander opened the door to his suite and gestured for her to come inside.

"Here we are," he said, his voice neutral, his body relaxed as he leaned a strong shoulder against the door to hold it open.

But those eyes, so piercing green and fierce. They sent a shiver down her spine.

"Morgan, Christian, I'll speak to you later." He made a small motion with his chin to indicate they should continue on down the corridor.

"Of course, Leander," Morgan said, sounding happy to oblige. "We'll see you later. And Jenna," she turned her head and spoke as she moved gracefully away, her long black hair rippling down her back like waves of dark water over a bed of smooth stones. "It was a pleasure meeting you. I do hope we'll get to see each other again very soon."

"No—wait, where are you going! You need to *stay*—"

But she only smiled and turned away, leading Christian by the arm, her cutout dress revealing a tanned expanse of back and a hint of the top swell of firm derrière.

Christian looked back at Jenna over his shoulder, but his face was layered in shadow under light thrown from the sconces on the wall. She could not read his expression. They both kept walking and went out of sight around the corner.

Without speaking, Leander raised his hand in invitation to enter the suite.

Jenna huffed, ignored his heated gaze, and moved past him, carefully avoiding any physical contact. She walked through the marble foyer into the sumptuous main room, admiring the exquisite furnishings, the broad expanse of marbled veranda visible through sheer curtains, the king-size bed.

Her gaze flew away from the bed before it could linger there.

Damn. She wasn't in control. She *needed* to be in control.

She was flushed and trembling. She somehow felt both exhausted and exhilarated, strung out and calm. Every fiber in her body was attuned to the room around her, to the warm air and the slanting light, and the beautiful, obviously dangerous man standing at the door, watching her, silent and so still she might have thought he'd disappeared.

Except for the beating of his heart. She still heard it and struggled to smother the staccato, pulsing beat from her mind.

"It will get easier in time," Leander said softly from behind her, his voice surprisingly tender. "You just need to practice."

Startled, Jenna turned so quickly she nearly lost her footing. She reached out a hand to steady herself against the back of a silk-covered chair, its polished wooden arms strangely cracked and splintered. *Control*, she admonished herself.

"What will?"

"The sensations. You could quite easily overdose on the glut of information your senses will be able to pick up, but it can be managed. After a while," he said, moving away from the door to let it swing shut with a soft click behind him, "you'll be able to control it. You'll hardly notice it at all, unless you want to."

He took a few steps toward her with great deliberation, his eyes focused on her face.

"No," Jenna said, taking one step back, forgetting for a moment that he had known she could hear his heart. "The door stays open. That was our agreement."

"No, that was your demand. However," he said, still advancing with that suggestion of coiled power in every movement, a look of slowly simmering sensuality darkening his features. "I think it would be wiser to keep the door shut for the moment. Especially with what I'd like to show you."

Jenna's heart began to pound with such ferocity she thought she might faint.

Instead she jerked away until her behind hit the desk against the wall. She kept backing up as he continued to advance, stepping around the desk, moving farther into the room, until finally her shoulders came to rest against the smooth silk paneling of the far wall.

"Stop!" Her voice cracked in panic. He smiled, awfully, and kept on. Her gaze flew around the room for something to leap at, to stab him with—was that a knife on the desk— no, a letter opener—

But then he was standing right in front of her, a razor-thin slice of electrified air vibrating between their bodies.

Jenna froze. She felt burned by the heat and muscled tension of him, the aching strain of awareness between their bodies. She struggled to control her breathing, to control the butterflies in her stomach, to stand without fear and look up into his eyes.

What she saw there made the butterflies dance.

"I believe you wanted answers," he murmured, raising his forearms to rest against the wall on either side of her head. She turned her face away and tried to flatten herself even farther against the wall to escape what was between them, that glowing dark burn.

"I don't see how this—" she broke off as he lowered his head and trailed the tip of his nose slowly down from a spot just under her earlobe to where the pulse beat at the base of her throat.

He inhaled deeply and made a low, masculine sound in his throat.

"—is any kind of answer." She said it on an exhalation of breath, fighting back the ripple of pleasure the touch of his skin had sent flooding through her body.

He chuckled, low and amused, and spoke without lifting his head, his breath warm on her skin. "It's not," he agreed. "I'm just indulging myself."

"Well, you can stop it, please. *Now*," she added severely, trying very hard to sound convincing.

He tipped his head back, looked down at her through half-lidded eyes, and smiled. A line of light from the veranda windows caught the shadows in his hair, turning it shades of mink and chocolate brown under the thick, shining layers of ebony.

"Do you really want me to?" he murmured, that lazy smile deepening. His eyes glowed green, and the line of slanted light cast rippled shadows across the arch of his cheekbone, showing the detail of his skin: perfect, poreless, and burnished gold.

"Beautiful girl," he whispered, looking deep into her eyes. "Tell me the truth."

Jenna preferred the truth; she'd spent her entire life trying to discern it. But now, for the second time today, she very much appreciated the value of a good lie.

"Yes, I do," she said coldly, with as much blunt force as she could muster.

"I see," he said, unaffected, his smile growing even deeper, a hint of whimsy there. "So you would not like it if I, for instance, did this."

He lowered his face and brushed his lips against hers with a bare, languid lightness, back and forth, touching but not touching, sliding and slow.

Jenna gasped and tried to turn her head away, but he caught her by the jaw, his strong hand firm against her face, and turned it back.

Her mind was instantly filled with images not her own, her skin burned with the stinging hot pulse of him, his desire, his memory, his *essence*. "Stop!" she cried.

"You can learn to control it, Jenna," he said roughly, moving his lips against hers. He pressed his body hard against her so she felt the heat of him scorch straight through her clothing, burning her chest and abdomen and thighs. Her body arched against the wall, flexed hard against him, aching and wanting and full of need. Her hands made fists and she wasn't sure if she meant to hit him or if it was to keep from pulling him harder against her.

"Try to control it," he said, fierce and adamant.

He flicked the tip of his tongue out to stroke over her lower lip and she was flooded straight through with crystal clear pictures of herself in passionate surrender, pictures snatched straight from his mind.

Feel me, Jenna.

Lie back, let me taste you.

Tell me what you want. Do you like this? And this?

Say my name, whispered hot into her ear as he thrust deep inside her and she shuddered and climaxed beneath him. *Say it and belong to me.*

"Leander," she whispered, just as her knees gave out.

He caught her up in his arms as she fell, as easily as if she weighed next to nothing, and swung her around. He carried her over to the bed and gently laid her on it, then settled himself on the down coverlet next to her in one fluid motion, warm and masculine and solid against her side. One finger brushed a lock of stray hair from her eyes, leaving a trail of images burning vividly over her skin, and though it was crazy and wrong and impossible, his body beside hers felt so *right*.

"Just focus on your breathing," he said, his voice stroking and soft. "I swear you're safe with me, Jenna—I won't cause you any harm. Nothing will ever cause you harm again."

He nuzzled his nose next to her throat and breathed in, a deep inhalation that sprouted goose bumps all over her skin. "I only want to protect you," he whispered, his lips brushing her neck, "to keep you safe. Trust me, Jenna. Trust me. Let me take care of you."

That was his hand at the small of her back, fingers spread, pressing her body closer to his. That was her knee drawing up to allow the weight of his muscled leg to fit between hers, the hem of her dress slipping up, leaving her bare thigh exposed. Those were her fingers digging deep into the soft down coverlet as his lips moved over her collarbone, as he murmured words in a flowing language she didn't understand. That was her hand stealing up to glide over his arm, his shoulder, touching the warm skin of his neck, sliding into his hair...

"Leander," she protested, her voice caught between a whisper and a groan, already beginning to surrender herself to the flush of hot pleasure his hands brought, his lips brought. Her physical reaction to him was overwhelming: instinctual, pure, and primal. Another few seconds and her body would take control of the decision making. "Please, I can't think—"

But he cut her off with a kiss, deep and hot, and rolled half over her body so she was melting down into the soft, welcoming luxury of the mattress.

He pulled back, panting. "Don't think," he said, husky. "Just feel."

And then he kissed her again and she couldn't help herself—she kissed him back.

Leander made a sound deep in his throat, a rumbling low growl, like an animal's. He put his mouth against her ear and rasped out six words that made her heart clench into a fist.

"I want to be inside you."

He slid his open palm down her bare thigh, curled his fingers over her hip, and rocked his pelvis against hers. She felt the length of his arousal, hard and insistent, and desire slammed into her with so much force she moaned. A hot, eager lust that demanded satisfaction swelled up in her and began to rage and burn.

He caught her wrist in one strong hand and lifted it over her head, pressing it down, captive, against the pillow. He lowered his head against the column of her neck and fastened his lips against her skin, licking, sucking, making her arch against him.

Then he bit her.

It wasn't hard, nothing that would break the skin or leave a mark, but a native, untapped burst of energy flashed to life inside her under the fleeting sting of his bite. A blinding white current of feral awareness shot through her muscles and blood and nerves as if she were a pile of dry leaves touched by a torch and doused with accelerant...

...As if an animal sleeping just under her skin had awoken to barbarous, savage joy.

Jenna opened her eyes and stared hard at the ceiling and felt something dark within her gather into storm.

NINE

One moment she was velvet and fire and flexed tension in his arms, the next she dissolved completely into mist.

Leander supposed it shouldn't have surprised him. He knew this was coming, after all. From the first moment he'd laid eyes on her, he'd sensed the latent power that simmered just beneath that ivory skin—he knew she would Shift, as surely as he knew his own name.

But it wasn't only the suddenness of it that left him frozen, staring down at her empty dress still settling back against the bedcovers with a faint rustle of silk, the perfume of her skin still lingering in his nose.

It was the fact that she'd Shifted *now*—it was still days before her birthday.

In the entirety of a recorded history that stretched back nearly two thousand years before the appearance of Christ, Leander had never heard of a half-Blood making the turn before turning twenty-five.

It was an immutable, scientific fact. When fused with its human counterpart, *Ikati* Blood was diluted, warped, corrupted from the state of purity that allowed their specific genetic characteristics to flourish. The first Shift would generally occur anywhere between twelve and sixteen for an *Ikati* child, but for a half-Blood...

Twenty-five years to the minute from birth, and the Shift either happened or it did not.

If it did come, only a tiny percentage survived it.

And so there were unmarked graves near the outskirts of every *Ikati* colony where the bones of those lesser creatures were cast into the ground. The Law was clear: Shift or die.

But Jenna had made the Shift effortlessly and had done it early. Leander didn't quite know what to make of the anomaly she was proving to be.

He looked up to the ceiling where she had spread out against the white plaster. She moved silently toward the chandelier in the center of the room, a fine plume of white mist that hovered and dipped and flowed, a curving ghost slinking through the air.

"Jenna," he said, his breath still coming as a ragged pant from the pleasure of her lips under his, of her body so feminine and lush. "Come back."

He watched as she gathered herself around the chandelier, moving over it, learning its edges and cool planes as she sifted through the shining drops of crystal. His gaze skipped to the veranda doors and his heart missed a beat. He'd left one of them cracked open.

He pushed off from the bed and went to stand under the chandelier.

"Please come down." He stared up at her as she hovered above, the most beautiful phantom. "Just think it, *down*, and it will happen." He watched her form and unform, ripple and flow and stretch out so thin he glimpsed the ceiling beyond.

She dropped down from the ceiling in an elegant column of ruffling white mist and Shifted to woman just under his nose. To a completely nude woman, save only for strands of that cascading mass of honeyed blonde hair, which covered a few inches of bare skin as it draped over her chest but left very little to the imagination.

His breath caught in his throat as he caught sight of the rise of her breasts beneath her hair. He took a step back and tried to look straight into her eyes.

Her eyes were wide as saucers, glowing green and yellow, staring at him with a combination of horror and flat-out elation.

"You're all right," he said. "Don't move."

He snatched the soft cashmere throw from the end of the bed, spread it open and wound it in a lush expanse of dove-hued softness around her body. She was trembling. He rubbed his palms up and down her arms to get her blood circulating and thought about baseball to distract himself from the straining ache of his erection, from thinking about what pleasures were hidden under that blanket, how just one yank would leave her entirely exposed—

"Leander," she whispered. Her voice broke over his name.

"Yes."

"I just—I just—"

He had to clear his throat before he could speak. "You just Shifted," he said.

She looked into his face, a clear and concentrated look, her wide-set eyes gleaming phosphorous green from under extravagantly long lashes. A faint stain of color bloomed over her cheeks. It was like watching a lovely piece of marble flush to life.

"Shifted…"

His heart skipped a beat. Even in a haze of confusion she was so beautiful it made breathing difficult. "You're a Shifter, Jenna. *Ikati*. Like your father. Like me," he murmured, drawn into her eyes.

She blinked once, and her shaking slowly stopped. She released all the breath in her lungs in one long, quiet exhalation, and along with it all the tension in her limbs dissolved.

"*Ikati*," she repeated, rolling her tongue over the unfamiliar word.

"It's an ancient word from our motherland, it means you can manipulate your human form to become…something else. Something more."

"More than human." She stared without blinking so deeply into his eyes he felt as if every corner of his soul was exposed, as if he was a mystery, *her* mystery, that she was trying to divine. Her lips began to lift into a smile, but they paused, then turned down. She frowned.

She then regarded him with an eyebrow raised, that look of defiance he was beginning to recognize settling over her face, thinning her mouth into a firm, stubborn line.

"I think I need to sit down now," she said.

He moved instantly to drag the ruined silk chair over to her. He positioned it behind her and she sat, her back ramrod straight, her naked body swathed securely in deep folds of cashmere.

She gazed out the windows toward the veranda and the city skyline beyond and didn't make a sound.

"I know it must be shocking for you. Unbelievable, most likely," Leander said, unnerved by this unnatural calm. He couldn't begin to imagine what was behind it. The first time he'd Shifted, at eleven years old, he'd run screaming with joy in circles over the lawn at Sommerley.

But then he'd been prepared. He'd known his whole life who and what he was. He'd always wanted it. While Jenna...

He dragged the other side chair across the carpet and sat down across from her in it, while she only continued to stare out the window, silent, still as stone.

"I think I owe you an apology," he began, uncomfortable with her continued silence. "I didn't actually know you would—it's not your time yet, you see, we still have a few more days—I thought I would have more time to explain. I only thought to show you how *I*—" He checked himself and ran a hand through his thick hair when he couldn't think of anything else to say.

Jenna gave him a long, frozen look that stripped away every pretense of softness between them. "What else can I do?" she demanded, cool and controlled. Accusing.

He was taken aback by the difference in her. Only a moment ago she had been pliant and soft in his arms, she had kissed him so passionately he'd felt himself melting. He still had the taste of her on his tongue. But now she was sitting soldier straight in her chair and glaring at him with daggers in her eyes.

"I don't know yet. I'm not sure exactly *what* you'll be capable of—"

"But you have an idea," she interrupted, her voice still the same low, guarded cadence that twisted his heart into knots. Her lovely features hardened into a mask of wariness.

She looked at him as if he were a stranger.

As if he were an enemy.

He longed to reach out to her, find her hand under the layers of cashmere, gather her into his arms, slide his hands into the cool weight of her hair. But he knew she would only recoil, so he remained in the chair, an unhappy clench in his stomach.

"If you can make the Shift to vapor, you'll be able to Shift to panther as well," he said. "It's what we are. It's what *you* are."

This time she didn't even blink. Her eyes were clear and dark and fathomless. Her gaze flickered down to his lips, then she turned her head away again, raised her chin, and gifted him with her profile.

"A panther," she said, without inflection.

"Yes."

A slight pause, then—"A *cat*."

"Technically, yes. A cat."

A little huff of air escaped her lips, which could have been either amusement or disdain. She watched the heat of the day bend the air into shimmering waves over the rooftops of the city beyond the windows and her nose delicately wrinkled, as if she smelled something bad.

"Wonderful. What else?"

Leander leaned back in his chair and debated how much he should tell her. This air of bored civility might be the way she normally reacted under stress, or it could be the calm before the storm broke. He didn't know her well enough to judge.

He *hated* that he didn't know her well enough to judge.

"Not just any cat, Jenna, and certainly not the average domesticated house variety. You are a predator, and a lethal one at that. You'll have the speed and agility all felines possess, but you'll be far faster, far stronger." He watched the light play over the contours of her face, watching carefully to see her reaction. To see *any* reaction. She gave none.

"You'll be able to see clear as day through a night pitch black. You'll be able to hear a whispered conversation half a mile away, smell a rainstorm a week out, and sense everything around you with perfect, unbroken clarity. You'll be in tune with nature in a way no other creature on this planet can ever be."

Through all of this, she remained a sphinx: beautiful and cold and unmoving.

His voice dropped to a murmur. "You'll be able to feel the very heartbeat of the earth."

That seemed to get through to her, barely. Her lips twitched and she inhaled deeply, then let out the breath silently through her nose.

"I assume you've known about some of these talents for years. You must have known you were different," he continued, wondering what it must have been like for her to hide who she was, to try to act like the rest of the people around her, though she was so much more.

He pictured himself living a life among all those cow-witted humans and suppressed a shudder.

He leaned toward her in the chair and rested his elbows on his thighs. "But now that you've Shifted to vapor, they'll be exponentially stronger. And once you Shift to panther, the surge of sensations will be almost overwhelming. In order to thrive, in order to *survive*," he emphasized, "you must learn to regulate how much you let in."

His eyes searched her face. Jenna sat mute, expressionless. It was thoroughly unnerving.

"Also, every Shifter has talents individual to himself—or herself—which will vary in strength. You, for instance, can obviously read minds with a touch of your hand. Anything else you may be capable of will reveal itself to you when the time is right."

"And you?" she said, barely audible.

Her hair glinted gold and honeyed blonde in the light, casting a warm gleam over the rose-cream clarity of her skin, lighting her features with a glow so bright it was almost incandescent. It did nothing to warm the ice in her eyes, however.

"I can Shift to vapor as well—"

"Can't they all do that? All the *Ikati?*" she interrupted.

"No. Only a very few, only the most Gifted. Most of our kind are earthbound."

"Could my father Shift to vapor?"

Among other things, he wanted to say. But that didn't seem prudent. "Yes."

She gave a little, satisfied nod, then turned her face away to gaze out the window once again. She crossed one leg over the other, sending a tiny whiff of the warm, wind-clean fragrance of her skin to his nose. He watched one slender bare foot begin to dance up and down.

The cashmere blanket covering her legs moved higher over one knee, rising up her unclad thigh, but she didn't seem to notice. He gritted his teeth.

"Morgan? Christian?"

He didn't particularly care for the sound of his brother's name on her tongue. "Neither can Shift to vapor. Morgan has the power of Suggestion—"

"Suggestion?" she repeated, her voice rising an octave. Her head swiveled around sharply and she fixed him with a wide-eyed stare. "Like *mind* control?"

"Didn't you see that when you touched me?" Leander said, surprised.

He realized instantly it was a poor choice of words. She winced and closed her eyes for just longer than a blink. "I was too busy seeing everything else," she muttered as she turned her head. All at once the unnatural poise and calm seemed to flow out of her like water down a drain, leaving only a pale shadow of barely concealed distaste flattening her lips.

She fell silent once again.

He forced himself to remain relaxed, willed himself to be calm, fought his instinct to pull her back into his arms. After long minutes of watching her breathe and gaze numbly into the heat-glazed horizon, he spoke.

"Is there anything else you want to ask me, Jenna?" He waited patiently for her to respond.

He waited for a very, very long time.

Jenna stared out the bright windows. She listened to the faint hiss of traffic on the streets below, caught the scent of heat-baked stone and wilting roses rising up from the rose garden, tasted the ashes of her former life in her mouth. She stared out at everything, but saw nothing at all.

Her mother had warned her something was coming. And now it was here.

The sensation of her corporeal body dissolving into mist was the most exhilarating—and frightening—thing she had ever experienced. Cushioned on an updraft of heated air, her back flattened against the cool plaster of the ceiling, she saw and heard everything as before, yet it was all amplified a thousandfold. As vapor she was free as a ghost to move over and through anything she wished, she had only to will it and she could drift in any direction.

A song of joy pierced her straight through as she realized her body was gone. All the cumbersome heft of muscle and bone disappeared, the pull of gravity evaporated completely, leaving nothing but lovely and weightless air. It was like coming home to paradise after being imprisoned in a dark cell for the whole of eternity.

She thought she might die from the sheer bliss of release.

It wasn't the first time, of course. It had been happening in fits and starts since she was ten years old, since the day her father disappeared. Her mother had told her he'd never be back, and she'd shut herself in her bedroom and simply disintegrated into nothingness. It was just for a moment, and she half-believed she imagined it, but then it happened again, and again, and always when she was angry or somehow out of control.

It was the main reason she never had a long-term relationship with a man. Once her emotions got involved, once she let go of her vigilant control, it was all over. It hadn't happened at all in years now—she'd been much too careful.

But this was entirely different, this Shift. It felt like a million fevered dreams of release, it felt like home. She would have gladly left the world behind and stayed as vapor forever.

It was only his voice calling her from below that brought her back from the beautiful edge of oblivion. There was a weight underscoring the velvet tone of it that pulled her back down to earth like ballast. It was as if he was in command of her will, as if the mere sound of his voice could affect her so deeply she would turn away from anything to obey it, even the sweetest pleasure she had ever known.

That had been the frightening part. She did not want to consider what it meant.

Jenna slowly filled her lungs with air and said a silent good-bye to everything that existed for her before this moment. Because now she intended to keep her promise to Leander, now that everything had changed, now that the key had been pushed through the keyhole, the tumblers turned in the lock, the door pushed wide open.

Now that she was Alice, down the rabbit hole.

She understood precisely what he meant when he said she'd have to learn to control the sensations she let in; she thought she'd learned how to do that years ago. But now everything was even brighter, even louder; her surroundings pummeled her harder than they ever had before.

Every breath he took now was a rasp in her ears, every sunbeam that sliced through the windows seared her eyes, every scent in the room and pouring through the open patio doors hammered her relentlessly.

Sun-warmed skin, stale wool and perfumed silk, polished wood, scented soap, freshly laundered sheets, cut grass, car exhaust, arid air. Fecund earth and heated sky and every animal for miles around, pulsing hot with blood. But underneath it all, something new and dark and very unpleasant. The rotten scent of human desperation threaded through like a stain, rising up from the people moving over the earth below to sting her nose with its savage, acrid bite.

Sorrow. Loneliness. Grief. Remorse.

More than anything he said, this moved her, very nearly to tears, though she wouldn't let him see it. For she was human still, only half the *Ikati* he spoke of. Her mother's blood ran true in her veins, just as her father's did.

It was her mother's pain she smelled in all those people below. And her father...

"Do you know where my father is?" she asked Leander in a fierce whisper, still looking out over the city.

He answered without hesitation. "I do."

She bit her lip hard to force back the sob of relief that wanted to escape her mouth. She couldn't crumble now, that wasn't even her most important question. She watched a peregrine falcon circle lazily in the bottomless azure sky. It soared on an updraft, hunting, feathers ruffled gray and black by the wind. She felt its eyes of piercing jet flicker over her for a moment, then it banked and soared away.

She swallowed, gathered her courage, and lifted her gaze straight to his. "Is he alive?"

Leander didn't answer in the affirmative, nor did he answer in the negative. He only gazed at her in silence and drew a weighted breath.

This she took as the answer she dreaded. Her father was dead, years dead, had been so since he vanished like ether when she was a child. She closed her eyes against the hot tears that welled up and fought to swallow around the fist that formed in her throat.

She didn't know how much time passed before she could speak again. She just repeated one thing over and over in her mind.

You will not let him see you cry. You will not.

When she finally spoke, it was a whispered directive. "You will take me to him."

"I will take you anywhere on earth you want to go," he said, his eyes soft.

She nodded back at him, a numbness like frostbite beginning to sink icy runners into her heart. "There are others there—at Sommerley—others like my father. Others like you and....me. There are more of us there?"

"Many more," he said. That look of wolf-hunger illumed his face again, the thump of his heart rang strong and clear in her ears.

She felt his desire, hot and thick as maple syrup. She smelled his skin, tasted his lips, felt the ghosted heat of his hand branding the small of her back. And she wanted him too, though it was reckless and crazy: he'd come to *kidnap* her. She couldn't ever trust him.

So she decided she simply wouldn't allow herself to feel anything for him at all. She wouldn't ever let him in.

With an effort of will she didn't know she had, she blocked it all out. His desire—her own as well—the crush of noises, the assault of smells and sensations. Hardest of all was smothering the sound of his heartbeat. Its echoing beat refused to fade in her ears, though she concentrated so hard she nearly stopped breathing.

"I'm going to require something from you now, before we go any further," Jenna said softly. She let her gaze trail over his face one final time, memorizing its carved and perfect planes and angles the way she had memorized those of her father's face, so long ago.

Another beautiful memory she'd had to erase to survive.

"Yes," he answered, his voice rough. He sat forward in the chair, coiled so tight he seemed ready to spring. His eyes glittered bright, unearthly green. "Anything."

She looked at him, at his eyes, at his lips, at his body so strong and muscled. His beauty was almost sublime, but now she felt nothing. In the space of a single moment, her heart had turned to something cold and barren. Lifeless.

Jenna nodded, satisfied. This deadness was good. This would help her move forward.

"I require your word now, Lord McLoughlin. Actually, no," she corrected herself with a tiny jerk of her head that sent waves of honeyed blonde cascading over the cashmere wrap. "I require your *oath*."

"Anything," he repeated, instinctively lifting a hand out toward her.

"Promise me you won't ever touch me again," she said, hard and cold like the glacier inside her.

His hand frozen in the air between them, Leander stared into her eyes and found a new, resolute hardness staring back at him. He realized with an unpleasant shock that turned his mouth to dust that she was dead serious.

His hand lowered slowly to rest on the cool wood arm of the chair. He considered her in a beat of silence and everything seemed to grind to a slow, molasses stop. Dust motes coiled lazily in a shaft of sunlight from the windows, suspended in the air, suspended like his heartbeat.

He had found her. He had wanted her. He had failed to move her. Now that she'd made her intentions clear, he had only his duty to return her to Sommerley left.

He allowed his rigid body to lean against the solid, grounding back of the chair. His answer came soft and very low.

"If that is what you require, Jenna, you shall have it."

A fraction of the tension she held in her body disappeared. She even smiled, small and tight. "Well then," she said, a little brighter. "When do we leave?"

TEN

"….and the beluga," Morgan said between mouthfuls of the glistening white caviar, "is exceptional. You really should try it."

Jenna wrinkled her nose at the mound of gelatinous fish roe and looked back out the rain-streaked pane. They were descending. Vast swaths of emerald forest interspersed with fields of rolling green hills and low stone walls rose up to meet them. Thunderclouds heavy with rain boiled overhead in the dark sky, and off in the distance, a lone spike of lightning scorched the air with a fleeting, electric brilliance.

"I thought caviar was supposed to be black," Jenna said to the window, wondering if the lightning was a bad omen. "Or red."

"The cheap stuff is," Morgan replied with a shrug that rustled the black taffeta stretched over her shoulders. The blouse was low cut, tight, fronted with a row of delicate pearl buttons. It showed off more than a hint of décolletage, while her miniscule skirt showed off what seemed like ten miles of tanned, bare leg. With a set of carved cheekbones, a fall of shiny, sable hair rippling over one shoulder, and a cherry-red pout, she was intimidatingly beautiful.

"The older the sturgeon, the lighter the caviar is in color, the more exquisite the taste. This is Almas, from the Caviar House & Prunier in London. It's the best money can buy."

She swallowed another bite spread thick on a lightly buttered toast point and sighed in pleasure. "It's heaven, nothing less. Let me make you one." She dug the tiny mother of pearl spoon into the crystal bowl set in front of her on the dining table. It smelled faintly of salt water and hazelnuts.

But Jenna had no appetite for food.

It wasn't the eleven-hour flight from Los Angeles on Leander's private jet that was bothering her. That had been an introduction to the kind of luxury Jenna had never been exposed to: burled walnut tables and desks, lamb's-ear soft leather seats in tones of chocolate and beige, a huge flat-screen television mounted above the sofa. Even the carpet below her feet was beautiful; plush and thick and the color of desert sands.

The open and elegantly appointed interior of the cabin mimicked the great room of the most comfortable, luxurious manor. They even had a butler.

It was the hour drive south to Hampshire from the Heathrow Airport that worried her.

Leander hadn't spoken a word to her since they boarded the plane, except to say the butler was available for anything she might need. Then he'd retreated to the far corner of the cabin and spent the entire flight reading, his face stony whenever she snuck a glance.

It shouldn't have bothered her. It *didn't* bother her. Only now all four of them would be driving to Sommerley together, in the same car. She'd be forced to talk to him, forced to sit next to him, possibly.

She'd be captive to his scent. To his proximity. To her smothered, agonizing desire.

She stretched in her chair and looked away from the window just as the captain came over the loudspeaker to say they'd be arriving in London momentarily and should buckle their seatbelts and remain seated for the rest of the flight.

Damn. She'd been just about to jump up and pace. Again.

Morgan looked at her from under her lashes and returned the spoonful of uneaten caviar to the crystal bowl. "Relax," she murmured, the barest of whispers. "Once we get to Sommerley you won't have to be so close to him. You'll have your own quarters. The place is really quite enormous—you may not see him for days at time."

She sent her a slow, knowing smile and winked.

Jenna felt the blood climb into her cheeks. "I don't know what you mean."

Morgan pushed away the platter that held the bowl of caviar, the buttered toast points, and an iced glass of vodka and began gathering her things from the open seat next to her: black cashmere overcoat, patent leather Kelly bag, a stack of glossy fashion magazines.

"I mean he told us why you agreed to come with us. And what you required from him to do so."

She couldn't think of anything pithy to say in response. "Oh."

"Yes, *oh*," Morgan mocked her gently, a smile warming her face. "And I completely understand. He can be a royal pain in the—"

She cut herself off and glanced over to where Leander was sitting. He leisurely turned a page of his book and ignored them both. Her voice dropped even lower. "Although I can't say that Christian was at all bothered by that news."

Now Morgan shot a glance toward Christian, who reclined with his arms folded over his chest on the leather sofa across the cabin. He was staring at the ceiling, unblinking, his big body tense as a plank. Every so often, a muscle would flex in his jaw, but that was all. Watching him, Morgan's smile faded just a bit.

Jenna's gaze darted to Leander. His hand had stilled on the page.

"Well, that's good to hear," Jenna murmured, her gaze still on Leander's face. "About how big Sommerley is, I mean. That will make it easier for everyone, I'm sure."

Leander gave no indication he heard her. He continued to stare at the book in his lap. Then one finger began to tap a steady, silent rhythm against the back cover.

Jenna realized that if she wanted to keep something from him, she'd have to start passing notes.

"So how does this work?" Jenna turned her head away to stare once again at the dark landscape rising up to meet them. A suburb now, lighted houses and tiny cars moving over rain-swept streets. "All the *Ikati* live in one big house together, like a commune?"

Morgan's derisive laugh made Jenna look over.

"Oh, please." She made a face, just a dainty curl of her upper lip. She glanced at Leander then went on in a lighter tone. "Sommerley is just like any other small town, except it's more…hidden away. I like to pretend it's an exclusive resort, like an island retreat only a privileged few can visit." She smiled, almost melancholy. "Which, I suppose, it is. There's the main square and schools and shops and everything else you would expect in a town. It's also vast dark forests and rolling green hills and a sky that goes on forever."

She tossed a lock of dark hair over her shoulder and looked out the window. "I've been told it's one of the most beautiful places in the world, but…" She shrugged, and her sad smile faded, leaving her face pale and somber. "I really wouldn't know. I've got very little to compare it to."

A sigh escaped her lips. "Anyway, everyone lives in their own homes, just like humans, except we have a lot more space. We're not exactly pack animals, we need our own territories. The Alpha lives on the main estate with Christian and their sister, Daria—"

"The *Alpha*," Jenna interrupted, eyebrows arched. "That's what you call Leander?"

Morgan regarded her with a look of cool, green-eyed amusement. "That's what he *is*, Jenna."

Ah, yes. It was sometimes very hard to believe that underneath that elegant, refined exterior beat the heart of a beast, a creature of vapor and fangs and stone-cold sorcery. She glanced over once again, forgetting for a moment her vow of indifference, and simply admired him.

"So he's…the leader, then. He's in charge?"

Morgan flicked an electric green gaze over Jenna. "Of course. You couldn't tell?"

"And exactly how many of you...of us...are there? Why England? I mean, aren't panthers from tropical forests?"

"Originally, we were, yes. Africa, the legend goes, though panthers can survive in any forested area with plenty of prey. I'm not privy to all the particulars because I'm a—" She checked herself and made a small, helpless gesture with her hand. "I never paid much attention to the tribe elders and their creation stories."

Somehow Jenna didn't believe that. "But why aren't the *Ikati* everywhere then? Why are you three the only other ones I've ever met? Beside my father, I mean."

A shadow of something Jenna couldn't identify crossed Morgan's lovely face. "Because unlike humans who breed like rabbits, many of the *Ikati* are infertile. Most of them, in fact. And it's getting worse with every generation. Less than a half dozen colonies exist now, scattered throughout the globe. Nepal, Canada, Brazil, and Sommerley."

"And Leander is Alpha of all of them?"

She smiled, amused. "I'm sure he wishes he were. But no, each colony is held together by an Alpha and an Assembly of their most powerful tribesmen." Her smile deepened. "I would say tribes*people*, but as far as I know, I'm the only woman to ever serve on an Assembly."

"And no one knows about any of it," Jenna marveled. "You live right out in the open and no one can tell you're different."

Morgan's smile vanished. "Not in the open. Never in the open. We can't."

"Why not? Wouldn't it be easier, or better? Just to be... out, as they say?"

Morgan tilted her head and gazed at Jenna. Her eyes glittered in the dim cabin light. "It must be nice to believe human nature would be anything but cruel toward something so different from itself."

Jenna felt vaguely insulted. "You never know. You might be surprised at how kind people can be. There's a few bad eggs, sure, but overall—"

"Don't be naïve," she interrupted quietly. "There is nothing the human mind despises more than diversity, no matter what you're led to believe. You are either the same, or you are Other." Her voice went flat. "And being Other equals being the enemy."

Jenna thought about all the nice people she'd known in her life, albeit none of them for very long. "I find that hard to believe."

Morgan slanted her a look, gently scornful and sad. "You'll just have to take my word on this one."

A jolt as the plane touched down. Morgan's hand flew to her throat.

Jenna frowned over at her. "What is it?"

She shook her head a little and swallowed, then waved her hand in the air, a dismissive gesture. "I hate flying. I feel so out of control—you can't *see* anything."

"Really? God, I love it," Jenna replied. "We moved around so much as a kid I used to think we owned our own airplane. I'd always ask for the seat next to the window so I could look out at the clouds and pretend I was alone, flying free on the wind. My father used to tell me I had the soul of a bird."

She paused, the memory of her father triggering the bitter taste of salt in her mouth. The taste of tears. "I always wanted to be a falcon," she murmured. "Then I could just fly away and leave the world behind, all its secrets and misery."

From the corner of her eye, Jenna saw Leander's head come up and tilt in their direction.

"Well, it's only my second time on an airplane," Morgan said, leaning over to grab a small bag at her feet. "I'll be glad when I can get my feet back on the ground." She sat up and kept her eyes averted. Jenna sensed it was deliberate.

"Let me guess. Your first time was the flight out to L.A."

Morgan's mouth twisted into a wry smile. "I don't really get out much," she said, her voice shaded with quiet sarcasm.

The plane shuddered to a stop. In one swift movement, Leander unbuckled his seat belt and leapt to his feet. He moved silently through the airy corridor of the cabin toward the front of the plane and disappeared behind the galley wall.

"You can stop boring holes into the fuselage with your eyes now, Christian." Morgan looked toward where he lay stretched out at the front of the cabin. She stood and gathered her coat and handbag. "We're here."

He turned his head and gave Jenna a long, searching look before standing. It was the same look she often saw Leander give her, and it made her flush in exactly the same way. She looked away quickly and concentrated on unfastening her seat belt and gathering her things.

She needn't have worried about the car. By the time she, Morgan, and Christian made their way down the jet's lowered steps to the wet tarmac below under enormous black umbrellas held aloft by the butler and one of the crew, Leander had been whisked away in one of the two sleek black limousines that waited just steps away.

"Ass," Morgan muttered under her breath as she watched the smudged red taillights of his car disappear into the night. Tires slicked back rain in a spray that caught the light and turned it to a shower of rainbow crystals.

Jenna pretended to ignore the compression she felt within her chest as she watched his car speed away. She drew a deep breath, letting the dark, unfamiliar scent of wet peat, heather, and moss settle over her skin, permeate her nose. It was at once cool and inviting, familiar and alien.

"Well," Christian said, standing just behind her. "All the more room for the three of us."

He snapped his fingers and flashed a quick, hesitant smile at Jenna as a uniformed driver jumped out of the car. The driver rushed around to their side and opened the heavy black door of the limousine, then stood at attention, stoic and unblinking, not meeting any of their eyes.

Christian gestured to the open door, his eyes penetrating. "My dear lady," he murmured. "After you."

Leander had called ahead to make sure he would have a car to himself. He guessed he would need a quick escape after eleven hours confined in a small space—luxurious though it was—wrapped in her scent and the quiet, pleasing sound of her voice.

He'd been absolutely right.

He rubbed a tired hand over his face and let his head fall back against the cushioned headrest of the sedan. God, his head ached. Staying in one place for that length of time, willing himself to remain motionless against every instinct that raged within him had produced a throbbing vise around his skull that inched very near a migraine.

He wasn't used to sitting still. He wasn't used to being denied what he wanted.

He watched the night flash by in patches of muted color and light, blurred with the sheen of rain and the speed at which the driver was taking the narrow roads, and wondered what it was about Jenna he found so compelling. So intoxicating.

Naturally there had been other women. Scores of them, if truth be told. His youth had been spent in study and sports and the rubric of the tribe's tradition, but there had been plenty of time to steal away into the woods with some fetching young thing, plenty of time to explore.

And explore he did.

For the son of the Alpha, one day to be named Alpha himself, there was no shortage of willing partners. Beautiful creatures with burnished skin and brazen eyes, beckoning him shamelessly with mouthed invitations across candlelit rooms, propositioning him with words and eyes and slender-limbed bodies. He knew all the best pockets of the woods, all the darkest corners with the softest grass in which to roll.

But for all their wiles and beauty, none of those lusty panther girls of his youth had ever moved him beyond a youthful excitation. He had yet to fall in love.

He'd watched his parents for clues. Theirs had been a happy union. After thirty-five years of marriage, they still held hands, still kissed and gave each other warm and lingering looks.

It was the way with their kind. They were monogamous. They mated for life. Once wedding vows were exchanged in the tiny red-brick chapel at Sommerley, nothing could separate man and wife. No affairs, no divorce, no midlife crisis plagued the *Ikati*.

Only death separated them.

In a way, his parents had been lucky. Horrible though the accident was, they'd gone together. He thought his father would have had the worst of it, if he'd been the one to survive the crash without his mother. Leander pictured him wandering the empty halls of Sommerley, lost as a child, sobbing into his teacup.

They'd been inseparable in life. Somehow it seemed fitting they were inseparable in death.

He passed a hand over his throbbing head and urged the driver to go faster. He wanted to be back in his own bed tonight. He needed sleep, a *good* sleep. He was wrung dry from the constant ache of desire Jenna aroused in him, an ache that grew sharp as a blade when she was near and dulled to a chronic buzz of discontent when she was not.

She was lithe and rash and strong, lovely beyond description, reckless and valiant yet full of a vulnerability that moved him. She was obstinate and clever, she was heat and fire and cool, feminine mystery, she tasted of wild roses and rain, but she was not his.

Nor, as she had so clearly demonstrated, did she want to be.

His head dropped back against the headrest once more. He pressed his fingertips into the hollows of his eyes and let out a long breath.

When they finally pulled to a smooth stop before the massive, scrolled iron gates at the bottom of the long drive that led up to Sommerley, Leander's hopes for a good night's sleep were dashed.

A small square of fabric was posted above the stone pillar on the left, whipping hard in the wind.

It was a red flag. The Assembly's sign for danger.

ELEVEN

Jenna found the button on the armrest that operated the tinted black window. The smell of sodden grass and rain-cleansed country night invaded the warm, dimly lit interior of the limousine as the window silently retracted. She leaned out to stare in wonder at the ten-foot hewn stone walls, the bank of security cameras, the razor-sharp barbed wire artfully concealed beyond the gates by the grove of ficus trees, their gleaming dark foliage trimmed to precisely the right height.

"It looks like a fortress," she said, awed. The rough stone walls fell away from the main gate in either direction for as far as the eye could see, fading into murk as they marched away from the floodlights. "What are you trying to keep out?"

"The world and all its secrets and misery," Christian replied softly, his voice a languid caress from the front of the sedan.

He reclined, long legs sprawled casually before him, against the seat behind the driver. He faced her and Morgan, who sat together on the long, leather seat at the rear. The smoked glass window between the main compartment and the driver was rolled up, flaring into a dark corona around Christian's head as it caught the lamplight from the windows and reflected it back.

His face was swathed in shadow, but the sheen of his perfect, white teeth glinted as he smiled. Even through the darkness, she felt the particular heat of his stare and felt a twinge of panic. Was she insane for coming here? Were these *Ikati* going to eat her alive? But then she was distracted by Morgan, muttering under her breath beside her.

"It's more like what we're trying to keep *in*." She shifted her weight on the seat next to Jenna and crossed her slender arms over her chest.

Jenna frowned. The closer to Sommerley, the more morose Morgan grew. She snuck a peek at Morgan, who stared out the other window, stiff and pale-faced, her lips pursed.

"What does that mean?" she asked.

"You'll see," Morgan replied ominously, still looking away.

A squawk of static from outside startled her. The driver spoke into a microphone box mounted on a slender post beside the driveway. The static cleared to a tinny voice then an electronic clink as the iron gates were automatically unlocked.

The gates swung slowly inward past the stone gatehouse, its black windows staring out like empty eyes. The limousine rolled forward.

Sommerley manor was as she remembered from the images snatched from Leander's mind, only it loomed far more vast and intimidating now that she was standing on the white gravel of the circular drive, oblivious to the liveried servant—*Ikati*, she sensed, like the driver—who stood slightly bent at the waist as he held the door open behind her.

It was intimidating, and also exceedingly beautiful.

Here were manicured gardens jeweled with raindrops and edged with groomed borders of fragrant herbs, burbling alabaster fountains and statues of nudes, an enormous rounded portico with marble Palladian columns washed in deep umber from spotlights hidden in shrubs beneath. Behind the sprawling main house stretched wild, deep vales shrouded in gray-blue mists that wound in thick fingers and curls to a dark horizon beyond. The forest.

The moon was an ivory pearl in the sky, casting her pallid glow over everything.

Serenaded by crickets sawing and frogs croaking and the crunch of gravel underfoot, they were led inside by the white-gloved servant through iron-studded doors twice the height of a man, and Jenna couldn't help but gasp at what lay within.

She was astounded from the moment she stepped through the doors, hammered by beauty and voices and echoing footsteps, Christian and Morgan ahead and the servant behind, the confusion of a dozen different exotic perfumes in her nose at once, dazzled by the silk-covered

walls and baroque vaulted ceilings and chandeliers sparkling in icy cold brilliance overhead.

The sheen of parquet floors was interrupted constantly
by thick Persian rugs, a marble fireplace burned bright in
every room they passed, Chinese porcelain and cut-crystal
bowls filled with fragrant peonies and masses of orchids
adorned marquetry tables, a vast drawing room was lavished
in gold. Clocks ticked and fabrics rustled and voices murmured from deep within the labyrinth of the mansion, and
always the potent reminder of the creatures that walked the
halls of this magical place:

There were statues of panthers—slinking and
hunting and prowling in polished onyx, marble, and
bronze—everywhere.

"Please allow me to lead you to your chambers, Lady
Jenna."

Another liveried servant was speaking to her, bowing at
the waist while he kept his gaze down and gestured toward
dual winding staircases that climbed to the second floor. He
also exuded the fine, humming power of *Ikati*, and Jenna
guessed everyone at Sommerley was, even the servants.
Judging by how Morgan spoke of Others, humans would be
the last creatures invited here.

"Oh, please," she said to the bowing man, "you can just
call me Jenna."

This seemed to startle him, though he recovered quickly,
blinking just fast enough to let her know this was a most
unusual request. "Yes, madam, if it pleases you," he murmured, then glided silently away toward the stairs.

Jenna frowned at his retreating back. Lady Jenna?

"They've been expecting you," Morgan explained,
pausing to pluck a fig from a Waterford crystal bowl on a

cherrywood console a few feet away. She turned it in her fingers, lifted it to her nose, then set it back down in the bowl with a sniff. "I'm starving. That little bit of caviar I had on the plane didn't even put a *dent* in my appetite."

She brushed an invisible piece of lint from the sleeve of her black taffeta blouse and sighed, glancing over the gilt-edged mirror above the console, the wall painted ivory and cream, the vaulted ceiling towering above. Her expression soured.

"Who's been expecting me?" Jenna asked.

"Why, everyone," Morgan said. A smile stole over her face, and Christian, standing beside her, arms crossed and legs spread wide, gave a gentle snort.

"We have a meeting to attend, Jenna, please forgive us for leaving you for a while," he said, shooting Morgan a look. She nodded. "But we'll be having a late supper afterward, if you're hungry. Or you can ring the kitchen to have something brought to your room."

Morgan called a farewell over her shoulder. "I have to freshen up. See you later, Jenna." The servant holding Morgan's bags snapped to attention as she passed, then fell in two steps behind her, a lethal creature outfitted in black stiletto heels, taffeta, and cashmere, down the airy corridor toward a set of carved doors inlaid with panels of mother-of-pearl.

"Stay out of trouble now," she said with a low laugh as she closed the doors behind her.

Jenna looked to Christian.

His body vibrated with a crackling, electric tension that seemed to heat the air all around them. He smiled at her with an intensity that lent fire to his eyes and made her heart skip a beat.

"I'm sure I couldn't get into any trouble here," she said, vaguely embarrassed, though she didn't know why.

"Really?" His gaze was steady. "Out of the frying pan as you are?"

She made a little noise of irritated disbelief. "Is that your way of trying to make me feel better? Because it isn't working."

There was a long pregnant pause, then he stepped closer, slowly, fire still burning in his eyes. He stopped just feet away, almost as tall as Leander, muscled and substantial, and she had to look up to hold his gaze.

"It's my way of saying be careful, Jenna," he said. "Alphas are known for getting what they want. By any means possible."

Embarrassed by that, her face flamed. "Duly noted. And not that it's any of your business, there's nothing between Leander and me, and I have no intention of letting that change."

Christian stared at her for several seconds, head cocked as if weighing the truth of her statement. Then hesitantly, with a conflicted look as if he didn't want to but just couldn't help himself, he reached out and lightly touched a finger to her hot cheek. She stiffened, and seeing her unease, the expression on his face changed from conflicted to pained. He dropped his hand and his eyes grew terribly sad.

"He doesn't need your permission," he murmured. "You're in his world now. There's no one that will stop him from doing anything he likes." His gaze drifted over her face, down her throat, to the open collar of her white silk blouse, and his own cheeks grew ruddy. "Anything at all."

She resisted the urge to step back and instead squared her shoulders. "I can take care of myself."

His gaze flickered back to hers and he nodded. One corner of his mouth lifted. "I know you can." The lopsided smile disappeared and his brows drew together. His next words came out in a fumbling, disjointed rush. "But...if you need...anything...I'm here for you...I'd be happy to...you can always...what I mean to say is that I want...I want..."

He stammered to a halt and she frowned at him, waiting. He flushed even redder, looked away, and blew out a hard breath. Then he cursed and hid his face behind a hand as if he was embarrassed, and that was when several things fell into place at once.

She realized Christian was offering her more than just his assistance.

Her pulse went jagged. She was caught between empathy—she knew the terrible toll loneliness and longing could take—excruciating self-consciousness, and the strong desire to run away into the moonlit night and leave all this insanity behind.

Answers, she reminded herself. *I came here for answers, and I'm not leaving until I get them. No matter how weird this gets.*

She put on her resolve like armor and remembered what her mother would say when things got especially rough— "Remain calm and carry on." She groped for the right thing to say, and it wasn't until she spoke that she knew she really meant it.

"Thank you," she said.

Christian's head snapped up and he stared at her, expectant.

"I mean..." She was momentarily distracted by his molten aura, flaring bright as danger between them, and tried to compose herself and say something coherent that wouldn't make the situation worse. "I mean I hope we can be friends because I need all the friends I can get. And you seem like someone I can trust."

She was immediately sorry she chose that particular phrase.

His eyes closed for just longer than a blink and an urgent sorrow contorted his face, here then gone. He opened his eyes and his gaze raked over her figure with a naked hunger so palpable she felt it like a hand on her skin.

"You shouldn't trust me," he said, his voice rough. "If I were Alpha I'd have already claimed you for my own, regardless of what you wanted. At least my brother is showing some restraint." He paused, his breathing gone ragged. "I wouldn't."

Now she did step back, not just one step but two, thankful suddenly for the servant waiting by the stairs who was looking quite pointedly down at his own shoes.

"I don't believe that," she said, startled. "You're a gentleman."

He laughed, a dark, ruthless sound, and closed the distance between them in one long stride. He loomed over her, large and male and menacing. "Am I?" He snatched up her hand, pulled open his shirt with one hard yank that sent buttons popping, and pressed her palm flat against his bare, muscled chest. He held it there when she gasped and tried to pull away. "You can read minds, so tell me what you see, Jenna," he said, eyes searing. "Tell me *exactly* how much of a gentleman I am."

She managed to disentangle herself and stumble away, hand to her mouth, both faint and furious, the lightning strike of images still burning in her mind. They were a jumble of carnality and tenderness and vivid color blurred by speed, pictures of her and him locked together in passionate kisses and even more passionate lovemaking, images of children that looked like the two of them combined and a few odd, fuzzy scenes of a great many people bowing down to her over bended knee that were quickly crowded out by the overwhelming flood of pornographic depictions of her lips saying yes as she was astride him, beneath him, arching against him in ecstasy.

Seeing her obvious shock at his split-second metamorphosis from benign to not, Christian's lips twisted into a joyless smile. "Don't mistake us for humans, Jenna. The *Ikati* are animals. And like all animals, we're concerned with only three things: hierarchy, territory, and procreation." That searing gaze traveled over her body, lingering, and when he looked into her eyes again her mouth went dry with dread. He opened his mouth and said, "But every time I'm close to you I can only think about one."

Then he turned on his heel and stalked away, leaving her speechless and shaking in the cold, echoing hall.

"Another body has been found," came the terse voice of Viscount Weymouth as Leander entered the fire-warmed confines of the East Library. He paused at the door and looked at the gathered men, every one gray-faced with fear, wearing the look of interrupted slumber: bleary eyes, disheveled hair, unshaven faces.

They all had wives and children, homes and livelihoods. They all had something precious to protect.

Leander hadn't bothered to unpack or eat or even remove his traveling clothes. He'd come directly from the limousine. He knew they would be waiting, most likely been waiting for hours, and it was his duty to make decisions.

Swiftly.

With a shrug of his shoulders he was out of his heavy woolen overcoat. He slung it over a side chair on his way to take his place at the head of the rectangular mahogany table. He didn't sit but gripped the carved wooden back of the Alpha's chair, stared at the silent congregation, listened to the crackle of dry wood as it burned and the thumping, frightened heartbeats pounding against the ribs of the men of his tribe.

He nodded to Morgan as she came through the door and took her usual seat, then frowned as Christian, grim and tight-jawed with his blue Oxford unbuttoned halfway down his chest, followed only moments behind. Without glancing in Leander's direction, Christian went to stand in front of the fireplace, crossed his arms over his chest, and stared down at the flames.

Leander turned his attention to Viscount Weymouth. "Tell me," he commanded.

"Outside the Quebec colony this time, frozen stiff in a lake just beginning to thaw. They think it may have been there since winter." The viscount slid a French newspaper to him across the long table. A blurred photograph showed the naked body of a man being pulled from the lake by a team of local officials.

Like the first body discovered in March outside the Bhaktapur colony in Nepal, this one was headless. What he couldn't tell from the picture was if it had been burned too.

Leander did a quick calculation. Two bodies in a few months, possibly even less depending if they could establish a time of death for this new one. Both found very near an *Ikati* colony, both headless.

It was the indelible calling card of their ancient enemy, the Expurgari. Torture the victim, burn him alive, cut off his head. What they did with the heads, none of the *Ikati* knew.

But if they had been discovered, why not more victims? Why not a direct attack?

"Has the body been identified?" Leander asked, pulling the paper toward him, almost dreading to touch it. He squinted at the picture and read the caption beneath: *Body of missing activist found in frozen lake near Mt. Tremblant.*

"Yes," Viscount Weymouth replied, frayed nerves ringing in his voice. "It was Simon Bennett."

Leander felt the blood drain away from his face.

Bennett was a vocal environmental activist, fighting for tougher laws on pollution, championing clean energy and a move toward more earth-friendly life-styles, working to bring man and animals and the planet in harmony with one another. Working to stop overpopulation, stop wasting natural resources, stop the destruction of their mother, planet Earth.

Working, very vocally and in the public eye, to stop the habitat encroachment on the local population of cougars, lynx, and jaguars. Panthers.

Like Viscount Weymouth, both men killed were Keepers of the Bloodlines.

Leander slowly looked around at the faces in the room, faces he had known his entire life, men he had grown up with or looked up to as a young boy, as the son of the Alpha. Men he had sworn to protect once he became the Alpha himself.

If the Expurgari had obtained any information from these men before they were killed, if they had tortured these men who knew every secret of their colonies, every member within it, every location of their kind throughout the world...

He now felt the same seed of fear he saw on the faces of all these men plant itself firmly into the soil of his heart, take root, and push up an evil, dark leaf.

"Guard the colony. Take every precaution. No one comes in, no one goes out. Edward," he said, turning to look at the pale face of Viscount Weymouth, "convene a meeting of the Council of Alphas to take place immediately, here at Sommerley."

He drew in a long breath that felt like acid scoring his lungs and spoke the words that acknowledged their fears, that would change all their lives from this moment forward.

"They've found us again. Prepare for war."

TWELVE

Jenna awoke slowly in a soft square of sunlight that poured like honey through the dormered windows into her second-story room. Eyes still closed, she inhaled a deep, cleansing breath, the scent of morning and freshly laundered cotton soft in her nose. She languorously stretched her arms and legs beneath the smooth sheets, curling her toes, flexing her fingers.

So comfortable, this bed, so large and deliciously warm. So pillowed with down and fine linens, she felt as if she had slept on a cloud.

It was quiet in the neighborhood today. No noise from the boardwalk, no garbage trucks rumbling over the asphalt in the early morning hours, no muffled conversations overheard through the thin walls of her apartment. The only sounds were the sheets sliding over her naked skin as she rolled onto her back and the warbling of a lone songbird, a pure note held high and trembling in the dewy, pink-tinged dawn.

The stillness was unbroken, idyllic, and *very* unusual...

A frown ruched her eyebrows. Was it a holiday? A Sunday? Why was everything so hushed?

Her eyes snapped open. A swath of shimmering fabric warmed by sunlight swam into focus overhead, saffron and apricot organza threaded with gold, folded and tied between four mahogany posts with heavy silk tassels.

Jenna bolted upright and stared around the room in a fog of confusion. She recognized nothing.

Walls painted coral and vanilla, overlaid in a delicate scroll of trompe l'oeil gardens, climbing ivy and jasmine in lavender and green. Furnishings at home in a palace: a French *secretaire*, a raw silk settee, hanging tapestries, carved wood chairs, and velvet pillows in disarray upon a divan.

It took seconds of heart-stopping panic before her memory flowed back and she could breathe again.

England. Sommerley. Her room. *Ikati.*

Leander.

She remembered she'd dreamt of him, here in this gilded room as the sunlight stole over the horizon and warmed the darkness beneath her closed eyelids to burnished ambers and golds. Dreamt of his face and his eyes and the silky-sweet timbre of his voice as it rolled over the vowels in her name.

She'd dreamt of him and of the dark forest beyond her windows, a forest that beckoned to something deep and dark inside her, a forest she explored with him by her side, a muscled, ebony panther who moved through trees and bracken and undergrowth without a sound except the whisper-thin noise of wind sliding over sleek fur.

Don't mistake us for humans, Jenna. The Ikati *are animals...*

She was going to have to do something about both Christian and Leander, and she had no idea what that something might be. She'd fled to the relative safety of this lavishly feminine room last night after her confrontation with Christian and hadn't emerged since, not even to eat.

Coward.

Aggravated, she flung back the heavy duvet and picked up the sheer robe of ivory silk left by the maid who had turned down her bed. She swung it over her shoulders and, with a jerk, tied the sash around her waist.

She felt plush carpet then cool marble beneath her feet as she padded through the sun-washed room into the adjoining bathroom. She reached for the curved handle of the sink faucet to wash her face, but her hand stilled midreach as she saw a quilted cosmetics bag on the marbled countertop next to a soap dish that looked like solid gold.

Her cosmetics bag.

She straightened and frowned at it.

Leander had waited outside her apartment in the limousine yesterday while she packed. He'd given her twenty minutes. She had flung everything she thought she'd need for a short trip into a single leather suitcase, but hadn't remembered until this moment she'd left her cosmetics bag behind.

Not that it mattered, because it was somehow *here.*

She picked up the bag, letting her fingers trail over the familiar fabric, the quilted stitching. She unzipped it; everything was packed neatly inside.

Jenna turned and eyed the frosted glass door to the walk-in closet. She set the bag on the sink, pulled the silk sash tighter around her waist, squared her shoulders, and walked over to the door.

Four pairs of jeans, a half dozen T-shirts, underwear, socks, two pairs of shoes. That's what she'd thrown into her carry-on yesterday. That was all that had fit.

But what she stared at now—folded in fluted mahogany cubbies, tucked into rolling shelves, hanging from polished wood dowels, nestled into sliding racks row after row—was her entire wardrobe.

Every item of clothing she owned was arranged in perfect order, color by color, shirts and dresses and handbags and shoes, all lined up and tucked in and laid out within this walk-in. Her jewelry, ensconced in velvet trays within four sliding drawers of a large center island. Her panties, folded like handkerchiefs and arranged by color in drawers on the other side. Even her lingerie hung in rainbow colors in one section, categorized lightest to darkest, then by length within the color spectrum.

In addition to everything she owned, there were things she didn't recognize. Formal dresses, cocktail dresses, and evening gowns filled a length of wall, overcoats and jackets in every style and color took up another. A third section was dedicated entirely to handbags and shoes, many which she recognized as designer and extremely expensive.

It didn't really surprise Jenna much when she peeked at the tags on these strange and beautiful clothes. Everything was her size.

She stood motionless in the center of the large room, trying to decide what to do. She pressed her hands hard against the sides of her head and closed her eyes with a heavy exhalation.

It was in exactly this position Leander found her.

"Let me know if that helps a headache," he said. "I've found nothing to cure my own."

Because she smelled his particular fragrance of musk and exotic spices long before she felt the faint tremor of floorboards under his step travel up her spine to lodge in a knot of tension under her stomach, Jenna didn't turn at the sound of his voice.

"I generally find," she said, looking sourly at a fire-engine red Valentino gown with a thigh-high slit, "that throwing something heavy against a wall is a satisfying way to relieve a tension headache. Especially if it should be so accommodating as to shatter into a million pieces."

She looked over her shoulder at him.

"My, my." He leaned against the doorframe with a wan smile. "I had no idea you had such violent tendencies. If you like I'll have a porcelain vase sent up. I imagine that would do the trick."

There were faint shadows under his eyes. He wore the same black silk shirt and black trousers he wore on the plane, except now both were wrinkled. Beneath his golden complexion, he looked pale.

"Or maybe it would help if you just told me why all my clothes are in this closet."

He gazed at her. "Because it's your closet. Where else would they be?"

The tremor in her stomach began a slow burn.

"At my home. Where they should be," she said. A vein pulsed in her forehead and she fought the urge to press her fingers against it.

"Which is exactly where they are," he replied, soft as silk.

She stared daggers at him. "Don't play games with me, Leander, please. Putting aside for a moment the logistics of how my entire wardrobe arrived here overnight, just tell me why it's here and who the rest of this stuff belongs to."

It was incredible to her that although he didn't move or twitch a single muscle as he leaned casually against the door, he still managed to exude a current of rapacious action, like a bubble that engulfed everything around him.

Yet today there was dark tension beneath his veneer of effortless elegance, a hint of something she'd not seen before. Worry?

"I thought you would need a more extensive wardrobe than you brought with you, so," he shrugged, the picture of cool composure, "I asked Morgan to find a few things for you. She loves fashion and she loves to shop, as you may have noticed."

Jenna's palms went clammy, but she was determined not to let him see her rising panic. She might be a coward, but she certainly wasn't going to let him in on that little fact. "How generous. But that was hardly necessary, seeing how I'll be leaving in a few days. To go home."

He slowly raised his eyebrows.

"My actual home," she clarified, breathing steadily against the blood surging through her veins. "Where I *live*."

Something feral glimmered in his eyes but subsided as his smile deepened, bringing out a dimple in his cheek. "I hope everything fits. Though I must admit," he murmured, letting his gaze drift over the clinging silk of her dressing gown, "I quite enjoy this particular *ensemble*."

And there it was again, the thing that always sprang up between them, the warmth and the pull. In spite of her best efforts to the contrary, there was no ignoring or dimming the desire that rocked between them. Now that she'd tasted him, now that she'd felt the taut, muscled weight of his body above hers, she had only to look at his gently curving lips to feel something scorch through her stomach.

Now she knew what he could do for her, and so did the beast clawing under her skin.

She stilled a moment, concentrating on the throbbing pulse of heat between them, trying with lasered focus to make it disappear.

"Is it my navel you're so seriously contemplating?" he said, amused. "Because I'd be happy to remove my shirt and show it to you—"

"You can't keep me here," Jenna enunciated, each word clear and exaggerated as she squared off to face him. "You can't keep me against my will."

"Against your will? Are you here against your will?" he inquired gently. "Because I believe it was you who asked me to bring you here. Demanded it, in fact."

Blood flushed deeper into her cheeks, but she didn't allow herself any other reaction. "Like a cat, toying with its prey," she said quietly. "Playing with a half-dead mouse until it bores of the game and devours it whole."

"What a charming opinion you have of me," he said, unruffled. "Though I assure you, I have no immediate plans to devour you. And you, my dear, are no half-dead mouse."

He smiled that dangerous, languid smile, taking in her look of black fury. "No, you're something more treacherous than that, aren't you?" he murmured. "Something that could charm the birds right out of the trees with the bat of an eyelash, even with those eyes of frost."

"Whatever I am, I'm nothing like you," she shot back.

His smile faded. "Yes, love, I'm afraid you are," he said. "I'm afraid you're *exactly* like me."

They stared at each other, tension aching between them, until a loud rumble interrupted the silence. Jenna's stomach, growling with hunger.

"Forgive me," Leander said, pushing from the doorjamb to stand erect. "You haven't eaten. Why don't you dress and join me for breakfast?"

"Do I really have a choice?"

He turned with a suppressed smile and walked to her bedroom door. "I'll be waiting just outside," he said. "Take your time." The door closed behind him with a soft click.

The room they dined in was elaborate, like everything else in this place, festooned with colorful hanging tapestries on one long wall and a gallery of gilt-framed portraits lit from above along the opposite. There was china edged in gold, crystal glasses filled with freshly squeezed orange juice, baskets of sugar-dusted pastries and raspberry scones, a platter mounded with red grapes and razor-thin slices of creamy Camembert that melted on her fingertips.

There was enough food to feed a small army, yet there were only three of them at the table.

The woman who sat across from Jenna stared demurely down into her bone china teacup, her delicate hand fluttering around her throat like an agitated butterfly as she watched the steam curl up like tiny fingers from the hot oolong. Though it was first thing in the morning, she wore pearls and a gown of ivory satin piped with intricate gold stitching that sparkled under the light thrown from above. Her hair was blackest ebony threaded with silver, pulled away from her fine-boned face. A few loose tendrils curled around her cheekbones as if they refused to be tamed.

She appeared a rare and precious bauble, just removed from a locked vault.

"Leander tells me you are a connoisseur of fine wines, Jenna," she said softly, lifting her lashes to look at Jenna above the rim of her raised teacup. She took a delicate sip and set the flowered cup back onto a matching saucer, her gentle gaze lingering on Jenna. Her eyes were a paler, cooler green than either of her brothers'.

She had been introduced by Leander as his elder sister, Daria. Leander sat silently to Daria's right, frowning at his plate as it if offended him.

"Well, that may be a slight overstatement," Jenna replied carefully, watching Leander tear apart a scone with his fingers. He had eaten nothing since they'd been seated. "I love wine. I appreciate everything that goes into it—the passion, the hard work, the artistry. But I don't have the disposable income to be a real collector. I have a friend who does, though." Jenna smiled, thinking of Mrs. Colfax. "She taught me everything I know about wine."

Daria smiled back, lending a bit of warmth to her eyes. "Yes, it is good to have friends," she replied. "People who can help you in times of need." She dropped her gaze to her plate, grasped her fork lightly between her fingers, and speared a piece of cantaloupe on the golden tines.

"Indeed," Leander murmured. He motioned to the footman, who stepped forward with a silver bowl and dished some of its contents onto Jenna's plate: slivers of beef carpaccio drizzled in olive oil, so thin they were nearly transparent.

"I couldn't agree more," Jenna said. "Though I sometimes wonder how I can tell friend from foe. It's so easy to be fooled by wolves in sheep's clothing."

Jenna watched Leander's mouth twist into a sardonic smile. The scone in his fingers was now thoroughly demolished, strewn over his plate in tiny bits of pale, raspberry-studded fluff.

"Quite so," Daria agreed. "People can be rather unreliable, can't they? But one can always count on family." She smiled again at Jenna, her expression open and engaging. "You'll be meeting more of them at your party," she added lightly.

Jenna looked at her, perplexed. "More of who?"

"The family," Daria responded, still light and ever so enigmatic.

"Morgan insisted we throw you a party, Jenna, if you recall," Leander interrupted. "I hope you don't mind, she doesn't get to do this kind of thing very often. Once she gets her mind set she can't be budged."

"One does need a distraction from the monotony," Daria said. She smoothed the flat of her hand over her skirt as Leander glanced at her, a muscle in his jaw flexing. "Hopefully you can find something in your closet to wear," she added, sending Jenna a sidelong glance. Her cheek lifted, as if she stifled a smile.

Something in Daria's manner reminded Jenna of her mother. She had the same effortless elegance, the same charming manner, a way of setting you at ease though you were perfect strangers. To her deep surprise, she liked her.

Jenna set her fork down and picked up the crystal glass. As she swallowed a sip of tart, cold juice, Leander spoke again.

"I definitely wouldn't wear the red Valentino if I were you, though. I've asked Morgan to return it. I don't think it would particularly flatter your skin."

Daria looked at him with raised eyebrows. "*Très gentil, mon frère,*" she murmured. "*Charmante comme toujours.*"

To conceal the anger that flared under her breastbone at Leander's offhand insult, Jenna tightened her fingers around the stem of her glass. She glanced at the oil paintings along the opposite wall and had no trouble reading the words that were etched on the small gold placards below the portraits.

"Just out of curiosity," she said, swallowing a bite of the delicious carpaccio, "why do you have a portrait of Marie Antoinette on the wall?"

Daria and Leander shared a glance. He nodded, almost imperceptibly.

"The doomed *Reine de France* was an ancestor of ours, my dear," Daria replied, patting a corner of her rosebud mouth with a linen napkin. "The last full-Blooded Queen of the *Ikati.*"

"Queen of the *Ikati.* Right." Jenna tried to keep her face neutral, composed. "Of course. And the portrait below hers, the one of Michelangelo?"

Now it was Leander's turn to speak. "You really thought the Sistine Chapel was created by something so—simple—as a human?" He looked vaguely disappointed.

"Silly me," Jenna murmured as her eyes moved over the gallery of portraits. Her surprise turned to shock as she read all the names.

Amenemhet I; Cleopatra; Michelangelo; Sir Charles Darwin; Sir Isaac Newton...

"We call this the Gallery of Alphas, Jenna. The portraits you see are a pictorial history of our most potent leaders, back to the beginning of our line, or at least as near as we can figure."

Daria picked up her teacup and took another delicate sip. "We used to live quite in the open, but after those dreadful Romans took notice of us..." She shrugged unhappily and set her teacup back down. "We began to be hunted. We were driven out; most of our kind were killed. We've never really been safe since."

"Hunted?" Jenna said, startled. "You were hunted by the Romans?"

Daria paused for just a hair longer than a heartbeat. "Among others, yes."

"Driven from our homeland," Leander said softly, studying Jenna's face, "declared enemies of the state to be terminated at all costs. So we went into hiding."

"We learned to blend in," Daria agreed, stroking a finger along the delicate curve of painted flowers and bone china under her hand. "We interact with humans when necessary, of course, for trade or other purposes, but we never let them know what we really are. It's far too dangerous."

"But that was hundreds of years ago," Jenna protested. "Thousands. Don't you think it might be different now? So much has changed since then, things are so much better in so many ways—"

"People have not changed since the beginning of time," Daria stated simply, still staring sadly down at her cup. "It's only gotten worse for us with the passing centuries. In the thirteen hundreds, legends arose that witches could transform into cats to disguise their activities and demons rode to midnight meetings on giant black panthers. Because they didn't understand us, they cast us as witches, consorts of the devil. That's when the Expurgari were first formed—"

"The Expurgari?" Jenna interrupted.

Daria lifted her pale gaze to Jenna's face. "The *purifiers*," she said in a hushed tone, as if merely saying the word would invoke them. "They're a small branch of the Church—trained assassins, very brutal, very militant, with unswerving faith in their dogma of death. All across Europe cats were burned, drowned, tossed from church belfries, used as archery targets. Once again the *Ikati* retreated into secrecy to survive. Though our strength and wiles have helped us thrive, though we've amassed wealth and our leaders have risen to become *Sir* and *Your Honor* and *My Lord* in the human world, we are not safe. And we never will be. So though it may seem incredible that creatures such as we have been forced to do so, we've endured the centuries by simply...hiding."

Jenna was overwhelmed by this. She thought of her parents, how they ran, year after year, how they suffered. A sharp pain bloomed under her ribcage.

"Hiding is never the answer. I can tell you that from personal experience." She raised her gaze to Leander's face. His beautiful eyes narrowed. "Whatever you're running from will eventually find you, whether you like it or not."

He drew in a long, deliberate breath, staring at her, his face impassive.

"I certainly hope you're wrong," Daria said quietly, going a shade paler than she was before. "Because what is looking for the *Ikati* is very nasty indeed." She shivered lightly, then nodded to the hovering footman to remove her plate.

Jenna looked again at the wall of portraits, ignoring Leander's piercing stare, and let her gaze wander over the rows of elaborately framed oils, moving down toward the end.

Last in the row on top was a portrait of Leander, in severe charcoals and burnt umber, all stern brows and shadowed cheekbones. Only the pleasing curve of his full lips softened his expression. The plaque below read *Leander McLoughlin, 7th Earl of Normanton.* Next to his, second from the end— *Charles McLoughlin, 6th Earl of Normanton.*

He was a handsome man, only slightly less arresting and leonine than his son, with the same blistering green eyes and a wide, intelligent forehead. *His father,* she thought, surprised that someone so fey and otherworldly had been formed in such a normal way. He seemed so self-sufficient and effortlessly in control of himself and everyone else, she couldn't imagine him as a child, being taught how to walk, how to speak, how to read. It seemed far more likely he had once been formed of space and stars and merely willed himself into existence.

Her gaze flickered over to Leander, who now stared at her with a look of odd anticipation. She frowned at him, and this earned her an amused smile.

With a sniff she looked again at the wall and her eyes fell on one name carved in slanting gold that stopped her short. It was a portrait just next to Leander's father, third from the end, which perfectly captured that look of stoic resignation she knew so well.

Rylan Moore, 13th Duke of Grafton.

The crystal glass slipped from her fingers and shattered like a bomb on the parquet floor.

THIRTEEN

Jenna couldn't stop apologizing for her clumsiness, though Daria brushed off her stumbled explanations with an elegant wave of her hand and another sharp look at Leander.

"Your surprise is perfectly understandable, Jenna. I had no idea you'd not been told. I assumed Leander had explained it all to you before you arrived."

She watched as the footman brushed the last of the crystal shards into the dustpan and moved away behind a recessed door before she turned her gaze once more to Jenna. "It's only a glass, after all." She smiled, pushed back in her chair. "I hope you'll excuse me, but I must be off. My husband, Kenneth, frets if I'm gone too long, especially now…"

Leander stood beside Daria and offered her a hand as she rose in one fluid, elegant movement of slender limbs and rustling skirts. "Dolt," she murmured under her breath as she accepted his hand with a chilly smile.

"*Merci*," Leander murmured back, keeping his face carefully neutral. He knew neither of them would be pleased if he allowed himself to smile.

Though he was. Pleased, that is.

Albeit in a wretched sort of way. He felt immensely satisfied he'd finally gotten a reaction from Jenna, and equally mortified by the pain he saw in her eyes when she recognized the portrait of her father. He'd only meant to rattle her enough to peer beneath the icy exterior she'd formulated; he'd chosen this room for their breakfast with a great deal of deliberation.

But she now seemed utterly disoriented and shaken. She had the wide-eyed, startled look of a deer in headlights. A deer just about to be run over by a very large truck.

"I'll leave you to it then," Daria murmured as she turned away, glaring at him from the corner of her eye.

She had always been the one with the keenest sense of justice, his older sister. Always the one who insisted they play fair, even if it tipped their hand or gave away their advantage. She was softhearted and kind to a fault, very much like their mother had been.

She turned back to give Jenna a warm smile. "It was lovely to meet you, Jenna. I hope we can spend more time together after the Council of Alphas convenes."

"The Council of Alphas?" Jenna echoed. She was looking at the table, at the food, at the footmen lined along the wall, but she wasn't looking at him, and she definitely wasn't looking at the portrait of her father on the wall.

With a small, hissed exhalation of breath, Daria spoke through her teeth. "I see you have much to discuss with Jenna, Leander. Try not to leave anything out," she said, her pale eyes like ice above her serene smile.

She released his hand and turned away, gliding past the tapestries and footmen and portraits, the scent of tea roses and hand cream lingering behind her. Her head was held at the stiff angle that told him he'd be in for an earful later.

Leander turned back to Jenna still sitting in her chair, all pink and gold and dreamy, sorrowful distraction, her perfect poise fracturing around the edges.

Daria is right, he thought with a sudden stab of guilt, *I am a dolt.*

"Perhaps a walk in the garden," he suggested briskly, tossing his napkin onto the table. "It's a beautiful morning. Maybe you'd like to get outside?"

"Outside…" she murmured, pulling back from her contemplation of the seedless grape she held between her fingers. She dropped it onto her plate and stood abruptly, scraping the chair across the parquet with a screech.

She blinked at him, at last awakening. "Yes. Outside would be…better."

Through the maze of corridors that led from the gallery to the French doors at the rear of the manor, Jenna remained silent, moving gracefully by his side, ignoring the veiled, speculative looks of the servants as they passed.

Though their heads were always lowered, faces impassive, every one of them was profoundly, instinctively interested in her.

Everyone at Sommerley had felt her arrival by now. She was new, and different, and potent. Even the servants were atwitter with gossip and guesswork. Everyone knew who she was and why she was here, and he couldn't stop their instinct to see her, to look at her, no matter how many hard, silent looks he threw.

Twice he felt her glance at him, but when he turned his head, she had already looked away.

They strolled through the French doors into the cool, dewy morning, footsteps striking lightly against the marble slabs. He looked to the sky and the profusion of white and lavender clouds floating gently there like tufted fleece, emptied of their burden of rain. A knot of starlings scored the pale horizon, a skein of silver-gray and black as they rose from the treetops, flashing in the light like quicksilver.

It felt bloody good to get a lungful of fresh air. He'd been confined to the East Room the entire night, arguing strategy and logistics with more than a dozen other sleep-deprived and agitated men, breathing air that had been inhaled so many times it was stale and humid.

Leander had set his guards at the perimeter of their territory. The few who could Shift to vapor floated overhead as small, drifting clouds, patrolling in tandem with dozens of sleek and lethal beasts concealed in the shadows of the forest. His orders were explicit.

If you see anyone new, anyone who isn't Ikati, kill them.

His gaze slanted to Jenna. He couldn't take any chances, not now.

She wore a sleeveless dress of pale blush cotton, tea length, cinched around her slender waist, one of the few ladylike things Morgan had chosen for her. It was feminine and soft and lent color to her ivory cheeks.

It made him think of cotton candy and hand-churned strawberry ice cream and a great many other pink and delectable things he'd like to run his tongue over.

"Am I the first human to ever come here?" Jenna asked as a pair of housemaids who'd been watering baskets of scarlet and purple flowers froze, dropped swift curtsies then fled, wide-eyed and whispering, through the French doors Jenna and Leander had just emerged from.

"You're not human," Leander corrected, "you're a half-Blood. Those are two very different things." They moved down the marble steps of the shaded colonnade onto the green expanse of the lower lawns. The air parted around him, sweet, thick with moisture and the scent of rosemary and garden roses, free of the smog that had choked his lungs in Los Angeles.

"But everyone else here is like you."

He inclined his head.

"Then how do you decide who's in charge? How do you decide who's a servant and who gets to be on the Assembly?"

"When we first settled here generations ago, everyone was assigned a particular job according to his or her Gifts. The most Gifted were members of the Assembly, the least Gifted were servants, with a dozen different layers in between. It's stayed mostly the same since then. Many of the maids and cooks and foot-men here now had great-grandparents who served my great-grandparents."

"And I suppose no one gets a vote in all this? The Alpha's word is law?"

Leander's lips twisted into a smile. "This isn't a democracy."

"So I've been told," she said, dark, but didn't add any-thing else, and he wondered what Morgan had told her on the ride from the airport. Nothing good, he'd bet.

He paused beside a groomed hedge of rosemary and turned to look at her. "There's something else you should know."

"Only one thing?" she replied, staring straight ahead at the wall of the forest that began in dappled sunlight beyond the dells and vales and turned to dusk a few yards in. "How reassuring. I was inclined to think there were several things I might need to know. If there's only *one* thing, why, I feel so relieved."

He sighed.

She looked at him and smiled, green eyes bright. "How bad could it be, if there's only one little thing?"

He studied her. She was remarkably resilient, this iron-willed female who looked about as tough as a frosted marzipan rose.

But then she'd had to be tough, he thought suddenly, *hadn't she?*

"The *Ikati* are under attack," he said, drinking in her creamy complexion, the elegant line of her throat, the soft rise of her chest. Her skin was as dewy as the morning, pearlescent, shining in the sun. "At least we have very good reason to believe we are."

"Attack?" Jenna repeated, just as calm. She gave him a measured, assessing look before turning to gaze once more at the dark line of forest in the distance. "Well, how very inconvenient for you. I know how you hate to be on defense."

He looked away and stood with his hands clasped behind his back.

For a long while, neither of them spoke.

"That's true," he finally said, quietly and without a shadow of sarcasm. "More true than you know, Jenna. I've been groomed to succeed my entire life, expected to lead and make decisions, trained to *win*. I take neither my responsibility nor my position lightly. I can't. I'm the Alpha. There are scores of people who depend on me, women and children and families I must protect, at any cost. It's a privilege, yet also a burden, because I've no one to share it with, no one who understands how I fear losing. If I fail, the *Ikati* fail. If I lose…"

He turned toward her. "We all lose."

"Losing," she mused, turning back toward the forest, eyes hazy and unfocused. Morning light glowed against the slope of her sculpted cheekbone, caught the tips of her long eyelashes, warming them gold. Her gaze flickered back over him, assessing. "I wonder if someone like you has any idea what it *really* means to lose."

"We all have things to lose, Jenna, even me. Especially me. My people are in danger, our way of life is in danger." He angled a step closer, inhaling the soft scent of dew and roses that clung to her skin. "*You* are in danger," he said, his voice roughened. "And that is something I simply will not tolerate."

Jenna didn't protest or step back, as he expected. She accepted his proximity without comment, without moving away, but she turned her head and lowered her eyes.

"You're right," she murmured. "We all have things to lose." A flush crept over her cheeks. "Things like faith, trust, hope—all the things we were taught to believe in. All those make-believe saviors, like knights in shining armor. Like second chances." Her voice lowered to the barest of whispers and was shaded with sorrow. "Like true love. And as for the danger…" She slowly raised her gaze to his face.

Leander heard everything around them for twenty miles: the air whispering through the pines, the river Avon flowing swift and deep over granite rock and polished stones, the birds in the sky and the squirrels in the trees and the moles rustling deep in their underground burrows.

But most acutely he heard her heart, beating strong and true, flush with heated blood, a squeeze and thump so compelling he wished he could drown in the sound of it.

All his worry for his people, all his rage at his enemies seemed to melt away, and in their stead there was only Jenna, the drum of her heartbeat, the cool embrace of the morning.

"I'm not afraid of danger," she said. "Or I never would have come here with you. What I am afraid of...is something only you can give me, Leander. And I hope..." She closed her eyes. "Even though I know it's going to hurt, I really hope you'll give me what I want." She opened her eyes and fixed him with a raw, hungry stare.

He stood mesmerized as an errant breeze lifted a lock of golden hair and sent it fluttering over her bare shoulder and down her back.

"Anything," he murmured, dazed, his heart clenched in sudden agony. *I would give anything just to have you look at me like that for one second longer.*

"The truth," she said firmly. "Whatever you haven't told me so far, whatever you haven't wanted to tell me, that's exactly what I need to hear. And I need to hear it right now."

She pinned him in her gaze, the smoky-sweet timbre of her voice sliding like satin into his ears. He could barely breathe with her beauty, with the desire pounding through his veins.

"The truth," he repeated, still muddled, trying to focus on her words.

She spoke very calmly. "What happened to my father?"

"Your father was..." *executed*, he almost said. He caught himself just in time, bit his tongue to hold the word back. After another, steadying, breath...

"An amazing man."

Her eyes widened. "You *knew* him?"

"Every *Ikati* across the globe knew him. He was a legend."

He saw how startled she was, saw how she tried to hide it. "Because he was the Alpha." Her eyebrows drew together. She pulled her lower lip between her teeth and he wanted to free it with his finger, with his tongue.

"Because he was the most powerful leader our kind has ever seen. His Gifts were unmatched." Leander looked away, over the vast stretch of ancient forest where his guards prowled, the trees smoky-blue in the morning sun. "And because of the sacrifice he made."

"Sacrifice," she repeated, a chill in her voice. "What sacrifice?"

Leander felt her stare though he wasn't looking at her, felt the way her body became both stiff and still, heard her heart skip first one beat, then another. She was beautiful, and precious, and new to the world of the *Ikati* and Sommerley, though he planned to keep her here—with him—forever.

He was loath to hurt her.

And so he couldn't say he had watched her father die, as had his father and brother and every other Alpha from all the tribes across the globe, every *Ikati* in his colony. He couldn't tell this creature staring up at him so rapt and lovely that he had stood by and watched in impotent horror at what had been done to Rylan Moore, how he had been made an example of by the Assembly, so they would all know how outlaws were treated, so they would all see the consequences of breaking the cold and unchanging Law.

His death hadn't been swift, and it hadn't been merciful. The Expurgari themselves would have approved of what had been done to the disgraced Alpha.

"*Ikati* Law is immutable, Jenna," he said softly, still avoiding her gaze. "Adherence to the Law, to the will of the Assembly, is what keeps us together, what allows us to survive in a world that would destroy us. No matter the position of the *Ikati* who breaks the Law, no matter the transgression itself, punishment follows."

"Punishment?" she whispered. She took a step back.

"It is forbidden to marry a human," he said, carefully watching her face. "It is forbidden to have a child with a human. The punishment for this is…" *Death.* "Imprisonment."

"Imprisonment?" she repeated, her voice small, like a child's. "For how long?"

"Forever," he said simply.

She took this in with a quick inhalation of breath, two spots of pink high on her cheeks. She stared at him, her lips slightly parted, sunlight haloing her hair.

"It wasn't long for him, however," he went on because she was frozen in place and he had to do something to distract himself from the urgent need to touch her. "He refused any food or water, refused to be…caged."

This was true, still so real in Leander's mind that he saw Rylan, chained and defiant even in the face of imminent death, shouting at his father and the whole Assembly that they could go straight to hell and he wouldn't change a thing if he had to do it over.

That had made such an indelible impression on Leander—on the raw edge of eighteen, poised to become Alpha after his own father someday—he often wondered, in the years that followed, what it must be like to love a woman so much you would willingly give your own life to protect her.

With a shock of recognition akin to plunging naked into a lake of icy water, Leander realized he had finally begun to understand.

"So that's why we were always on the run," she said, her voice tremulous and too high. "Because their love was forbidden. Because *I* was forbidden." She cleared her throat, the pink spots on her cheeks darkening to crimson while the blood seemed to drain away from her skin everywhere else, leaving her pale, ghostly white.

"And all that time, every single day of my childhood, you're telling me we were running from…*you?*"

Leander was experienced with women, so he knew, judging from the tone of her voice and the look in her eye, that no matter what he said next, it wouldn't be the right answer. Nothing he could say would help her pain, anything would fall far short of what she needed.

So he accepted this lack of control like a bitter pill he had no choice but to swallow and spoke the truth.

"Your father was a man of great courage. A man I looked up to, a man of pride and valor and honor. I didn't agree with what was done to him, but I was young, powerless to change his fate. And the Law is ironclad. What your father did was forbidden. If we allow even one exception, we risk the destruction of our way of life, of our existence. It's our way. We must live in secret, we must stay together, we must adhere to the Law."

He drew in a long, slow breath. "Or we must die."

She stared at him, lips still parted as though she had something hard in her mouth she was unable to chew. He thought he felt a compression about her, as if her skin were tightening over her muscles and bones, as if she were drawing invisible armor around herself.

Her eyes narrowed. "He wasn't just imprisoned. Was he, Leander? He didn't just die of natural causes."

He wanted to lie. God, how he wanted to lie to her. But he couldn't.

"No."

Her body went completely still. It didn't even seem she was breathing. "Say it. Just say it. Tell me what happened."

"Jenna—"

"Tell me!" she hissed.

The look on her face gave him the kind of pain he imagined someone run through with a sword would feel. For a second he debated with himself, knowing this would be the final nail in his coffin. She'd really hate him after this. But she deserved to know. If the truth was all he could ever give her, even if it meant she'd never speak to him again, so be it.

"He was executed," he said, low, holding her gaze. Her nostrils flared, but she didn't move or speak. She waited for him to continue, just watching him with those wide, beautiful eyes. "There were...other things done to him first, but in the end..."

"In the end?" she prompted when he faltered.

He wanted to pull her up hard against him and bury his face in her hair and beg her forgiveness, beg for a chance to somehow make it right. But that was only wishful thinking. He took a breath and steeled himself for what would come.

"A full-Blood *Ikati* can stay in animal form forever if we want to because that's what we really are. It's our true nature. Our human shape is a disguise, a clever adaptation that's allowed us to live alongside our enemies, to survive.

We can only hold our form as human or vapor for so long."
He drew another slow breath, measuring his words. "Days,
weeks maybe if you're strong enough. But you have to Shift
back sometime, and when you do…"

He stood there struggling, remembering.

"Though he was ordered not to, your father Shifted to
vapor to relieve the pain after he was tortured on a machine
called the Furiant—"

Jenna made a small, horrified noise. All the color
drained from her face. She lifted a trembling hand to her
mouth.

"He was recaptured as vapor and put in a box, a special
steel box designed to seal on entry so he couldn't escape."
His final words were almost whispered. "It was a very small
box."

Her lips parted. He saw her pulse pounding in the hollow of her throat. "So when he Shifted back…"

It didn't need further explanation, but he nodded
anyway.

She stepped back and stood with one hand over her
mouth and the other pressed to her heart and stared at
him, swaying, her eyes fierce with unshed tears. It was several moments before she spoke.

"Do you know what I think?"

Her tone was so cold he imagined icicles falling from the
shape of her words to shatter into a million frozen pieces
against the stone beneath their feet.

"No."

"I think maybe it's *better* to die than live like you do," she
spat, clipped and hard, eyes flashing eerie citrine against
the pallor of her face. "Hiding like fugitives, trapped in
a gilded cage." She made a wide, sweeping gesture that

encompassed the lawns, the gardens, the smoky forest, and the sprawling mansion behind them. "Turning against one another in the worst possible way for the sake of your precious *Law*. It makes me *sick*. *You* make me sick!"

Pain exploded under his collarbone as if a nail had been driven there. He closed the distance between them with two short steps. "Jenna—"

"*Don't*," she said, breathing hard and stepping back. "Don't you *dare*."

Jenna Shifted to vapor just as he reached for her arm, leaving him grasping at nothing but air. Leander watched helplessly as her empty cotton dress slithered to the ground, a castoff ghost curving pink and soft to lie in mournful silence against the dewy grass.

FOURTEEN

Jenna streaked like a bullet into the cool sanctuary of the forest.

She had never moved like this before, had never thought it possible. Nothing but the sheer animal force of her will propelled her straight ahead through the thicket of towering trees. Sunlight slanted down from above as she flew, a shooting arrow filled with rage and a despair so deep it was bottomless.

Her father. Those bastards killed her father.

She sped on under primal instinct, darting through misty air and dappled shafts of sunlight, startling a family of deer into flight, flashing over fallen logs and mossed bracken, scattering a trail of dead leaves high in her wake. She sliced through a delicate, dew-heavy spiderweb and felt its silken fibers cling to her until they sheared away, one by one, torn off by her velocity.

She was grateful she didn't have the capacity to cry now, folded in vapor as she was. She was grateful she couldn't feel her heart throb, feel her guts twist into knots.

She was grateful she couldn't scream. Because if she started, she didn't think she would be able to stop.

"If they ever find you, run," her mother had emphatically said, a few months after her father had disappeared so many years ago.

"Who?" she'd asked, suddenly alert, abandoning the show she'd been watching on television in the living room and turning to look at her mother, who was staring out the front window of their house, her gaze darting this way and that as if she expected someone to jump from the bushes at any moment. A large glass of clear liquid was clutched in her shaking hand, and even from where she sat cross-legged on the floor a room away Jenna could smell the alcohol.

"It was too late for me by the time I found out what he was," she answered, cryptic, still peering out the window. "I was already in love with him. A real Romeo and Juliet kind of love too, quick and deep and star-crossed, with everyone and everything against us." She took a long swallow from the glass, ice cubes clinking, then pressed it against her forehead and closed her eyes. "Not that I would change it," she whispered. "Not that I would go back and change a thing."

"Mom?" Jenna said, afraid of the incoherent rambling, the dark, desolate tone in her voice. Her mother turned from the window and Jenna saw for the first time the deep grooves around her mouth, the furrow between her brows, the lines fear and mourning had carved into her face. Though frail and ill, she was still beautiful—statuesque and elegant with a mane of long blonde hair she'd inherited from her own mother and passed along to Jenna.

"And no more sports," she said abruptly, her voice changed from desolate to fierce. "No more gymnastics, no more soccer, no more track. You can't risk standing out like that. You have to blend in, try to act like everyone else—"

"I won a trophy in track!" Jenna cried, leaping to her feet. "Gymnastics too! I'm way better than those other girls—"

"Oh, honey," Jenna's mother said, her eyes welling with tears. "That's because you're not like those other girls. You'll never be like them."

Those words held a ring of prophecy, and it had struck Jenna speechless. She stood looking at her mother, tall and blonde and pale, just like she was, but broken, and felt the earth turn under her feet.

"Who am I like, then?" she asked, already knowing.

A lone tear tracked down her mother's cheek. She didn't bother to brush it away. "You're like your father," she said, and the desolation was back. "You look like me, but you're like him, strong and fast and…different. And like him, you'll be hunted. So you need to learn to pretend to be something you're not, because I won't always be around to protect you."

There was nothing in Jenna's short time on earth to prepare her for that. Not only the thought that her mother might eventually leave or die or otherwise cease to take care of her, but also the admission that she was like her father, who she worshipped as something close to divine, and the proclamation that she was going to be hunted.

Like him. Her father was *hunted*. Her body went cold with horror.

"What happened to him?" she whispered, terrified her mother might actually tell her this time. But she didn't. She only took another drink from her glass and turned back to the window. It was a long while before she answered.

"He's gone, and he's never coming back," she said, and Jenna had never heard such anguish in another person's voice. Her mother drained the final ounce of liquid from the glass, set it on the windowsill, and stared at it, *through* it, as if she wasn't seeing it at all.

Jenna sank to her knees on the bare wood floor, shaking so badly her legs wouldn't support her anymore. Her cheeks were hot and wet, and she realized she was crying.

"Why not? Why won't you ever tell me what happened?"

"When you're older," her mother replied in an eerie, dead tone, still staring at the glass. "I'll tell you when you're older."

That became a promise that was never fulfilled. And now Jenna was flying like the wind through a forest that once belonged to her father, fleeing from the answer to a question that had gnawed and hurt and grown unchecked like a cancerous tumor for fifteen years.

She covered miles of primeval undergrowth until finally she tired.

Drifting down against the rough bark of a sapling, she pooled, exhausted, in a watery plume into a fork in its branches. She listened to the sounds of the forest, leaves rustling, branches creaking, squirrels chattering, the patter of tiny, unseen feet scraping over the dirt below. A redthroated sparrow alighted on the branch above her and began to whistle, feathered belly expanding sweetly in song.

She couldn't think of what to do. She could hardly think at all. She had wanted answers so desperately, had felt as if the world would be righted if only she knew all the details of her past, if only she knew the *why* and the *how* and the *when*. But even the small piece of information Leander had given her hadn't helped her world align in any way—it had only served to throw it even further off its axis.

Execution. A very small box. The thought of it made the sparrow blur into a shape she didn't recognize, a blob of color stark and sharp against the haze. She reared up against the branch, flattened herself over the peeling bark as she lost her balance. The sparrow flew away with a shriek into the forest.

She surged up through the canopy of branches and looked down over the treetops, spread thick and verdant green for miles around. She spotted a crumbling ruin in the distance, just beyond an outcropping of lichen-covered granite, and angled herself down, heading toward it. It was an old stone cottage, with empty windows and a roof half-collapsed, almost reclaimed by the forest.

Covered in climbing ivy and blue trumpet vine, it looked exactly as wretched and forlorn as she felt.

Jenna funneled down and Shifted to woman beside a low, crumbling wall. She hesitated a moment, her senses surging back. Her heart pumped to life, the scent of wild mint and cedar resin filled her nose. A chill erupted over her naked skin as a cool, misty breeze stole over it.

She put a hand on the rough stone wall to steady herself, leaned over, and threw up.

When the last of the heaving was over and she had finally emptied her stomach, she wiped her watery eyes and nose with the back of her hand and spat into the dirt. She knelt there awhile, staring at a small pile of dead leaves on the ground, feeling slime and mud ooze through her fingers, the dull ache of her bare kneecaps against the cold ground. She filled her lungs with air, forced herself to do it again, and again. When it began to feel as if they would remember to do it on their own, she hauled herself to her feet and scraped the mud from her hands against the rough wall.

The cottage was dark and even cooler than the forest. When she stepped inside she had to wrap her arms around her nude body for warmth. Grasses and ivy had overtaken most of the stone floor, but in one corner opposite the collapsed roof there was a blackened brick hearth, and beside it were a lantern and a rough blanket, folded atop a pillow. Someone else had found refuge here, but long ago—a fine layer of dust covered everything.

Shivering, Jenna unfolded the blanket, shook it out, and wrapped herself in it. It was coarse and scratchy, it smelled of must and rotting wood, but it was thick and warm and fell past her knees. She sank down on the cold stone hearth and felt like a lost pilgrim in some forgotten fable: friendless, soulless, outcast, and abandoned by everyone and everything. She looked around at her sad little sanctuary. The crumbling walls, the mossy stone, the shadowed and lonely interior.

Meager though it was, it would have to do. She planned on staying here awhile.

FIFTEEN

Morgan watched with mounting amazement as Leander, for the fifth time in four minutes, paced the length of the East Library, spun on his heel, and paced back again. He paused next to an overstuffed armchair, then sat down heavily into it, propped his elbows on his knees and clenched his fingers into his hair.

Holy shit, she thought, astonished. *He's losing it.*

After all he'd been through—the grueling strength and agility trials to confirm his Gifts and worthiness for the title of Alpha, the rigors of commanding a pack of unruly and feral beasts, the shocking death of his parents—he'd never lost his composure, had never once allowed a glimmer of anything less than total control to be seen by anyone close to him.

And now this...unraveling. It was as unthinkable as the earth ceasing to rotate.

"She won't be gone long, Leander, she doesn't have any food," Morgan said from her chair at the table. She adjusted her weight against the carved wood back, uncomfortable and uneasy. "Or clothing. How far could she get?"

"And she has an army of the best hunters on earth looking for her," added Viscount Weymouth, seated across from Morgan. They exchanged glances as Leander remained unmoving in the chair, staring at the floor. He let out a low, guttural moan—a sound that sent something unsavory crawling along her skin.

Definitely losing it.

In the three days since she fled from Leander, news of Jenna's disappearance—a single day after her much-anticipated arrival—had spread like wildfire though the colony. The daughter of the tribe's most Gifted Alpha, and its most notorious criminal, had vanished like a ghost.

A ghost that had absolutely no intention of ever being found again.

Along with a cadre of his most Gifted guards, Leander searched every nook and cranny of Sommerley—every low and hidden place, every knell and dale, all the miles of open fields and high bluffs and grass-covered banks of the winding river—but no one found a single atom of her scent to lead them to her.

He was attuned to her, he knew her scent better than any of them, but he found nothing of her in the woods, nothing of her near the road. No trace of her lingered to give him hope that she was still near, could still—somehow—be convinced to stay.

"And what if there is something *else* out there looking for her as well?" Leander raised his head to stare across the room. His eyes were fierce. There were fine lines around his mouth that hadn't been there yesterday, an expression of naked anguish he was doing nothing to hide. "She's alone, unclothed, with no weapons or food—she's completely vulnerable."

"We don't know that the borders of Sommerley have been breached by the Expurgari, Leander," Viscount Weymouth said soothingly, glancing once again at Morgan. He sat back in his chair and picked up a steaming cup of black coffee.

"We have no proof of that yet. If they are about, it's highly doubtful they're inside the perimeter, not with the number of guards you've posted, not with the security systems you've put in place." He lifted the coffee to his lips, all the while keeping his gaze trained on Leander. "An intruder would almost have to be *invited* in to breach our safeguards. I'm sure she's safe."

"For the time being," said Christian, tense and brooding at the far end of the table.

All eyes turned to him.

He too looked worse for wear. He'd worn the same shirt three days running, hadn't bothered to shower or shave in the last two. He ran a hand through his hair and huffed out a weary breath.

"She's new to these woods, new to Sommerley as a whole...she has no idea where our borders lie. And if she can Shift to vapor, as Leander *says* she can," he ignored Leander's steely gaze and continued, "she can simply fly away at will. Never to return."

"Thank you, Christian," said Leander, "for your very helpful input. Now shut up."

"I'm merely saying," he continued, speaking directly to the viscount and Morgan, "that not only does Jenna have absolutely no reason to want to make her home here, but she's been given good reason to loathe us all. In her place," he glared at Leander, his hands white-knuckled around the arms of the chair, "I would have done the same thing."

"Are you implying," Leander said, deadly soft, "I was *wrong* to tell her the truth?"

The viscount cleared his throat and set his cup down carefully atop the gleaming mahogany table. He leaned forward and adjusted his spectacles. "Perhaps it might have been a bit much...so soon..."

When Leander switched his gaze from Christian to focus directly on him, the viscount cleared his throat again. "Her ways are not our own. It must have come as a great shock," he added, a faint sting of chagrin in his voice.

Silence took the room. The warning call of a mockingbird rose outside the windows, harsh and razored, slicing through the sunlit room like a knife.

"Although I'm sure you had your reasons," the viscount finished lamely. The surface of his coffee suddenly became of great interest to him.

"We're not like the rest of them," Leander said, his voice hard. His eyes burned as they fell on each of them in turn. "We're not like the Expurgari or the humans or any of the other animals that walk this earth. We're stronger than all of them, we *face* the truth. We speak it. We've survived eons of persecution and envy by being stronger than they are, and Jenna is a survivor as well. I won't sink to their level and lie to her. We are *Ikati.* We are above them all, above their petty skirmishes and greed and lies."

"Indeed," Morgan said, examining her French manicure with acute interest. "I daresay we are." She raised her gaze to Leander's face and a pulse of anger sharpened her tone. "But we're not above making someone with good intentions and an innocent heart our unwilling prisoner, even if she doesn't quite realize it yet. Nor are we above forcing her to be subject to our Laws. Laws that are foreign to her, Laws that took the life of her own father."

She leaned back in her chair and crossed one long leg over the other, her manicure forgotten. "Laws that will make her no more than chattel if it's discovered she can breed. No," she said softly, her eyes narrowed to slits. "We are definitely not above any of that."

"We've been through this with you before, Morgan," interrupted the viscount before anyone else could speak. "Dozens of times, *hundreds,* I would wager." He leaned forward in his chair, visibly grateful for the opportunity to move the focus away from himself. He began to tap his index finger on the table, a staccato beat to underscore his words.

"The Law is in place to keep us from total disaster. It was created as the anchor that holds us fast against the raging river of temptation that would lead us into extinction. If it weren't for the rules we live by, we'd be hunted far more easily than we are now. We never would have lasted even the first *millennium*—"

"The *Law* is nothing more than control and oppression, *especially* for a woman, and if Jenna has any sense she'll keep as far away from this shining prison as she possibly—"

"Whether she likes it or not, *this* is her home, *this* is where she belongs—"

The huge wood door at the far end of the room swung open and hit the wall with a muffled boom. Two of Leander's guards stepped forward with a scullery girl in tow.

"Forgive me, my lord." One of them gave a quick bow before righting himself and motioning to the girl next to him, her arm held aloft in the firm grip of the other guard. "We thought you should hear this straight away."

"What is it?" Leander leapt from his chair and strode toward them, his back ramrod straight. "You've found something? You saw something? Speak up, girl!"

The guard gave the scullery girl a little nudge with his elbow and jerked his head toward Leander.

The girl curtsied and chewed her lower lip.

"I was in the kitchen, my lord," she began, meek as a mouse. Strands of her lank brown hair fell over one downcast eye. Her small hands fluttered over a striped apron until they settled, trembling, around her waist. She cleared her throat.

"Polishing the silver as I always do on Tuesdays." She twisted the apron in her fist, over and over, working the rough cotton into a knotted bunch. "It's a lovely silver set, my lord, all dotted about with tiny roses and vines and wee little birds. I love to work on the silver, it's really very—"

"Yes," Leander said. The word fell between them like a block of cement.

The scullery maid stopped speaking, looked up at him, and paled.

"It *is* a lovely silver service. I'm pleased to hear you enjoy working with it." He gazed down at her, his right hand flexing open and closed.

The scullery maid opened her mouth, then snapped it shut.

"But perhaps you could tell us—quickly—*exactly* what it is you saw."

"Just...just the blood, sir," she stuttered.

Christian rose from his chair in one swift unbending of limbs that produced not a single sound. Morgan cut her gaze to him. He stood stock-still, eyes trained like gunsights on the girl.

"The *blood?*" Leander repeated, aghast. "What on earth are you talking about? What blood?"

"Little splatters on the stone floor, sir. I only noticed because I'd bent down to reach a fresh polishing cloth we keep in a little bin below the cupboards next to the laundry. It's kept just so, sir, very neat and clean, the housemistress herself makes sure the kitchen and laundry are always in such good repair, so organized and run nearly like the military itself, sir, never a thing out of place. You can always find just what it is you might be looking for, whether it's polishing cloths or hand towels or just the right spice for the dish the cook is making for dinner—"

"The *BLOOD!*" Christian boomed, his face red. "What about the *BLOOD?*"

The guard held onto the scullery maid's arm as she leaned back in a half-swoon, her face round and white as the moon.

"Christian," Leander spat. "*Enough!*"

Christian kicked the chair away with the heel of his boot, pushed roughly by the girl and the guards, and strode out the open door, cursing.

"What the devil's got into him?" the viscount muttered to Morgan. His fingers were wrapped so hard around the fragile coffee cup the handle looked ready to snap in two.

"The exact same thing that's gotten into Leander," Morgan murmured back. She dropped her gaze when Leander's head turned sharply. He stared at her over his shoulder, eyes black with rage.

For one long moment, Morgan felt the burn of his stare on her face. If he hadn't been so unstrung, she'd have met his gaze head on, but now...now he was ready to snap. And that made him very dangerous.

He turned his eyes back to the girl. "Tell me all of it. Tell me *now*," he growled.

"There was blood on the floor, sir, in the laundry," she whispered in terror. "Blood that led through the kitchen, up the backstairs to the lady's chambers—"

Leander pushed past her before she even finished speaking.

"Leander! Wait!" Morgan shouted.

She leapt from her chair and crossed the room. She moved quickly to match his long stride, which had already taken him past the door and into the hallway. He shouldered past her, walking stiff-legged and stone-faced down the long corridor toward the curving staircases that led to the second floor. She had to almost break into a run to keep up.

"If Jenna's back, and she's hurt, she is *not* going to want to see you." She moved in front of him just as he placed one foot on the carpeted first step.

"*Goddammit*, Morgan—"

"*No*," she interrupted. She pulled him to a stop and stared right in his eyes. "Just this *once*, trust me. I'll go up first. You can follow in a few minutes if you like, but believe me on this, your face is not going to be the first thing she's going to want to see, not after the way your last conversation ended."

"If she is bleeding, if she is *hurt*—"

"Then I will come right out and get you."

Through the fabric of his shirt, Morgan felt the tremor beneath his skin. Tension that flexed tendon and bone into pieces of hardened flesh, poised for action, strained so taut she thought he might Shift to panther under her hand and fly up the stairs six at a time.

"Just a few minutes," Morgan said, more softly, realizing Leander was almost past the point of reason. His eyes, blazing unearthly green, were trained on the landing at the top of the curving staircases, the landing that led to another long corridor that led directly to Jenna's rooms. "I'll go in first," she persisted. "Just let me see her first. You can wait right outside the door."

He hesitated, breathing hard, still looking up the stairs. When he finally spoke, his voice was harsh, as if his vocal cords had been strained with silent screaming. "You have one minute before I break the door down."

He turned back to Morgan and she could see how much it took for him to grant her even this much. "*One.* I'm right behind you. Go."

He pushed her up ahead of him.

Morgan didn't have to look back to see him follow. She felt him at her heels, more beast than man, the song of his blood pounding hard in her ears.

SIXTEEN

The cut on the sole of her foot was small, at least at first.

Produced after she'd stepped on the atom-thin edge of a piece of broken obsidian outside the cottage, its edges were clean and razored: it wasn't deep. It bled more than it actually hurt. But it was the effect it produced that was most terrifying.

Since she'd cut herself, Jenna was unable to Shift.

She tried in every conceivable way to force the Shift, although before it had seemed to appear of its own will, if she was upset or frightened, or if she merely willed it, a single word in her mind to flee from the things coming out of Leander's mouth—*vapor*.

There was a glimmer of power, but the Shift wouldn't come.

She had no plan when she'd run away into the forest, nothing more than escape. The cottage seemed a good place to stay while she gathered herself to consider her next move. Clear, cold water ran from a little brook just twenty paces beyond the cottage, there was wild mustard and raspberries, and even a patch of morel mushrooms poked their pale heads through a scorched patch of earth from some recent fire. She had shelter, she had food, she had water.

What she didn't have was any sense of what she should do next.

The first day she spent choked in a kind of anger that felt outside of her, as if it followed her around as she moved, a thick haze of fury she was barely able to see through. She didn't feel anything inside of herself, no light or hope, nothing solid or substantial. It was as if the enormity of her emotions couldn't be contained within her body and had needed more space in which to breathe.

But *she* couldn't breathe. She spent long, panicked minutes gasping for air, sure she was having a heart attack, the pain in her chest was so great.

Twilight falling into the forest brought with it a loosening of the pain. A dull ache took the place of raw and hopeless anguish. The sky turned a brilliant shade of fuchsia as the sun began to sink below the horizon. Pink and violet and vast above her, she stared at it and thought of her home, her tiny apartment on the beach half a world away from this place. She missed it with a sudden, wrenching pang of melancholy. She missed Mrs. Colfax and Becky and her job at Mélisse and even felt a bit nostalgic for the hysterics of Geoffrey. At least those people were real and reliable, those things were home.

This wasn't her home. It could never be. And these people...Christian was right. These people were animals.

She fell asleep slumped against the cold stone hearth, shivering like a dog, listening to the small creatures of the forest come awake with the dark.

When she awoke in the morning, her neck was stiff and pinched but her head felt clear, as clear as the dawn breaking over the smoke-purple hills in the distance. There were no more answers to be had, at least nothing that would set this right or help her understand.

She decided understanding the past was less important than embracing the future.

She would leave. She would leave this place and its mythical beasts and the horror of all the secrets they held and find a new life for herself somewhere else in the world.

Somewhere they'd never find her.

She knew the ways to hide, taught well as a child by one of their own. She would disappear into the wind and be done with it all. She would finally be free.

But just as she'd made her decision and squared her shoulders to take to the air, she'd stepped on that damn rock. No matter how she tried, she couldn't Shift. She couldn't escape.

Jenna was now faced with two choices: live in the forest as long as she could, foraging for food, exposed to the elements, or walk back into the den of beasts. It took a full hour of debate with herself on the pros and cons of both situations before she'd made a decision.

Death by starvation and exposure was only *slightly* less appealing.

She'd spent the last two days trudging through the woods back to Sommerley, nude, starving, the coarse blanket around her shoulders filthy with a layer of mud from when she'd had to stop and sleep on the ground.

The cut on her bare foot worsened as she walked, tearing open ever wider over the undergrowth of fallen logs, rock, and stone she'd had to traverse. And now it was infected.

"How is it, I wonder, you were able to evade all Leander's guards in the forest and around the manor and walk right in without a single soul getting wind of your arrival?"

Morgan raised her gaze from the sole of Jenna's left foot, which she washed in a basin of warm, soapy water while Jenna sat, stoic and silent, biting her lip against the pain.

She shrugged, a defeated motion of her shoulders underneath the pale blue silk robe Morgan had thrown around her. "I could feel them. Where they all were, when they were close, and when their attention was elsewhere."

Except for her clean left foot, the rest of her body was still covered in grime from her trek across miles of woodland. Her shins were bruised, her ankles covered in scratches. Her hair was snared into an unholy mess of knots. She had snuck in through the kitchen, stolen up the long, curving staircase, and simply collapsed naked atop the bed in her room, falling asleep instantly when her head hit the pillow.

She'd been so exhausted she'd forgotten to lock the door.

She awoke with a start moments ago to find Morgan standing at the edge of the bed, clucking her tongue like a mother hen, covering her naked body with the robe.

"All of them?" Morgan looked startled. Her hand stilled in midair, the wet washcloth dripping into the silver basin in her lap. "You could feel *all* of them?"

"What difference does it make?" Jenna pulled her foot from Morgan's grasp. She set it down on the carpet, tightened the belt around her waist, and brushed a lock of grimy hair away from her eyes. "I'm back here now, I'm sure I'll be under lockdown—it won't matter who I can feel and who I can't. From what I understand of your *Law*, I'll never be able to leave this room again."

Morgan looked at her, green eyes pensive, head cocked to the side. "Actually it makes a great deal of difference," she said quietly and set the basin on the floor.

Morgan had already been to the bedroom door three times. The first to whisper something to someone standing outside, the second to lock it, the third to stop the pounding of a very strong fist with a hissed command.

The pounding started up again, louder than before. It shook the heavy door in its frame.

"Let me guess," Jenna said. She glanced wearily at the door. "Everyone knows I'm back."

"If they didn't before, they definitely do now," Morgan muttered. She stood and started toward the door again.

"Can't you just ignore him?" Jenna fought the pull of exhaustion, unwilling to face the owner of the pounding fist.

Morgan looked at her. "*Him?*"

"Yes, him. Leander."

She knew it was him. She smelled him, felt his particular brand of pulsating energy all the way across the room. Even the locked door did nothing to diminish the feral current it sent scorching across her skin. She hated that even in her current state of bedraggled fatigue, he still affected her so strongly. And his heartbeat...

She was beginning to realize she recognized the sound of it anywhere, as if it were a voice that spoke her name, over and over.

Morgan looked at her askance. "So you can feel each one of us *specifically?* Not just the general sense of an *Ikati* close by, but you can identify specific individuals?" She glanced back toward the closed door. "Without laying eyes on them?"

Jenna sighed. "No. Just him, specifically. With the rest of you I just feel this…presence. You're different from anything I've ever sensed before, so it's easy to pick you out from your surroundings. But with him…" She sighed again, annoyed with herself for even admitting it. "It's like this pulse, like the charge of electricity before lightning strikes. It was so strong the first time I felt it I passed out."

Morgan's mouth made an O of surprise. Her eyes were so wide Jenna could see the whites both above and below her irises.

"What?"

She glanced at the door again, looking confused. "That's why you fainted—at the store? Are you sure?"

"Well, yes. I felt it before I even saw him. And then when I finally did see him, that energy knocked me on my ass. I tried to pretend it wasn't him at the time, but unfortunately it appears it was."

Morgan made a sound of amused amazement. She lifted a hand and covered her mouth; Jenna could see the smile she tried to hide.

"Please don't make me guess what you're thinking, Morgan. I have no energy for guessing."

"No, it's nothing," she said airily, waving her hand in front of her face. "Really, it's probably nothing."

Jenna glared at her.

"Well, it's just that..." She trailed off, pressing her lips together.

"*What?*"

"It's just that only an Alpha can sense another Alpha like that. Specifically." She giggled, a lighthearted, girlish sound that seemed distinctly out of place for the circumstances. "And only with the Alpha to whom they're mated."

Jenna wished she wasn't so tired. She thought she could probably throw Morgan a good twenty feet across the room on any other day.

"If you ever say anything like that to me again, I won't be responsible for my actions."

Morgan made a gesture of acquiescence with her shoulders and hands, though her smile still wasn't helping Jenna's peace of mind.

The pounding on the door started up again, louder than before.

"All right. We've got about five seconds before he breaks down the door. I can't ignore it. What do you want me to do here?"

"Just tell him I'll come out later, for dinner. If I'm *allowed* to eat." Her upper lip curled.

Morgan's smile faded. She regarded Jenna with a look of peculiar, intense concentration for a long moment. "*That* I'm sure they'll let you do. As for the rest of what you'll be allowed to do..." She pursed her lips. "That's going to depend entirely on you."

Jenna closed her eyes and let her hair fall over her face as Morgan went again to the door. This time she stepped through it and closed it behind her for a moment before she came back in and slammed it shut.

"That ought to do the trick."

When Jenna opened her eyes, she saw Morgan standing with arms akimbo at the end of the bed. "I just told him if he didn't stop the pounding you were going to fly out the window, never to be seen again."

"That *was* the original plan," Jenna murmured. She stifled a yawn behind her hand and eyed the pillow, the fluffy duvet, the layers of satin sheets below. The soft bed called to her like a siren's song, lush and succulent and oh so inviting. This place might be a prison, but at least it was a sumptuous one.

"Well, little bird, you're grounded until that foot heals anyway," Morgan said.

Jenna came instantly alert. "Why?"

"Because we can't Shift when we're wounded. Even a little cut will do the trick. You're not going anywhere until that foot heals."

Something inside her stomach eased and softened, then bloomed into a tiny flower of hope. A shallow cut like this would heal quickly. A few days, maybe a week…

She turned away so Morgan wouldn't see her surprise. She stood, putting most of her weight onto her right foot, and hobbled over the plush carpet toward the bathroom.

"So you're saying I'm stuck here until this heals completely," she threw over her shoulder.

"I'm saying, my dear," Morgan said, utterly neutral, "you're stuck here permanently."

That stopped Jenna dead in her tracks. She turned slowly back to Morgan, holding a hand out at waist level for balance. Panic sprawled over her chest. "I knew it," she said, her mouth gone bone dry. "I *knew* I shouldn't have trusted him. He never planned on letting me leave, did he?"

Morgan's face held another inexplicable expression. Her eyes shone with a deep, hard thoughtfulness. Her gaze flickered to the window for a moment. "Unless..."

"Unless what?" Jenna said sharply.

She cut her gaze back to Jenna. When she spoke, her voice was urgent, a sudden rush of words falling from her lips. "How did you find your way back to Sommerley, Jenna?"

"I *walked*, I told you—"

"Yes, for two days. I know. Through woods you've never set foot in before, evading along the way an army of the best hunters on earth, and simply came in through the open kitchen door. But how did you know which *direction* to go?"

For some bizarre reason, Morgan's facial expression exuded an air of incredulous expectation as if she were just about to peek around a corner to see a unicorn standing in the middle of the room.

"I just..." Jenna struggled to find the right description for what had led her back. "I just followed the trail."

Morgan just stared at her with the same silent anticipation, so Jenna went on.

"There was a trail—"

"Your scent? You detected your own days-old scent?" Morgan interrupted.

"Well, yes, my scent was the obvious thing, but there was also...the light."

This was a wholly inadequate description for the pulse of energy she had detected when, as she knelt down to examine the cut on her foot, she closed her eyes for a brief moment and saw the concentric rings under her lids, a faint, glimmering trail of diamond-white and gold that led off into the woods. When she opened her eyes it was gone, but she closed them again and it came back, glittering shapes like circles with streamers trailing behind heading steady south, even as she turned her head to and fro to see if it would move.

She knew instinctively it was her, an impression left as she shot like an arrow through the forest. She knew it would lead her directly back to Sommerley.

"You could see your heat signature," Morgan said, unblinking. "You could smell your scent and see your heat signature, all from more than two days past." She lifted a hand to the chair against the wall and sank unevenly onto its stuffed silk cushion. Her eyes were very wide.

"I don't know exactly how to explain it...I guess that sounds right, though." Jenna took in Morgan's face, the sudden pallor on her cheeks, her slack jaw. "Why? What does that mean? Can't you do that too? Can't everyone here do that?"

"I...I..." Morgan cleared her throat and began to blink quite rapidly. The color flushed back to her cheeks in a rush of crimson. "And now—if you close your eyes now, can you see anything else?"

Jenna raised an eyebrow. "How did you know I had my eyes closed?"

"Just try it," Morgan whispered. "This is very important, Jenna—please, just try it."

"I am in dire need of a shower, Morgan, as you can clearly see, and am almost delirious with hunger and exhaustion. I hardly see how this is the time for me to play—"

"Marie Antoinette," Morgan interrupted in a hoarse whisper.

Jenna remained silent, wondering, as Morgan stared at her from her perch on the chair.

"She was the last *Ikati*—"

"Queen. Yes, yes, I know. Your doomed ancestor, the queen of France. What about her?" Jenna said, exasperated. Her foot was throbbing, her patience was fraying, and her stomach was clenched into a horrid little ball of empty, writhing air that seemed poised to begin cannibalizing itself.

Morgan appeared to be breathing regularly, but Jenna could hear her heartbeat drumming under her ribcage like a hummingbird's.

"The *Ikati* aren't dogs, Jenna. We're not like a wolf pack, though we have Alphas and hierarchies and rules upon rules upon rules," she said slowly. She swallowed before continuing. "We are *CATS*. And every pride of cats has a queen." She paused again. "Though the *Ikati* haven't had one since Marie Antoinette. She was the most powerful Alpha of her time, more Gifted than any male Alpha. She was our last true Queen."

"And look how well that turned out for her," Jenna said, humorless.

Morgan shook her head, disagreeing. "You are missing the point entirely. The queen of France was allowed to do as she pleased precisely because of who she was. She was in control of her own destiny—had she been any other *Ikati*, she would have been shackled by the Law, as the rest of us are. So I'm going to take a wild guess here, but if I'm right..."

Morgan inhaled a shaky breath. "Just close your eyes and tell me, tell me what you can see. Close your eyes and concentrate."

Jenna stared at her, confused. "Why?"

"Because it's...important."

Her eyebrows arched.

Morgan took another shaky breath. "Because it's *very* important?"

"This is completely ridiculous."

"Please?"

Jenna made a sound of exasperation. "I already *know* what I can see—the light! I told you!"

Morgan remained silent but clasped her hands together tightly in front of her chest in a gesture of mute supplication.

"Fine," Jenna said through clenched teeth. "But you're going to be disappointed. And you owe me one."

She closed her eyes.

At first there was nothing but the amber glow of sunlight against her lids. Two songbirds began to warble outside the window, a rising melody of piercing notes that wound together and lifted ever higher, lovely and sweet. She sighed in frustration and crossed her arms over her chest.

"Just relax, Jenna," Morgan murmured. "Just let yourself go and concentrate on your breathing."

Inhale. Exhale. She relaxed her body and felt her exhaustion so keenly she thought she might fall asleep standing on her feet. She didn't bother to cover her yawn with her hand.

She became aware of her heartbeat slowing. Something began to sink into her cells, softening time around her to a muted tick of the clock on the fireplace mantle, a hollow pale echo of Morgan's breathing. There came a warm, sliding sensation, like honey poured over her skin.

And then it arrived with a breathtaking, silent lucidity as if it had been poised behind her eyelids forever, as if it had only been waiting all along for her to *want* to see.

Picture: A night sky, black, perfectly clear and cloudless, deep in the countryside where no other lights could pollute the virgin dark. Silence. Then, after a moment of suspended anticipation, a glimmer.

A star.

First one winked to life, a bright spot of white against a velvet black canvas, so near it seemed she would be able to reach out with her hand to touch it. Another shimmering light, again very close, this one burning a strong blood red. Then another, still one more, glittering bright, all close to the first.

Then, all at once, thousands of stars winked to life.

They blazed against the darkness, burning and twinkling, calling to her with the most beautiful, aching song. It ran through her senses like an intangible zephyr, like a silken, living wind, and settled down into her bones as if it had been waiting for years and years to arrive, for her to listen.

Here were clusters of light, like galaxies across the universe, beautiful and ethereal and spread over a vast distance, all pulsing with heated power, every one unique in color and shape and size, every one crying out to her, every one her own.

The strongest song of all came from the glowing red star.

A shiver came over her.

It started in her core, in the very center of her stomach, and ran out along her arms and legs. The shivers turned to goose bumps, butterflies in her stomach transformed into scarlet bright flame, joy came up hard to consume her. She wanted to stare up at these stars forever, felt they were more than just brilliant points of light, they were something akin to...

"You can see them all, can't you?" Morgan said with an awed, whispered voice you would use in church. "All the *Ikati*. All of our kind, all across the globe."

Jenna opened her eyes and gazed at Morgan's face. She spun with dizziness and had to swallow a few times before she pulled herself together enough to respond.

"I didn't see anything." Her voice was more tremulous than she would have liked.

Morgan gazed back at her with something like reverence. Reverence...and awe. "Yes, you did."

"No, I did not." She paused for just longer than a heartbeat. "And even if I did, it doesn't mean anything. I'm just overtired."

"I'll tell you what it means." Morgan straightened her long legs and rose unsteadily from the chair. "It means that you are connected to *all* of us, you can find us anywhere, even through pitch black or blinding snow or at the bottom of the ocean. This Gift is the strongest of our Blood, a Gift shared by only a few of our kind throughout the ages, a Gift Marie Antoinette herself was blessed with. It means you are bound to us all, in a way we're not even connected to each other.

"As a matter of fact," Morgan inclined her head and sank into a low, proper curtsy, one knee bent elegantly with the other behind, "it *means* you are the Queen."

Jenna stared at her, blinking. "I'm sorry," she said slowly. "I must be hallucinating. I thought you just said I was the *queen.*"

"Yes," Morgan insisted. She rose up with shining eyes to look her in the face.

There was total silence in the room save for the longcase clock against the wall that ticked out the seconds in crisp, clicking notes. Five, ten, twenty...

"That is the most ludicrous thing I've ever heard."

Jenna hobbled back over to the bed, sank down heavily on it, and stared around the gilded room in a haze of confusion. She yawned again, fighting the tide of exhaustion that wanted to pull her down into an ocean of blessed rest.

She glanced over to find Morgan beaming at her.

"No, Morgan."

"Yes, Jenna."

"No. *No.*"

Morgan just stared at her, smiling enigmatically. It unraveled the last of her patience.

"I don't know what game you're playing with me, but I'm not in the mood for it! I only came here to get answers about what happened to my father, and first I find out he was…he was *killed* here—and not only that, but I'm a *prisoner*—and now you're trying to tell me I'm the—I'm a—"

"Queen," Morgan finished for her, calmly and quietly. "And yes, like it or not, I believe that is exactly what you are. And not only that, but Leander…is your mate."

Jenna collapsed onto the bed and curled up into a fetal position. "Please just go away now. I just want you to go away."

For a long moment, all Jenna heard was her own pulse pounding in her ears and the sound of Morgan's soft, erratic breathing. "Just so you know," Morgan murmured, "there are substantial benefits to being Queen of the *Ikati.*"

"I find it extremely hard to believe," Jenna said into the coverlet, her voice muffled, "that being the matriarch of a pack of wild animals who live in hiding and kill each other if they step out of line would have a single advantage I'd be interested in."

"Well…" Jenna heard the sound of rustling silk as Morgan nervously shifted her weight from one foot to the other. "Now they'll have to do exactly as you say."

Jenna barely had the strength or the interest to answer her. "They?"

"The *Assembly*," Morgan enunciated. "If you're the Queen, that means you can do as you please. It means you can come and go and live your life and *to hell with all of them*..." Morgan trailed off to a whisper, then gave a final, amazed sigh.

Something in her voice began to make Jenna extremely nervous. She sat up quickly and stared hard at Morgan. "You can't tell them about this. That you think this."

Morgan's mouth dropped open. "Don't be *ridiculous!* Do you know what this means for you? You'll be able to—"

"Promise me," Jenna interrupted. She leaned over and clutched Morgan's hand. "Promise me you won't tell them."

"Jenna! I have to tell them! You have no idea how important you are to us—to *me*—"

"No!"

"Why on earth not?" Morgan said, indignant.

Jenna dropped Morgan's hand and sat back on the bed. She took a breath and lifted her gaze over Morgan's shoulder. The color of the sky in the windows beyond was lifting to a bottomless, azure blue. "Because I don't want to be that. I *can't* be that."

"But," Morgan said, astonished, "*why?*"

She pinched the bridge of her nose between her fingers, hating the memory that surfaced. She kept her voice monotone when she answered, because at least she could control that, unlike the pain in her heart. Unlike the past.

"After my father disappeared, my mother drank herself to death. It took eight years. It wasn't pretty, and I was helpless to stop it. Every single day growing up, I would pray that whatever was making her so sick and so scared would stop. I think she was literally scared to death. By the thought of what was following her, the thought of who and what wanted to see her dead." She looked at Morgan. "The *Ikati*. And now you're telling me I'm supposed to be—what?—in charge of?—the leader of?—the very people—*things*—that killed her? The things that killed my father?" She shook her head sharply. "No. No way. Not a chance in hell."

Morgan gazed at her for one long, solemn moment. "I'm sorry about your mother," she said quietly. "I didn't know about that. All I knew—all any of us were ever told—was that your father deserted the colony for a human woman and had a child. And then he..." She moistened her lips, hesitating. "And then he..."

"Sacrificed himself so we could live. Yes," Jenna said. "Apparently he did."

"But he knew exactly what he was doing. He loved this place," Morgan said softly. "He loved his people, his position, our way of life. He didn't leave Sommerley because it was bad. He left because he couldn't have what he wanted if he stayed. Because of the *Law*. But you can have anything you want, Jenna. Don't you understand? Because you are who you are, you can leave, you can stay, you can have what I've wanted my entire life."

Morgan leaned forward and gently took Jenna's hand in her own and held it there with careful pressure.

"Which is what, exactly?"

"Freedom," she breathed. "You can have your freedom."

Morgan's words came back to her, spoken with such pathos the night they arrived in the limousine. *It's more like what we're trying to keep in.*

Jenna's body was now so heavy with weariness she felt she would sink right through the mattress to the floor below.

The urge to sleep seemed as irresistible as the pull of the moon over the tides. She fought it back for just a moment longer.

"I already had that, Morgan. I already *have* that, and there's nothing that's going to keep me here against my will, playing nice. No matter how Leander and the Assembly or anyone else tries to force me to, I won't play nice." She looked at Morgan, squinting and blinking as her face went in and out of focus. "And I think *you* don't want to play nice either, though you try to act like you do. I think you've had enough of their macho bullshit."

Morgan squeezed her hand, hard. Her face blurred as exhaustion seeped like a slowly hardening cement into Jenna's muscles.

"So promise me you won't tell them about this. At least not yet. Not until I can figure out how to get around it—or get out of it. Promise me and you have my word, I'll give you something in return. Whatever you want that I'm able to give."

"Anything?" Morgan asked, suddenly tense. "You'll give me anything? Do you promise?"

"I promise."

Jenna's eyelids drooped but flew open when Morgan's fingernails pressed into the flesh of her palm. She leaned in closer, her eyes very wide and dark, unblinking.

"I want what I've always been denied. What others take for granted. I want what you have, Jenna. *Freedom.* I want to walk away from Sommerley and never look back, never have to worry that they're coming for me. If you can get Leander to let me go, I won't tell them a thing. I'll even help you get out of here. You have my word."

The choked passion in Morgan's voice convinced her.

Jenna sagged over, her head hit the pillow. "It's a deal," she mumbled, already half-asleep. "Just don't tell them anything. Just keep this between us...for now...and I'll make Leander let you go...I'm sure I'll find a way to convince him..."

Darkness began to slide over her in a sweet, easy blanket of release.

She was nearly asleep when she heard Morgan whisper something to herself. Something anguished and self-loathing, something that sounded almost like a plea for forgiveness.

But before Jenna could ask what Morgan needed forgiveness for, she tumbled into black oblivion.

SEVENTEEN

The room was crowded.

Too bloody crowded, Leander thought as he let his gaze rake over the footmen along the gallery wall, the blazing candelabras, the ocean of satins and lace that rustled as the ladies moved. The wives of the Assembly members and visiting Alphas were done up in their finery for the occasion, a dinner party he'd argued strongly against.

Any other time. Fury climbed into his throat. *Any other time I'd have been able to stop this.* But with the Council of Alphas convened, he was simply outvoted. In his own home, no less.

This was pure madness.

This was no time for silliness and festivities, no time to have the entire leadership of the *Ikati* gathered together in one place, like sitting ducks on a pond. Over the past twenty-four hours, the Alphas from the other colonies had arrived at Sommerley with their families and envoys and entourage. They would stay for a day, a week, or a month, however long it took for them all to come to an agreement on what precautions were to be taken, what was to be done about the Expurgari.

Of equal importance: what was to be done about Jenna Moore, *Ikati* gone rogue.

At the behest of the Assembly—and against his express wishes—Jenna had been locked up like a prisoner in her rooms for the past four days. She was now considered a threat of unknown proportion. She had yet to Shift in front of the Assembly, had fled into the woods, had refused to answer any questions whatsoever or even meet with them.

One of the Assembly members had even floated the idea she might be connected to whomever was now stalking the *Ikati*. Motivated by anger or revenge, she had both the reasons and the wherewithal to stand against them.

Leander had been restrained from snapping the man's neck in two when this idea was forwarded. He'd very forcefully reminded them she didn't even know about her father until *he* told her.

She was guarded carefully by a rotating watch of four of their strongest men, was brought food and water on silver trays, was allowed to see anyone she chose, but she denied access to anyone but Morgan. It had been tolerated for the past few days, but he knew the Assembly was getting restless. He knew it wouldn't be long before she was forced to provide irrefutable proof that she was *Ikati*, she could Shift, she was friend and not foe.

So far Leander was the only one who had seen her Shift to vapor. In these perilous times, his word alone was not enough to convince the rest of them that she was indeed one of their kind.

We can't know her mind, Leander, the Alpha from the Manaus colony had said. *She remains a danger to us until she is proven otherwise.*

His neck had also been in danger of Leander's grip.

His gaze found Morgan standing across the ballroom. She was pale and erect with her back against an alabaster column, clad in an uncharacteristically chaste dress of simple ivory satin. She wore a guarded look, but he sensed her elation.

He frowned. Morgan hadn't seemed herself the past few days. Only planning this ill-conceived and hastily arranged dinner party had brought her—barely—out of her strange and fevered distraction. She remained silent through the Assembly meetings, through all their heated arguments about what to do with Jenna, wearing an enigmatic expression very close to the one on her face now.

She turned her head and caught him looking. With a Mona Lisa smile that lifted one-half of her mouth, she put two curved fingers to her forehead and inclined her head.

His frown deepened, but then he was distracted by someone laughing very loudly in his ear. He angled away. He ran a finger under the stiff collar of his shirt and pulled it away from his burning skin. Not only was the room overcrowded, it was overheated.

The Council of Alphas was scheduled to meet this evening at ten o'clock, after the dinner. After the—unbelievably stupid—dancing. The orchestra was already playing in a box of their own on the second floor, sawing on violins and blaring into horns under a set of branched candelabras that rinsed them in dancing pale light.

A brooding Christian sidled up to him. He wore a perfectly cut jacket of sable and fawn, an Italian silk shirt open at the throat, and clutched a large glass of single-malt whiskey in his hand.

Leander knew it was his fourth whiskey so far tonight. He'd been watching Christian carefully since Morgan's comment in the East Library. The comment that felt castrating with the horrible, cutting surge of jealousy it brought. The comment that made him so angry he nearly couldn't speak.

He'd never been in competition with his brother. Nor did he want to be. But he suspected, in a dark, abandoned part of his heart, that a competition was exactly what the two of them were ensnared in—albeit a silent, unacknowledged one. He couldn't describe the excruciating misery this brought him, both for himself and for Christian...for what it might mean to their relationship.

Leander had another suspicion he would never admit to himself. Doing so would be like unlocking Pandora's box to unleash the selfish, snarling beast inside him that had no thought for anyone but himself.

The suspicion was this: no matter the pain it caused them both, he would do anything to claim Jenna as his own.

Anything, including laying waste to all his familial ties and every Law that bound him.

"All the usual suspects," Christian said dryly. He lifted the glass to his lips and swallowed the amber liquor, draining it quickly. He lowered his arm and motioned to a waiter hovering nearby for a refill. "I think our friend Alejandro over there is going to challenge you to a duel later."

Alejandro, the Alpha from Manaus, Brazil, who had impugned Jenna's motives, glowered at Leander from behind a protective cluster of women who flitted about him like delirious moths. He was tall, as tall as Leander, though somehow lacking physical substance, as if you could put your fist into his abdomen and it would simply come out through his back, trailing smoke.

He had long teeth and a slick smile and wore his hair in the combed-back and pomaded style of a mid-century Sicilian mobster. His colony was small—as were all the other colonies in comparison to Sommerley—but his cunning and ambition were not.

"Good," Leander said, gazing at him evenly. He was the only other unmarried Alpha, younger than Leander by four years and a lifetime, conceited and pompous and too fond of himself for his own good. "Maybe then I'll get the chance to finish what I started in the Assembly meeting."

Alejandro dropped his gaze and turned his attention to one of his female admirers, a rotund woman cocooned in a dress two sizes too small, which caused her ample bosom to be in imminent danger of breaching the restraints of the delicately beaded neckline. He lowered his head and whispered something into her ear. She broke out in a flurry of giggles and waved her plump hand in front of her face.

And then a few strange things happened at once.

First, the orchestra missed two bars of the sonata entirely. The violinist pulled his bow in an awkward, off-key screech in between. They stumbled for a moment, unable to find their way back to harmony while Leander looked up at them, eyes narrowed.

Then a hush fell over the ballroom. People stopped talking in midsentence, stopped walking about and laughing, the ice in their drinks even seemed to stop clinking. Silence filled the room. The plump, laughing woman with

Alejandro lifted her hand to her mouth, clutched his arm, and sank her fingers so deep into it that Leander almost felt the bruise forming from where he stood.

Alejandro frowned down at her—all his teeth showing though he wasn't smiling—then lifted his gaze. He too froze in place, as if struck by an arrow.

At the exact same moment, Leander heard a hissed inhalation from Christian. His danger-sense rising to gnaw at his skin, Leander whirled around.

And there she was, an angel swathed in demon red.

Jenna stood poised at the arched doorway, one hand resting lightly against the head of a marble statue of a muscled panther in midleap. The other trailed slowly down the narrow, cinched curve of her waist outlined beneath the scarlet red Valentino gown he'd told her not to wear, but had known she would exactly because of it.

She was serene, smiling mysteriously as if she hadn't a care in the world, as if she were not facing down an entire room full of eager beasts ready to pounce on her at a moment's provocation, the living dark heart of the tribe gathered as one to bear witness to her glory.

Or her imminent destruction.

She was always beautiful, in his memories, in his best fantasies. But now she became, with the candlelight marking her skin and the shadows dancing over her face and body in layer upon silky layer, something magical and poetic, like the radiance of a sunbeam piercing a thundercloud.

She wore her hair madonna-loose, tumbling in gorgeous honeyed waves down over her bare shoulders, over the milky white contours of her throat and chest and arms that stood in perfect contrast to the vivid hue of her gown.

A part of his mind—the part that could still think, that was not dazed by her magic—noted her sensual, knowing smile, the look of calm control in which she took all of them in, a roomful of silent and deadly accusers.

She shifted her weight. The high slit in her gown slithered open, revealing one long, bare expanse of perfectly toned and curved leg, which ended in a delicate high-heeled sandal of crimson red. He felt the beat of his heart as his gaze moved over that finely turned ankle, up that bare calf and knee and thigh so familiar in his memory, familiar from the erotic, aching dreams that wrung him dry night after night like a poison that ate through his blood.

Mine, he thought, hungry. The word flooded him with something like despair.

Her eyes found his across the room. Her sensual smile now deepened to something distinctly provocative.

Christian exhaled through his teeth, a soft whoosh of astonishment, and it broke the spell.

Leander stepped forward, the blood pumping back into his heart. He crossed the silent ballroom, people falling back, agog, to let him pass. He came to a stop a few feet away from her, close enough to smell her subtle perfume of fresh air and winter roses, close enough to reach out and stroke her arm.

With concentrated effort, he restrained himself from touching her. He gave a little bow instead. "Jenna," he said, smooth and light, "you've decided to join us. I'm happy to see you."

Her lips quirked. A fleeting shadow crossed her face, then disappeared. She reclaimed her composure with a toss of her head. "Well, I do hate to miss a party," she said, equally light. She fixed him with a level gaze, her chin lifting. "And I was growing tired of the enforced solitude."

Someone new approached, but Leander was unable to look away from her.

She was safe. She was here, standing so blithe and beautiful in front of him, having somehow gotten past her retinue of guards. She appeared unhurt—more than unhurt, she appeared luminous. Exquisitely so. And oddly confident. Recklessly confident, he would say, in light of the current circumstances.

He felt every eye in the room burning like firebrands into his back.

But she remained as if separated from them all by a layer of glass: serene, unperturbed, as if she thought herself nothing more than a curiosity in a museum case, a shrunken head brought back from the deepest bowels of the Amazon, on display for all to see.

He looked at her and raised an eyebrow.

"Careful, love," he said, his voice stroking. "They're all looking for any reason to lock you up and throw away the key. Don't give them one."

Jenna raised an eyebrow in return, cool and haughty as Cleopatra before the Romans. "They? Not *you?*"

He smiled, very slightly, in spite of himself. "My reasons are different from theirs, of that I can assure you," he murmured. He held her gaze for what felt like an eternity, willing her to respond, to give him any clue she felt anything at all for him.

But naturally she gave him nothing but a chilly smile and her perfect profile as she turned her head to the person now upon them.

"Jenna." Morgan glided to a stop next to his elbow. "You look lovely." Leander saw the two of them exchange a secret, knowing smile.

"It's my favorite, I think," Jenna said, offhand. She smoothed her palm over the layers of ruched silk gathered just under the bodice, at the swell of her breast where it met the upper part of her ribcage. "I've never been partial to red, but this one...well, the fit is perfect." She glanced side-long at Leander, her smile warming almost imperceptibly. "For some strange reason, I just love it."

"May I get you something to drink?" Morgan asked her, deferential.

"Champagne?" Jenna replied, still smiling. "That seems rather appropriate, don't you think?" Morgan nodded, her lips mashed together, and drifted away toward a waiter.

"You two seem to be forging quite the friendship," Leander said, watching her go. There was something amiss here, but he couldn't put his finger on it. She and Morgan were close now, it seemed...and how the hell had she gotten past the guards?

Every minute fissure and crack in the room had been sealed off before her arrival. Even the door was protected with invisible sealant to block her from Shifting to vapor and escaping. No precaution had been spared, but some-how it hadn't mattered.

The music started up again and people were beginning to talk, if only in hushed whispers. Every eye in the room was still trained on the two of them.

Jenna's smile deepened, became mocking. "I've been told, by a very reliable source, that it's good to have friends." The green in her eyes turned a shade darker. "People whom you can trust in times of need."

Morgan returned and handed Jenna a glass of champagne, its crystal bowl filled with madly roiling bubbles. She did it so politely Leander imagined an invisible curtsy with the gesture. Another look passed between them, and Morgan placed her fingers lightly on Jenna's forearm before turning to move back into the crowd, toward a still-gaping Christian.

His gaze was fixed firmly on Jenna's leg, still insouciantly jutting from the high slit in her dress. It then traveled slowly up her waist, her breasts, her face.

Christian realized Leander was staring at him at precisely the moment Morgan reached his side.

Leander met Christian's eyes with a cool, steady look of his own, until his brother dropped his gaze and turned away. Morgan said a few words into his ear. Christian nodded stiffly, then stalked off into the crowd.

"Are you? In need, that is? Of anything?" Leander asked, turning back to Jenna.

"I am...well." He thought he saw something in her eyes, something that might have been either pain or anger, swiftly erased.

"Yes, Morgan said as much. Though not much else," he added, pointedly.

She only smiled, still mysterious.

"You weren't badly hurt?" he prompted.

"My foot wasn't badly hurt, no," she equivocated, moving her gaze over the gathering in the ballroom. "It's healed now. Thank you for your concern."

"So quickly?" he pressed, unconvinced. "There seemed to be a great deal of blood—"

"Morgan is a very good nurse," she replied vaguely, peering over his shoulder.

This polite, sterile conversation was beginning to make the palms of his hands itch.

What had she been doing for the last four days? Why had she not spoken with him? With anyone else but Morgan? When could he speak with her alone? Why the hell was she being so *remote?*

"Just out of curiosity, who is the tall, handsome man standing with all those women against the far wall?"

He didn't have to turn his head to know who she was referring to. He answered her through clenched teeth. "Alejandro. Alpha of the Brazilian colony."

Her eyes came back to his. "You don't like him." She seemed amused by this.

"No. I do not like him."

She smiled. "Well, you might want to leave, then. He's headed our way."

Leander turned just as Alejandro, oblivious to everything else around him as he honed in on Jenna like a bloodhound on the hunt, shouldered through a cluster of whispering Assembly wives. They fell back as one, shocked, twittering.

Leander cupped Jenna's elbow, lightly, and began to turn her away toward the door. "Perhaps we should go somewhere more private to talk," he murmured, noting with no small surprise that she didn't draw her arm from his light grasp.

"Oh, no," she answered. "I'd love to hear what he has to say. After the last few days of enforced solitude, I'm in desperate need of some stimulating conversation." Her gaze flashed to his, sharp, then darted away.

"Madame."

Alejandro was suddenly there, pushing past Leander with a stiff shoulder, purposely ignoring him. He broke

Leander's grip on Jenna's elbow with a practiced bow: low, obsequious, and swift.

"You are…" He cleared his throat, let his gaze drift over Jenna's figure, lingering on her décolletage. "*Muito bonita.* Even more stunning than I have heard."

Leander had to work very hard not to smash Alejandro's face in with his fist.

"How very suave," Jenna said, smiling coyly.

She shocked Leander by lifting her hand toward Alejandro. He bent over it, his lips barely stroking over the surface of her satiny skin. "That seems to be a rather rare quality these days," she added lightly, looking down at his helmet of shining dark hair. "Although one I *so* enjoy."

Alejandro straightened, still holding Jenna's hand, and shot a victorious look at Leander. His gaze slithered back to her face. His eyes were wide and unblinking and he wore a swooning, torporous expression, as if he'd gorged himself on a rich dessert and was finding it exceedingly difficult to digest.

"*Obrigado,* beautiful lady," he purred. "I'm afraid not all of us are born with the ability to be pleasant to others. But as I always say, *um charme pouco vai um longo caminho.* A little charm goes a long way."

"Well said. I completely agree," Jenna replied smoothly, allowing her hand to rest in Alejandro's palm as if she might never remove it. They gazed at each other for a moment, both of them smiling. Jenna wore an expression of slightly amused curiosity, and he hoped to God it was only because of Alejandro's hair.

Fury erupted within him, white hot, a firestorm of deadly, devouring flame.

Jenna moved her gaze once again to a place beyond Leander's shoulder. She frowned, then recovered her placid expression and tossed her hair back over her shoulder with a graceful shake of her head. "Wonderful. Here comes the cavalry," she murmured, barely moving her lips.

Four men were behind him now, crowding in, then eight, then twenty. Leander felt them all, their concentrated energies focused with lasered precision on Jenna, who still smiled as if she hadn't a care in the world.

The Assembly. The Alphas. The firestorm grew, a merciless howling inside his skull.

"Lady Jenna," a voice said over his right shoulder.

LeBlanc, the Alpha from Quebec, damn him to hell. They wouldn't even give him one moment alone with her, to talk to her, to *warn* her.

"Perhaps you would care to join us in the drawing room for a moment. I'm afraid we have much to discuss before we can continue with our party."

"Gentlemen. Of course," Jenna replied easily. She disentangled her hand from Alejandro's pinched grip, took a delicate sip of her champagne, then lowered the glass and licked her ruby lips, deliberate and slow. She smiled at the group of men, looking at each in turn.

Leander watched two of them rock back on their heels, the rest too gone to even react with more than stunned stares.

"I would hate to interrupt your festivities by being unaccommodating. Please," she said sweetly, her hand held out toward LeBlanc. Her smile was beautiful and dazzling and utterly without warmth. "Lead the way."

She moved her gaze back to Leander's face, her eyes glacially pale.

Something dark and reptilian moved inside his chest. He suddenly remembered a piece of advice his father had given him long ago, when he was still a boy, a lesson about the nature of woman.

Do not ever underestimate a woman, son, or make the foolish mistake of trying to bend her to your will. She may flatter you and smile and even seem to agree, but in the end she'll cut out your heart, feed your body to the wolves, and then enjoy a good night's sleep.

With another twist in his gut, he slid a step away from Jenna and allowed her to be led by the hand out of the ballroom and down the long corridor toward the drawing room. He watched a thicket of silent, jostling *Ikati* trail in her wake like a school of hungry parasites.

"We are going to require some *proof* of this," LeBlanc insisted again, his fingers pressed against the polished surface of the mahogany tabletop, his eyes a sharp, frozen green. "And we are going to require it now."

The drawing room was silent except for the faint echo of the orchestra drifting in from the other end of the manor and the irregular breathing of agitated men. It was much darker here than in the rest of the house, and cooler. There were no windows to let in the light during the day, no fireplace to blaze against the chill of the evening.

They were seated in chairs pulled hastily from every corner of the room, a rough circle of nineteen with three of the four Alphas at one long table like judges on the bench.

Jenna stood alone before them, her skin pale and luminescent against the carnelian gown and the blue and charcoal shadows surrounding her. Here in the dim, close confines of the drawing room, she glowed like a morning star.

But her eyes, Leander thought, watching her carefully. Her glittering eyes collected the dim light and sent it flying back at them all like the flash of knives in a cave.

For the past twenty minutes, Jenna had feinted and danced around their questions, seeming to enjoy the growing tension and frustration of the men seated before her. Aside from Leander, she was the only one standing.

She had refused LeBlanc's direction to take a seat with a simple, succinct no.

She seemed to have absolutely no idea of the danger she was putting herself in. He had seen *Ikati* imprisoned and punished for far, far less than this brazen display of disrespect.

"Are you?" Jenna mused. She raised her eyebrows, a shadow of disdain curving her lips.

"Yes," LeBlanc said, adamant, sitting forward. He pressed his palms on the table now and began to rise to his feet. "You simply *must* Shift in front of the Assembly. We cannot just take your word for it—"

"And what about the word of the Alpha of Sommerley, Lord McLoughlin?" Jenna interrupted. Her disdain for the man flattened her lips, thickening the air between them. She let her gaze drift to where Leander stood against the far wall of the drawing room. He leaned, arms crossed, tense and silent, in the shadows cast from a large breakfront, shadows that would hide his expression—and his eyes.

"Won't you take *his* word as proof? Are you calling him a liar?"

Leander heard LeBlanc grind his teeth together and smiled in grim satisfaction to himself. She was clever. Whatever LeBlanc's answer, he either conceded defeat or admitted treason. The Law didn't allow for Alphas to openly challenge each other without provoking a fight to the death.

Another voice interrupted, and the room turned to him. Viscount Weymouth.

"No one is impugning Lord McLoughlin here, Lady Jenna—he has vouched for your ability, as well as your motives. But the Law demands proof, and your continued objection puts you in quite a precarious position. We are living in dangerous times…we must know your loyalties and learn your Gifts, if you have any, especially since it will be so easy for you to provide any kind of proof. You are either *Ikati* or you are not. You are either with us or against us."

Murmurs of assent were heard around the room. Leander saw nodding heads and smug looks of congratulation passed from face to face.

With a flush of anger that brought the blood to his face, Leander curled his hands into tight fists. Morgan was right. These men were nothing more than posturing idiots, enamored by the sound of their own voices, too complacent with unchallenged control and authority to have any empathy or humility left. They ruled only for themselves, for their own pleasure and comfort and egos.

For the first time in his life, Leander felt that perhaps it was time for a change.

"The *Law*," Jenna repeated, mocking. "Right. You can never escape the death grip of your perfect, shining, barbaric *Law*."

She stared at them all with eyes of frost…then her gaze found Leander across the room.

All at once the calculated nonchalance seemed to drain away from her face, leaving it open and naked, as if the layers of an onion had been peeled back to reveal its tender core. Her eyes shone clear and bright, her smile faded to the barest, melancholy lift of her lips. Her voice, when it came, hovered just above a whisper.

"I almost feel sorry for you. You don't know what you're missing. You don't know how amazing it is to be...free."

A giggle from another dark corner of the room. Leander knew at once it was Morgan, though he didn't turn to look.

"Leander has told the Assembly that you Shifted *before* your birthday, Lady Jenna," someone said sharply, ignoring the muffled laugh from Morgan.

Leander cut his gaze to the heavily accented voice.

Durga, the Baron Bhojak, Alpha from Nepal.

He sat in front of Jenna, in the center of the table, his hands folded across the swell of his belly, legs splayed out in front of him, his posture that of someone bored entirely by the proceedings. But Leander knew better. Durga had earned himself a reputation for running his colony with an iron fist. He was old-school, a hard-liner, a purist. The Law above all.

"Did he?" she murmured, still looking at Leander with those glittering eyes. It sent a tremor straight through his core. *You don't know what you're missing...*

"Yes. This is...unusual. Highly unusual. Incredible, actually." Durga brushed an invisible piece of lint from the lapel of his black suit jacket and kept his gaze lowered as he continued. "I do not recall, at least in my lifetime, a single instance of a half-Blood *Ikati* Shifting before their twenty-fifth birthday."

There was an open challenge in his voice. Leander watched as she moved her gaze to Durga and tilted her head to the side, considering him in silence.

Alejandro sat in a chair slightly angled toward him. Even from across the room, Leander felt the desire pulsing off the man in waves. He couldn't keep his eyes off Jenna. They trailed up and down her body, over and over. He stared at her with his lips pursed and brow furrowed as if he was trying to memorize a highly difficult equation.

Leander pushed away from the wall and lowered his fists to his sides. His lungs tightened under a band of steel that made it hard to breathe.

"Well," Jenna said lightly, brushing her hair over her shoulder with a graceful, feminine move of her hand, "it wasn't the first time."

Leander, forgetting Alejandro completely, blinked at Jenna.

It wasn't the first time?

No one moved. The silence was deafening.

"The first time was when I was still a child. And there have been other times since then, though not in years, I've been too careful..." She stopped herself, her eyes flickered over to him. A faint blush of pink rose up on her cheeks.

Leander was the first to recover. "How old were you the first time?" he asked into the raw and hungry silence.

"Ten," she said, her voice wavering. She cleared her throat. "I was ten. It was the day my father disappeared."

Not a sound was to be heard in the drawing room. Not even a single breath was drawn.

Ten.

Leander felt all the blood drain away from his head. He had first Shifted at eleven, the youngest of his peers, the youngest of his entire colony. No one else he knew had made the turn before twelve. And like him, all the others were full-Blooded *Ikati*.

But if she had been Shifting since she was *ten*...

"Impossible," Durga scoffed to a chorus of agreement from the gathered men. Their voices were first tentative, then grew more confident as he repeated it again. He crossed his thick arms over his chest and shook his head. "That's simply *not* possible!"

Only Viscount Weymouth remained silent, gaping at her. Alejandro leapt from the chair as if it had burned him, as did two other men, staring hard at Jenna with faces ominous and tight and filled with a pinched, dark desire—animal, wholly dangerous.

"If this is true..." Alejandro didn't finish his sentence. He lifted an open hand toward Jenna, then dropped it, his mouth working silently like a fish out of water.

Leander took a step away from the wall. He never moved his gaze from Alejandro's face.

"It is a lie," Durga said, flatly. He pushed to his feet, straightened his dinner jacket, and peered at Jenna with a sneer, disfiguring his face. "Do not forget who this is, gentlemen—this is the offspring of tainted blood, sired from an illegal union. She is the daughter of a *criminal*. She is half *human*, clearly inferior, clearly a danger to all of our tribes!"

He pointed a stout, accusing finger at her, his face hard and red. "No half-Blood Ikati has *ever* Shifted at that age. That is a fact. Not only is she lying, she simply is—"

"*I am my father's daughter.*" Jenna's voice rang out through the close and suddenly suffocating room, its pitch clear and strong. "I am not a liar and I'm not inferior to anyone. Especially *you.*"

She stared at Durga with a look of such vitriol he paused with his finger in midair, as if shock had muddled his brain, making him forget what he was doing there.

He blinked once, astonished, and Leander knew exactly what the man was thinking. He was simply flabbergasted she would dare speak to him this way. To *stand up* to him. He most likely could not remember the last time anyone had done so, if ever in his life.

He was Alpha of the *Ikati*, a leader of beasts that paraded as men, a deadly, revered warrior, a lord and a master and a ruler of all he surveyed.

He was absolutely, unequivocally beyond question, beyond reproach. It was their way. It was his birthright. It was the Law.

And she was nothing but a *woman.*

"You will prove to us all, right this minute, whether or not you are one of us," another man from the circle insisted. This drew nods of agreement around the room. "If you do not—"

"Show them," Leander said roughly, moving out of the shadows to pace toward her. He felt the rising tension in the room, saw the looks of cold calculation on the faces of the men, sensed something ugly and dangerous beginning to unfold.

"No."

Her eyes met his, but her face had closed off, the stubborn defiance was there again. She wouldn't listen to him, he knew. But he had to make her listen, because she was putting herself in terrible jeopardy.

"If you don't, there will be consequences, my dear," Viscount Weymouth said, his voice wavering. He looked stricken by some unnamed terror. He hadn't moved from his chair, though by now the entire room was on its feet, energized by the growing conflict. He cleared his throat and spoke again, his tremulous voice now gone quiet. "Very, very unpleasant consequences, I'm sorry to say."

"Jenna," Alejandro began, his tone soft and capitulating though his face was dark with something Leander didn't like at all, "*meu caro,* perhaps you do not understand."

He moved a step closer to her, reached a hand out toward her but thought better of it when she stepped back with a grimace. He smoothed the hand over his hair instead and smiled to hide the fleeting look of anger that crossed his face.

"We mean no disrespect. We do not wish to alarm you, or to harm you, for that matter. We are only here to get a few answers, as *friends.*"

He slanted a calculated look toward Durga, who took the hint. He lowered the arm he still held out toward Jenna and sat down heavily in his chair with a look of astonished outrage. But Leander knew it was all a ruse. They *would* harm her if she didn't obey, and quickly. He was at her side in ten paces, angling his body between her and the roomful of silent men.

He had to make her understand. He had to protect her.

"I'm well aware of how you treat your friends," Jenna said coldly just as Leander reached her.

"Don't do this, please." He said it low into her ear, his fingers resting on her forearm. "All they need is a simple confirmation of the truth. There is no need for this."

"I'm not afraid of them." Her eyes were as sharp as her voice.

"You would be wise to be very afraid of them. They don't know you as I do. To them you are only a threat, an unknown quantum. They are not as...fond of you as I am. And they will not be as lenient with you. They won't be lenient at all."

She hesitated, lowering her gaze to his fingers on her arm. Then she looked up at him, her gaze clear and guileless, all traces of anger and posturing gone. "They want the truth? I asked *you* for the truth, and look where that got me," she said, her voice gone small. "I don't know if the truth is all it's cracked up to be."

With a flash of intuition, Leander knew what he had to do.

"Sorry, love," he said roughly, tightening his fingers on her arm. "But that's the wrong answer." Then in one swift motion he pulled her hard against his chest and kissed her.

For a moment there was nothing between them but her body rigid with anger and shock, her lips flattened, her face twisting away. He held her face in his hands, hearing the murmurs of surprise from the gathered men and the sharp intake of breath from Alejandro, and kept his lips pressed against hers.

He felt her heartbeat, pounding wild, angry. He heard the little sounds of protest she made in her throat, felt her hands balled against his chest, trying to push him away. He thought she would never relent.

But then something softened between them, just barely. A shade of tension eased from her neck, her lips turned from stone to velvet. Her arms, braced so hard against his chest, began to release, then draw up around his neck. Her body arched against him and she drew in a breath through her nose.

Her lips parted.

She took his tongue into her mouth, and he slid his hands into the glossy weight of her hair, cradling her head, feeling the warm, lush length of her body against his. She slid her fingers up his neck. They tightened in his hair, drawing his head down further, deepening their kiss.

She made another low sound in her throat, but this one was purely erotic.

He forgot his hasty plan to save her, forgot his jealousy and worry and everything else in the universe. Only a single thought remained as he tasted the honeyed sweetness of her mouth and held her in his arms, so slim and firm and real against him. Unbelievably real.

Mine.

She finally pulled away, her eyes still closed, her lips brushing against his as she breathed out a single, ragged word.

"Bastard."

And then, for the second time in four days, Leander was left staring at Jenna's empty dress as it slithered to the ground at his feet.

E IGHTEEN

In all her life, Jenna had never been so humiliated. Or so angry. He *kissed* her. He *forced* her to Shift. In front of *everyone.*

But the worst part, the most agonizingly wretched part, was the way she had responded.

She hid her face in her hands and groaned as she remembered it. The way her skin began to tingle and flush even as she was trying to fight him off, her mouth opening to accept his tongue, his scent filling her nostrils, his hands an inescapable vise around her face, the hard length of him suddenly pressed against her, holding her captive.

Arousing her. Making her lose control.

In front of them all.

Damn him.

Thank God it was dark in here. She didn't have to look at herself in the mirror; she didn't have to meet any more jeering, hostile eyes. She could hide. She wished she could hide here forever.

She buried her face into the arm of a heavy wool over-coat. She burrowed into it, slipped it off the wooden hanger, wrapped it around her naked body. She folded up the collar and turned her nose to the silk lining. It smelled like him. She groaned again and fell back into the dark, plush haven of the row of hanging coats, their heavy folds providing layer upon layer of sanctuary and warmth.

Even in the pitch dark confines of Leander's cavernous dressing room, Jenna knew her face burned bright red.

She knew she'd be safe here for a while at least, much safer than in her own rooms. Though the guards outside her door would protest, if questioned, that she was still inside, that she hadn't gotten past them. It wasn't really their fault. Morgan had pushed them into her will with the power of Suggestion, telling them all to let her pass and forget they had seen either of them.

Which, of course, they so obligingly did.

And escaping to the forest, well, she might as well just send out a flare to announce her whereabouts. With the number of *Ikati* in the drawing room, in the ballroom, swarming through the entire mansion, following her into the woods would be easy.

But here, in Leander's chambers, no one would follow, even though they must sense she had fled here. There was no way the rest of the Assembly would dare breach the confines of the Alpha's inner sanctum.

At least that's what she hoped.

She just needed time to think. She needed time to decide how exactly she was going to keep her promise to Morgan, how she was going to convince Leander to do something that would basically amount to treason on his part. She hadn't come up with any brilliant ideas yet.

Tonight was supposed to be her debut, as Morgan kept calling it. The cut on her foot was fully healed, she could Shift again. And she had been on board with the idea, had thought it might actually work. Just tell the Assembly, just show them a little something, like maybe one foot turning to vapor, her arm or a lock of her hair—just enough proof to get them off her back and allow her to drop off the radar and escape back to her old life. And escape was exactly what she was planning.

But the minute she'd seen their ominous, arrogant faces as they gathered to lurk behind Leander in the ballroom, she knew she wasn't going to show them anything.

Because they planned to *force* her to.

And then Leander, with that kiss...well, he took the choice right out of her hands.

She was a fool. She knew it, as sure as she knew the sun would rise tomorrow. She was a fool to keep thinking of him, hour after hour, day after day, thinking and dreaming and wanting even as she tried her best to stuff it all down into the pit of her stomach.

She knew he was exactly like the rest of them. All he wanted was her cooperation, her submission, her *obedience*. There was no way in hell she was going to be obedient to a single one of them.

Especially *him*.

"I thought I'd find you in here with a pair of scissors, shredding up my entire wardrobe," an amused voice said, low and silky soft, from a few feet away. "Not trying it on."

Jenna's head snapped up. He was right there, his out-line barely visible in the middle of the darkened room. She smothered an angry gasp.

How had she not heard him? How had she not heard his heart?

"I was hoping you wouldn't find me at all," she retorted hotly, moving one step back into the row of coats, her hands clenched around the wool collar, drawing it closer. Another step and her back hit the closet wall.

"Don't be ridiculous. You're one floor up from the draw-ing room. I can easily hear your heartbeat from there."

Through the murk she saw the sheen of Leander's teeth as he smiled. Then his scent hit her, spice and smoke and virile man. His heartbeat pumped to life in her ears, an echo of her own. She realized with a start she hadn't heard it before because he had entered the room as vapor and Shifted back to man.

Which now meant he was standing there nude. As nude as she was under this coat.

"And just for the record, I'm not trying it on," Jenna snapped. "I'm…" She floundered, hating herself for letting him get under her skin. "I'm just trying to stay warm!"

He stepped forward, put a hand out to push away a dove-gray cashmere overcoat that was partially blocking her face. The skin of his sculpted chest was swathed in shadows, but she saw its polished gleam as he moved. A ripple of dusky light fell over the muscles in his abdomen; ambers and char-coals and deepest grays outlined the planes and angles of his flesh. She pulled her gaze away before it drifted farther down.

"I can think of better ways to keep you warm," he murmured.

"I'm sure you can," she said acidly, unnerved. Did he have to be so masculine? So muscular? So damn good looking?

Jenna blew out a little breath between her teeth, not realizing they'd been clenched together. "Like throwing me into a pot of boiling water. Or staking me to the ground in the desert. Or pouring honey all over my body and dumping a beehive over my head. Or—"

He tsked. "You have my intentions entirely wrong, love. Except possibly the honey part."

She caught the phosphorous glow in his eye as he smiled, slow and languid. "Minus the bees."

She swallowed and tightened her fingers around the coat. Her heart began to hammer in her chest. "Well, then you're the only one. The rest of your friends are hell-bent on doing something nasty to me because I won't—"

"But you did," he interrupted, still with that same silken, caressing tone that sent tremors over her skin. "And now they've got their proof. You're no longer in any imminent danger."

"From *them*," Jenna peeped as he moved another step closer.

He dropped his hand and curled his long fingers around the collar of the wool coat. His other hand came up and grasped the lapel. He pulled her closer until their bodies, separated by only a fine layer of wool, grazed.

She looked up at him and time slowed to a crawl.

He was a head taller than she, radiating heat from his unclad skin, his face hidden in shadow and locks of thick ebony hair that fell over his forehead and cheekbones. The hard and substantial muscles of his shoulders and arms were folded in darkness, outlined black against the meager light.

But his eyes were clearly visible, wide and unblinking and glowing fiercely green.

"You could never be in any danger from me," he whispered. "You know that. Tell me you know that."

"Only in danger of losing my ability to *think*," she murmured, then bit her tongue. She dropped her gaze to his mouth, to the pleasing full arc of his lips, then merely squeezed her eyes shut, realizing there was nowhere left to look that would dull the ache that was eating her inside.

"And why would that be?" he asked, husky, amused. "If you hate me so much?"

She should run. She should push him away and turn to vapor and get the hell out of—

"Jenna."

His thumbs were on her jaw, tilting her head up. Her eyes fluttered open. She peeked up at him through her lashes, then bit her lip to keep it from trembling. She felt panicked. She felt frozen. She could not look away.

He said her name again, barely audibly, bent his head, and now the amusement was gone. "*Do* you hate me?"

She hesitated, then shook her head once, quickly. "But I *should*, after what you did to me downstairs."

He laughed, a low, relieved exhalation. "I'm sorry I made you Shift, but you are the most stubborn creature I have ever met. You'll put yourself in mortal danger just for the sake of making a point. I couldn't stand for that."

She felt his warm breath on her neck as he whispered into her ear. The skin on her arms rose in gooseflesh. Over her pounding pulse, she heard herself say, "How did you know...how did you know that would work? That you could make me Shift like that?"

"I gambled." He stroked a finger lightly over the soft spot under her earlobe. "Unlike any other half-Blood, your trigger seems to be linked to your emotions, especially the strong ones. Including murderous rage." He chuckled, then nudged her hair aside with his nose and breathed deeply against her neck.

Jenna held perfectly still as the tip of his nose trailed down her throat. His unshaven jaw was a surprising rough scrape against her bare skin. She willed her hands to stay where they were and not wind up around his shoulders, willed her shaking knees to support her weight.

"That wasn't fair," she said, her voice cracking. "And I hate being forced to do anything. I hate bullies."

"I know," he murmured. He stroked one thumb across her jawbone, back and forth, light as a feather. "Which is why I'd like to ask your permission to do something."

Jenna knew he heard her heart beating wildly in her chest, just as he heard her uneven breathing, felt the way her body was primed tight as a bowstring under his touch. The knowledge that he could, in all likelihood, almost *taste* the depth of her arousal filled her with an exquisite flush of shame.

"You promised," she said, stiff and breathless, knowing what was coming.

"Yes," he agreed, unmoving. "I did. So this time I'm asking your permission."

The sound of his breathing seemed suddenly deafening in her ears.

"I want to kiss you again," he said quietly. "Will you let me?"

She didn't answer because she could not speak.

She breathed steadily through her nose, willing herself to say no and mean it. She clamped her eyes shut, fighting her desire, fighting her fear, fighting the knowledge that her entire future might hinge on whatever she did next.

He bent his head to hers and whispered against her cheek. "Will you?"

She meant to shake her head back and forth, but found herself nodding instead.

He didn't move for a moment, and she nearly bolted. But then his thumb lingering on her jaw moved up to trace the outline of her lower lip, the corner of her mouth.

The urge to flee grew stronger. She began to turn her head away, but he spread his hand around the back of her neck and brought his lips to hers.

This time it wasn't forceful, it wasn't demanding. It was the slightest brush of skin over skin, a caress so light it was merely a breath of air. His tongue traced the curve of her lower lip. She shivered, frozen to the ground. He sucked on her lip and gently drew it into his mouth.

He began to massage the tension in the back of her neck with his hand, making the tightness in her muscles slip away. Caution began to crumble, a little piece at a time, like tiny butterflies alighting from a flower to scatter into space.

Her lips parted and she began—tentatively—to kiss him back.

He pushed one strong hand into her hair and wound another around her waist, gently, slowly pulling her closer. Her fingers were still clenched around the collar of the coat, her forearms pressed against his bare chest, but the coat had slipped open and she felt his skin branding hers, the warmth of one naked hip and muscled thigh and only the merest strip of fabric between the rest of his body and hers.

His kisses grew deeper, longer, more demanding. His free hand ranged over the outline of her body over the thin barrier of the coat, learning the curve of her waist, the shape of her bottom.

Leander slipped his hand inside her coat and put his hand against the small of her back, urging her nearer.

Her blood began to rise.

She'd dreamed of this, over and over, caresses and stroking that she wanted so badly—even as she fought to push every thought of him from her mind. For four long days she hadn't seen his face, for four interminable nights she'd been tortured with an awareness of his proximity in the manor like a beacon that shone through the darkest night. Away from his presence, she'd nearly been able to convince herself the molten, tangible desire that existed between them was a figment of her imagination.

But for those erotic, tormented dreams.

But for that heartbeat.

Like the call of a siren, it always beckoned to her, every minute through the long days and nights, a thump and echo so compelling it seemed to meld into her blood, driving her insane with want, calling her to the edge of oblivion, where she teetered, looking down.

It was only through hours of practice with Morgan that she learned to block it at will, that and the cascade of thoughts that would crowd out her own at his touch. But every time she closed her eyes she could still see him, a red star on the dark horizon, strong and close and burning with heat.

And now that he was here, with his hands and mouth and heat burning every inch of her skin, she knew she'd only been fooling herself. She was drawn into the circle of his warmth, his arms, the feel of him so right it clashed with what her mind wanted, which was for her to run.

"Don't put yourself in danger like that again. Please. I can't take it. It's important to me that you're safe, Jenna." His arms tightened around her, hard, and his voice dropped to a whisper. "It's more than important. It's *everything*. I would give everything I have to make sure nothing hurts you."

"*You're* the one that can hurt me," she protested, hating how weak it sounded. Ambivalence and euphoria were doing battle within her, and euphoria was quickly winning. She shook her head, trying to clear it. "I know you think you can keep me here—but I won't be locked in a cage, Leander. I won't be your prisoner."

He dragged his lips over her neck, down to her collarbone. His teeth pressed against the tender flesh there so hard it stung.

"I can't deny I want to keep you with me. And I want you to *want* to stay. But...I would do anything to make you happy. Even if it means letting you go, if that's what you want. Even if it means breaking every Law there is. I'll do anything, Jenna. I'll do anything."

Though his voice was hushed, muffled against her skin, she recognized the truth in it, the raw emotion, and she started with the abrupt realization that he would put himself in danger for her.

He was willing to release her, protect her, and take the consequences, with nothing in it for himself except pleasing her and inciting the rage of all those snarling dark beasts.

It pierced her in the center of her chest, an unfamiliar sweetness that brought a prick of tears to her eyes. She had forgotten sweetness, had forgotten what it was like to be touched and held and cherished, and it opened something in her, it melted her like sunlight on snow. When she next exhaled, all her fears and hesitation sifted away with her breath, leaving only warmth and certainty behind.

She loosened her grip on the collar of the coat and slid her arms up around the hard strength of Leander's shoulders. On their own, her fingers twined into the thick, silken strands of his hair.

He made a low sound in his throat as their bodies met. The coat slipped open to let skin meet heated skin. Her breasts pressed against his chest, his erection pressed hot and throbbing stiff against the slope of her hip.

"Don't let me go," she whispered, dizzy, delirious. "Not yet. Not tonight."

He kissed her then, fiercely. His hands held both sides of her face, the friction of his tongue and lips against hers was so sweet and erotic she thought she would die with the sheer bliss of it. "Love," he whispered, and kissed her again.

Just as she was convinced her knees would give out, he broke the kiss and bent in a half-crouch to nuzzle her chest. His hand rose to cup her breast, his thumb grazed her nipple. It hardened instantly under his touch. Jenna gasped as he pulled it into his mouth and suckled, a pull of teeth, a lap of tongue, a delicious, aching pleasure that spread through her body like a wash of sunlit honey.

His hand moved down over her belly, stroking its rounded softness, dropped lower to trace over her hipbone, then down to the flesh between her thighs.

He kneaded and pinched and stroked her skin, his fingers brushing against her mound, teasing lightly around it. She whimpered in her throat as he knelt down in front of her, his mouth against her stomach. His hands lifted up to cup her breasts.

He dipped his tongue into her belly button, pressed his teeth into the flesh of her hip, slid one hand slowly down her body and found her center, damp and hot. She gasped and sunk her fingers into his shoulders as he pushed a finger inside her. He touched her and stroked her until his fingers were slick, until she moaned and slid her fingers into his hair.

Her eyes blinked open at the sound of something heavy slithering onto the floor with a muted rustle. Leander straightened, then captured her lips again as he pulled another plush overcoat from its hanger to fall at their feet, then another.

After four more, he gently pushed her down to the floor by her shoulders and watched as she lay back into the bed he'd made, a deep pool of wool and cashmere and silk to cushion her body.

He knelt beside her and pushed the wool overcoat away, leaving her naked and exposed on the floor before him, only her outflung arms still hidden by fabric. The light was nothing but indigo shadows and pale glimmering grays that melted to velvet black, yet she clearly saw his fevered gaze drinking her in, devouring her.

He brought his gaze back to her face and she saw the hunger raging through him, the same hunger that made it feel as if she was conducting fire through her veins.

"All I think about is you," he said, husky, staring straight into her eyes. "All I've wanted is you, since the first second I saw you. I've never wanted anything else so much in my life."

Jenna knew he saw the blood rise in her cheeks even in the spare, silvered light of the room. But now she didn't care. Now she wanted him to see everything.

She sat up and shrugged out of his coat, letting it fall behind her, another warm blanket to pillow her body, to cushion his weight above her. She lay back again against the floor, spread her hair out in a fan behind her head, her body cocooned in luxury and filled with an aching that bit down deep into her core.

"Leander." Her gaze never left his. She held her arms out. "Come here."

Leander saw himself in her eyes. His thoughts, his moods, the unbridled need that tore through his blood, barely checked. Like him, she was vapor and fire, passion and smoke, headstrong and willful and bold. Like him, she was alone and accustomed to it, though not suited for loneliness. She needed a mate as much as he did, a strong and loyal partner to share a life with, to dream with, to love.

Mine, he thought again as he stared in hunger at the glory of her naked body spread out before him.

He needed to taste her. He needed to feel her and claim her and hear her moans form the shape of his name. He felt hot and alive and inflamed, her eagerness for him tipping him over the edge of reason to a place where he would lose himself, a place where the urgency that raged through his blood would block out the rest of the world and leave only the two of them, joined at last.

But he made himself wait.

He restrained himself as the fire rose to boil his blood and simply put one hand out and skimmed it slowly over the velvet perfection of her skin. His fingers traced the curve of her breast, the shape of her ribcage, the dip of her waist, the creamy plush flesh of her thigh. Her lips parted as he stroked her, her eyes fluttered closed. Her back arched to meet his touch. Her arms dropped to the floor behind her head.

He lowered himself over her, balanced his weight carefully on his elbows. She cradled him with knees and arms, turned her face toward his. He brushed a kiss over her cheekbone, her eyelids, the perfect arch of her brows.

Her palms stroked up his bare back to his arms, restless. She sighed, the smallest exhalation, her breath warm against his cheek, and his heart leapt at the sound. "Love," he whispered again, everything he felt for her contained in that one word.

He bent his head to her neck; she tipped her jaw to allow him better access. He took it, stroking his tongue up the heated column of her neck, tasting her flowery skin and the barest hint of salt. He felt her move beneath him, her chest arching to meet his.

He lowered his head to her chest, to the satiny flesh of her breasts, the exquisite puckering of her nipples, dusky pink against her gleaming pale skin. His teeth bit her gently, and she breathed his name with a catch in her throat.

Leander smiled, his head lowered, his teeth bared against her skin. A fierce, savage joy scorched through him. *Mine.*

He drew his tongue down her body, between her breasts, over her belly, down to her thighs. He bit her there too, heard her make a small, restless moan as his teeth tested her succulent flesh.

He found her center, the slick ruby between her legs hot and wet under his tongue.

She gasped and stilled, her breath ragged. He dug his fingers into her bottom and reveled in her. Her musky-sweet taste like maple syrup, the muscles of her legs smooth and flexed and feminine against his shoulders, her hips and bottom so round and soft in his hands.

He kissed her and stroked her with his tongue until she writhed beneath him, her hands twisting in his hair.

"Leander," she gasped, her voice broken, breathless. He didn't stop. He wanted—he *needed* to hear her say it again. Another lap of his tongue with his fingers stroking her now, teasing, probing inside her heat and tight wetness. She moaned, her back arched.

He pushed his fingers deeper, and she gave him what he wanted with a sharp intake of breath.

"*Leander!*"

In one swift motion, he drew himself up her body and sank deep into her.

She shattered around him.

Her climax was abrupt and gorgeous, a delicious, shuddering clench and throb that nearly sent him over the edge at once. She cried out, her thighs trembling, her body a lovely taut bow beneath him. He clenched his teeth, willing himself to hold back against the enormous tide of pleasure her orgasm gave him, willing himself to be still as she rocked and gasped beneath him, her head thrown back, her eyes squeezed shut, the sensation of her body so lush and warm and pleasing he had to bite his tongue against it.

In a moment she relaxed underneath him. Her head lolled to the side. She breathed out, sighing again, her legs and arms slackening around him.

Still ardent and throbbing inside her, barely controlled, Leander tipped Jenna's face toward him with a finger. He kissed her tenderly and her eyes fluttered open.

"Better?" he asked, low, gently teasing.

She smiled at him, blinked slowly with half-lidded eyes, flushed cheeks. "Almost."

She ran her hands down his back, palms open against his skin, urging him closer. Her knees slid up, her ankles crossed at his waist. Her smile now was something utterly feminine, knowing and sensual. She arched into him and drew him deep with an erotic, fluid motion of her pelvis.

He breathed out with a moan, all teasing gone.

She lifted her hips and sank her fingers into his buttocks, and now he could not stop. He thrust into her, agony burning through him with the feel of her, lustrous and hot against his skin.

She gave a soft moan, her head tipped back, the heat of her burning him to his core. He reveled in the sight of her beneath him, her hair a ripple of silken gilt tumbled over the pile of cashmere and wool, the dim gleam of milky skin, slender thighs wrapped tight around his waist.

"Jenna," he gasped, caught between her pleasure and his own release.

She shuddered, said his name, formed other broken words that meant *yes* and *oh God, please* and *now*. She pulled his head down with both hands and kissed him hard. Her body strained against his, she met his every thrust with shivers and low, mewling noises in her throat that resonated all the way through him.

She gasped against his mouth and tilted her head back. Almond cat's-eyes fixed on him with a look of pleasure and ardor so intense his heart spasmed within his chest.

"Come with me," he commanded, hoarse, thrusting deep. He lowered his head and bit her on the neck, so hard he tasted the coppery tang of her blood on his tongue. He closed his eyes and let his hips take over, the thrusts harder and faster, electricity snapping along his nerves, shooting up his spine.

"Yes," she breathed, the faintest of sounds before her head fell back, before she stopped breathing entirely. Her whole body arched into his and he groaned, shuddering, feeling her clench around him as her orgasm hit. He pushed deep, so deep into her it must have hurt, but she only made a low, impassioned sound and tightened her legs around him. Her nails bit into his back.

His own orgasm began as a throbbing pulse that quickly expanded and exploded through his body, ripping another groan from him, this one deeper and more primal. He buried his face in her hair and put both hands under her bottom, squeezing and pumping and lost.

He gave himself to her.

His seed and his climax and things he had no name for, secret things deep in his heart he had never spoken aloud, love and longing and blazing desire knotted together as one, an upswell of pleasure and bliss fixed on this lovely creature beneath him, binding him to her.

She was his. She was his and nothing could change that now.

He thought for a brief, deranged second that were he to die at this moment, he would be the luckiest man he had ever known.

Against his chest, he felt the anthem of her heart, keeping time with his own, its frenzied beat not yet beginning to slow. They lay entwined together in the dark, upon the mess of coats, oblivious to the world for long, countless minutes. He let himself drift, let his panting slow, let the moment spin out to dreamy, lazy perfection.

When he could breathe again, he found her lips, kissed her gently. His hair trailed dark along her alabaster skin. He slid out of her and rolled her next to him, on her side, pulling her up hard to nestle in the warm space against his body, their chests and stomachs and thighs pressed together.

He stroked her face, pushed a lock of hair from her brow. A few bright strands caught the light like threads of gold. She burrowed down next to him, sighed prettily, her head cradled on his arm.

"*Now* I'm better," she murmured, drowsy and lax against him.

He bent to kiss her, smiling another pagan, barbarian smile. Elation, triumph, and a piercing, fierce pride washed over him, relentless and dark as a hurricane.

Mine.

NINETEEN

He'd carried her to his bed at some point during the night, though she hadn't woken up for that, or anything else, until this very moment. She felt as if she hadn't slept in years and was making up for lost time.

Jenna's eyes came open to the dove-soft sheen of dawn beginning to lighten the sky through the windows of Leander's bedroom. They were huge—like so much else in this manor house that was really more like a fortress—beveled panes of cut glass set in casements framed by heavy silk draperies showcasing the emerald-dark forest swathed in mist and shadows beyond.

His bed was massive as well, soft as eiderdown and deliciously comfortable. She felt warm and sated and utterly relaxed, like a ragdoll with loosened joints. She looked at

Leander, solid and substantial and still asleep by her side, and a scotch-warm flush spread through her stomach.

He was beautiful as no other man she had ever known, burnished skin and sculpted muscle and potent masculinity laid over with elegant manners, perfectly at ease in his own body. Confident. Even in sleep he looked confident; a little, pleased smile curved one corner of his mouth.

The diffused morning light flattered him, though he didn't need flattering, he was too perfect as it was. She lifted a finger and traced the outline of his dark eyebrow. The pad of her fingertip hovered just above the winged curve, close enough to feel the warmth of his skin.

Beneath her finger, she felt the echo of his dreams.

She closed her eyes and concentrated on his heartbeat instead.

In the four days she and Morgan had spent together in her rooms—*locked* into her rooms, she sourly reminded herself—Morgan had shown her how to drown out anything she didn't want to see or feel, to manage the glut of sensation that came flooding through her with the touch of flesh upon flesh.

Thank God she had. If not, last night—with Leander's hands and mouth and body over hers, inside hers—would have been something very different altogether.

Her gaze dropped to his lips. Her finger moved from his brow to linger over the dented curve above his top lip, a cupid's bow of perfect proportion.

She wanted to kiss him. She wanted to touch his body again, to spend long hours discovering it. She wanted to tell him all her secrets and fears and feel the hard length of him filling her, stretching and inflaming her until she lost herself to him, to the magic they made together.

She wasn't sure how to feel about this—whatever *this* was. She thought, frowning, she might happily forego any further thought on the subject for as long as possible.

Forever, preferably.

Last night changes nothing, she told herself firmly, dropping her hand from its ghosted exploration of his face. *Nothing at all.*

The lonely cry of a hawk gliding through the bleached sky drew her attention back to the windows.

A curious surge of desire pinged inside her stomach as she looked at the forest. It was deep and primal, like a bass note plucked once on a guitar string. But the note didn't fade; it held and grew and vibrated in her stomach as she stared at the line of trees rolling off into the distance over low hills. The sudden urge to feel the loamy forest floor underfoot was an itch, an almost irresistible compulsion.

"It calls to you," Leander murmured. He shifted his weight on the mattress, sending a waft of scented, warm air to her nose, the delicious smell of his skin folded within it. The heat of his hand was heavy and real on her hip. "Doesn't it?"

He opened his eyes and gazed at her with a look of hot, hungry knowing.

She blushed deeply, wishing she wouldn't. The memory of the pleasure he gave her with his body, with his hands and lips and tongue, became a delicious sweetness in her mouth.

"The forest? Yes, I suppose it does. I felt...safe there. At home."

"That's because it *is* your home." He stretched like a cat in the sunshine, drowsy and languid, yet capable of coming fully alert at any moment to devour a mouse.

Or her.

He settled back down against the mattress and slid his hand from her hip to trace a path up her spine, making small, stroking circles with his thumb. It sent currents of electricity coursing through her body.

"What do you mean?" she asked casually, trying to ignore the pulse of pleasure his hands gave her, even this—the barest stroke of his skin over hers. Here in the clarity of the morning sun, the memory of her wanton abandon from the night before seemed something very far away—and best forgotten.

He lifted up on one elbow to peer down at her with half-lidded eyes, a secret smile. Even partially hidden behind a fall of shining jet hair, his eyes gleamed like jewels refracting the light.

"You were born there."

She sat up abruptly in bed. The white satin sheets slid down to her waist, her skin prickled as it met the cool air. She stared down at Leander with wide eyes.

"*What?*"

He dropped his gaze to her naked breasts then lifted his lashes to gaze at her once again. His smile deepened. He raised a hand to her cheek, watched its path as he moved it down her jaw, over her neck. One finger traced the delicate outline of her collarbone.

"What a lovely creature you are," he murmured, bringing his finger down to skim languidly between the swell of her breasts. "Not yet five o'clock in the morning, and you're already shouting at me."

She pulled the pillow out from under his head and smacked him with it.

Leander fell back against the sheets with a muffled laugh. He reached out for her, found her waist, pulled her atop his body with the easy work of strong muscle. She scowled down at him as he pushed aside her hair and cradled her head with both hands. He gazed up at her face.

"Are you ever going to stop with the dramatic pronouncements?" she demanded.

Something in his face softened. He stroked a thumb under the fringe of her lower lashes then pulled her face to his, bringing their lips into delicious friction. She thought she might not be able to breathe with want, with the desire that rolled through her as she felt his warm body under hers, his lips against hers.

Then, as he stroked one hand down her back and traced a finger into the cleft between her bottom, she thought breathing might not even be necessary.

"I may have one or two more dramatic pronouncements up my sleeve yet," he murmured. His gaze, pale green veiled with shadows, angled to hers. "Perhaps something involving a bent knee?"

It took her a moment of stupefied silence before she found her tongue and willed it to move.

"I'm not sure I can take any more of your surprises," she said, unnerved. She lowered her head to his chest to avoid his gaze and listened to the steady thump of his heartbeat, trying to calm herself with the rise and fall of his smooth chest beneath her cheek.

"And besides," she said, tart, before she could stop herself, "things involving men and bent knees usually involve questions, not pronouncements. And large baubles. Specifically diamonds."

She swallowed, bit her lip, felt flame spread across her cheeks.

"All right then," he said, amused and unrepentant. He smoothed his hands over her head, combed his finger through the thick cascade of hair spread over her back. "I'll say something entirely neutral. Perhaps…good morning?"

Jenna breathed in and out through her nose, vexed and rattled, verging on hysterical. "You have exactly ten seconds before your head becomes separated from your body," she said with exaggerated care, concentrating hard on the real and grounding sight of an elaborate dressing table across the room, an elegant piece of burled walnut topped with Caraca marble and a shield-shaped mirror. "I was *born* here?"

He pressed his lips to her hair and she felt the laughter shaking him. "Hostile *and* demanding. The perfect duo. How irresistible. You are most definitely my dream woman."

She flung herself off him with a frustrated huff, but he caught her before she rose from the bed and pushed her back into the downy softness of the mattress. He threw one heavy leg over hers, caught her wrist, and pinned it to the pillow over her head.

"You are so endearingly literal," he said softly. Light spilled through his inky hair to paint the angles of his face deepest chocolate, espresso, and gold. She relished the heat and weight of his leg over her body, the firm muscles of his thighs and stomach and arms, the tickle of his hair against her skin.

She looked into his emerald eyes, filled with warmth and a deep, mischievous tenderness, and felt the cold and impenetrable thing that had been lodged inside her chest since childhood dissolve, like a block of steel lowered into a smelter.

She blinked up at him, dazed by an uncomfortable new feeling, something she hadn't felt in years, something that made her body feel so light it was as if she was filled with helium and was in danger of floating off the bed and drifting up toward the ceiling.

She had a terrible suspicion this uncomfortable new feeling might be happiness.

No, she thought. *Oh, dear God, no.*

"Literal?" she repeated weakly. Her pulse was a sudden, thundering roar in her ears.

You cannot fall in love with him. You cannot.

He drew his hand down her arm, stroking the skin of her wrist and the soft place inside her elbow, caressing her shoulder, then her neck. He brought his hand up to cup the side of her face and lowered his head. He brushed the tip of his nose against hers.

"The New Forest has succored the *Ikati* of Sommerley for almost twenty generations. It's kept all our secrets, allowed us to flourish and live undiscovered through hundreds of years. It's in our blood. It's in *your* blood. Your body may not have been born there, but your soul was, your spirit was. It's your home, Jenna," he murmured. "You're finally home."

"Oh." She laughed, a little too high and breathlessly, turning her face to avoid his eyes. "Is that what you meant?"

She'd never known exactly where she was born. It was just another of the many mysteries of her childhood, an unimportant fact lost in the shuffle of moving and hiding and pretending to be something she was not. "Somewhere near the water," was her mother's standard response, and whether she really didn't remember or just didn't want to say, Jenna never found out. And so it was tucked away with all the other questions that were never answered, frozen into the bitter cold that solidified around her heart so long ago. It was the kind of cold that burned like fire.

That's why you're here, remember? she reprimanded herself. *Answers. Nothing more.*

Leander lowered his face to hers. She exhaled and he stole it back from her lips, mingling their breath together. He drew his mouth over hers with a lovely, silken brush of skin against skin that made her shiver.

"My beautiful girl," he murmured, kissing the corner of her mouth. He spread his fingers around the back of her neck, his fingers warm and strong in her hair, stroking, possessive. "My lover." She felt the heat of his erection growing stiff and insistent against her hip. He bent his head and nipped the tender skin of her neck, pressed his lips gently where he had bruised the skin from the night before. "Say you're mine. Tell me you're mine."

No. No, no, no, no, no, no, no. NO!

She squirmed beneath him, trying to escape, but he only laughed low in his throat and pulled her even closer.

"So demure," he teased in that pirate's voice that made her weak all over. He slid his hand down to her chest and cupped the fullness of one breast in his palm. His voice dropped an octave. "You weren't quite so demure last night."

He pinched her nipple between his fingers and she fought back a gasp.

She leapt up from the bed and stood quivering and wide-eyed before him. "Show me!" she blurted out, desperate for any distraction that would restore her rapidly shrinking sense of control.

His eyes drank her in, her breasts and hips and thighs, all so softly rounded, all so lushly feminine.

"As you wish, dear lady," he drawled. He pulled the covers away from his body in one long, slithering rustle of fabric, revealing his naked body, the flat, hard muscles of his abdomen, his unabashed, impossible-to-ignore erection.

She blanched and yanked the sheet away from the bed with a hard pull, then wrapped herself in it, leaving nothing visible of her body save one bare forearm and her forehead and eyes, which blinked at him, fast and startled like a baby bird's.

"Not *that!*" came the squeak of her voice through the sheet.

He lay back against the mattress with his fingers laced behind his head, a wicked smile lazing across his handsome face. The morning light gleamed in molten streamers across his chest. He crossed his ankles and slanted her a look of mock distress. "It grieves me to hear you find the sight of my naked body so distasteful, love. I rather think I might cry."

"I meant the *forest!* I meant how to Shift to a panther!"

His body drew down to complete stillness at this. His eyes grew flat and dark, the smile vanished from his face. He sat up, ramrod straight, planted his feet on the floor and gripped the edge of the mattress. His legs were spread wide open, his stiff member jutted up to push against the reticulated muscles of his belly.

She looked away. His lack of self-consciousness, the perfect ease in which he inhabited his skin, struck her as more viscerally appealing than anything else she had seen of him so far. He exuded heat and untamed power, he was lithe and beautiful and unfathomable, he was utterly enticing and charismatic without one ounce of effort.

Yet she knew in her heart, for all his beauty and refinement and the poetry of his words, there lived beneath a primal creature, poised to pounce. A creature that had had a hand in her father's death.

She could never allow herself to be drawn into his world, no matter how skillfully he spoke words like *my beautiful girl* and *home* and *tell me you're mine.*

It seemed a very long time before he spoke. The room was still and cool around them.

"What you said last night," he began, his tone dark and controlled, "in front of the Assembly, about Shifting at ten years old."

Her gaze was drawn back to the startling, feral beauty of his face. A crackle of electricity fluttered over her skin. "Yes?"

"That was the truth, wasn't it?"

"Of course it was," she snapped, failing to keep the affront from her voice. The sheet slipped down to her neck. She clutched at it with stiff fingers, drew it back around her throat.

He only stared at her, gripping the edge of the mattress with those long fingers that had stroked her only moments before, and narrowed his eyes.

"And what else?"

"I don't know what you mean," she said, her lips flattened to a thin, stubborn line. She raised her chin.

"I mean," he said, with that same narrowed, assessing look, "that if you have been Shifting since you were ten years old—and successfully hiding that fact from everyone around you, including our scouts—you are, in all likelihood, capable of all manner of interesting tricks. I'd like to know what they are."

She ground her teeth together. *Don't let him bait you! Don't let him win!*

"I honestly have no idea what you are talking about," she said, plucking at the sheet to wrap it more securely around her body. "But if you prefer not to accompany me into the forest so I can try to Shift into something more substantial than a wisp of air, suit yourself."

She began to march toward the windows with her head held high, the sheet billowing out behind her like the train of a wedding gown. He stood quickly from the bed, strode over to her, and gripped her arm.

She turned to him, startled, and was instantly snared in the heat of his eyes. The slanting light from the windows turned them a pale, clear jade.

"You *can* trust me, Jenna," he said. His voice was surprisingly soft for all the hard, unyielding edges in his face. "In spite of what you may think, I do have your best interests at heart. If there is more to this story than you are telling us, if there is anything else you are hiding from me, from the Assembly, I need to know it now. You are out of danger from them now, but your place in the colony will not be secured until we establish exactly what you are capable—"

Jenna removed her arm from Leander's grasp with as much dignity as she could muster, dressed only in a ridiculous, trailing sheet, shaking from head to toe with outrage, with a naked and resplendent man by her side.

"There is no *securing* me, Leander. Not here, not anywhere else. I told you last night, I won't be locked up. I won't be your prisoner."

They squared off to face each other, unsmiling.

"Yes," he said. "I recall. But you have apparently forgotten what I told *you* last night."

But she hadn't forgotten. She was acutely aware that his promise to let her go was the one thing that had let all her fear and hesitation melt away. His promise was the one thing that had allowed her to surrender to the moment, to the desire that sang through her blood and shortened her breath and ate through her veins like poison. But now in the cold light of day the certainty of last night seemed foolish, wishful thinking, and was replaced by doubt.

"You would really do that?" The memory of her meeting with the Assembly brought the metallic bite of anger to the back of her throat. "With all your rules and restrictions and secrets, you would let me just walk back out into the world, back to my old life? When no one else can leave Sommerley without permission from you? When even Morgan, an *Assembly member*, can't be free to live her life as she pleases because she's a woman?"

Leander's face remained neutral, not a muscle in his face or body moved. But his eyes, oh, how his eyes burned straight down into her soul with such a fierce blaze of anger she nearly took a step back.

"Yes," he replied, his voice deadly soft. "I would."

She raised her chin another fraction of an inch, unwilling to be intimidated. "I don't think they would let you."

He gazed back at her, inscrutable and terribly beautiful, as magnificent and untamed as the vast black forest that stretched beyond the windows into infinity.

"I am the Alpha of this colony, Jenna. *They* don't allow *me* anything. I do as I please."

"And if there's a price to pay?" she asked, knowing there would be. Not even he would be exempt from the Law. Her father certainly wasn't.

His voice dropped and he said, "Then I will pay it."

She chewed the inside of her lip, unsure of what to say next. The sky outside the windows was going from pale gray to pewter, a silver dawn turning dark. Clouds heavy with rain floated on the horizon, waiting to drop their bounty of water to the trees and mountains and plains below. It looked cool and dewy and inviting, when everything in this room suddenly seemed so densely close and heated and filled with nothing but him.

"I came here for answers," she finally managed, after an endless, aching moment. "That's all I've ever wanted." She cleared her throat after a tickle made her voice crack. "That's what's most important to me. Finding out...who I am. Filling in all those missing holes in my past."

His eyes softened. He reached up and twisted a strand of her hair between his fingers. "I'm here to help you, Jenna, but you're keeping me at a distinct disadvantage if you don't tell me everything."

He lifted the lock of hair and stroked it over the slope of her cheek, down the curve of her neck. She shivered as he trailed it over the swell of her breasts, his gaze dropping to follow the path.

"Yet I have to think," he said, his voice lowered to a husky whisper, "that can't be the *only* reason you came here." He brought his gaze back to her face, dropped the strand of hair from his fingers, and lifted his hand to brush her cheek with his knuckles.

She felt the heat bloom over her cheeks under the weight of his frank, knowing look.

"Don't be so pleased with yourself," she said frostily, angered by his arrogant assumption. She'd had just about enough of everyone's assumptions about her and Leander.

"Of *course* that's the reason I came here." She turned away, clenching her fingers so hard around the edge of the sheet it pinched and puckered in her fist. "This was just," she said, waving a hand to indicate the two of them, the sudden, stifling heat of the room, the disarray of the unmade bed, "an unfortunate accident."

He dropped his hand to his side. It must have been her imagination that made the temperature in the room seem to drop several degrees. She chanced a look in his direction. The narrow, assessing look was back again.

"I see."

He turned his head, shifted his gaze toward the misted morning outside the windows. She was struck again by the sculpted, arresting planes of his face, the full, solemn mouth, the curve of long lashes so pure and perfect with the glimmering fairy-light catching the tips and turning them to silver.

He looked, she thought with a shiver crawling up her spine, exactly like what he was.

Dark magic.

Magnetic and dangerous and beguiling. Capable of anything.

"Well then," he said through thinned lips, "if it's only answers you're after…"

He slid away from her, moving toward the marble fireplace on the opposite side of the room. It hadn't been lit last night; the hearth was cold with day-old ashes. She followed his progress with her eyes as he paused with one hand propped against the mantel.

He turned to look at her. She couldn't read the expression on his face.

"It's answers you shall have. Follow me, if you please."

He Shifted to vapor and vanished into the black mouth of the fireplace. A wisp of trailing gray smoke curled out behind him as he rose up the chimney and into the gathering gloom of the morning sky.

It took only a moment before her surprise wore off and she Shifted herself. She dropped the sheet to a puddle of satin on the floor and darted up through the soot-crusted flue to emerge over the lip of the bronze chimney cap, but he was already quickly becoming invisible against the cloud cover that hovered over everything, swallowing the light.

He was a pale specter of fluid movement high in the sky, far beyond the green and manicured gardens of Sommerley, already breaching the first line of trees in the forest.

He was moving fast.

She surged forward, darting away from the roof and rising into the thick air as quickly as she could, pushing through the clusters of silver-gray clouds. The cool wind rushed over her, the moisture-heavy air slowed her and added drag to her progress, but she willed herself to keep moving, to keep him in sight.

But where was he going?

The ground became a blur of passing color beneath her, the ordered gardens of the mansion gave way to wild fields then low, rolling hills covered in heather and peat. Then the forest below, an abrupt line of dark trees so thick they appeared like a body of water, like a vast, ancient lake... placid on the surface, with danger and secrets lurking below.

Thunder began a long, distant rumble.

The first of the rain began just as she lost sight of him beyond the rise of a hill. A gentle sheeting of mist became something more definite, heavier drops that slipped through her, first softly then with more energy, slicing, pricking like a million tiny needles. She rose up farther into the sky, banked over the hill, and then paused, searching the leaden sky and the silent black forest below.

Leander was nowhere to be seen.

She caught his scent far to the south, perhaps a dozen miles, just a faint lure of spice and smoke wafting on the freezing wind. Only a few atoms of his presence still lingered in the air, but it was enough. She shot toward it, using it to guide her like clues in a game of hide-and-seek, until finally it became strong enough that she slowed at the edge of a meadow, searching.

But this wasn't a natural clearing, she saw as she hovered above. This was man made, with orderly beds of flowers and a low stone wall that ran the length of it.

Where was he? The rain now sliced through her so hard she had to concentrate on staying vapor. It was uncomfortable. She contracted, fighting the storm. She didn't know how much longer she could hold herself in this form.

But there—just across the clearing, next to a massive, dripping conifer—the gleam of water sliding over naked skin.

He was crouched low to the ground with one hand on the rough bark of the giant tree, the other sunk into the earth. He was looking up at her, unsmiling.

She skirted the perimeter of the clearing, staring down at the intentional beauty of the gardens and grasses and odd, flat pieces of moss-covered stones, and Shifted to woman just behind Leander. Relief flooded through her as she took air into her lungs and stretched her limbs. The scent of wet earth and rainwater and *him* hit her nose, followed quickly by the bite of freezing air on her unclad skin.

They were shielded from the blunt edge of the storm by the canopy of boughs above them, but she was still getting wet, and quickly. She padded over the soft layer of dead leaf and moss underfoot and crouched down next to Leander, her knees in the wet bracken, shivering with cold. They did not look at each other.

"Where are we?"

His voice came on a draft of frigid air. "The final resting place of the *Ikati*."

She came to her feet at once, forgetting her nudity and the cold and the wet and the storm raging above. He rose silently beside her and turned his face toward hers.

"You brought me to a cemetery?" She watched a drop of water fall from above to catch the rise of his cheek, then slide down over it like a tear. He did not blink. "Why?"

"I wanted you to see something," he said evenly, his eyes dark and unfathomable.

"What?"

A small flicker of emotion flared in his eyes, but was quickly extinguished.

"Your father's grave."

He turned and walked away from her, out into the open clearing and the raging storm. His naked body was soaked at once by the downpour, his hair blew slick and black around his shoulders, buffeted by the wind.

But she only stared after him, too frozen to move.

TWENTY

Daria was naked.

She was also gagged and blindfolded, her arms and legs bound so tightly with rope the skin beneath was chafed and bleeding. It wasn't the only part of her that bled. The long, cross-shaped gouge they carved in her upper arm with the tip of a hunting knife was still bleeding freely and throbbing.

She had been in the trunk of this vehicle for hours, since she had awoken with the blinding pain in the back of her head where they had hit her with something blunt and heavy. Her arms were tied behind her back, her knees were drawn up against her chest, her body was racked with uncontrollable shivering.

They would kill her. Of that she was sure.

Expurgari. Terror and fury roiled in the pit of her stomach, sending the acrid sting of bile rising up her throat.

She hadn't seen or heard them sneak up on her, which meant they were both sly and clever. She hadn't smelled them either, which meant they knew how to disguise their scent from the *Ikati.*

It also meant they had been waiting, watching, all the while right under their noses.

She'd been winded by all the dancing, taking turns with her husband and a flushed, distracted Christian and many other men of the tribe—friends and relations both—and had gone out to the rose garden for a breath of fresh air. She was alone for only a moment, leaning against a flowering trellis of jasmine, gazing up at the stars.

She was distracted, undeniably, with the news that had spread like buckshot through the gathered gentry that Jenna's Shift had been confirmed, in front of the Assembly, that Leander himself had made her do it—with a *kiss*, no less—then they both had disappeared.

To discuss things further, most likely.

She smiled, gazing up at the stars, thinking of a match between the two of them. For all his independent ways, she knew her brother longed for a partner who could love him, who would stand up to him and stand by him and challenge him to be his best. And Jenna seemed perfectly suited to that task. Perhaps she could even persuade him to allow the women of the colony a more active role in the decisions that affected their lives.

A cluster of stars in Virgo blinked down at her, millions of light-years away, winking with dreams and promise.

And then the hands closed hard around her mouth.

They were calloused and rough and covered in something tacky and viscous, like pine resin. There was a blinding stab of pain in the back of her head that sent scarlet and orange fireflies exploding behind her closed lids. A wave of intense dizziness hit her, followed very quickly by a rising swell of blackness, then nothing at all.

Until she had awoken to the fact of her limbs bound, her skin bruised and cut, her body lying atop a filthy, stinking blanket in the black prison of the trunk. The low, melancholy hum of spinning tires and the road rolling away beneath her sang a song of good-bye. She was being taken far from her home, far from any hope of rescue.

There would be no escape from them, she knew. She was smaller and shackled and weak with injury. She couldn't Shift. She bit her lip to hold back a sob and prayed she would be strong enough not to talk.

Though they would surely have gruesome ways of trying to make her.

Daria's heart began a painful throb within her chest as the car slowed, then stopped. She heard doors opening and closing, the crunch of boots on gravel, low, masculine voices muttering something she couldn't make out. A burst of cold air hit her naked skin as the lid of the trunk popped open.

She screamed against the gag as two pairs of big hands closed around her wrists and ankles and hauled her from the trunk.

TWENTY-ONE

Leander hadn't anticipated Jenna's reaction to seeing her father's grave. He couldn't have. Everything he knew of her until this moment was of a woman so strong and defiant you couldn't even tell her the time without garnering a swift contradiction.

Yet at the sight of the flat stone carved with her father's name, she crumpled to the ground like a discarded tissue and began to weep, great wracking sobs that shook her whole body as she knelt, her hair spread wet and thick over her shoulders and back like a dripping funeral shroud, her knees and fingers sunk deep into the sodden grass.

"Why?" she said in an agonized, hoarse whisper to the headstone. Her voice was nearly swallowed by the boom of thunder in the sky. "Why did you leave me?"

Leander knelt next to her and put a gentle hand on her shoulder, but she knocked it away, leaving a smear of mud on his wrist, dark splatters across his chest. She turned to him with wild eyes.

"You could have helped him!" she hissed, her face deathly white. She rocked back to her heels, her teeth bared, hot tears and cold rain streaming down her cheeks, mingling together to drip from the curve of her jaw. "You could have stopped it!"

He felt the animal in her, coiled just beneath the surface, a dark and deadly creature awakened by rage, ready to claw its way out.

"No," he said, careful and low.

He didn't move, he didn't look away, though the icy rain and the freezing air bit at his naked skin until it was painful. His fingers and toes were numb with cold, but he kept them where they were, sunk into the long grass and mud. He kept his breathing even and his face neutral. He didn't want to make any sudden moves that would push her over the edge.

If she Shifted to panther now, he was sure she would attack him without hesitation.

In their animal form, the *Ikati* were primal and dangerous, prone to sudden bursts of violence. Their human mind, every aspect of their human heart, was engulfed by this primal side. They retained the ability to reason, they retained their memory and core personality, but they became highly unpredictable, often lethally so.

In her panther form, with the amount of anger in her eyes at this moment, Jenna was fully capable of killing him, and quite easily. She would be full of fresh power, her emotions would be raw and overwhelming, her instinct to lash out at the source of her pain would be overpowering.

He held himself at the brink of the turn, blood rising, muscle and sinew humming with the effort of holding his human form while every nerve in his body screamed *danger!*

"I was not the Alpha then, Jenna. I was hardly more than a child."

A crack of lightning lit up the sky overhead in a brilliant blaze of white. It was followed by more thunder, then the rain, impossibly, seemed to increase. They were both drenched, and he knew she had to be freezing, exposed as she was with only her mass of hair to shield her from the elements.

But Jenna didn't move from her crouch. She ignored the rain and the thunder and the lightning and only stared at his face with an expression that hurt him so much it felt like his heart had been pierced by the tip of a dagger.

Hatred. She glared at him with unveiled, unmitigated hatred.

"*I don't believe you.*" It was nearly a growl, the snarl of an animal.

Cold and stinging rain poured over them both, bounced high off the grass, dripped from the end of his nose. He felt a sudden, hot frisson crackle between them, smelled that familiar scent of smoke and gunpowder sting the back of his throat, and knew what was about to happen.

"I would never lie to you, Jenna," he said roughly, knowing he was putting his own life in danger if he didn't Shift *now*, right now, before she did. "I swear to you, I would never do that."

Leander watched her, shaking and panting, begin to blink. Her eyes lost their focus, then found it again. They narrowed to sharp points of burning fell green, flat and dark with animal rage.

Her pupils turned to black, vertical slits, her eyes blazed to unearthly, phosphorescent malachite. The shaking in her body became more violent, her limbs twitched as if invisible ants crawled over every inch of her skin, but she didn't move. She vibrated hostility, coiled tight like a deadly cobra ready to strike.

He felt it now. He knew it was coming.

The freezing wind stole the breath from his lips.

Just as another crack of lighting tore through the sky to illuminate the rain-swept graveyard in which they knelt, Jenna Shifted to panther.

TWENTY-TWO

Earth. Sky. Trees. Rain. Him.

Everything, all at once. Perfect awareness. Perfect perception.

Power.

There was nothing before in her life to compare to this sensation, to this rushing great flood of feral electricity that scorched through her veins. There was a flash of acute pain as bone and muscle and tendon transformed—fleeting but terrible—then a sweet, aching surrender that glittered through her blood, smoldered over her skin. She was heady with it. She was staggered with the glut of raw power and sensation that vibrated through every molecule of her body.

Her new, streamlined, muscular body.

She recalled a pale human emotion from only moments before—anger or fear, she couldn't recall which—the residue of which still lingered in her nose like a cheap perfume. But she was so far beyond that now, pushed into a world so much better, so much finer, so filled with the utter, aching beauty of light and sound and taste.

Every breath she took now was pure and cold, like inhaling snow, every minute ray of light now pierced clear through the black clouds overhead like a million shining filaments in a light bulb, every scent for miles around flowered into her nose and over her tongue with a taste better than the finest of wines.

And she saw everything. *Everything.*

She opened her mouth to laugh with the surprising rapture of this feeling, a fierce joy that came from nowhere to grab her around the throat and shred every earthly care to pieces. The sound that came from her throat brought the man in front of her to his feet.

It was a rumbling, jungle-deep growl, rich and spine-chilling, vibrating with danger and potency and the warrant of a lineage fulfilled.

It was the most beautiful sound she had ever heard.

The man took another step back, held a hand out, fingers spread and hesitant. He said her name in a tone of whispered awe.

She knew him, yes, she knew he wasn't a danger to her. She knew he wasn't afraid though his eyes were very wide and he was hardly breathing at all. She knew he was Alpha; she smelled the ripple of power and sovereignty he exuded like some delicious perfume that wrapped around her, filling every pore, settling into every atom.

She knew his name, though it hardly mattered now. Only one word came to mind when she looked up at him, silhouetted large and male against the raw and streaming sky.

Mate.

She didn't know *how* she knew, but she knew he belonged to her, and she to him, and together they belonged to the fecund earth and the wild forest and the heart-piercing song of nature that cried out to her from everywhere around them.

The song was strongest behind her. Beckoning in sweet, rising thick notes that washed over her, unrelenting, undeniable, it called from the trees.

She turned her head to look at the forest—to the place where the song came flowing strong and high with a delectable, irresistible siren's call of HERE HERE HERE—then turned back to the man.

She tried to speak, but the only sound that came from her throat now was a strange, rumbling chirrup, a low, chuffing invitation that made the man's shoulders relax. He filled his lungs with air, the tension left his body, and he smiled at her, eyes shining, face exultant, astonished.

With one swift motion that occurred without thought or conscious effort other than she desired it, Jenna pushed off the ground from four strange, wonderful points of pressure, pivoted in midair, and landed in a perfect, noiseless crouch, facing away from the man. A long flash of pure white whipped by her head as she moved. With her nose low to the ground, she scanned the trees before her, smelling and tasting and hearing all the chatter of nature that swam around her, a buzzing that grew and swelled inside her head like a symphony, like an opus written just for her.

The forest called with the sweetest song she had ever heard in her life.

A song of sanctuary. A song of home.

Jenna pushed off from the earth and began to run in great, loping strides to the trees, her feet a blur beneath her as the welcoming arms of the forest came up fast.

She didn't look back.

He followed because he had to. His feet gave him no other choice.

Leander ran after Jenna, pumping his arms and legs hard as she became a blur of white streaking over the open meadow toward the trees. The animal in him roared to life, clawing out of his skin. He Shifted to panther in midstride, the rain now bouncing from sleek black fur and compact muscle, never breaking his gait.

His gaze never left her. Against the dark day and the darker forest ahead, she was impossible to miss.

She was pure white, as white as the most perfect pearl, exotic and luminous and rare.

He had heard of the legends of white panthers, members of their tribe in that lost, long-ago paradise where they lived like gods before it all came crumbling down to ruin. But to see her with his own eyes, to *feel* her—

He was so astonished he couldn't catch his breath.

The forest was gloomy and damp and thick with fog. Low tendrils of it swam just above the ground, higher up it swallowed the tops of the trees in a dense layer the pale light of day barely penetrated. This was the most ancient part of the woods, one never before breached by humans, hidden like a pristine jewel in the heart of the New Forest. The trees grew to heights of over three hundred feet, the forest floor was buried beneath a foot-deep layer of perfumed leaves and moss and pine needles, the silence was unbroken save for the calls of birds and the sound of water dripping from low boughs to pool in clear puddles or sink into the earth.

Far ahead of him, Jenna moved through the forest like a ghost, pale and beautiful against the dark woods, navigating the dense undergrowth as if she knew its every secret. She left not a single leaf disturbed in her wake. Only the fog moved around her feet, parting in silence as she passed swiftly by, swirling into eddies of pale, clinging mist.

He craned his neck forward and stretched his legs as far as they would go, his paws sinking into the loam underfoot, the ache of muscle and sinew making him bare his teeth as he pushed himself to his limit to follow her. She was swift and lithe, undulating with expert and beautiful precision over the remains of fallen trees, around thick trunks and glistening dark foliage, moving like an ivory zephyr through the ancient trees.

He'd never seen anything move so fast. He'd never seen anything so beautiful.

He stayed carefully behind her, listening to the patter of rainfall over dirt and stone as they moved through the forest, watching his beautiful phantom move like the wind, the scent of upturned earth and potent female in his nostrils, his body alight and attuned to her every move.

She needed to see. She needed to get high and look out over her forest.

There. That tree ahead. Huge, towering, trunk like a skyscraper, boughs up high lost in mist.

She leapt from the forest floor and landed easily on the tree trunk twenty feet up, claws sinking deep into fragrant bark. She held still for a fraction of a second, testing her balance, feeling the wind slip through her fur. She raised her head and looked toward the sky, toward the rain-soaked canopy of boughs and branches filtering wan light from overheard.

She pushed off, climbing straight up.

When she could climb no farther, she jumped out to a high branch as wide as a king-size bed and landed on all four paws, dropping into a perfect, silent crouch. She padded out toward the end of the branch as it curved up through an opening in the dense mass of leaves, the bark cool and rough beneath her feet.

An unobstructed view of the forest was spread before her like a banquet. She feasted her newly strong eyes on the rainbow beauty of sunlight glistening off wet treetops, rolling hills sapphire-dark with rain and mist and groves of fir trees, black woods and emerald moors and meadows thick with wildflowers bowing under the weight of rainfall.

She sat back on her haunches, lifted her nose to the west wind, and closed her eyes.

Owls nestled snugly into hollowed trees. Deer, close by, nosed through piles of dry leaves to capture fallen berries. Squirrels scabbered over bark, a woodpecker's staccato tattoo against a trunk, moss and stone and centuries of undergrowth. The scant vibrations of all the creatures for miles around. Rainfall, lighter now, pattered down through the canopy, slacking. The scent of fresh water slipped past banks of vetiver grass, over sandy, granite-strewn bottoms: the river Avon.

She was awash in the forest, immersed in it, drunk with it. She never wanted to leave.

Then a new scent, darker and warmer than the others, a faint touch of spice under the animal smell of hot blood and wet fur. A new heartbeat pulsing in time with her own.

She turned her head and opened her eyes to find him crouched there, at the base of the branch. His long tail snaked back and forth behind him. Canny almond-shaped eyes fixed sharp and questioning on her face.

And this was startling: the beauty of this creature was even more tangible and pleasing to her than anything else, even the entirety of her vast and pristine forest. The huge, wedge-shaped head with the long, tapering nose and even longer silver whiskers that caught the shadowed light, the fur shining so charcoal black it carried a tinge of royal purple, the body so powerful and muscled.

This animal was magnificent. Blessed with an undeniable, hard grace.

She leapt to all fours in one smooth motion and began to walk toward him, moving ever so slowly, carefully. Curiosity called, something warm and willful sang through her blood.

A sound in her throat now. A huffed chirrup, a questioning tone.

He made a low, rolling sound of acknowledgment that rumbled through his chest. She crept closer and stopped just a foot away.

He eased forward, elegant and deadly, perfectly silent on four huge, silken paws, and brought his face to hers. With the barest of pressure, he rubbed his cheek against her face. His whiskers passed over hers with an electric current that was close to a shock.

Startled, she drew in a breath and froze.

He froze as well, his gaze slanted down to hers. Another heartbeat, another moment that she didn't move, then he slowly lowered his head to hers again, stroking his cheek against her face. She closed her eyes and accepted the pressure, let him rake his face against hers a little harder, until he stepped closer and they were shoulder to shoulder and he was making a low growl of purring pleasure deep in his chest.

And oh, this feeling, this aching, this burning bright happiness—she'd never known anything like it.

She opened her eyes, took a sharp, cold breath into her lungs, and Shifted back to woman.

"Don't," she gasped, tottering with her hands held out, trying to find her balance again with human feet that seemed outrageously weak and frail.

He Shifted as well, a flash of black dissolving into vapor, which coalesced into the naked, muscled form she was beginning to know so well. He reached out and caught both her wrists as she flailed, teetering dangerously close to the sloping edge of the massive branch. A cool breeze ripe with moisture and the bouquet of the forest caught her hair, blowing from behind to lift it in heavy tendrils that reached out and flickered over his chest, caressing.

His voice was a spare, low growl as he fixed his fingers hard around her wrists. "Don't what?"

She looked at him. Time slowed to a standstill.

She looked at his beautiful face and his hooded eyes, staring aslant at her through a fringe of coal-black lashes. She looked at his shining jet hair stirring around his shoulders, one long strand caught at the corner of his full lips. She looked at his resplendent, nude body, dusky skin patterned with shadow and light, and nearly stopped breathing.

She took him in, all of him, fully. She suddenly felt this was the first time, the very first time, she actually *saw* him. Her heart jumped. The skin on her arms rose in gooseflesh.

"Stop," she whispered, her voice a thin echo of itself. "Don't stop."

And she stepped into his arms that easily.

He kissed her as if he had already pushed deep inside her, his hands wrapped hard around her waist and neck, his mouth open and hot, an urgent sound in his throat as their bodies came together. She slid her arms up around his shoulders, reveling in the feel of unyielding muscle under smooth skin, like silk poured over steel.

His body was a solid warm pressure against her chest and hips as they kissed, and the cool wind slipped past them, rustling through the trees and sending patterns of indigo fluttering across the amber glow spread beneath her closed lids. A smattering of raindrops fell from the leaves overhead as the wind passed over them, speckling her shoulders and hair with chilled, fragrant drops.

"I'm sorry." His voice was low and husky, breaking with unchecked emotion, an urgent murmur between kisses. "I didn't mean to upset you—I wasn't trying to make you Shift—I just thought you should see—"

"No," she interrupted, her mind foggy with sudden, overwhelming want, a pounding, relentless ache that cut deeper with every breath she took. The animal in her was still so strong, so powerful, cresting just beneath her skin, straddling the threshold between control and complete, sweet abandon...

"Don't apologize. It's not your fault. I'm the one who should be apologizing. I'm just—I'm out of my mind. And you're…you just keep giving me the answers I asked for, the answers I wanted…"

Her voice dropped to a whisper as he slid his hand up her waist, her hair bunching and slipping under his heated palm. He angled her head to his with his thumbs under her jaw.

"…all along you've given me what I've wanted…"

She felt so strange, like a dreamer wandering through a beautiful fairy tale, never wanting to wake. A coil of new pleasure unwound in her core as he lowered his head to her neck, inhaled deeply against her throat. He pulled her head back with his fingers twisted in her hair and stared at her.

"Have I?" There was something challenging now in his tone, something disbelieving. His eyes grew dark.

Jenna opened her mouth to answer him, but Leander slid his hand down her back, over her waist, shoved it without preliminaries between her legs. He found her center, the damp folds of her flesh parting under his invading fingers.

"And this?" he said, suddenly rough, demanding. "Is this something you want?"

TWENTY-THREE

He pushed a finger inside her—*God, so hot and wet*—and caught her jaw in his hand, forcing her to look at him. He pushed his finger deeper, in and out—and in—and she made a wordless sound, her eyelids fluttering with every stroke, her brows knit.

His voice dropped, his tone becoming astringent. "Or will this just be another unfortunate *accident?*"

Her tongue flicked out to lick her lower lip, and he nearly lost himself to a rush of pagan lust, wanting to lift her up in his arms to spread her legs open and bring her roughly back down, impaled.

His blood beat a thunderous call of *Jenna, Jenna, Jenna,* so loud he wondered she couldn't hear it herself. But he held himself back, concentrated fiercely on containing the animal that wanted to force her, here and now, that wanted to take her in this open air temple, whether she gave her permission or not.

He needed this to be her decision. He needed very desperately to know that she wanted this as much as he did, that she felt the same agonizing need for him that he felt for her, that she had surrendered her heart and soul—and not just her body—as he had.

Her offhand rebuff this morning had caused him surprising, swift pain. It was a sensation he didn't care to revisit, nor one he needed to interpret. It put everything into crystal-clear perspective.

He was in love with her.

Hopelessly, awfully, violently in love.

Without answering, without taking her eyes from his, Jenna dropped one arm from his shoulders, reached down between their bodies, and closed her hand around his stiff shaft.

He sucked in a breath and froze. His heart stopped, then restarted with a painful throb as she rubbed her thumb over the tip, feeling the ridges and satiny skin. She spread her fingers down his hardness, exploring his shape, his heat, her nails lightly scoring his skin.

She slid her fingers down to the base, turned her hand, and brought it back up over throbbing veins and rock-hard flesh, stroking and squeezing, listening to his breath grow ragged and watching his eyes grow hot.

He couldn't think. He couldn't breathe. He could barely stand upright under the magical agony of her soft, sorceress hand.

"Jenna," he warned, checking himself from savaging her with a thread-thin resolve. He dipped his head and brought his mouth back to the poem of her throat, feeling her pulse warm and vital against his lips. He inhaled the perfume of her skin, allowing the animal inside him a swift jubilation, then slid another finger inside the tight velvet of her body.

A tiny cry of pleasure wrung from her throat. Her hips made small, excruciating circles against him.

"I can't have you regretting this, regretting *me.*" He felt his own will fracturing away, chunk by chunk, falling down into oblivion as she moved against him, sensual and enticing. "No matter how much I want you, no matter how much I want this to go on forever, you need to be sure this is what *you* want…I won't coerce you. I won't force you. This needs to be your decision."

Sweet, hungry lips found his neck, his jaw, his earlobe. His fingers pushed deeper inside her, earning him a soft, ardent moan that reverberated all the way through him.

"Is this what you want? Am I what you want?" he rasped against her neck.

She slid one thigh up to his hip, her muscles taught and supple against his. Her knee came up to his waist and she opened to him like a rose in bloom. It took him to the very edge of reason.

Still she said nothing.

"Jenna, God, Jenna…tell me what you want…say yes or say stop…say *anything…*" he demanded. He heard the raw emotion in his voice, all pretense stripped away, the scent of her hair and her skin and her hot, ready sex driving him quickly insane.

"Please," she said softly against his neck. He pulled back to look at her face, her velvet soft eyes, her lips so ripe and red like a plucked cherry. A small, mischievous smile stole over her cherry mouth and she tightened her hand around his erection.

"Please...?" Leander repeated tightly, rigid and barely able to speak.

Her voice dropped to a throaty, amused whisper. "Please stop talking."

And she kissed him.

Every thought fell away at once.

He turned without breaking their kiss and pressed her back against the rough bark of their ancient tree. Her arms encircled his shoulders, her legs encircled his waist. He helped her, lifted her, grasping her bottom, sinking his fingers deep into her tender flesh. She was light in his arms, hardly a weight at all. She arched her back, and for one beautiful moment he saw her bowed in the dappled light, raindrops scattered over her chest and throat like glittering jewels.

He found her entrance, shoved himself into her heat with a chest-deep groan. She answered it with her own visceral sound of pleasure and tightened her legs around him, slender muscles held taut, pressing her heels into his spine.

They held still, unmoving for long breathless moments, wrapped in each other. Their blood pumped together, their hearts beat as one, while the sounds of the living forest and the slackening storm filled the world around them.

She softly exhaled and tightened her arms around him. Like a man sprung from prison, he was suddenly, exquisitely free.

They began to move together, rocking in their perfect embrace, his sex hard and impaling, hers wet and stretched around him. He'd never known anything like this, never known he could make love to a goddess in a forest, high up on the limbs of a tree, and lose himself to her and to the rain-swept sky and to the forest so dark and vast around them.

Mine, the animal inside him hissed. *Mine!*

"Tell me you're mine," he whispered, rough, into her ear. He pumped deep into her, spreading her wider. His skin began to tighten. Every inch of his body began to ache with such intensity his chest hurt with piercing exhilaration and a dark flame of secret fear. Fear he would lose her and lose himself, fear for what would happen to him if she turned away.

"Say it," he panted, burying himself in her, lost and ablaze. "Say you'll stay with me. Say you belong to me, Jenna."

She clenched her fingers into the muscles of his shoulders and shuddered. A soft moan escaped her lips. Her hair blew in golden ripples across the lichen-covered bark and he felt her body tighten, felt the coming of her release. He tangled his fingers into her hair, forcing her face to his, forcing her to look into his eyes as he thrust inside her and claimed her as his own.

"For the love of God, woman," he groaned. The air had turned to fire. "*Say it.*"

She stared deep into his eyes, her pupils wide and black, then tilted her head forward. She brushed rose petal lips against his cheek.

"You know how I feel," she breathed, low and husky.

He stilled, panting, buried inside her heat and wetness, and shook his head. "Not...good enough," he said, teeth clenched against his release, features whetted, eyes ferocious. He pressed his face to her neck and growled like an animal. "Tell me. I need to hear you say the words."

She stilled as well, a flame held aloft and silent except for her pounding heart, entwined with him, her body a lovely, perfect arch around his. She brought a finger to his lips, made a small, circular motion of her hips. He moaned with the sensation, her dark, sweet magic, her breath against his cheek.

Another rocking motion of her hips, a tremble in her thighs, and he nearly lost himself. His fingers clenched against her bottom, his eyes slid shut.

"Leander," she murmured. "You already know."

A sudden spike of anger shot through him. Very well, then. He'd have to play dirty.

He gritted his teeth, pulled himself away, slid almost completely out of her. He reached down with one hand and grasped his hard shaft, pushed the tip against her slick opening. She moaned, protesting. Not allowing himself to slide back in, he rubbed himself against her, back and forth, his head against her swollen nub, his heat and straining hardness against her wet lips. She moaned again and began to rock her hips in rhythm to his strokes.

She opened her eyes. He saw the desire there, the passion, along with the resistance.

"You belong to me," he whispered, nearly panting. "Your body doesn't lie. Your eyes don't lie. Tell me the truth."

She shook her head. "Stop this," she said between clenched teeth and closed her eyes.

He leaned his head down and caught the bud of her hard nipple between his lips. He suckled deeply, pulling her taut areola into his mouth, and heard her gasp, felt her body stiffen against him. He thrust himself into her, deep and hard, then pulled out just as quickly.

Her moan was broken now. He thrust into her again and felt a sharp contraction of her muscles.

"Yes, please, yes," she whispered. Her nails bit into the flesh of his shoulders.

He pulled almost all the way out of her and stilled completely. He held her up with his hands clenched into the tender flesh of her bottom, panting against her shoulder.

"You belong to me, woman. Admit it." He caught her mouth and kissed her deeply. He drove into her once, then again, until he was completely buried inside her, until he could not go any deeper.

He felt her jerk against him, felt the bounce of her breasts against his chest. Against his mouth, she gasped his name. He brought a hand up to her jaw and held her face to his.

She breathed raggedly for a moment through parted lips, blinking, trembling. He held still and their eyes locked.

A single, erotic rocking motion of her hips and he almost lost himself. She sucked in a breath and he felt the rhythmic, squeezing pulse of her orgasm begin.

She said it in a ragged, clipped rush as her head fell back against the tree trunk. "Fine—yes!—I belong to you! *I'm yours.*"

It didn't matter that she said it with her teeth gritted, defiant.

It finished him.

He thrust into her, pushing deep, pressing her down to him so hard it was an unbearable pleasure almost tipping over to pain, the best pain he'd ever felt. He couldn't get enough of her, her gleaming pale skin that tasted like flowers and smelled like heaven, her erotic, feminine moans against his shoulder, her mystery and fire and rash courage that scored a burning path deep into his heart.

He came in a violent, blind rush, his teeth clenched, his toes dug into the rough bark beneath his feet, heady with the feel of her lush body wrapped around his. Jenna moaned and convulsed against him, coming again. He covered her mouth with his, stealing the sound from her lips, claiming dominion over her heart and her body, over even her breath. He spilled his seed into her and forced his tongue into her mouth as she made a low sound of surrender deep in her throat.

He saw cold white light against his closed lids, bliss and agony and fierce rapture wringing through him with the feel of her so lustrous and hot and throbbing around him, every inch of her open and raw to him, her heart and soul laid bare, her body wanton and abandoned.

Surrendered. Finally, fully *surrendered.*

When he could breathe again, when he opened his eyes to the sight of her face—eyes half-lidded, skin flushed with a lovely pink glow—everything seemed new, everything seemed different. Even the gloom of the forest around them seemed brighter somehow, lit by the magic they had made together.

She dropped one leg from his waist, tentatively, finding her balance, then the other. All the while he kept himself inside her, not wanting this to end. Not wanting it to ever end.

He cupped his fingers around her jaw, tilted her head back so he could see her face better, so he could see her eyes. He smelled wet bark and fragrant pine and the frank, musky scent of sex all around them, warming the very air itself.

They didn't speak for a long while, a suspended moment spent gazing at each other as the forest drifted back to reality around them. He finally pulled himself from her with a lingering kiss.

"I hope you realize," he drawled, tightening his arms around her, his eyes avid on her face, "I'm not going to let you take that back." He smiled down at her in gorgeous, dazzling victory. "Even if you didn't really mean it, you said it. And I'm not going to let you take it back."

Jenna, looking up at him with their bodies still pressed together, was sated and sore...and utterly enthralled. A luxurious, golden pleasure had spread through her with his first touch, a pleasure that captured her and took her to her knees.

And now—as he gazed down at her with the cool wind slipping by their bare bodies and the skin of her back stinging from scraping over bark as he took her against the tree—she realized she had finally discovered what she'd been looking for her entire life.

More than just answers, more than mere information or facts.

Completion.

She opened her lips to speak, to tell him that she actually *had* meant what she said, but something stopped her, something strange and new.

It was a scent, the faintest hint of copper and salt carried on the breeze. She frowned, gazing up at him, trying to place it. She knew this smell, she knew that dark, metallic tang burning faintly at the back of her throat. And it was overlaid with something else, something sweeter, something floral...

Tea roses.

Tea roses...and blood.

Jenna gasped.

Leander reacted at once. She felt the way his body responded to the shock on her face, his muscles instantly tensed, his eyes honed in like a hawk.

"What is it? What's wrong?"

She blinked and felt a chill pass over her skin. The forest around them, moments before so welcoming and warm, suddenly pressed in, close and dark and dangerous.

"Daria," she whispered. "It's Daria. She's hurt."

He didn't wait for her to say more. He grasped her wrists in his hands, looked west toward where Sommerley awaited, then turned his face back to hers, his eyes gone to stone. Wordless understanding passed between them.

They Shifted to vapor as one and twisted up through the canopy of boughs, out into the open sky.

TWENTY-FOUR

They returned to Sommerley the way they left, filtering through the chimney that opened to the enormous fireplace in Leander's bedroom. He Shifted to man just as Jenna funneled out its marbled mouth and dropped in a ruffled column to turn to flesh before him.

He pushed her toward his closet, their feet hardly touching the ground, and pulled a pair of his beige trousers and a white linen shirt from wooden hangers. He handed them to her without a word. She dressed quickly, rolling up the flopping sleeves and too-long pant legs, watching Leander as he pulled more clothing off hangers for himself.

She eyed the rumpled pile of coats still bunched on the floor from their lovemaking last night and watched his face grow tighter and darker with every passing second.

Jenna guessed he could smell the stench of spilled blood now too. It was stronger here, nipping the air like the sting of biting insects. She could find its source if he let her, if only he gave her a moment, but he was already pushing her out the door, down the curving staircase. She stumbled after him in bare feet as he dragged her along through the winding corridors of the mansion toward the sound of gathered heartbeats and strained voices.

They burst into the East Library through the carved mahogany doors, and the room fell into arrested silence.

All the men were gathered here, the leaders of the *Ikati* and his own Assembly. They sat in rigid shock around the long rectangular table, scattered throughout the room in small, staring clusters. For some reason, all the windows were open, thrown wide in their casements. The room was nearly frigid. Morgan sat alone in shadow in one corner of the room, her arms wrapped around herself as if for protection. She stared first at the floor, then up at them in relief.

Her look of relief was followed quickly by something like terror.

Christian was the first to speak.

"You're safe," he said, his voice cracking. He looked straight at Jenna. His gaze dropped to her hand, clenched in Leander's fist, then raked over her tousled hair, her swollen lips. His face turned crimson.

Her face turned crimson as well when she realized that in addition to probably looking like she'd just enjoyed a thorough ravishment, she was most likely marked with Leander's scent. Which everyone would be able to smell.

"We didn't know where you had gone—no one could find either of you—" he sputtered.

"What's happened?" Leander interrupted, hard. "Where's Daria?"

"She disappeared sometime during the party, we've been looking for her all night. We tried to find you too. We thought you *all* had disappeared—"

"She's been hurt—"

"We *know!* We found the blood and footprints leading away from the East Gate. Two guards were found, killed—"

"*How the hell did they get in!*" Leander thundered, gripping Jenna's hand so hard it hurt. "I've got a hundred men on guard, we've got sensors, cameras—"

"Isn't that *your* job?" Christian spat, breathing heavily. "Make sure no one gets in or out?" His gaze darted back and forth between Jenna and Leander, down to their clasped hands and up to their faces again. "Or are you a little too *distracted* to bother?"

"We need to focus on getting her back now," someone interrupted. "We need to focus on securing the rest of the colony—"

The voices of the men began to churn over one another, rising in a chorus of noise that created a confusing wall of sound in Jenna's head.

But one voice was mysteriously silent. Its absence drew Jenna's attention like the pull of a magnet as a new scent began to bloom in her nose. It was a fetid, dark stink, like something had died and was rotting there among them.

She recognized it immediately.

Guilt. It was the cloying, tangible, awful scent of guilt.

Despair gathered into an evil knot in her chest as Jenna's eyes found the source of the smell. Something clear and terrible dawned over her, sinking into the pit of her stomach. She felt as if she had just swallowed a vial of poison.

"Morgan!"

Her voice echoed off the wood-paneled walls of the room. Its tone of horror startled the gathered men into another abrupt silence. Leander's fingers tightened into a vise grip around hers as thirty pairs of surprised eyes flickered to her, then over to Morgan, who sat frozen and whey-faced on her chair.

Jenna's voice dropped to a hoarse, accusing whisper. "What have you done?"

Morgan was silent for one long, endless moment, her eyes wide and staring, her hair spilling in a lovely dark waterfall over her shoulder. Tears welled up in her eyes and began to track down her cheeks.

"It wasn't supposed to be *her*," she moaned.

The room erupted into chaos.

A snarl of fury tore from someone's lips, a tall man Jenna hadn't seen before. He was pale and gaunt, eyes hollowed with worry. He leapt across the room toward Morgan and barely missed closing his hands around her throat as four other men caught him by his coattails. They pinned his arms and dragged him away as he howled in outrage and twisted like a madman in their hands.

"Kenneth! Get a hold of yourself, man!" someone shouted to the thrashing figure.

Daria's husband, Jenna realized. Her heart pinged with empathy. How horrifying to lose your mate. How she would bleed if anything happened to Leander, how she would die if anyone ever hurt him...

Mate.

Her stomach did a painful, twisting freefall. All the breath left her body in a single, violent rush.

Her gaze shot to Leander. He stood taut and menacing by her side, emanating danger and barely checked rage as he stared in cold fury at Morgan. She was weeping openly now, her chair surrounded by a circle of men.

But Jenna couldn't look away from Leander's face. She couldn't breathe. She couldn't move.

For one long, interrupted moment all she could do was stare at him, frozen, openmouthed. She felt her past and her future slipping away, felt her heart throb and twist as if in its death throes inside the confines of her chest.

If they ever find you...run. And now she was—what?

Not in love? She couldn't be in love with him?

A chilled draft from the open windows stole over her skin. It prickled the hair on the back of her neck as if someone had walked over her grave.

She blinked and came back to herself just as two men picked Morgan up by her arms and hauled her out of the chair to her feet. She didn't fight or protest as they began to drag her toward the door, spitting words like *traitor* and *monster* and *whore.*

With knees weak and trembling, Jenna loosened her fingers from Leander's grasp. She had to shout over the din of angry male voices.

"Stop!"

Everyone froze. Leander's head swiveled in her direction. She took a tentative step forward, then another, feeling raw and exposed in Leander's ill-fitting clothing. The frigid hardwood floor leached the warmth from her bare feet with every step.

"Let me talk to her."

Alejandro's dulcet voice floated to her from the other end of the room as if in a dream. "*Meu caro,* please do not interfere. We have no time for dallying, she must be questioned—"

"I'll only answer to Jenna!" Morgan sobbed and leaned heavily against the arms that bound her. "None of you bastards will ever make me talk!"

"What the hell is going on here?" Leander's voice from behind, cutting and hard. "Why will she only speak to you, Jenna?"

Jenna took another step toward Morgan, ignoring him. "Where did they take her?" she asked gently, slowly advancing across the frozen room, feeling every eye on her like brands burning into her skin.

Then Durga's voice, growling like thunder across the chamber.

"You have not the authority to question this traitor, Lady Jenna, no more than you have the authority to enter this meeting."

He shouldered through the men to stand before her, swarthy and substantial, blocking her path. His eyes glittered dark and baleful. "You have no authority *whatsoever*," he sneered. His lips curled back to reveal a row of startlingly even, white teeth. He crossed thick arms over his chest. "In fact, I must insist you take your leave."

Jenna felt Leander take a step forward behind her, felt his fingers make a possessive span against her shoulder, felt his intention to crush Durga's windpipe so acutely she imagined it in vivid detail. His gurgling death on the rug at her feet, hot blood coagulating on the cold wood in thick crimson pools, fingers clawing at the air, grasping, finding nothing.

"*I* am the Alpha of this colony, Durga," Leander hissed near her ear. "*I* give the orders here. This woman is under my protection. *Choose your next words wisely!*"

Before Durga could form a reply, Morgan's voice rang out high and clear behind his back.

"The Queen of the *Ikati* has every authority granted under the Law!"

That's when the air in the room actually turned to ice.

Leander's fingers spasmed, sunk deeper into her flesh. No one moved. No one spoke. Jenna didn't think anyone even breathed. Somewhere off in the distance beyond the open windows, a dog began to bark.

She suddenly felt as if she were watching herself from above, floating as a fine sheen of vapor, free and disembodied, hugging the ceiling. She was curiously detached and a bit light-headed. Her blood seemed to have stopped circulating throughout her body and pooled in a great heated mass at her feet. She thought she might actually faint if it weren't for the pressure of Leander's hand on her shoulder, the real and painful sting of his nails sinking into her skin.

Out of the frozen, astonished silence, Christian's voice rose like the chiming of a bell. "I knew it!"

Durga's eyes, horrified, found her face. "No. Impossible! She's a half-Blood—"

Viscount Weymouth immediately interrupted, his voice wavering. "Daughter of the most powerful Alpha in all our history, *the skinwalker himself*—"

"A traitor!" Durga shouted. "Who married a *human*! Her mixed blood is impure, she cannot have even one-tenth of his Gifts! She cannot be Queen!"

"Skinwalker?" Jenna murmured to no one in particular, still floating, still free, the shouts of the men bouncing off the walls and the protective bubble of shock that had settled around her.

Alpha.

Half-Blood.

Queen.

"It's happened before, Durga." Weymouth's blue eyes, pale and rheumy, fixed on Jenna, his face ashen. "Cleopatra, the last pharaoh of Egypt, was a half-Blood Queen. You recall *her*, I assume?" His voice dropped lower and lower as he spoke. "The saying is as old as our kind. *Blood follows Blood.* If the Blood is strong, the Gifts are strong."

He lifted his hand and pointed a shaking finger right at her. "And *her* Blood is the strongest of them all."

Skinwalker.

Jenna's protective bubble of shock burst wide open.

Now the blood began to rise up from her legs, rise up under her skin, scorching like fire through her veins as they all stared at her, a roomful of flabbergasted men ahead of her and one furious one behind, his anger growing and pulsing and focused now on her, his eyes like sandbags on her back.

She didn't even have to look at Leander to feel the burning gaze he leveled her with.

"THIS IS RUBBISH!" Durga roared. He turned blazing eyes toward Leander. "Complete fantasy! How do we know this woman doesn't have some kind of involvement with the dogs who took your sister! She kept herself locked in her rooms for days with the *other* one—" He jerked his thumb toward Morgan, who had dropped to her knees on the floor as the men who held her stared in shock at Jenna, their anger forgotten. "A *female* who just admitted treason, a *female* you allowed onto your Assembly, a *female* who now knows *everything* about us—our defensive strategies, our logistical strengths and weaknesses—*everything*!"

He leveled Jenna with a look of such pure, unmitigated hatred she nearly took a step back. "She cannot be Queen! She can't even be trusted! The two of them were probably planning this all along!"

"No," Christian said flatly. "She knows nothing of this."

Durga growled, a low snarl of hostility that rumbled through the room. "We cannot know that! They *both* should be taken and questioned and we then can determine what to do with—"

"Jenna." Leander's voice came from beside her, spare and hard. "Is there something you need to tell me?"

She turned her head to look at him and saw it like an ugly blemish that marred his beautiful face.

Doubt.

He doubted her. And she had just realized what he meant to her, she had just begun to admit to herself how much she wanted and needed and cared for him and now... now he doubted her.

"Jenna," he said again, an imperative.

Weak sunlight angled through the high windows, spilling pale across the gleaming floor, falling warm across his features. But there was no warmth in his eyes. They glittered diamond hard and cold.

He waited, silent. For all the gold in the world, she couldn't find her tongue to speak.

"Just tell them, Jenna!" Morgan sobbed. "Just *show* them what you can do!"

Leander's hand slipped from her shoulder, he slid one step away. And all the while, one thing hammered in her head, drowning everything else out with a cruel irony that would have made her smile if she didn't want so very badly to weep.

Mate.

"You can't possibly think I had anything to do with Daria's disappearance, Leander," she said as strongly as she could manage while everything inside of her was weak and floundering. All the new joy she had found in the forest was being sucked away, inch by inch, by a vacuum, a massive black hole of pain. "You *can't.*"

He continued to stare at her, his eyes assessing and full of swift calculation, his face too savage, too far beyond human touch to be tamed. "You wanted nothing but the truth from me, do you recall?" he murmured. "You demanded that much, and now..." His voice was so soft, ever so dark and controlled, revealing nothing. "Now I must demand it from *you,* love."

Not a sound was heard in the chamber. Not a muscle moved, not a breath was drawn as the Alpha of the *Ikati* turned to face her fully and pinned her in his green gaze, clear and cold as a dragon's.

"Is there something you need to tell me?"

It was a curious pain she felt, witnessing the awakening on his face, the way doubt bloomed into something deeper, something darker as she kept her breathless silence while the seconds ticked slowly by. Leander held her gaze without blinking, without smiling. The curious pain burned and burned and yet she could say nothing. She couldn't speak.

Leander finally turned away, and Jenna felt something within her chest fall and shatter, like the glass she had dropped to the floor. She lost herself then, lost the feeling of completion and satisfaction she knew only a short time ago, wrapped in his arms, his body filling hers, their forms fitted together as perfectly as if they were made one for the other.

She lost the only fleeting happiness she'd ever known.

She controlled her breathing. She controlled her shaking legs. She even controlled the bile that wanted to rise up into her throat as she turned to Morgan, who knelt pitifully on the floor, still surrounded by stunned, gaping men.

"Tell them what you know, Morgan. Tell them where she was taken."

"I don't know!" she wailed. "They didn't tell me anything—I was only contacted once—they promised me they would just take the Keeper of the Bloodlines, just him and no one else!"

Viscount Weymouth gasped, then took two swift steps toward Morgan and slapped her very hard across the face.

Her head rocked with the impact of his blow, but she whipped it back and glared at him, her face streaked with tears and mascara, her pride not yet defeated.

"How did they get to you?" he demanded, trembling in fury. "*Why would you betray us?*"

Morgan smirked, her lovely face twisted into a mask of hatred. "*Why* would I betray you?" She let out a cold, mirthless laugh. "When every decision about my life is not my own? When even who I should marry is determined for me, *by the Keeper of the Bloodlines*, forced upon me and every other woman of our kind so we make a proper Blood match? We're nothing more to you than *breeders!*"

Viscount Weymouth slapped her again, this time so hard she fell back to the floor on one elbow. A drop of blood welled up on her lower lip. She licked at it, then wiped the back of her hand across her mouth. The blood smeared over her chin.

"Do you have any idea what you've done?" Weymouth shouted. The other men began to advance around Morgan, staring down at her with flexed fists and faces black with fury. "*They'll kill us all!*"

"Then let us die!" she screamed back at him. A dozen hands reached out for her, closed hard around her wrists and arms and waist. She was hauled to her feet. "We live on our knees as it is, shackled by your precious, goddamn *LAW*—"

Weymouth reared back to slap her once again, but his arm was caught in midswing.

"Do *not*," Leander said very softly, his fingers closed in an iron grip around the other man's wrist, "do that again."

The viscount wrenched his wrist away and began to step back, panting and wide-eyed, rubbing his other hand over the spot where Leander's fingers had dug into his flesh.

"You will take Morgan to the holding cell to be questioned," Leander continued, his tone still soft and infinitely dark. He motioned to Morgan with his head but did not remove his gaze from the viscount. "And you will wait for me there. You will not begin without me. She will not be touched again without my express permission. Is that perfectly clear?"

The viscount nodded, still backing away.

"And what of *her*?" Durga demanded, pointing one shaking finger at Jenna.

Leander turned his head to consider Jenna, just the one elegant motion of his neck, and for a swift, horrifying moment, she was sure she would be dragged to prison along with Morgan. She kept her heels hard against the floor, kept her spine straight and her face impassive. But the look he gave her, the blade-thin smile as he examined her under his lashes, sent a spike of dread straight through her heart.

All the warmth and softness that had been there in the forest had now been replaced by something alien and cold. It sliced through the air between them, slick as steel, predatory and dangerous.

"Christian, Andrew." His gaze flickered to his brother and another, much larger man, then came back to her face. "Escort Jenna back to her chambers. Don't let anyone else in. Wait for me there until I return." He took another step away from her.

"You'll never find Daria without her!" Morgan screamed, struggling to free herself from the hands that bound her. Someone twisted her arm behind her back and Morgan grimaced in pain. "She's as good as dead without Jenna!" she screamed again.

But no one paid her any heed. Nearly every gaze had settled back on Jenna.

Jenna didn't protest as Christian came up and took her arm gently, she didn't speak as he and Andrew led her from the room. She held her head high, she kept her face straight. She wouldn't let them see her fear.

But as she passed through the doorway, she couldn't resist another, final glimpse at Leander.

She craned her head over her shoulder to see him, standing alone in the middle of the room. Motionless, taut, gazing straight back at her.

Gazing back at her with unblinking eyes of dead-cold flint.

TWENTY-FIVE

Christian stared out the row of massive windows in her pink and gilt room, silent, his back turned to her, his hands clasped behind his back. Her gaze skipped around the room but she saw nothing except the repeated pattern of ivy on the wallpaper, which made searing impressions of red against her eyelids when she closed them.

She'd done this often over the past few minutes.

The chair she was sitting on seemed oddly insubstantial, as if she had only to shift her weight and it would disappear beneath her in a puff of smoke. Nothing, in fact, seemed to hold any weight any longer. Even her hands in her lap seemed poised to evaporate into nothingness. It all seemed like something from a dream.

From her time spent here with Morgan, Jenna knew this room was sealed like a vault. She'd been over it a hundred times as vapor, searching for any escape, any exit, but there was none.

No handles to open the windows, no cracks in the panes, no fireplace and chimney that led to the freedom of the roof. Not even a breath of air flowed past the doors. They were fitted perfectly with a custom lead jamb that allowed no gaps and locked her in with the finality and airtight seal of a tomb.

They'd prepared well for her arrival. There would be no escape until Leander decided to let her out. *If* Leander decided to let her out.

If they ever find you...run...

How she wished she had listened to her mother. What a stupid, reckless fool she had been.

He didn't love her, he didn't trust her, he didn't even allow her to speak in her own defense before sending her away under guard to await his return. She knew he imagined her in league with Morgan's plans to destroy the *Ikati*, he imagined her a traitor. And now she knew with vivid clarity what happened to those who ran afoul of their savage, unyielding Law...

Her mouth went dry.

The longcase clock in the corner began to chime the hour in low, haunting notes.

"I know you had nothing to do with Daria's disappearance," Christian murmured, bringing Jenna back from her dazed inspection of the backs of her hands. He turned his head to consider her through half-lidded eyes. Against the fall of the silk curtains and the dark oyster clouds beyond the windows he seemed as cool and remote as the rainfall that slanted over the emerald forest in the distance.

"I appreciate that, Christian," Jenna answered quietly. "But your Assembly doesn't seem to share that opinion." Her voice dropped even lower. "And neither does your brother."

Leander, oh, Leander, how close we came.

She still smelled him on her skin, she still felt his hot breath in her ear and heard his moans of pleasure as he found his bliss inside her. She almost tasted the velvet sweetness of his tongue as he thrust it into her mouth.

But now it was gone, all gone with the blink of an eye, and nothing could ever bring all that sweetness back.

Christian continued to gaze at her with an inscrutable expression. His eyes and face were shadowed as the gray light from the windows flared into nimbus around his head.

"Do you love him?" he suddenly asked, his voice too loud.

It startled her. She stared at him across the silent room and realized there was a distinct possibility she would be sent to a traitor's death within the hour. She wouldn't be a coward now, here at the end of everything.

She wouldn't lie. To him, or to herself.

"Yes," she rasped, her throat closing around the word.

He only blinked and turned back to the window. He seemed to contract into himself, drawing down like a flame in an airless room, a phantom of a man fixed in a room of feminine frills and very tight locks.

"How do you know?" he murmured, gazing out upon the rain-swept day to some faraway point she couldn't see.

Because every time I see his face, I feel like I could fly.

She didn't realize she'd spoken aloud until Christian slowly turned and sent her a small, pained smile. "Yes," he said, holding still, his eyes fiercely bright. "That I understand."

They stared at each other in weighted silence for a moment. He turned away once again.

"What will he do to Morgan?" Jenna heard her voice from the far-off dream place she still moved within.

I love him, oh, God help me, I do.

"Most likely kill her."

This ripped through her waking dream like a knife through flesh. Blood flooded her cheeks. "Of course," she said, hard. "Why not? After all, she's disposable—she's only a *woman*."

"It has nothing to do with her gender," he said, staring out the window. "She's a traitor, Jenna. She admitted it herself. Because of her, at least one man has died—I expect she was the one responsible for the deaths in our sister colonies. And now, if the Expurgari know where we are, if they know of all our colonies around the world...we're all in grave danger. She hasn't only betrayed Viscount Weymouth. She's betrayed us all."

Jenna thought of betrayal, of revenge, of how much Morgan must have hated these men, the way they controlled every aspect of her life. She understood her anger, her powerlessness. She thought of her father and how he left this place because he wasn't allowed to love as he pleased.

When she thought of Leander pain came stealing back, spiraling up from her gut to sink icy claws into her heart. She felt her nails digging into her palms and was glad for the pain there. It lessened it everywhere else.

"And what is it, I wonder, that *you* are going to do now?" Christian asked, interrupting her thoughts. He lifted his hand and trailed one tapered finger very slowly over a beveled pane of glass, leaving a trace of gathered mist from the warmth of his skin.

She looked away, found the familiar sight of her hands clenched pale in her lap. She drew in a deep, bitter breath and flexed her fists open. There were little red crescents where her nails had broken the skin.

"You say that like I have a choice in the matter. I'm probably going to sit here in this room, watched over like a bird in a cage, until the Assembly decides my fate."

Maybe they would imprison her forever. Maybe they would kill her and bury her next to her father.

Or maybe...maybe they would torture her.

She imagined it would be Leander who would do it. She imagined his beautiful face hard as he beat her, as he whipped her and flayed her skin and made her blood run onto the ground.

And maybe they will all burn in hell. She fought back sudden, bitter tears.

"No," Christian said. Jenna looked at him, blinking past the moisture in her eyes. "No, that simply won't do." He stared at her, fierce and hungry. "Not for *you.*"

He smoothed one hand over his mess of thick black hair, straightened his shoulders beneath his ivory linen shirt, and bent down to pick up a marble-topped accent table near his feet. He threw it straight through the wall of windows.

The room exploded into noise.

Jenna covered her face on instinct as great, jagged chunks of glass flew in every direction, glinting through the air like a thousand miniscule blades. The dust of shattered marble and destroyed lead casings sifted around them, settling in her hair and on her arms, drifting down after a moment into thin, unnatural silence as she sat frozen in shock.

A shout from outside the door, the sound of the handle being tried. It didn't open, he'd locked it. Jenna stared openmouthed at the door, then at Christian. He stood amid the rubble of the demolished window with his hands hanging loose at his sides. His serene expression hadn't changed, but his eyes shone ferociously green from the depths of his shadowed face.

"Leander is Alpha of the *Ikati*, Jenna." His voice was full of ancient sorrow and such forsaken need it chilled her skin. "But *you* are the Queen. Whether they recognize it or not, whether you wish to rule or not..."

A faint, melancholy smile curved his lips. His voice grew soft. "Whether you choose to love one brother over another, that fact remains."

He motioned with one hand to the windows, to the gaping hole and the cool breeze that stole in to disturb the curtains and send them lifting and flapping in heavy silken ruffles around his legs. "I've never been more than the second son, the second best. But above all else, I am *Ikati*. I'm bound by the Law. I'm goddamned *defined* by it. And on this, the Law is perfectly clear."

He drew a long breath, the muscles in his jaw working. "You are the Queen. I believed Morgan because I've known it from the beginning. Anyone just has to look at you, to feel you, to know. They're all just afraid of what it means for them. But you are the Queen, and your life is your own."

Jenna breathed in and out, blinking in shock and abrupt understanding. Sunlight crawled along the threaded colors of the rug beneath her feet. A pair of starlings rose into the sky beyond the windows and winged off, zigzagging drunkenly into the silvery-blue horizon.

She stood without thinking, crossed to him, touched her hand to his unshaven cheek. "I knew you were a gentleman," she whispered.

His small, sad smile made another appearance. Angry fists began pounding on the bedroom door. Neither of them moved.

"But I can't let you do this." She stared into his eyes, shaking her head. "They'll have your head for this. You know they will."

He lifted his hand and gently pressed her fingers to the side of his face, covering her fingers with his own. He turned his nose to her wrist and inhaled. "My head…" his voice faltered. "My head is not your concern." He squeezed his eyes shut and pressed his lips, very briefly, to her skin. "But yours is of great concern to me. Please, go. Quickly."

"Jenna!"

Leander's enraged voice tore through the door. His fists kept an intense, throbbing rhythm on the wood. "Christian! What's going on in there? Open this door! *Open this goddamned door!*"

"You can't go home," Christian said calmly, lifting his head to gaze at her, ignoring the thundering racket. "They'll look there first. Go somewhere they can't find you and live your life."

He smiled again, only this time it was bittersweet, filled with longing and regret, and did not reach his eyes. "Somewhere warm. That's where I'd go, if I could." He turned to the shattered window and stared off into the distance. "Somewhere without all this dreadful fog."

"Thank you, Christian," she whispered, blinking away the moisture that blurred her vision. "Thank you."

She kept staring at him as the pounding on the door grew louder. She knew it would be the last time she'd see his face, a face that was as flawless and carved as all the rest of his kind, a face full of a pain that nearly broke her heart, a face she would never be able to erase from her memory...

...a face so like Leander's, the man who'd captured her heart and inflamed her body and wanted to see her dead.

The sound of wood cracking under pressure snapped her out of her reverie.

"Go," Christian urged, backing away, his gaze fixed to her face. "*Go!*"

Without another word, Jenna Shifted to vapor and surged out the broken window into the windswept sky just as the door splintered open and five men burst into the room.

Leander was the first one through the ruined door, but she was already gone.

TWENTY-SIX

The house was nondescript, deceptively so. Red brick and white shutters with a tiny green lawn and a picket fence, just like its neighbors to the left and the right. Nothing stirred beyond the lace-curtained windows, no voices were heard above the chirping birds and the evening traffic and the faint whine of the jet airplane that tracked a line of pearl gray across the indigo sky overhead. No lights shone from within to indicate an occupant.

It had taken all day to find this place.

The neighborhood was good, if unfashionable. She gathered from the older model cars lining the streets that the people who lived here were hard-working but not affluent. The gardens were small but well tended, the houses modest but kept in good repair. The suburb itself was altogether forgettable, like one of thousands found everywhere, on every continent on earth.

It was a place where you could blend in, if you had a mind to.

But it wasn't where Jenna had chosen to blend in. It was where *they* had.

The stink of the Expurgari was all over it.

It was a rank, vicious scent of violence and jealousy and greed, with an underlying bloodlust that was unmistakable. It lay thick on the grass in the rose garden where Daria was taken, and it oozed from the benign-looking house like an evil vapor. It made her skin crawl.

She'd never been to London before in her life. She'd never tracked a murderous band of psychopaths either. But today, she thought bitterly, staring at the brick house from her hiding place behind a reeking Dumpster in the alley across the street, today was a day for all kinds of firsts.

First time to Shift to a wild animal.

First time to fall in love.

First time to be accused of treason by a pack of rabid beasts pretending to be men.

She'd wanted nothing more than to fly away and forget him—forget all about him and his underhanded, arrogant Assembly with their ancient, feudal, *ridiculous* Laws—Laws that would have most likely had her head on a chopping block if Christian hadn't intervened—but she'd caught the scent of tea roses and blood as she'd lifted into the air above Sommerley and couldn't help herself. She'd twisted on an updraft of air and followed the scent as it led far away from the pastoral perfection of Sommerley into the smoggy, noisy mess of humanity and clogged streets that was London.

No one had helped her father. He'd died a traitor's death. Friendless, forsaken. But she wasn't like them, she was *nothing* like them. She wasn't going to leave Daria to die, not if there was something she could do about it. She would prove to them that their prejudice against humans was just as wrong as the prejudice leveled against them.

And then she would be done with them all.

It had taken hours of strenuous flight, holding herself in vapor form, mingling with rain-thick clouds and polluted city air, until she finally found this place. She'd gone on smell alone. She couldn't sense Daria at all, she couldn't summon her under her closed lids or feel her heartbeat anywhere near. It was as if she had vanished, but for her scent.

And now she was hunched low, naked and hungry in a filthy alley that smelled of rotting garbage, hiding behind an overflowing trash bin, inhaling the stench of men so vile they exuded a fetid fog around themselves.

She'd spent the better part of the past hour mentally castigating herself for yet another massive show of stupidity. This little side trip was most likely going to get her killed.

There was no way in. From the inside, there would be no way out. Not a hole in a brick, not a crack in a window, not a single loose tile on the roof. Along with the distinct smell of Daria and evil, this was how she knew she was in the right place.

The front door of the house opened. Jenna hissed a sharp breath between clenched teeth and shrank back against the metal Dumpster.

A man looked out. Tall, wiry, and rachitic, he wore head-to-toe black and held a slim silver briefcase in one hand. His eyes raked the quiet street. He didn't move for one long moment, but then, seemingly satisfied there was no danger, he stepped out onto the porch and motioned with his head for someone else to follow. He walked quickly to the waiting car in the driveway, got in, and turned the engine over.

Another man followed him, dressed also in black, but this one had enormous biceps and thighs that strained against his clothing. He carried a zippered nylon shoulder bag. He paused at the door for one final glance inside, then turned and began to close the door behind him.

Just before the lock slid shut in the bolt, a fine sheen of mist drifted above the man's head for an unseen, silent moment, then slipped between the lead-enforced jamb and the door. It disappeared like a sylph into the foreboding gloom of the house.

TWENTY-SEVEN

Once upon a time, when he was a boy of fourteen, just beginning to understand the world he lived in and his future role within it, Leander ran away from home.

He hadn't planned it. He awoke in the dead of a particularly balmy spring night with the glow of the moon so bright through his windows it lit the entire room with a magical, pearled brilliance. He slid out of bed and crossed to the windows, looked out over the foggy, leafy shire, and felt the overwhelming need to feel the dewed grass under his bare feet.

He'd always been stealthy, even more so once he'd begun to Shift three years before, so it was effortless to steal down the long curving staircase of what was then his parents' manor house and slip out through the back kitchen door, the one with such well-oiled hinges they never squeaked when opened.

He couldn't Shift in the house. His father would have sensed it. Discovery was inevitable.

So he waited until he was deep within the fragrant borders of the chest-high rosemary hedges that surrounded the marble fountain of Triton in the back gardens and Shifted then.

He remembered how he felt, roaming, running, Shifting back and forth at will between animal and human and vapor, ruler of the velvet-dark forest, prince of the star-studded skies, king of the beautiful, magical world:

Free.

It thrilled him, this stolen freedom. It sent the blood pounding through his veins as he skipped over soft dirt and silken grass, the breeze murmuring through the ancient trees, moonlight dripping down to crown him in opal and pearl.

He was never alone like this. He could never play and explore and run until his lungs hurt and his legs burned. There was always someone watching, someone to make sure he didn't fall, he didn't fail, that he did as he was told and toed the line as befit his position.

Freedom was something new and foreign to him.

It was also exquisitely intoxicating.

Hours later, at the far edge of Sommerley, as he perched naked atop the towering hewn walls that marked the end of their territory, he stared out into the vast, unknown world on the other side and it suddenly came upon him.

What if I keep going?

The thought arrested him. For one blind moment, he teetered between an agonizing, heart-wrenching need to flee his future and his people and his heritage and every-thing that came with these things...and the yoke of duty that had hung around his neck since birth.

He was Alpha heir. He was the future of the colony. With all the privilege and power that accompanied his position, he was bound and tethered in ways none of the others were.

He stared into the sultry sky, at the fat, perfect moon overhead. He envisioned a future for himself that included freedom and romance and swashbuckling adventures...and just like that, the decision was made. He smiled up at the moon, straightened from his crouch, and was just about to Shift to vapor...

...when his father reached out and, very firmly, grasped his wrist.

"Before you go," he said lightly, "a moment of your time."

Leander spun between shock and indignation and twitched out of his father's grasp.

Unfortunately, and to Leander's eternal chagrin, his father was one of the few others in the colony who could Shift to vapor. His Gifts were unmatched, his senses pow-erful. Leander had been caught, more than once, in some boyish act of insubordination precisely because of it.

"I wasn't going anywhere," he huffed, dropping his gaze from his father's face, enigmatic and shadowed by the can-opy of alder trees that spread their boughs overhead.

"No?" his father answered, laughter warming his voice. "I rather thought you were."

Leander didn't answer. He turned away and stared sullenly at his feet, breathing heavily through his nose. Humiliation and anger washed over him in awful, pum-meling waves.

"At any rate, you should know a few things before you make your decision."

"It's not as if you'd really let me go anyway," Leander said, sullen and indignant. "I never get to do anything *I* want."

A car drove by in the night, unseen, somewhere far off in the black distance beyond Sommerley. Just the low-pitched hum of tires moving over asphalt on a road he'd never seen was enough to make him ache with longing for all the things he'd never be allowed.

"We're very alike, you and I," his father said softly, studying his son's face. "It was hard for me, and it will be hard for you. Even harder, I think. Terrible things are required to lead our kind. Things that would devour the weak."

Leander crossed his arms over his chest and glared at his father, defiant, unrepentant. "I don't want to be a leader. I just want to be left alone."

His father gave him a sidelong glance and a smile filled with compassion.

"Things change, Leander. Day by day, the future comes nearer, the past recedes. Whether we like it or not, change is inevitable." His father's gaze slid to where the light from the gatehouse pooled saffron and gold on the cobbled road leading away from Sommerley. His gaze followed the road until the light dwindled and the cobblestones were swallowed by shadow.

"Your time is coming, son. And I know you'll be ready. But if you are unwilling to live the life that's set before you" —his father lifted his hand to the night, a simple gesture filled with grace and authority—"then go."

Leander stood frozen on the wall. The night breeze rustled the trees around them, the smell of elderberry and wet grass was crisp and cool in his nose.

"Deserters are considered one of the worst threats to the tribe," Leander said slowly, thinking it through. His mind turned, leaping ahead. "They're desperate. Uncontrolled. Dangerous. Almost as dangerous as…"

But he didn't say the word. It hung in the air between them.

"Yes," his father answered.

He chewed the inside of his lip. "The Assembly would come after me."

His father smiled serenely. "Yes."

"I'd have to find somewhere forested, somewhere I could live and Shift without being noticed…"

"I daresay you would be able to take care of yourself, to find a way to survive alone. You're the bravest of my children, by far the most resourceful. Though you're young, I've no doubt you'd manage. And the world is full of wooded places, to be sure."

Leander sent a glace back toward Sommerley, toward where his home lay deep in the wild and beautiful woods. His heart seized with sudden emotion—elation or remorse, he couldn't tell. "Mother would kill you."

His father nodded ruefully. "Undoubtedly."

Leander's temper snapped. "Then why! Why would you do such a thing! Why would you let me go when it's against the Law—when *no one* can leave, not even you, the Alpha!"

His father suddenly looked older. His handsome features betrayed the burden of a lifetime of leadership in the lines around his mouth, in the furrows carved in his brow.

"Because you are my son, and I love you. You have a choice, as do we all, but you must be willing to pay the consequences. You must be willing to forsake everything you have, or ever will have here at Sommerley: your friends, your family, your home. You must be willing to walk away from your heritage and your future and any kind of security. You must be willing to be chased, and possibly—most likely—caught and punished severely by the Assembly.

"You must be willing to be hunted by our enemies, to run from place to place like a fugitive, to feel like an outsider everywhere you go on this earth. You must be sure that whatever it is you are pursuing by abandoning your home is worth all these things."

His father sighed then and turned to the edge of the wall they perched atop. He peered down into the dark meadow spread below, filled with alpine flowers and dozing mice and the sweet, ripening smell of the summer to come. "To my mind, there is only one thing worth that kind of sacrifice. Only one thing in all the world."

"What is it?" Leander whispered, enthralled with a curious, creeping dread.

The amber glow reflected from the gatehouse lanterns warmed his father's profile as he turned his head slightly and smiled down at him.

"Love."

Leander blinked, confused. His father's smile only deepened. "Are you in love, son?"

Leander wrinkled his nose and snorted. "*No.*"

"Ah. Well, then. Perhaps it's not worth the risk. But I leave that to you to decide."

His father began to dissolve into vapor from the feet up, slowly, in parts, his body shimmering and turning, evanescing into the warmed air like steam curling up from water, until only his shoulders and head remained. It was a trick Leander had seen before, when his mother was angry with him about something and he'd wanted to soften her with a bit of whimsy.

Leander crossed his arms over his chest, unmoved, and glared at his father.

"Whatever your decision, son, I'd like to ask you one favor."

Silence. An aggravated sigh. Then—"What?"

"If you do come back tonight, let's keep this conversation between the two of us. If your mother finds out I didn't try to stop you," he chuckled as his chest and neck disappeared into vapor, winding up around his head in fine ribbons, pale as smoke, "she'll kill me."

With a wink, he dissolved completely, leaving Leander alone in the succoring dark.

All these years later, Leander remembered his father's words as he stood looking over the crowd gathered on the curved driveway in front of Sommerley manor. His friends and his kin and the leaders of his kind from around the globe, most of the people from the village, hundreds upon hundreds of *Ikati* stood silent and grave on the groomed white gravel, getting wet in the steady rain that had started up again.

Only Christian was missing from the crowd. He'd been thrown into the holding cell with Morgan.

His father and mother were dead, his brother had defied him, his sister was in the clutches of their ancient enemy, possibly being tortured or raped or killed at this very moment. His people were on the brink of falling into chaos, their tribe was on the edge of war, and he was on the verge of losing his mind.

There is only one thing worth that kind of sacrifice—only one thing in all the world.

His father had known he wouldn't really run away, Leander understood that now. Or perhaps he knew all Leander really needed was the choice. No man could truly lead if it was forced upon him, if the need to serve and protect was not as much a part of him as the heart that beat within his own chest.

And on that night so long ago he'd chosen to stay, because Sommerley was his kingdom and his heritage and his lifeblood. He loved it. He realized he would never forsake it, nor would he forsake those who depended upon him.

He had a job to do. He'd been raised to do it, he'd been groomed for this moment and this fight. He had to protect his people and lead them to safety and exterminate the threat to their way of life.

Yet for all he had lost and all he had yet to do, for all the fury and vengeance and wrath that scorched through his veins, for all the terror he saw in the eyes of his people and the danger that had descended so abruptly and savagely upon them, at this moment Leander thought of only one thing.

Jenna.

She was his passion. She was his fire. She was his heart.

He would find her. He would find her because she was his mate and his queen and his future bride, and death itself could not keep him from her.

"Our defenses have been breached." From his elevated position on the top step of the marble staircase that led to the massive iron doors of the manor, his deep voice carried easily over the gathered crowd. "Our secrets have been discovered. Our enemy is finally at hand. Every one of us knows what is at stake."

The cold wind picked up, sending dry leaves skipping through the legs of the crowd. It lifted the hems of long skirts and jackets, flicked his dripping hair against his cheeks and jaw. The sky boiled slate gray overhead, choked with ominous clouds that dropped rain in slanting sheets to the forest. The trees poked up like dark claws into the wet bowl of the sky.

His gaze raked the crowd. "Let them come. We are *Ikati.* We have survived the eons, we will survive this."

His lips curved into a smile, cold and beautiful. "We will slaughter them all."

Nothing stirred. Nothing made a sound, and as far as she could tell, nothing breathed.

She was alone. For how much longer, she didn't want to consider.

She lingered as vapor on the cool plaster ceiling of the small foyer for a moment, looking down and around at the heavy wood furnishings, the blood-dark Spanish tiles layered over the floor, the baroque mirrors hanging in groupings on opposite walls. Their gleaming slick surfaces reflected what meager light permeated the shuttered windows back and forth, so she glimpsed a thousand mirrors and dark rooms cloned over and again like in some awful carnival funhouse.

Except for the video camera mounted on a tripod in one corner of the living room and the computer and printer set on a massive oak desk in what appeared to be a study, the house had a sly, ominous, medieval feel. There was even an ancient-looking suit of armor propped up against a glass-enclosed steel case, the interior of which held an astonishing, comprehensive collection of antique weaponry.

The case engulfed one entire wall of the living room. It frightened her deeply.

Jenna crawled across the ceiling as slowly as she could toward the back of the house, her senses open for any sound or movement. Once she went through an arched doorway, she was in a long corridor, lined with closed doors on both sides.

The doors were lead. Though painted white to fool the eye, she felt the hard coldness radiating from them like black ice, slick and treacherous. The ceiling here was sprayed popcorn, rough and bumpy. She sensed nothing behind these reinforced doors, no heartbeats or warmth, no sign of Daria or of *them*.

She crept forward, rolling and gathering in as fine a mist as she could manage on the uneven ceiling, trying to be stealthy, trying to be brave.

The door at the end of the hallway emitted the faintest scent of copper and salt.

Blood.

Jenna slid down the door. She spread herself over first one jamb and then the opposite, chilled at once by its icy surface, trying to find a crack to slip through. There were none. This door was lead, like the others, every opening around it was tightly sealed.

She looked at the handle. She knew the door was locked, knew they wouldn't be so stupid as to leave a key lying around, conveniently untended...

She hesitated, floating in midair for a moment of inde-
cision, then Shifted back to woman. The Spanish tile felt
unnervingly slick beneath her feet. She knelt down and
peered through the door handle, then allowed herself a
grim smile.

She didn't need a key after all.

Jenna Shifted back to vapor and began, slowly, to sift
through the keyhole.

Leander went alone to Jenna's empty room to stand before
the ruined window with the cold and the rain blowing in.
Shards of glass and marble crunched like broken bones
beneath his boots.

His men had their instructions, his colony prepared for
war. They had been hiding for millennia, but had never forgotten how to fight.

They were *Ikati*. They were warriors. Fighting was in
their blood.

And they would win. Even if he had to kill each and
every one of the Expurgari with his bare hands, he would
ensure that they won.

He lifted his eyes to the east, to the cold, sterile sun
veiled behind storm clouds, and caught a trace of her on
the wind.

She was still here, lingering like a ghost, her cool scent of
winter roses and fresh air sparking memories of the softness
of her skin, the shape of her breasts and hips, the intense
pleasure of her body yielding to his.

It murmured to him in soft welcome, the scent of his
beautiful panther girl, so vulnerable and reckless and brave.

Find me.

He summoned her through his memory. He closed his eyes and let her sink beneath his skin, the warm, feminine traces of her forming pieces to the puzzle of her disappearance. He opened his nose and his ears and his heart and let the animal take over, the great cat that hunted by night with its nose to the wind, that brought swift death with sharp fangs and claws, that lived ever long just under his skin, waiting and watching for the chance to blaze forth.

He inhaled deep and found her there, the female he claimed as his own.

Her scent was as potent to him as the day he first saw her, that initial, arrested moment he glimpsed her through glass doors, the burning heat of summer paling in comparison to the fire she kindled in his body, in his heart.

Then, it was compelling. Intriguing. Exciting.

Now it was an absolute necessity for survival.

Nearly a vibration, almost a tangible presence, her scent aroused something he could not name that lived deep within him, the part of him that was all animal, all hunter, and only that.

She was his. She belonged to him. And he *would* find her.

He breathed the ghost of her for a long moment, a deep, aching hunger eating a hole through his chest. Then the Alpha opened his eyes, Shifted to vapor, and surged out through the shattered window into the threatening sky.

TWENTY-EIGHT

The blood soaked through the white sheets in widening, erratic circles that went from brightest scarlet to claret to some grisly color near to coagulated brown. Jenna had never seen so much of it, all in one place.

She held little hope the source of it was still alive.

"Daria," she whispered, reaching out to touch a finger to the cold, pale cheek. "Daria?"

She was naked, spread-eagled on the bed, her wrists and ankles handcuffed to the scrolled iron frame, her hair spilling in tangled dark rivers around her head.

Wounds marked every inch of her pale flesh.

Ugly purple and black bruises bloomed over her legs and arms, deep gashes sliced through the flesh of her thighs and abdomen, a trail of small black burns with ashy residue marred the tender skin around the nipples of both her breasts.

Cigarette burns.

Anger came up hot and hard to eat through her chest as she stared at the macabre scene, at Daria's lifeless body so slashed and battered, at her face, white as death and covered in bruises and blood, yet still eerily, glowingly beautiful.

Daria's eyelids fluttered. A small moan escaped her swollen lips.

Thank God. She was alive. Jenna sat gingerly on the edge of the bed and lifted Daria's arm. It was so cold, her pulse was so weak.

"Get out," Daria whispered, moving her head slowly and deliberately, grimacing in pain. She licked her cracked lips with a dry, pale tongue. Her eyes fluttered open. One pupil was dilated wider than the other.

"Jenna, get out—"

"Don't move. Don't talk," Jenna insisted, gently brushing a lock of blood-encrusted hair out of Daria's eyes. "I'm going to get you out of here. You're going to be all right."

This was a bald-faced lie. Jenna had never seen anyone who would be *less* all right.

"I didn't tell them anything…" Daria's voice came in a broken whisper. "Not yet…"

Her fevered gaze fell on something behind Jenna's shoulder. Though it didn't seem possible, her face went even whiter. Her eyelids fluttered closed again. With a shudder that wracked her whole body, she fell silent.

Jenna made a swift, visual inspection of the room. Another video camera stood on a tripod in the corner, three wood chairs sat against one wall, a bedside table held an open briefcase, a lamp, and a bloodied set of tools on a glistening stainless steel tray. A leather strap, pliers, serrated and sharp-edged knives. The floor was raw concrete, with an open drain in the center. There were no windows.

Jenna felt a deep, gnawing fear begin to supplant her anger.

Fear was replaced by absolute horror when she turned and spied the five-foot-long curved, serrated saw with handles at both ends that leaned against the unpainted wall next to a tall rack of raw wood posts. The rack was composed simply of two seven-foot legs nailed to a top crossbar. Iron ankle shackles dangled down from the middle of it.

She'd seen this before, this gruesome apparatus, in a History Channel episode of torture devices popular during the Inquisition. It was appropriately named "The Saw"; the victims' bodies, tied in an inverted position, were sawed in half through their spread legs until a confession was made. Or they died.

Inevitably, they did both.

She sprang from the bed, heart pounding, and headed for the desk, looking for a key to the handcuffs. The stink of those men and Daria's blood and their cruel, incomprehensible intentions hung so thick in the air it was palpable. It sickened her.

What had the *Ikati* ever done to these men that could justify such depravity? What crime could ever account for this?

There was no key. Not on top of the desk, not in the briefcase, not in the drawers she pulled out and roughly dumped to the floor. She pawed through papers and bound notebooks and found a thick stack of Polaroids rubber-banded together. She nearly gagged when she glimpsed the one on top.

It was a photo of Daria, naked, surrounded by four men. Her nose was bloodied, her eyes wild. She crouched in obvious terror against the far wall of this spartan, harrowing room.

One anonymous, wiry, black-clad man with his back to the camera held a long knife in one clenched hand, a lit cigarette in the other. There was a tattoo on the inside of his wrist. Though small, she saw it clearly.

It was a headless black panther, run through with a spear.

She didn't bother to look at the rest. They tumbled through her fingers to the floor.

Three long strides and she was back at the bed. A solid yank with two hands and one foot braced against the iron frame, then another. The headboard didn't give. She swore loudly, planted both feet on the floor, shoved her hands into her hair, and bit down hard on her tongue so she wouldn't scream.

Just give me this, she prayed, staring at the ceiling. Panic and desperation and sheer animal horror crushed her lungs so she could barely breathe. Her hands shook so badly she was terrified they would be useless. Daria lay on the bed, silent and broken, waxen and gray as a corpse. *Just give me this and I swear I will never ask for anything ever again.*

She willed herself to breathe, to remain clearheaded, to *think,* and curled her fingers around the cold iron frame again. She lifted her bare foot and braced it against the bed frame, leaned all her weight onto her hind leg, and slowly, deeply inhaled.

She closed her eyes and heard her father's voice in her mind.

You are a princess...a princess who will one day be a queen.

"I need you," she whispered fiercely to the dead room. "I need your help. *Please help me!*"

She yanked hard. A shrill, moaning protest of bending metal, the bed shivered, the headboard gave by an inch. Daria's head lolled back and forth on the pillow and she made a low, choked sound in her throat.

Jenna yanked again and it tore free from its moorings on the frame with a loud metallic screech, sending her staggering back with a chunk of twisted metal in her fist. One of Daria's arms slipped free of the ruined headboard and dangled over the edge of the bed. The silver handcuffs that still circled her wrist twisted and winked in the light.

"Well, well," a voice drawled from behind her, languid and amused.

Jenna spun around. Her heart seized when she saw a man standing in the open doorway. He was dressed all in black, his long legs spread open, thin arms crossed over a narrow chest. He smiled at her, confident and cunning. He stepped forward and three other men came in, much larger and more animalistic than the first. They had terrifying, hungry faces.

"Another stray pussycat to join our party." He spread his arms in a fluid, sinister gesture of greeting. "Welcome."

With her heart pounding under her ribs, she spied the small, black tattoo on his inner wrist. Her mind registered several things at once.

The Smoking Man from the photo.

The leader.

The enemy.

She became acutely aware of her nudity, her hair falling down over her shoulders and chest, the piece of heavy, twisted metal in her hand.

His cunning smile grew wider as the other three men, rabid and bristling, began to move toward her.

TWENTY-NINE

Jenna was either dreaming...or dead.

She knew this because there wasn't any pain, not any longer, and also because her father was there, just as handsome and lithe and young as she remembered him. It was dark and humid here, the air perfumed with jasmine and plumeria. A beautiful, typical night in Hawaii. Her father prowled barefoot and silent around the unlit lanai of their small house, gazing down to the empty beach below.

Through the glass patio doors she saw how the palm trees rustled in the breeze, how the moon sparkled off the ocean and haloed his waving dark hair in a wash of pale, shifting elf light. She watched him pace to and fro from her secret place under the stairs, the one with her stash of pillows and blankets and her old friend Teddy.

Happiness shimmered through her like sunlit honey, pure and golden and perfectly sweet. Her father was here, he would protect her, she didn't need to be afraid any longer.

Even when he turned to a cloud of misted vapor, dropping his clothing to a pile of empty denim and linen slowly leaking air on the woven rug, then morphed to an enormous black crow that flapped its wings and landed on the glass-topped lanai table, she didn't need to be afraid.

As long as he was here with her, everything would be all right.

The crow turned its head and fixed her with a steady, intelligent gaze from piercing black eyes. It hopped sideways on the table, ruffled its feathers, and blinked at her.

Jenna crawled out from under the stairs, crossed without noise through the dark living room with Teddy under her arm. She stepped out onto the lanai, feeling the humid air cling to her hair and skin like a lover's caress. She lifted her arm out, whispered to the crow.

"Daddy...what are you?"

The crow made a harsh warning squawk, took another sliding sideways step over the table, and turned into a butterfly with wings of burnished amber and gold.

He hovered for a moment over her head, beyond the reach of her outstretched hand, bobbing silently through the heavy, fragrant air, then flew with bumpy grace over the edge of the lanai and off into the tropical, starlit night.

Jenna watched him go, a fire scorching through her heart. The pain that had subsided while he was here was returning, with a vengeance now, ripping through her mind and her body and every dark, hidden place in her soul.

The pain was how she finally decided she wasn't dead.

Death should be restful, not this endless, searing agony. She wasn't dreaming either, at least not this. She realized she was remembering something from so long ago it had been buried, lost and forgotten like so much else.

She'd seen him Shift as a child, more than once. And to more than one thing.

Something in the night sky caught her attention. Red and pulsing, glittering with color, burning bright as a drop of blood against the bottomless indigo. A star. And she didn't know what this meant, this star she'd seen somewhere before, somewhere in another life.

It was so hard to think over the waves of pain. Was she still dreaming? Was she hallucinating? Was she in hell?

A thumping sound began somewhere far off, somewhere beyond sight or ready touch, the rhythmic noise of blood pumping fast through hollow, squeezing muscle. Through a heart. It was a sound she would recognize anywhere.

A wordless moan of recognition, then the fire and pain began to pummel her deeper, to throb against her skull and scrape against her skin like a set of vicious, tearing teeth.

"She's coming 'round."

The voice was male, low, without a trace of inflection. A second, equally emotionless voice answered it.

"Finally." The sound of boots scraping against cement, a chair being pushed back. "Let's begin again."

She recognized the sound of flint striking metal, the flume of paper and tobacco catching fire, the acrid sting of smoke in her nostrils. Before she could speak or wake or open her eyes, another pain, newer and infinitely worse, sliced through her dreaming death like a thousand heated knives pressed into the tender skin of her inner thigh.

Then the sickening, awful smell of burning flesh.

Her flesh.

The scream tore from her throat before the pain really took hold, before it became so bad she thrashed helplessly against it, desperate for it to stop. But she was shackled, restrained by unseen bindings around her ankles and wrists that held her in place. Her scream went on and on, just like the pain did.

The flexed fist that cracked hard across her cheekbone stopped it short.

"Shut the fuck up or say good-bye to your tongue, you stupid bitch!" The second voice, hissing and spitting into her ear.

She fell into dazed, agonized silence. The thumping heart grew nearer, and nearer still.

"Now," the voice began again, this time in a reasonable tone, "I'm going to ask you one more time. And this time, I suggest you tell me what I want to know."

She turned her head toward the voice, sending needles of pain shooting into her closed eyes. She squeezed her lids against the stinging needles, then blinked them open.

The room swam into view. The bare walls, the scratched wood table, the gleaming tray of tools. A lamp affixed to the ceiling hummed and flickered, smothering the room in blunt fluorescent light.

The Smoking Man towered above her, smiling down with flat, expressionless eyes.

Daria...where was Daria? She recalled a fleeting struggle, the Smoking Man's arm lashing out in a blur, the hideous popping sound her abdomen made when the knife punched through it. It happened so fast, she didn't have time to Shift, though she'd split open one of their noses with a hard, well-timed swing from the fist that clenched the piece of the iron bed frame.

They had beaten her and cut her and burned her, but she had been spared the final brutality of rape. When they tied her to the bed and she'd screamed and shrunk from their rough hands, they laughed and made crude jokes about how sex with her would be worse than bestiality.

Something wet and sticky was spread on the sheets beneath her, something warm still oozed from the open wound in her stomach. Blood, pools of it, though she couldn't, for some strange reason, smell it. All she smelled was cigarette smoke and scorched flesh and the fetor of unwashed bodies.

"Shall I repeat the question? Or do you think you have an answer ready for me?"

He lifted his cigarette to his lips and inhaled against it, drawing the tip into flame, then exhaled. The smoke plumed from his nostrils like a dragon. Through the swell of pain that pounded through her body like waves pummeling the shore, she noticed his fingernails were grotesque. Chewed to pulpy stubs, ragged and yellow.

Thin and spindly as a spider, he leaned over her and let the smoke drift and curl like ghostly fingers around her face.

"Where is the fourth colony, pussycat?" His voice was playful, stroking, light as an afternoon breeze. "We know about Quebec, and Sommerley, and the one in Nepal, and we know there is a fourth plague land where the rest of you repulsive animals live, but we don't know where it is. And we can't put our plan into action until we do. I must say, your so-called 'Keepers of the Bloodlines' have been remarkably tight-lipped."

His malevolent smile lingered. He held her in his keen, hollow gaze. "Even when we cut off their heads with a kitchen knife," he said softly. "A very, very dull one."

Snickers from the unseen men. She wanted to spit in his face, but her mouth was too dry.

"There's a lovely display case at our headquarters in Rome where we keep all the heads. A trophy case, you might say," he calmly explained. "It's quite impressive; we've been collecting for centuries. Formaldehyde truly is a remarkable preservative. If I'd known we were going to have *two* guests today, I might have made a slideshow for you."

He sat back into the chair and smoked, calm and controlled, watching her with those glittering eyes. "Though most of them are women and therefore not as valuable to us. It's the Alphas we really want."

The small gesture he made with his cigarette seemed somehow regretful. "As the old saying goes, cut off the head of the serpent and the body will die—your entire species being the body in this case. We needed the Keepers to tell us who the really *important* pussycats are. For some reason, though, it always seems to be the females of your kind who are the most eager to talk."

The glittering eyes narrowed. "Although your friend in the other room hasn't been much help. Yet."

His tiny, vicious smile continued on and on as if it were permanently affixed to his face.

"But perhaps you will be more accommodating, yes? I'll make a bargain with you. Tell me now and this will all be over quickly." He made a sweeping gesture with his arm to indicate the room, the set of tools, her naked body laid out on the bed. He leaned forward in his chair and slowly lowered his arm. He didn't blink, his smile didn't waver.

"Or, if you prefer, I can take all the time in the world."

The cigarette sent up lazy whorls of smoke just inches from her right eye.

"I…"

It came out a pathetic, broken thing, a humiliating whimper. Jenna stopped herself and licked her lips. The Smoking Man raised his eyebrows. He waited, patient and inscrutable, until she tried once again.

"I do have something to tell you."

A broken whisper again, somehow less pathetic, but weak and pain-drenched nonetheless. The Smoking Man's flat gaze flickered briefly away to the men she sensed on the other side of the room, then settled back on her.

"Well." His smile deepened. He straightened and reached for a chair to drag next to the bed. He sat down and she stared at his face, his bald, gleaming head, the small black image inked on the inside of his wrist. The dead eyes.

"I think…" she began, trying to stay afloat on the river of agony that wanted to swallow her whole. The sound of the pounding heart was so close now, booming in her ears, rushing through her blood, drowning out even the sound of her own heartbeat.

The Smoking Man leaned in, waiting. He spoke, a sibilant hiss, and she almost couldn't hear him over the noise in her head.

"Yes? What is it, my helpless little pussycat? Tell me what you think."

She opened her mouth again and he leaned even closer, so close she saw the tiny red blood vessels snaking through the whites of his eyeballs. He hadn't shaved recently, he had a bit of meat from his last meal caught between his front teeth, and he was in dire need of a bath. He leaned in even closer, reached out, and touched one long, clammy finger to the pulse at the base of her throat.

She looked him up and down through her lashes and smiled at him, sweetly, without a trace of guile.

"I think you're even more stupid than ugly," she whispered. "A bitch is a female *dog*."

There was a suspended beat of silence before he registered it, before he stood up abruptly, dropped his cigarette on the floor, and kicked the chair over backward with his boot.

She felt a weary, thorough satisfaction that—*finally!*—his spidery smile had vanished. She began to drift, carried by a current of pain that flowed and tumbled and held her in its clutches, spiraling her down into the waiting blackness.

Little Miss Muffet sat on a tuffet. Eating her curds and whey. Along came a spider. And sat down beside her, And frightened Miss Muffet away…

"Give me the pliers," he snarled with his hand out. Another man, still hovering just out of sight, jumped to comply.

Before he reached the tray of tools set out so neatly on the wooden desk across the room, Leander smashed through the door.

He flew into the room—a blur of black fur and outraged snarling and long, sharp teeth—and landed first on the Smoking Man. He sank his claws into his chest and his fangs into his throat and with one hard shake and a wet, tearing nose, snapped his head off. It went bouncing into a corner of the room.

Leander Shifted to vapor just as a knife went hissing by his head and landed with a thunk in the drywall behind him. The body of the Smoking Man slid to its knees, then collapsed on its side on the floor.

Leander turned and saw the lead door was demolished completely. Though reinforced with steel bars from both sides, his impact had sheared the bars in half and taken out huge chunks of the drywall and a portion of the ceiling with it. Two men stood in the ruined doorway, shouting something at him as he floated above the room in a roiling mass of white mist.

He saw Jenna like a broken china doll on the bed below him, naked and wounded and covered in ribbons of dark, slick blood. Her wide green eyes stared up at him from a face white as snow.

A blinding fury tore through him like a hurricane, and all he thought over and over was *I will slaughter you all.*

A shout from the back of the house and he knew a third man was coming. Leander didn't wait for him to arrive before he Shifted back to panther and attacked.

Jenna, slipping in and out of consciousness, watched it unfold around her from her prison of chains on the blood-soaked bed. There was a bizarre, slow-motion quality to the action, almost amusing in its soundless, languid violence, like some video game gone horribly wrong.

There was the massive black panther flying across the room, its muscled forelegs reaching, stretching, long claws out, pointed fangs bared. It made a terrible roar that sounded like it traveled to her from under a body of water.

There were the silently screaming men, with their gaping mouths and bulging eyes, collapsing like paper dolls as he landed on them with the fury of his full, snarling weight. There was the faint, echoing snapping of bones like the crunching of dry leaves underfoot. There went a huge spray of crimson, arcing through the flickering light, splattering in a dripping long curve across the ceiling.

It's almost pretty, she thought, gazing up calmly and with restful detachment at the streaks of blood and gore above her. *It's almost like...art. Performance art.*

She couldn't feel anything anymore, not her arms or her legs, not the pain, not even a trace of horror or alarm or anything resembling emotion. She cast about for a description for this lassitude and realized she simply felt...resigned.

That's how she knew she was going to die.

And suddenly a third man was upon the sleek black form, slashing down with a blade that winked in the light. The man's heart was torn out by a powerful pair of jaws that ate through his chest, ripped out the pumping organ, and tossed it aside. More spurting blood, more silent screams, the dagger still on a downward trajectory that abruptly ended as the panther turned back to a man—a very beautiful, naked man—and the blade sank into his chest.

He stumbled back. The heartless man crumpled to the floor. Everything fell still.

She thought she must be very close to death now because her father was here again, sitting in the chair by the wooden desk, gazing at her somberly. He looked as if he wanted to tell her something, as if he was just about to open his mouth and speak, but the panther had turned back to a man, a very beautiful, naked man, and was leaning down beside the bed, blocking out everything else in the room with the shape of his golden, muscled body.

"Stay with me, Jenna!" he shouted, snapping the chains that linked her handcuffed wrists to the bedposts. There was a wound on his chest, a long smear of blood beneath it. Two more snaps and he'd freed her legs. "*Stay with me!*"

She tried to tell him it was all right, she was going somewhere else now, somewhere she could see her father again and there wouldn't be any pain or any confusion or any more secrets or lies or running away—or spiders—but all that came from her lips was a sigh.

She gazed up at him, at his trailing dark hair sliding over his shoulders and glorious face and his panicked, pleading eyes. He was shouting something else, his lips moving in slow motion, but she couldn't hear anything, and she thought maybe it didn't matter anyway.

Only one thing mattered. She wished she had the strength to say it out loud.

I love you, she thought, falling, floating, feeling the swirling black water rise up her chest, her neck, rushing over her chin and her cheeks and her nose, blocking out the sky and the moon and all the twinkling stars.

Leander, I love you.

She hoped he understood.

Then she closed her eyes and sank down into that dark river that had been waiting to claim her all along, hearing it echo over and over like a refrain, like a reverie, those three little words she just couldn't find the strength to say.

I love you.

THIRTY

Jenna didn't die.

Neither did she recover, not exactly. She lingered for over a week in a state of restless slumber, tossing in her bed. Only the occasional low moan broke her ominous, pallid silence.

Leander—who watched her day and night from the chair by the door or the settee at the end of the four-poster bed or pacing back and forth through the confines of her room—was in a matching state of arrested development. He couldn't grieve, he couldn't rejoice. She was here but she was not, and the doctor couldn't tell him much of anything useful.

"She's strong, Leander. But she's had a bad time of it. Her mind and body both need time to heal. Luckily she has no infection from her wounds. When she's ready, she'll awake."

Luck. He didn't believe in it. He put no stock in the word.

Courage. Valor. Stubborn, *pigheaded* bravery. These were words he valued, these were words that described this woman lying so still and deathly pale on the bed, her long flaxen hair lying in silken waves over the pillows.

His sister was still alive—barely—because Jenna had been brave enough to try to save her. She'd put herself in harm's way for someone she hardly knew and had, in all likelihood, saved Daria simply by diverting their attention. He owed her a debt beyond measure, but his gratitude was far eclipsed by the sheer, raw, aching love he felt for her, a passion and respect that had increased with the passing of every day since they'd met, yet remained lodged within his throat like a fist.

She was his heart and his fire, and he loved her with every fiber of his being, but he couldn't fathom how he would tell her. Not after what he put her through.

Naturally he blamed himself for everything. For every mistake and misstep and missed opportunity that had led her to this point, he crucified himself every single day. And he couldn't stop the memories. They haunted both his sleep and waking hours.

He'd pulled her from that ghastly torture chamber first, then retrieved his sister, wrapping both of their battered bodies in rough blankets, cursing like a demon, wearing a pair of blood-soaked pants stripped from a dead man's body. He drove like a madman back to Sommerley in a car he'd purloined from the Expurgari.

From the *dead* Expurgari. May they burn for all eternity in the fires of hell.

But there were more, he knew, many more than those few he'd killed in London. This was only the beginning. He'd spent days making battle plans to secure his colony, preparing himself and those he relied upon to dig in for a long and ugly fight. The Assembly had been convened every day; the machine of war had lumbered into gear.

And every day he was distracted and on edge and nearly overwhelmed by the terrifying possibility that Jenna would never rise from her troubled sleep.

He watched her in the mornings as dawn came and went, lavender and pink and silver crawling silently over the duvet through the slit in the drawn curtains. He touched his finger to the pulse at her wrist as the longcase clock chimed the noon hour. He sat with her during long, moonless nights, brushing his lips against her forehead, silently begging her to wake.

Eventually she did.

It was eight days before she opened her eyes, another ten before she was strong enough to get out of bed. But she remained silent and pale and took halting, slow steps around the mansion on his arm, or on Christian's.

Leander had let him out of the holding cell, asked his forgiveness for putting him there in the first place. He'd gone mad when Jenna left, had needed to lash out at anything, anyone. But now he couldn't bear any more discord among his family, he couldn't prepare for war when everyone he loved, the very glue that held him together, was broken to pieces at his feet.

Impossibly, Christian forgave him, said he completely understood.

Leander didn't know if he would be so forgiving in his place.

"You don't deserve her, you know."

They sat in the empty East Library after breakfast one warm morning, watching Jenna through the tall windows. She stood motionless in the rose garden, her face turned up to the clear summer sky.

Leander only nodded at Christian's offhand comment, wordlessly agreeing. He watched her bend and pluck a rose from the stem, an azure silk shawl snug around her shoulders, the hem of her skirt fluttering in a breeze. She straightened and winced—he saw it even from this distance, the way she sucked in a quick breath, the way she favored one side as she moved—then slowly exhaled and lifted the blossom to her nose. She closed her eyes.

Her shoulders relaxed and so did his own. He realized he'd jerked forward in his chair when he'd seen the fleeting pain cross her face. He let out a long, measured breath and sank back into the chair, his vision blinded by cold fury.

They would pay for what they'd done to her. All of them. *Every. Last. One.*

Seeing his reaction, Christian smiled sideways at him. "Well, you *mostly* don't deserve her."

Leander shook his head slowly back and forth, watching her still. "Doesn't matter anyway," he said, almost to himself. "She'd never have me. Not after all I've put her through. Once she's healed...she'll leave. There's nothing keeping her here."

Christian smiled his sideways smile and lifted a teacup to his lips. The dainty porcelain cup with its tiny yellow painted flowers seemed in imminent danger of being crushed to dust between his fingers. "You're not nearly as smart as you think, big brother," he murmured.

He took a long draught from the cup, held it stiffly away from his body with a frown as if it had somehow offended him, then set it aside on the marble-topped table with a sharp *tink*!

"Just out of curiosity," Christian added, his voice very calm, very modulated, his fingers now white-knuckled and clenched together in his lap, "have you told her of the Assembly's resolution yet?"

Leander sent him a small, sour smile. "Don't forget who we're talking about. She doesn't give a damn what the Assembly has to say. She'll never live by their rules." He shrugged, a weary motion of his shoulders. "And I don't blame her."

Jenna turned and looked directly at Leander through the window, as if she felt the weight of his stare. Her face was very pale and shadowed within the shining golden mass of her hair, spilling down in waves that lifted and fluttered in glinting locks around her shoulders.

Only her eyes were clearly visible, wide and unblinking, her gaze a level, cool green.

For a moment their eyes clung together. He wanted to leap from the chair and run to her, gather her in his arms, rain kisses over her hair and cheeks and lips—but then she dropped her lashes and turned away. She pulled the silk shawl closer and tucked a strand of her hair behind her ear in a gesture that seemed at once dismissive, indifferent, and entirely vulnerable in its simple, girlish elegance. The rose-bud fell in a streak of painted silence to the gravel beneath her feet.

"Well." Christian rose from the chair. He shot one last glance at Jenna before turning his gaze to Leander. "You never know. It might make a difference. You should tell her."

Leander felt his brother's fingers press a light squeeze against his shoulder as he walked behind his chair. He turned to watch him walk slowly from the room, gait heavy, shoulders hunched. When he looked back to the windows, Jenna had moved out of sight.

As the days passed, Jenna retained her silence and the ivory pallor of her skin, and she kept so somber and apart Leander knew he was right. She would leave as soon as she was able.

It was only a matter of time.

He found her early one evening dozing in a rocking chair in an unused bedroom on the second level of the manor. A book was open in her lap. A small fire muttered in the fireplace, lumpy piles of orange and yellow kindling cooling to embers and ash. He watched her gravely from the doorway, her face tinted with the last of the setting sunlight, her chest rising and falling in a slow, even tempo.

Her bare feet poked out from under the edge of the knitted afghan thrown over her lap and legs. Seeing how pale and vulnerable they looked against the dark wood floor sent an unexpected lance of anguish through his heart.

"You do that a lot, you know," she murmured, rousing. She turned to gaze at him through heavy-lidded eyes, her hair a tousled fall of honey around her bare shoulders.

"What, exactly?" he asked, leaning against the doorframe.

Her lips quirked. She looked him up and down once before answering.

"Stare at me."

"I do? Well, I beg your pardon. I wasn't aware that I did."

A crystal vase of garden roses dropped scarlet petals over a bureau near her chair. Their scent filled the air. He crossed to it, moving casually, and took a blossom between his fingers. He imagined her picking them from the garden, filling the vase with water, bringing it up to liven this deserted, silent room and wondered what—if anything— that could mean.

"Well, you do. You've even been watching me sleep," she softly accused.

He turned to her before he could cover his surprise. She watched him through chocolate lashes, her expression either curiosity or malaise or burning disdain. They stared at each other across the room as the dying sun sent orange and ginger and gold in gleaming bright prisms across the polished floor. She dropped her gaze to her hands, to the book open on her lap. She shut it with a firm snap and set it aside on the rosewood table next to her chair.

"How did you know?" Leander kept his voice even with a monumental effort. "You were awake?"

She smiled, a little sadly he thought, looking off into the fiery horizon, then shrugged. "Awake or asleep, it seems I can always...feel you," she said softly. She folded her hands together in her lap, then slid them up to clench bloodless against her upper arms.

"Ah. Yes."

He inched closer to her chair, the rose still velvet soft in his grasp. He rubbed the petals between his fingers and imagined the silken firmness he touched was her skin.

"Morgan told us about your Gift. Your quite...extraordinary Gift."

He stopped next to the window and looked out at the sky, at her reflected back at him like a ghost dancing in the panes. "You can see all of us, then? You can feel everyone? Everywhere?"

She adjusted her weight in the chair and he turned to look at her. She'd lowered her head so her hair tumbled forward, covering her face in a fall of gilded, shifting light. "Some more than others."

He didn't miss the innuendo, but his ego required her to say it aloud.

"Meaning...me?"

She drew her knees up under her chin, her cotton flowered sundress bunching and slipping under the afghan that protected her bare legs from the drafty room, and wrapped her arms around her shins. "Yes," she murmured to her knees. Then, darker, "Especially you."

He waited a moment for more, but she remained as she was, lowered eyes and silence and a veil of hair across her face.

"I didn't kill Morgan," he finally said.

"I heard," she said. Her fingers dug deep into her upper arms again. "But you didn't let her go either."

Was that condemnation in her soft tone? A fleeting distaste in her half-hidden expression?

"Her betrayal has cost us a great deal, Jenna. Some of our finest men have been lost, our defenses have been breached. Our protected existence is over. Who knows what the future holds for us. And you—"

He stopped himself abruptly. When he spoke again his voice was very low. "She almost cost you your life. What would you have me do?"

"I've been thinking a lot about that," she said quietly and looked up at him. "And to be totally honest...I don't know." Her eyes were clear and almost colorless in the light. He could not read her expression. "But I made a promise... a promise I have to keep. Somehow."

She stopped speaking and he frowned at her, waiting. She said nothing more, only glanced up at him, expressionless.

Doe eyes raked his face and then his chest, where a white bandage peeked above the open collar of his shirt.

"You're injured," she murmured.

He gave her a very dry smile. "I'll live, I'm afraid. It wasn't very deep, nothing like..." His smile slowly faded. His jaw began to work and he looked away from her, to the petals crushed in his fist. He opened his hand and they tumbled slowly to the floor.

"How is Daria?" she asked softly, after a time. "Christian told me she's doing well, better than could be expected but..." She swallowed and dropped her lashes. Her arms tightened around her legs. "She looked so bad. I thought he must be trying to cheer me up with a little finessing of the facts."

Leander raised his gaze to her face. She had her lower lip caught between her teeth and rocked, very slowly, in the chair.

"It's too early to tell. The probability of permanent injury is there, the doctor tells me. And," he added, sharper than he intended, "there will be scars aplenty."

She pressed a pale hand over her eyes. "God. If only I had gotten there sooner," she whispered. "It took me so long to find her, nearly all day. If I had gotten there faster..." She drew a ragged breath and shook her head. She squeezed her eyes together. A line of tears beaded her lashes. She swiped them away with the back of her fingers.

"Jenna," Leander said, his voice roughened. "It's *not* your fault. If you hadn't found her, if you hadn't gone looking for her, she'd be dead. What you did, back there…"

He lost the words.

Staring at her now, so beautiful and fragile and visibly despondent, twilight sliding like a lover's touch across her face, sent a terrible ache through his body, a fierce burning through his lungs that left him stunned and breathless. He tried to inhale, he tried to catch his breath, but he couldn't seem to manage it.

How long did he have? How many more days or hours or minutes until she left him behind with a gaping hole in his chest where his heart used to be?

The thought of living without her was like acid in his throat.

"So…" She drew in a long breath, gathered herself, and sat up straighter in the chair, folding her hands primly together in her lap. She gazed down at her hands and spoke in a small, quiet voice. "When are you going to do it?"

The hopelessness in her voice snapped him back to reality. His eyebrows ruched.

"Do what?"

She sent him a dark, resigned look. "Imprison me."

He stared at her, aghast.

"With Morgan," she explained, when he still didn't speak.

"Who…why…*what?*" he sputtered.

She waved a pale hand in the air in front of her face, weakly dismissive. "You don't have to put on an act for me,

Leander." She sighed. "I know you think I helped Morgan. You accused me of it, that day in front of the Assembly. On top of that, I ran away—again—and broke the Law—again. That's your job, isn't it? Enforce the Law? Protect the colony?" She stared at him, her gaze grim and unflinching. "Punish the enemy?"

"Jenna," Leander said, choked, his eyes full of shock. His face had gone very pale. He knelt down on the floor in front of her and grasped her hands, pulled them into his. "How could you ever think such a thing? How could you ever think I would hurt you?"

"Because you"—she began slowly, blinking—"you said it yourself, in the Assembly meeting that day. You said—"

"I *asked* if you had anything *to tell me,*" he broke in before she could finish. "You hate bullies, remember? I hoped you would stop hiding from me, stop keeping secrets. I was just giving you a chance to tell me yourself. You were always so stubborn, always so defiant. I wasn't going to force you into anything, not again, not when you should have just admitted to me then and there what I already knew—"

"What you *already knew?*"

She pulled her hands out of his grasp and stood up. The afghan pooled in blocks of primary color around her feet. She stepped over it, crossed to the bed, and sat down on the edge of the mattress with her back, rigid, to him.

Her voice came strange and unsteady across the room. "What is *that* supposed to mean? What exactly is it that you already knew?"

He came to his feet. His heart pounded against his ribs. "What you are. *Who* you are."

She turned her head a fraction of an inch and he caught a glimpse of her profile. Pinched lips, flushed cheeks, long, downswept lashes. Fingers clenched into the glossy fur coverlet.

"And who might that be, Leander?" she said past stiff lips.

He crossed to her in slow, measured steps, never taking his gaze from her face. The scent of roses and *her* was warm in his nose, the glow of the sunset flooded the room, lighting her hair to fire. He stopped just in front of her and put a finger under her chin. Her head came up.

She lifted her eyes and a sunbeam fell across her face. It illuminated her eyes to a fierce, brilliant green, shining and lucent like an emerald held to the light.

"Well…" she whispered. "Who am I?"

"You are Queen of the *Ikati*," he murmured, holding her gaze. "*My* Queen. My heart and soul…my true love."

Her lips parted. She didn't blink. She said nothing.

"You are the woman I've waited for my entire life, the woman who makes me want to be a better man, who makes me think I have a *chance* to be the man I've always wanted to be."

He sank down next to her on the mattress, framed her face in his hands, turned her body to his. "You are everything I've ever wanted, and the thought that you're going to leave—that you're only waiting until you're well enough—makes me want to die."

She stared at him, openmouthed, pale as a sheet. The fire popped and sputtered. A log fell through the grate. Somewhere outside, a nightingale began to sing.

"Well," she finally managed, blinking away tears, "and here I thought leaving wasn't an option." She dropped her gaze, but he caught the tiny smile that crossed her lips, fleet and wry.

"On the contrary." He allowed himself a smile to match hers. "The Queen is allowed quite an astonishing array of liberties." He gently lifted her wrist to his lips, then spread her hand against his cheek.

She pressed the smile from her mouth. "There's that word again," she mused, her eyes still downcast. "I don't think I want that title." She paused. "I definitely don't *deserve* that title."

"The Assembly thinks you do," he said. He brushed his cheek down her forearm to the crook of her elbow, inhaling the scent of her skin, then kissed his way back up to her wrist.

Jenna looked up at him, startled.

"They put it to a vote, taking into account several important things. First, there is the matter of your powerful Blood. As your father was the only skinwalker—"

"What the hell does that *mean?*" Jenna pulled her wrist from his grasp and leaned forward to stare at him with piercing eyes. "Edward said that to me before, that day in the Assembly meeting—what does it mean?"

Leander stared back at her with his eyebrows raised. "You must have known," he said. "You must have seen it before, when you were a child, your mother must have told you…"

Jenna shook her head no.

Leander folded her hands very gently in his own. "It's a term we borrowed from the Native American lexicon…the only appropriate thing we could think of to describe what he was, what he could do."

"What could he do?" Jenna breathed.

Leander hesitated. He rubbed his thumbs back and forth over both her hands, stroking, warming. "Jenna, your father could Shift to anything he chose," he said softly. "Not just vapor. Not just panther. Any animal on the planet, any human he wanted to resemble, anything organic in nature, anything elemental, anything inanimate. Wind. Water. Fire. A tree. A lamp. Anything."

She stared at him, breathless, the sound of her pulse banging away in her ears. She made a noise that wasn't quite coherent as she thought of that night on the lanai so long ago: Her father. The crow. The butterfly.

Leander smiled as he saw recognition dawn across her face. He lifted his hand to stroke her cheek.

"Where was I? Oh, yes, secondly, Morgan's disclosures of your own quite astonishing Gifts were taken into account, and finally the fact that you risked your own life to save Daria—which, even Durga had to admit, is something only the pure of heart would ever do—they've made the formal proclamation that, pending proof of all your Gifts, you are the Queen."

Jenna swallowed and blinked, breathing unevenly. "Pending proof of all my Gifts? But I...I can only Shift to vapor...and just that once to panther."

His finger stroked over her cheek, back and forth, back and forth. His smile deepened. "The Ikati have an ancient saying, *Blood follows Blood.* What your father could do...that could be in your Blood too. Most likely it is. Needless to say, we're all quite eager to find out."

A dimple flashed in his cheek. "Some of us more than others."

She stared at him. Her mouth made several odd shapes, but nothing came out.

"I...I..." she finally managed. She dropped her eyes back to the bed and drew lazy circles with her finger on the fur coverlet between them. "I see. Well. That's all very...

interesting." She took a long, shaky breath. "To say the least. But—"

She lifted her eyes straight to his and gazed at him steadily, her eyes cool, quiet green.

"I don't want to be your Queen."

"Another title, perhaps?" he murmured, watching her closely. "Duchess? Empress? She Who Must Be Obeyed?"

Her expression soured. "You Englishmen are way too fond of your titles."

He waited, not speaking, holding her gaze.

"What good is it to…rule…over people who have no say in their own fates, people who can't even decide who they're going to marry? People who hate you for having what they don't have—*freedom*." She dropped her gaze and shook her head. "I told you before. You have no idea how wonderful it is to be free. If I'm the…whatever you want to call me…and I have a choice—I choose my freedom."

"So you have no desire to make changes to the Law, then," Leander said, matter-of-factly.

"Changes?" She frowned at him while he remained gazing at her benignly, handsome and enigmatic with the light sketching patterns of gold and red over his skin. "What do you mean, *changes?*"

"Well," he drawled, perfectly serene, raising his eyebrows at her. "Who did you think would be able to make changes to the Law, if not the Queen?"

It was a full thirty seconds before she comprehended him. The blood began rushing through her veins like wildfire.

"Ah. *Changes*. Yes. Well." She cleared her throat. "I've always thought the Law was too strict. Despotic, in fact."

He nodded solemnly. "Archaic."

"Yes, exactly. In dire need of a few...updates."

"Adjustments," he agreed.

"Hmmm. Yes, the Law is in need of a few revisions. And if only the Queen can make those kinds of changes..." One shoulder came up. Leander watcher her lips purse, ripe as cherries against the glow of her rose-cream skin.

"Think of it as an opportunity to right the wrongs of an imperfect system," he murmured. "To bring liberties to the oppressed. You could bring the Law of the *Ikati* into the twenty-first century."

Her lowered lashes made a silken dark curve against her cheeks. "I never pictured myself a crusader for change..." The tiniest of smiles played around her lips. "Although I must admit, *liberties* are something I am particularly fond of."

"Not to mention trouble making and rule breaking," he added. She looked up at him. His face was placid, but his eyes were bright, laughing green.

"Don't forget baubles," she said.

His smile deepened. He slid his hand up her arm and over her shoulder, his palm skimming over her bare skin. He curled his hand around the nape of her neck, buried his fingers into the cool weight of her hair. "Large baubles, if I remember correctly," he said, husky.

His eyes took on a new light, burning and intent, as he bent his head toward her.

He brushed a kiss across her cheekbone, her temple. He nosed her hair aside and nuzzled her neck. "And the ever-popular bent knee," she said breathlessly.

He laughed low into her ear and put his arms around her, pulling her close. Her arms wound up over his shoulders. "I was just getting to that," he murmured, tightening his embrace. A slight, mocking sigh left his lips. "How much easier my life would be if I weren't in love with such a head-strong, demanding woman. I think you're going to be very bad for my blood pressure."

"Yes," she agreed, tilting her head to his. "I'm afraid I am going to be a very difficult wife. 'High-maintenance' I believe is the correct term."

Wife. His heart began to swell in his chest, so big he thought it would burst.

"A real hellion," he murmured, pressing his lips to the corner of her mouth. He felt her smile, curving and taut against his kiss.

"That's Queen Hellion, to you, my love," she breathed, lying back onto the pillows. She stretched her arms out to him, and he leaned down over her and smiled, a genuine smile this time.

"God, yes," he whispered. He bent his head to kiss her neck, the fine skin of her throat. His lips skimmed the rise of her breasts exposed in open invitation above the neck-line of her dress. "Say it again." His fingers discovered the delicate pearl buttons of her sundress. He worked the top few open.

"Queen—" She broke off as his tongue probed the flesh the opened buttons had exposed. She twined her fingers into his hair, turned her head to his neck. "Queen Hellion?"

"No, the *other* part," he murmured with a low laugh, dropping kisses over her skin. He lifted his head and gazed deep into her eyes with his hand spread against the side of her face.

"Oh, let's see." She pretended to think, looking at the ceiling and drawing her eyebrows together. "I'm a bit tired, my memory isn't quite clear—"

"*My love*," he insisted, scowling down at her. "You said 'my love.' And I want you to say it again."

Her eyebrows climbed. "And *I'm* the demanding one?"

"Jenna—"

"And as for headstrong—"

"*Jenna.*"

"My love," she whispered, relenting, her eyes shining and unguarded. "I admit it. You are my love and my life, and there is nothing in the world that could ever make me leave you. Not even your ridiculous titles."

"My beautiful girl," he breathed. He surrendered his caution, eager for her supple, feminine body, for her passionate heart. He pressed his lips to hers, and the animal in him awoke and stretched and roared *I want, I need* until he could hardly hear the words that left his own mouth. "Large baubles and bent knees will only be the beginning. I am going to worship you every day for the rest of our lives."

And he lowered his lips to hers once more.

Later, much later, after the fire had burned down to embers and ash and a huge, glowing moon had climbed into the sky, Jenna watched Leander sleep.

He slept on his back, one arm around her neck, his face turned to her hair. She lay on her side next to him and trailed her fingers over his muscled chest, over the edges of the white bandage. His skin sent up heat everywhere she touched.

She had that aching feeling again, that feeling she knew was happiness. It seemed not only unfamiliar but terribly fragile—and frightening. She wondered how people managed to live with it. Like a skittish wild animal, it appeared poised to bolt at any moment.

She smiled ruefully. She was beginning to understand wild animals. Very well, in fact. Maybe one day she would fathom this unpredictable beast called happiness too.

"Whatever you're thinking, keep thinking it," Leander murmured, opening his eyes to gaze at her with a drowsy smile. He rolled onto his side and turned her to her back with his hand against her hip. She settled against the smooth satin and angled her head to see him better. In the gloom, he was reflection and shadow, hooded green eyes against warm umber skin.

"It wasn't anything important," she said, skimming her fingertips over the unyielding muscles in his bicep, his shoulder. "You know, the nature of reality, the meaning of existence. Light stuff."

He bent his head to nibble at her lips, his hair soft and fragrant against her throat. "That sounds dreadfully boring." He took her hand and gently pushed it under the sheets, down between his thighs. His erection was already stiff against her hip. "I'm sure we can come up with one or two more *exciting* topics."

"Some people would find discussing the meaning of existence very exciting, I'm sure," she smiled with slow, sensual mischief.

"No one in this room," he countered, trailing kisses along the crest of her collarbone.

"And what about the future? Maybe we should be discussing that."

He paused, lifted his head to stare at her with a guarded look. "You're not going to tell me you've changed your mind about us, are you? Did I fall asleep too quickly? Did I say something wrong?" He struggled to sit up. "Do I snore?"

She pushed him back to the pillows, smothering a laugh. "*No*, you didn't say anything wrong, and you don't snore." She lowered her gaze and fingered the edge of his bandage, letting her hair drape over his face. "Although I must admit, you do fall asleep really fast. Like, in five seconds. You might want to see a doctor about that."

"It's not *my* fault you're so goddamned beautiful I have to have my way with you," he said, relaxing again. He lifted his hand and brushed her hair from her face. She nestled in under his arm and he smiled down at her. "Vigorously and repeatedly," he drawled. "Until I am completely exhausted."

"Until you pass out," Jenna corrected, blinking at him from under her lashes.

He lifted his finger to trace over a ragged red seam that marred the flesh of her shoulder, his fingertip following the path of a knife blade. His teasing smile disappeared.

"Tell me I didn't hurt you," he murmured, leaning over to press a whisper-light kiss to her shoulder. "Tell me I didn't lose myself and forget to be gentle." He lifted his eyes to her face and she saw the self-recrimination there, the pain. "You're still hurt, still fragile—I should have been more careful, I should have waited—"

"If you had waited, I might have had to throw myself at you, and that would be very unbecoming for a queen." Jenna raised her hand to trace the planes of his face with her fingertips. "I'm fine, Leander. Just a bit sore."

"From me or from…"

He left it hanging between them. She thought she'd never seen him look so troubled or so beautiful, his hair capturing the light in midnight colors, onyx and mink and deepest indigo.

"You did not hurt me," she slowly enunciated, raising both her hands to press against his face. "In case you couldn't tell the difference, those were moans of pleasure, my love."

He released a breath through his nose, pressed his eyes closed, and tilted his head down to hers. "Nothing can ever hurt you, not ever again," he whispered against her ear. "Not me, not those bastards. When I saw you there, chained and pale as death, all that blood..."

He buried his face in her hair and didn't speak for a long while. She pressed her hand against his chest, feeling his heart thump strong and erratic under her palm.

"I almost lost my mind," he finally said, tightening his arms around her. "I *did* lose my mind. And then when you didn't wake up for so long..."

She lay against him quiet and still, feeling his heat, the strength of his arms cradling her body.

"I will make them pay for what they've done," he whispered fiercely. "*They will pay in blood.*"

"Yes," Jenna said softly. She stroked her hands over his back, trailed her fingers down his spine. "I know. And we are going to win this war, or whatever it is, because we're stronger than they are. Smarter."

"*Better,*" he said, rough.

She nodded against his shoulder. "Also better informed."

He lifted his head to consider her in silence, waiting.

"One good thing happened back there," she said, serious and soft, gazing up into his face. "That day I went to find Daria. The day they...caught me. One very good thing."

His face went dark. "I find that extremely hard to believe."

"He touched me," Jenna whispered.

"I'm well aware of that, Jenna," Leander said stiffly. He rose from her side to sit upright with his arms crossed over his bent knees, the sheets rucked up in folds around his waist. "I'm well aware of what they did to you."

She sat up next to him and slid her hand up his back, feeling hard muscle under smooth skin, the silken hair at the nape of his neck. "No, I meant—he touched me. Their leader. With his bare hand."

It took a moment of silence before he comprehended her. He twisted around to stare at her full in the face, the moonlight pouring through the window behind him so she couldn't see his expression.

"Are you saying...?"

"Yes," she interrupted, nodding. "That's what I'm saying."

"So you could—?"

"See everything. His memories. His thoughts." Her voice darkened. "His plans."

His breathing was the only sound in the room aside from the small, restless murmurs of the dying fire. After a moment he leaned over and, with his palm on her shoulder, pushed her gently back to the mattress.

"Tell me," he said softly, raised to an elbow over her. His eyes glittered bright.

"It won't be easy," Jenna began haltingly. "There's a lot of them. They're very organized and very well"—she grimaced, then went on, determined—"trained. The leader of that little cell wasn't even that high up in their organization.

They know about all the colonies except one, and they're very driven. Driven to infiltrate, to attack. Driven to wipe us out of existence, at all costs."

She turned her cheek to his shoulder and closed her eyes. "They hate you...us...so much."

"Now can you see why we had to stay hidden all these years?" he whispered. He brushed her lips with his fingers, trailed them over the curve of her cheekbone, her jaw. "People hate what they can't understand, what is different from themselves. They hate it and they want to eradicate it. Violence and intolerance are woven through the fabric of human nature like a scarlet thread."

"My mother was human, and she wasn't like that," Jenna protested. "I've known a lot of people who aren't like that. You can't just keep this prejudice going from generation to generation—it's holding the *Ikati* back. We'll never be able to live in the open, we'll never be able to *advance* if we can't let go of the past."

He smiled down at her. Moonlight found the slopes of his face and slid over his skin in pale crystal streamers, magical and glimmering like fairy dust. "Silly of me to think you would agree with me," he murmured, lowering his face to touch his nose to hers.

"I'll always disagree with you when you're *wrong*," she said, turning her face away.

He caught her chin in his hand and turned it back, held her face captive in his hand. "I may be wrong about many things, but one thing I am completely sure of," he said, stroking his thumb over the side of her face.

"And what is that?" Jenna asked tartly.

"You are the most completely stubborn creature I have ever met."

She huffed and pulled her chin out of his hand, but he caught it again and rolled halfway on top of her, pinning her chest and part of her legs with the weight of his body. His laughter shook them both.

"I wasn't finished! You are the most completely stubborn creature I have ever met—"

"You already said that!"

"*And* I love you. I love you, Jenna. Awake or asleep, arguing or agreeing, through hell or high water, I love you." He gazed down at her, his body pressed full against hers, his gaze solemn and tender on her face.

"Oh. Well. Maybe you should have said that first." Her lips twisted into a tiny smile. Her lashes dropped. "And just for the record," she said softly, hiding her face in his shoulder, "since I haven't technically said it yet…I love you too. I finally feel like I'm home. You're my home, Leander." She closed her eyes and pressed a kiss to his chest. "Life is pain and we all must die," she whispered, remembering her mother's words, "but true love lives forever. And it can show you the way home."

His hand stroked over her arm and back, feathered kisses rained over her neck and shoulder. He brushed more kisses over her cheeks, stroked his lips very lightly against hers. He adjusted his hips to move over hers and settled his weight between her legs. A slow, slow burn began in her stomach.

"I should tell you more about what I saw…" she murmured, then gasped as his mouth lowered to her chest, found her nipple. Hot tongue and silken lips drew against her skin. "I need to tell you about…about their plans…"

"Tomorrow," Leander murmured, lifting his head, his gaze dark and serious. "Tomorrow we can plan strategy and plot vengeance and wage war. Tomorrow we can do all of those things. But right now..."

He kissed her, hard and delicious, until she lost her breath and her chest went tight. Her body arched against him.

He looked down at her between half-closed eyes and smiled. "Right now we have other things to attend to, great Queen."

"Actually," she murmured, sliding her hands around the back of his neck, "I think you were onto something with 'She Who Must Be Obeyed.' That has a really nice ring to it."

His laugh was muffled against her neck. "Well then, I suppose..." He brushed his lips against hers. "Your wish is my command. How may I be of service, my lady?"

"Oh, I'm sure I'll think of something," she said innocently. "In fact, I can think of several things just off the top of my head."

He tipped his head back to look down at her, smiling like a wolf.

She offered him a feral smile of her own and lifted her legs up to wrap tightly around his waist.

Acknowledgments

A big thank you to Marlene Stringer of the Stringer Literary Agency for being the first person to say what every writer wants to hear: "I loved it!" You've been a great advocate. Also big thanks to the team at Montlake for being so wonderful to work with. You guys rock. To Melody Guy, who helped me refine Jenna and Leander's story with some amazing suggestions, this is me giving you virtual hugs and a shout-out for your insightfulness. To the Wednesday night book club "ladies," Anthony, Don, Stephen, John, and Gene, big kisses. Here's to many more years of drunken debauchery and table pounding. I love you like the sisters I never had. And to Jay, who puts up with the insanity of living with the writing-obsessed and has taught me how to be a better person. You're my hero. I'd be lost without you.

About the Author

Photo by Jay Geissenger, 2011

J. T. Geissinger is an author, entrepreneur, and avid wine collector. A native of Los Angeles, she currently resides there with her husband and too many cats.

Printed in Great Britain
by Amazon.co.uk, Ltd.,
Marston Gate.